THE CROSSING

THE LAST CAVALIERS, BOOK 1

THE CROSSING

GILBERT MORRIS

CHRISTIAN LARGE PRINT
A part of Gale, Cengage Learning

GALE
CENGAGE Learning™

Detroit • New York • San Francisco · New Haven, Conn • Waterville, Maine • London

GALE
CENGAGE Learning

LIBRARY OF CONGRESS CATALOGING-IN-PUBLICATION DATA

Morris, Gilbert.
    The crossing / by Gilbert Morris. — Large print ed.
        p. cm. — (The last cavaliers ; v. 1) (Thorndike Press large
    print Christian historical fiction)
    ISBN-13: 978-1-4104-3751-8
    ISBN-10: 1-4104-3751-5
    1. Amish—Fiction. 2. United States—History—Civil War,
1861–1865—Amish—Fiction. 3. Large type books. I. Title.
PS3563.O8742C76 2011
813'.54—dc22   2011005111

ISBN 13: 978-1-59415-376-1 (pbk. : alk. paper)
ISBN 10: 1-59415-376-0 (pbk. : alk. paper)

Published in 2011 by arrangement with Barbour Publishing, Inc.

Printed in the United States of America
2 3 4 5 6   15 14 13 12 11

ED140

■ ■ ■ ■

PART ONE:
THE RETURN
1855–1858

■ ■ ■ ■

CHAPTER ONE

"I feel like a bag of sticks in a bunch of gaudy Christmas baubles." Daniel Harvey Hill, normally of a dry and caustic humor, still glanced at his wife with a look of tenderness in his eyes.

"Don't you dare call me gaudy, Harvey," Isabella Morrison Hill retorted, "after you practically forced me to buy this material for this dress." She was a pretty woman, as were her two sisters who accompanied them in the carriage.

Isabella was the older sister, with ash brown hair and dark eyes set in a small oval face. Her younger sister, Mary Anna, had a more quiet beauty. Her hair was a darker, thicker chestnut brown and her brown eyes were soft and warm. The youngest sister, Eugenia, was vivacious, with sparkling eyes and a bow-shaped mouth that looked as if she were always smiling. All three sisters were small-boned, petite women.

On this fine snowy day of December 12, 1855, D. H. Hill, in his somber black suit, had indeed almost disappeared in the finery worn by his wife and two sisters-in-law. His wife, Isabella, wore a scarlet dress that showcased her tiny waist, with a touch of white fur on her collar and cuffs and hem. Anna Morrison wore a festive holly green trimmed with frosty white lace. Her bonnet was velvet and framed her face perfectly. Eugenia Morrison Barringer wore a daring winter white trimmed with black velvet. Instead of a traditional bonnet, she sported a skullcap hat bordered by rich black sable, and her black gloves and hem were trimmed with the same expensive fur.

"You look lovely, my dear," Hill said gruffly. "You all do. Very festive. Puts me right in the Christmas spirit." His looks belied his words; he was a rather severe-looking man with sandy hair and a stubborn chin.

"Wonderful!" Eugenia, the saucy one, said. "So you won't be so grumpy, brother?"

"I'm never grumpy. I'm just matter-of-fact."

"Here's the bookseller's," Anna said, always the peacemaker. "Perhaps we may find a thesaurus, and each of us can pinpoint our particular dispositions. For myself,

8

I do agree that brother Daniel is always factual and to the point."

"Pointy, you mean," Eugenia said merrily. "As for me, I believe I am of a spirited disposition. Isabella is good-humored and personable, and you, Anna, are reserved and of an intellectual nature."

"Boring, you mean?" Anna asked, her eyes twinkling.

"Never, sister," Eugenia said. "You're much too smart to be boring. So, shall we go in? If we don't settle all of this soon, we'll be late for Uncle William's party." Their driver opened the carriage door and pulled down the steps.

Anna started to step out and was surprised to see a hand extended to her and a gentle voice ask, "May I be of assistance, Miss Morrison?"

"Why, yes, Major Jackson. How wonderful to see you!" In spite of her reserve, Anna flushed slightly and her eyes lit up.

He helped her out of the carriage then gallantly handed down the other ladies.

D.H. shook his hand heartily. "Thomas, it is very good to see you. It's been far too long. You do look well."

Thomas Jonathan Jackson was thirty years old. For almost four years now he had been at Virginia Military Institute as professor of

9

natural and experimental philosophy — at which he was an indifferent teacher at best — and instructor of artillery tactics — at which he was uncannily expert. He still wore the uniform he had worn during the Mexican War, where he had learned his artillery skills and, along the way, had been breveted a major for gallantry at Chapultepec, where he showed conspicuous courage and bravery. This uniform was not, however, made to show him off; it was a rather dusky blue, much worn and mended, double-breasted with two modest rows of buttons and the one oak leaf of a major on his shoulder flashes. The breeches were shiny at the knee, and the red stripe down the side was much faded. He wore his old cavalry boots and army-issued blue-caped greatcoat.

He was about five-ten and weighed one hundred seventy-five pounds. His complexion was smooth, his forehead broad, his nose aquiline. His hair was dark brown, soft, and had a tendency to curl. Jackson's most striking feature, however, was undoubtedly his eyes. They were of a lightning blue, such a bright color that they seemed almost to glow at times when he was feeling strong emotion. One of the nicknames the cadets at the Virginia Military Institute had given him was "Old Blue Light." His manner was always dignified and somewhat stiff, with an undoubtedly military bearing. In spite of this he was a forthright man, natural and unaffected. When he spoke to a person, his full attention and that frank gaze were fixed unerringly upon them.

"Thank you, D.H.," he answered. "As do you. But I must say that you lovely ladies positively brighten the day — even the whole town. Miss Morrison, that particular shade of green becomes you very much. Mrs. Hill, you look so much like a Christmas spirit that I wish it was Christmas today. Mrs. Barringer, as always, you are positively sparkling."

The ladies murmured their thanks.

D.H. asked, "Thomas, are you going to the bookseller's? Or have you already been?"

Jackson had a brown-wrapped parcel under his arm. For a moment he looked slightly uncomfortable. "No, this is a picture. That is, a daguerreotype. Of me." Next door to the bookseller's was a photographer's studio.

"Really?" Anna exclaimed. "Oh, may we see it?"

"I — I wouldn't deny you any pleasure, Miss Morrison," Jackson answered, obviously flustered. "But I think that would not be a very great pleasure. Besides, it — it is wrapped securely for my trip home."

Now Anna was embarrassed. "Of course, Major Jackson, it must stay — wrapped. I wasn't thinking."

Jackson bowed slightly. "But if you are going to Parson's Books and Reading Rooms, may I beg to accompany you all? I didn't have any particular book in mind, but I love to browse around."

"Please do, Major," Eugenia insisted prettily. "We are going to dinner at Uncle William's tonight, and we wanted to stop and get him a book for Christmas. We were thinking about *A Christmas Carol.* Don't you think he's much like old Mr. Fezziwig?" The sisters' uncle William Graham was a merry gentleman, a Whig of the old school who wore antique knee breeches, ruffled shirts, silk stockings, and heeled shoes with silver buckles.

Thomas smiled broadly and his eyes burned brightly. "So he is! A delightful old gentleman, if I recall. It has been, I think, two years since I've seen him."

"He looks the same," Eugenia said mischievously. "He always looks the same. I think he was born looking like Mr. Fezziwig."

"Then *A Christmas Carol* it must be," D.H.

said. "Though he will never get the joke. My dear?" He offered Isabella his arm, and Jackson gallantly escorted both Mary Anna and Eugenia into the shop.

It was much like booksellers' shops everywhere, comfortably crowded with books both careworn and brand-new. The shop smelled like aged leather and old paper.

Mr. Parsons was a short, balding man with glasses perched on the edge of his nose and a perpetual slight squint, probably from reading almost continuously for at least forty-two of his forty-five years. He welcomed them and urged them to take tea or coffee in one of the reading rooms. Mr. Parsons was not a grasping man; he loved books so much that he had included two parlors attached to his shop that were far too inviting to promote quick sales. He barely made a profit on his shop, but he didn't care. He loved reading and avid readers and encouraged his customers to sit in one of the comfortably overstuffed chairs by the fireplace to peruse the books at their leisure.

The group wandered about the shop, Jackson to find Shakespeare and Hill in search of Dickens.

Eugenia was heard to exclaim, "Oh, look

sisters! It's the newest *Godey's Ladies' Book*!"

The three sisters crowded around the magazines then went into the nearest parlor to spread them out on the library table so they could all look at them together. Jackson selected a copy of Shakespeare's sonnets then followed the ladies. The parlor was a large room, with four armchairs grouped comfortably around a brisk, crackling fire. The library table was large enough to accompany twelve people, and the sisters were grouped at one end, excitedly talking about the newest ladies' fashions. Jackson helped himself to hot tea from a sideboard then sat down by the fire.

Soon D.H. joined him, with his newly purchased copy of *A Christmas Carol*. Hill and Jackson had been friends for almost ten years now, because they had served together in the Mexican War. Hill, who in 1851 had been professor of mathematics at Washington College in Lexington, had recommended Jackson to the post at VMI that he had been awarded. The previous year, in 1854, Hill had joined the faculty of Davidson College, near Charlotte, North Carolina. In the last year he and Jackson had not corresponded much, both because Hill had moved and because of the tragic death of

Jackson's wife, Elinor. She had died in November of 1854, giving birth to a stillborn son.

Hill settled into the armchair next to Jackson.

Jackson looked up and smiled, a sad and lonely smile that had been his customary expression for more than a year.

"How have you been, Thomas?" Hill asked quietly.

Jackson sighed. "It has been very difficult, I admit, D.H. I miss my Ellie more than I can say."

Hill shook his head. "I cannot imagine the trial, Thomas. I am so truly sorry."

"God has given me comfort, but you're right. It is indeed a trial. I know that Ellie and my son are waiting for me in Paradise . . . and sometimes I wish I could join them." He stared into space for a moment then continued, "But I have found solace in my work, and in my home."

"You are still living with Mr. Junkin?" Hill asked. When Elinor and Thomas had married in August of 1853, her father had built onto the family home for them.

"Yes, and he is a pillar of strength. And my sister-in-law, Margaret, has also been a great help to me," Jackson answered. "Sometimes I wonder at the enduring faith

15

and love that seems to strengthen women more than men."

"I agree," D.H. said. "I also think Isabella is much stronger than I am, in so many ways."

Jackson brightened a bit. "She and her sisters are all such lovely ladies. A man would be blessed to have a wife from the Morrison family."

"So true, my friend," Hill agreed.

Carelessly Thomas commented, "I'm surprised that Miss Anna has not married. She is such a lovely lady, so intelligent and engaging."

"She is, and she has had two offers that I know of," Hill said. "But she wasn't the least bit interested. It seems that it must be very difficult for a man to persuade her to have him."

"Mmm," Jackson hummed noncommitally. "Most of the time the things that are hardest to obtain are the more precious to have."

With some negotiations about exactly how many *Godey's Ladies' Book*s to buy, and whether or not to also purchase *Bleak House,* which Isabella had never read, the group finished their book shopping and returned to the carriage.

Once again Jackson escorted Anna, but

Eugenia was walking with Isabella, still talking excitedly about their new magazines. Anna asked, "Won't you let us drive you home, Major?"

"Thank you, but no, I prefer to walk. In spite of the cold, it is a lovely day."

It was true; Lexington looked like an idyllic greeting card. The small village had feathery pillows of snow, but the sun was shining beatifically. Far on the horizon were more snow clouds, but they only served to accentuate the brightness of the late afternoon. The walks had been shoveled by industrious boys who earned a nickel from the town's treasury. They had done a fine job, pushing the snow up into neat snowbanks bordering the streets.

Anna agreed. "It is a beautiful afternoon. But I'm afraid if I walked too far I might muss my hem." Her hooped skirt was floor-length, as was fashionable, and it took particular care to hold it up without exposing a glimpse of a forbidden ankle.

Jackson smiled down at her. "In that case, Miss Morrison, I would be obliged, like that gentleman Sir Walter Raleigh, to cast my cloak at your feet. But I'm afraid it would be a sorry carpet for you." Jackson's blue caped coat, like his clothes, was worn and thin.

"I would still be honored, sir," Anna said. "I would be glad to tread on your cloak any time."

He handed her up into the carriage, and D.H. stopped at the open carriage door. "Thomas, won't you join us for dinner? Not tomorrow — Isabella and I have a prior engagement — but what about on Friday night? Rufus and Eugenia and Anna and I would, I think, make a merry party."

"That you would, D.H.," Jackson gravely agreed. Glancing at Anna he added, "It would be a very great pleasure, and I will be sure to bring my cloak."

The Hills, Anna, and Eugenia and her husband, Rufus Barringer, were staying at the Col Alto Manor House. All of them had relatives in Lexington, but instead of imposing on them for their Christmas visit, they had decided that it would be much easier to stay at this comfortable boardinghouse.

Col Manor had been built in 1827 and was a gracious two-story home with spacious bedrooms, two parlors for guests' use, and an elegant dining room. Col Alto was very well-known, too, for its fine food and was one of the locals' favorite places to eat.

Thomas Jackson joined them in the dining room, which was sumptuously lit with dozens of candles. It was a large room, but the tables were so discreetly located that it gave each party a feeling of privacy. Two enormous fireplaces faced each other across the room, and on this frosty night, the fires, continually tended by servants, snapped and sparked. The smoky scent of aged Virginia oak mingled with the delicious aromas of food cooked fresh and served hot. The D.H. Hill party was seated at a table in a corner, with the fireplace pleasantly distant enough so that they could feel the warmth but not to excess.

D.H. Hill introduced Thomas to Rufus Barringer, Eugenia's husband, whom Thomas had never met.

Barringer was a neat, compact man, balding, with light brown hair and a fine-trimmed mustache and beard. His blue eyes seemed to continually twinkle with good humor, and his mouth was wide and appeared, like his wife's, to be always on the verge of a smile. He was a man of good humor and patience, which served him well in his marriage to the spirited Eugenia Morrison. Barringer said, "Sir, I have heard of your famous artillery expertise, both in the Mexican War and at Virginia Military Institute. It's a pleasure to meet you."

"You're too kind," Jackson said. "But I

must agree that both the study and the practice of artillery gives me a great deal of pleasure — much more, I'm afraid, than the study of natural and experimental philosophy."

"I admit to considerable ignorance," Barringer said. "My study has been confined almost exclusively to the law. What, exactly, is natural and experimental philosophy, sir?"

"I don't know," Jackson answered, deadpan.

There was a long silence at the table, and then the entire party — except for Jackson, who only smiled — laughed.

They were a merry party that evening. Jackson and the other two men were wearing the only acceptable fine evening attire — dark suits, black ties, and white ruffled shirts. The women, in contrast, looked like colorful little birds in a drab wood. Isabella looked regal in royal blue, Anna glowed in a deep rose, and Eugenia wore a golden brown that made her complexion look like pure ivory. The candlelight cast a rich aura over them; as was the fashion, their shoulders were bare and their hair was gracefully swept up. Isabella wore a golden comb, and Anna and Eugenia wore dainty tortoiseshell. Anna rarely wore jewelry, but on this festive night, she wore pearl drop earrings that her uncle William Graham had given her years before, stating that they were such purity as became her naturally.

The party was seated at a round table, which served well, in that the matching of Anna and Thomas was not so obvious. Thomas Jackson exerted himself to be lighthearted company, but he was obviously still mourning the loss of his wife. Often when there was a pause in the conversation, his face took on a distant look, his fire blue eyes dimmed, and he stared into the distance as if searching for something far away. But throughout the long and delicious meal, he was for the most part amusing and perfectly cheerful.

Rufus Barringer questioned him about his service in the Mexican War, with his brother-in-law, D.H. Hill, as a fellow soldier.

"I prefer to remember the pleasant things about Mexico, and there were many," Jackson answered. One corner of his mouth gave a tiny tug. "The senoritas were particularly cordial. Not, of course," he added with a mischievous air, "to Major Hill, as he was engaged to you at this time, Mrs. Hill, and he never compromised his affections and loyalties to you. He was, however, uncommonly fond of quince . . . and that did get us into some trouble, as I recall."

Over Hill's protestations, Eugenia asked slyly, "And so this was a Senorita Quince, Major Thomas?"

"Eugenia, really," Anna scolded her. "That is — there was not a Senorita Quince, was there, Major Jackson?"

"No, no, there was not," Jackson hastily replied. "Quince is a fruit. It looks like a pear, but it is much more tart and crisp. All of us loved them, because they were so refreshing in that hot, dry climate. Once, I'm afraid, this hunger for them forced me and Major Hill to climb an adobe garden wall for fresh quince, and I believe we came closer to getting killed by the owner of the home than we ever were in battle. And there was a senorita involved . . . at least she made a good deal of noise, and I think that her father thought that we were more interested in her than in the less dangerous fruit. I think that is the fastest that I've seen D.H. move, climbing back across that garden wall."

Isabella glowered. "And you, Harvey, did you know this senorita? Is that how you came to know about the quince tree?"

"No! No!" he vigorously protested. "It was all Jackson's fault. He had seen the very tip-top of the tree the day before, and he said the gardener would never miss two or three of the fruits. But as it happened, he did object most strenuously."

"But after all this, did you get any fruit, Major Jackson?" Anna asked, smiling.

"We did, but it was at a high price. D.H. skinned his knee terribly in our shameful retreat, and I fell off the wall on the other side and twisted my ankle so badly I could hardly get my boot on the next day. But the quince was very good," he added, his blue eyes light and fiery as he glanced slightly at Anna, "and so I may say it was worth it. Most of the time, the things that are hardest to obtain are the more precious to have."

The First Presybterian Church was a solemn edifice, two stories of graceful Greek Revival architecture of white sandstone, with five lofty columns guarding the entrance and a great steeple with a clock tower. Thomas Jackson had joined the church in 1851. Before he joined he had visited with Dr. William S. White, the pastor, many times and had found him to be a dedicated scholar of the Bible and servant of the Lord.

Once again Thomas found himself escorting Miss Morrison as she and her sisters and brothers-in-law attended church with him. He wondered again at Anna. She was an attractive, modest, intelligent woman of a quiet, sweet wit, and it was unusual for a woman of such family and virtues to remain unmarried by the age of twenty-four. He had known her for five years now, having met her several times, as he had been a popular visitor to D.H. Hill's home when he had been at Washington College. He had always thought her a mildly pretty woman and an interesting one, but he had been so very much in love with Elinor Junkin that no other woman touched his mind except in passing.

Even now as he thought of Ellie, his thoughts, mind, and heart wandered. It had been over a year, and yet the grief and the feeling of loss was still so raw that, unknowing, he drew in a deep, ragged breath, stopped walking, and stared off at the distant blue hills to the east. The Blue Ridge Mountains were wreathed in mysterious smoke as always, and he longed to lose himself in that far place where, it seemed, everything and everyone must be immortal — forever beloved, unhurt, and undying. . . .

Anna stopped as Major Jackson paused and watched him with sympathy, for the expression on his face bore some sadness.

She recalled the first time she had met

him. It was at D.H. Hill's house, on one of Thomas's many visits to the Lexington house where D.H. and Isabella had entertained on any opportunity permitted. Thomas was generally her escort by default, as Isabella was engaged to D.H. and her younger sister, Eugenia, had many suitors to escort here anywhere and everywhere. Anna admired Major Jackson. He was a true man, it seemed to her, and a strong and genuine person.

In fact, she wrote to one of her acquaintances:

More soldierly looking than anything else, his erect bearing and military dress being quite striking; but upon engaging in conversation, his open, animated countenance, and his clear complexion, tinged with the ruddy glow of health, were still more pleasing. . . . His head was a splendid one, large and finely formed, and covered with soft, dark brown hair, which, if allowed to grow to any length, curled; but he had a horror of long hair for a man . . . he was at all times manly and noble looking, and when in robust health he was a handsome man.

When Thomas had announced his engagement to Elinor Junkin, Anna had appeared to wish him the best goodwill, as did her family. She never spoke of her private feelings to anyone. Her sisters did know that she admired Major Jackson, but Anna was reserved, so they never dreamed of intruding upon her by questioning her of her feelings about his marriage. Through those two years of Jackson's marriage, and the death of his wife and his subsequent mourning, Anna had conducted herself with great aplomb; but whenever she saw him again, she had a sparkle in her soft eyes. She spoke of him often to her sisters and to D.H., but it was always impersonal, regarding the last time they had seen him or reminiscing about old times.

Anna was reluctant to interrupt his reverie, but it was almost time for the service to begin. Softly she said, "Major Jackson?"

He came alive again, from that far-off land, and they went into the church, arm in arm.

Anna hoped that one day he would look at her with that same tender regard she had seen as he stared at the faraway Blue Ridge Mountains.

D.H., Isabella, Rufus, Eugenia, and Anna left Lexington on Monday, December 17, a week before Christmas. At the train station, Thomas Jackson discreetly asked Anna if he might correspond with her, strictly as a loyal friend. Anna agreed heartily.

Over the next months, Thomas wrote her nice little letters, about the goings-on at VMI and the coming spring and the beauty of the Shenandoah Valley. In summer he wrote about the great riches of his farm — corn, tomatoes, snap beans, peas, turnips, carrots, squash, celery, and beets. He wrote, mildly and oddly noncommitally, about the growing tensions between North and South on the question of secession.

Anna saw nothing more of Thomas Jackson until July 1856. Virginia Military Institute planned a particularly extravagant July Fourth celebration. Urged by Uncle William Graham and many of their cousins, D.H. Hill and Isabella decided to take a large party to Lexington to celebrate.

Without fanfare, Thomas escorted Anna to the festivites. They watched the fireworks and the immaculate artillery performances by the VMI cadets. As the merriments were winding down, he turned to her and said, "Although I realize it might be forward of me, I have a gift for you. Would it be too presumptuous to ask you to receive it?"

"Not at all, sir," she answered, blushing in

spite of herself. She took his arm and he led her to his horse, which was in the institute's stables.

Out of his saddlebag he drew a brown-wrapped parcel. He handed it to her, then closed his hands over both of hers as she grasped it. "I would very much prefer if you would keep it until you go home and then unwrap it," he said quietly.

"Of — of course, Major Jackson," she answered. "Certainly. I thank you very much, and I'm sure that it is a gift I shall cherish."

"I hope so." He led her back to her family.

They returned home, the Hills and Barringers and Anna back to Col Alto, Thomas Jackson back to Junkin Home.

Anna did not open her gift that night. She was tired and slightly drained, and she thought that whatever it was, she would appreciate it much more when she felt well and energetic. And she had the most curious feeling about the gift — great anticipation on the one hand and a sort of dread that it would be disappointing on the other. Though she was extremely curious, she still could not bring herself to open the gift. She told herself that she could deal with the emotion — whichever extreme it was — if she were at home.

The next day was July 5, the day they were to return back home to North Carolina. Anna had packed the brown-wrapped parcel tightly and securely in her trunk, between her brown velvet day dress and her green velvet evening dress. Major Thomas Jackson did not come to the railroad station to see them off, as he had said his good-byes the night before.

The next day at Cottage Home in North Carolina, Anna finally summoned the courage to open her package. It was Major Jackson, his daguerreotype from that December. There was no note attached. To her, he looked very handsome, and his light blue eyes had a hint of sadness in them. But they seemed to look forward, to new days, instead of the grief of the last year. She was extremely happy with her gift and treasured it, though she kept it in a bureau drawer because she felt it would be too much anticipation of the future to keep it displayed by her bedside.

On that same evening, July 6, she received a telegram. Major Thomas Jackson had written to tell her that he was gone to Europe, on a grand tour including Belgium, France, Germany, Switzerland, England, and Scotland. He hoped that she would be amenable to him corresponding with her. A few days later she began receiving his letters, which she answered immediately.

Once he wrote in more flowery language than she had ever heard him use:

> I would advise you never to name my European trip to me unless you are blest with a superabundance of patience, as its very mention is calculated to bring up with it an almost inexhaustible assemblage of grand and beautiful associations. . . .

Anna wrote back that she did, indeed, possess much patience.

He returned in October. His letters had grown steadily more personal and even showed some affection. So though Anna expressed surprise, she wasn't really shocked when he shambled up on his horse, unannounced, to call at Cottage Home. After visiting with her family, Thomas asked if he might speak to Anna alone.

There were many endearments expressed, although neither Anna nor Thomas recorded all of them. On one knee, holding her hand and looking up at her with a forgotten warmth and hope in his eyes, he asked, "Miss Anna, would you do me the greatest honor and consent to become my wife?"

"I will," she answered with tears in her eyes. "And sir, you do *me* great honor."

Anna Morrison had been kissed a very few times before, but Major Thomas Jackson's kiss celebrating their engagement was the sweetest, and the most poignant, she had ever known.

They were married at Cottage Home on July 16, 1857.

CHAPTER TWO

Yancy Tremayne leaned over the bank, as motionless as the stones in the stream below. He had held that position for ten minutes, but now with a flash of movement, he grabbed a fish and flung it on the bank behind him. He whooped with triumph, for it was the biggest fish he had ever caught; it was fifteen pounds at least, a striped bass. He strung it out and started back to the camp.

Even at the young age of twelve, he was half a head taller than any of the Cheyenne boys his age, and he already had matured more so that he had taken on a sort of manhood. He had dark eyes and an olive tint to his skin, and his hair was as black as the darkest thing in nature. He had a straight English nose and a cleft in his chin exactly as did his father, Daniel. Like all the Cheyenne, Yancy wore buckskin breeches, moccasins, and a buckskin vest with intricate beading. He had taken that off when he was fishing so that it wouldn't get wet.

He hurried back, for he always liked to bring his trophies directly to his father. Suddenly a Cheyenne boy named Hinto jumped out onto the path. Hinto was the son of the Cheyenne chief, White Buffalo. Hinto was his eldest son and was much indulged. Although he had handsome features, as did the Cheyenne people, he tended toward chubbiness and was a bully. He was sixteen years old and much bigger than Yancy. Now he blocked Yancy's way. "I'll take that fish, Yancy."

"No, you won't! This is my fish."

Hinto grabbed the fish, and Yancy let it go. Hinto turned, and Yancy picked up a smooth round river stone and hit him in the head, knocking him flat. Yancy picked up the fish and looked at Hinto, noting that he wasn't hurt badly or unconscious, only befuddled. "You go catch your own fish," he taunted then ran lightly down the path.

He reached the camp made of tepees covered with buffalo hide, which were scattered over an open meadow, but he ran by them like a fleeing deer and circled back to the riverbank. There his father had built a log cabin, insulated with river mud daub. It had only one room, with a loft where Yancy slept, and he headed there to find his father.

Daniel Tremayne sat outside, rocking in a chair he had made from Lake Essee's fine oak timber.

"Look at the fish I caught!" Yancy cried, holding up his prize.

"That is a right nice fish you got there." Daniel, at the age of thirty-two, was over six feet tall and was very lean and muscular. Ordinarily he wore a fur cap, but the summer was hot, so he wore nothing on his head. His long reddish blond hair was tied back with a rawhide thong. His face was handsome in a rugged way; his jaw was lean, and his cheekbones sharp. In the bright sun he had sun-squints at the corners of his blue eyes. He had a small scar beside his mouth, and a livid red one ran from his left jawbone down to his shoulder blade. His buckskin vest was much finer than Yancy's, for the beading was from the V-shaped front all the way to the shoulders and was very intricate. His buckskin breeches had a long fringe, and his knee-high moccasins were also beaded. He reached out and took the fish, holding the mouth with his thumb. "This fellow ought to feed us until we get sick of eating fish."

Yancy was pleased with his father's praise.

He was telling his father how he had caught it, relating every second, when they were interrupted by White Buffalo and his son Hinto, who had a bloody forehead.

White Buffalo growled, "Look what your boy did, Tremayne."

Daniel got to his feet and looked at the son of the chief. "What happened, Hinto?"

"While I wasn't looking, Yancy came up behind me and hit me with a rock."

"That's a lie!" Yancy argued, and stood up very straight to face Chief White Buffalo, his fists clenched by his sides. "He took my fish away from me, and when he turned around I hit him with a rock. I had to to get my fish back. He's a thief!"

White Buffalo was tall and well formed, a strong man. Since he was war chief, very rarely did anyone press him or argue with him. He crosssed his arms and frowned darkly at Yancy.

Daniel Tremayne grew alert. He knew the man had a fiery temper and was an expert with any weapon. White Buffalo carried only a knife at his side now, but he was always dangerous.

"You should teach your son how brothers behave," White Buffalo muttered.

"I'll take care of my son, you take care of yours, White Buffalo. Hinto stole Yancy's fish, and he had a right to get it back."

White Buffalo was angry to the core. He had never liked Daniel Tremayne, who was a far better shot with a rifle than he was. Also, when they were much younger and before White Buffalo became chief, they had a fight during which the two had bloodied each other thoroughly. It was, in fact, because White Buffalo had insulted Daniel's half-breed wife, Winona. In that altercation Daniel had emerged the victor.

Now White Buffalo grunted, "Your boy isn't a true Cheyenne, and you aren't of the people yourself. The boy's mother was only half Cheyenne. The other half was white trapper." He spat on the ground disdainfully.

"He's Cheyenne enough to make his way," Daniel said quietly and civilly.

White Buffalo had said what he came to say. "Tremayne, why don't you go to your own people? Neither of you belong here. Neither of you are true Cheyenne." He turned abruptly and walked away, followed by Hinto, who looked back and made a childish face at Yancy.

Daniel watched them leave until they disappeared over the path toward the Cheyenne camp. Then he sat back in his rocking chair and motioned for Yancy to sit down on the rough bench beside him. "Yancy, there's something we need to talk about."

Yancy sat and waited, his eyes fixed on his father. He was disturbed by the reference to his white blood. It was something that the pure-blooded Indian boys taunted him about often. His mother had been only half Cheyenne. Her father had been Pierre Charbeau, a fur trapper. The Cheyenne felt only disdain for anyone not of pure blood, although they did not — like the Comanche or the Sioux — torment or sometimes kill the mixed breeds. They just didn't include them, which was difficult for the mixed breeds in the tribe. The Cheyenne creed meant very strong and loyal family ties to their own, and to be left out of this close circle was painful.

The Cheyenne had been, perhaps, more accepting of Winona because she tried hard to fit in with them. She could raise a good tepee, she could fish, she made wonderful soft buckskin breeches and shirts and vests. Her skill in beading was the best in the village; often the chieftains bought beads at the trading post at Cantonment and paid her in fish and deer meat and rabbit to do her beading on their garments.

She had lived alone, because her mother had died when she was fifteen and her father had disappeared during trapping season, going off to the distant Ouachita Mountains, never to return. When Daniel Tremayne had first met the Cheyenne, she had been seventeen. He had loved her the minute he set eyes on her. They had married, in the Cheyenne way, and a year later she had Yancy. When Yancy was ten, she contracted cholera and died.

Now as Daniel remembered her he was saddened, because this place had always been Winona's home; but he knew that it wasn't his home, nor was it meant to be Yancy's home. "Yancy, we're going to be leaving this place."

Yancy stared at his father, his dark eyes suddenly narrowing. "Why would we do that? These are our people."

"No, they're not, as you just heard. When your mother was alive, we were a part of the Cheyenne people because of her. But you and I . . . we don't belong here."

"But, Father, these are my people, the Cheyenne! You've always taught me to be proud of my mother and what my Cheyenne blood meant!"

"Yes, Yancy, and I believe I've done the right thing. I always want you to be proud of your mother and your blood." He shrugged slightly. "Maybe if your mother had lived and I had completely adopted the way of the Cheyenne, it would've been different. But I am a white man, and though I loved your mother very much, we lived as white people. Just look at our cabin. I could never live in a tepee that you could just pick up and move from one day to the next. I don't have the wandering plains thoughts that your mother's people do. I need roots, and family, and a feeling of being permanent. And though you don't realize it, you sometimes show me you feel the same way."

Yancy looked as though he might cry, though he never had and certainly never would — at least not in front of anyone. "But, Father, where would we go?"

"I've thought about this for a long time, son, and we have to go back to my people," Daniel answered quietly and with some sorrow. "My parents are getting old, if they're still alive. I have many regrets, because I ran away from home . . . and I wasn't much older than you are now. I want us to go back to them and be a family again. That is, if they'll have us."

"Why wouldn't they have you, Father?" Yancy asked curiously. His father had often told him stories and the history of the Cheyenne, but he had rarely mentioned his own family.

"Because my people belong to a group called the Amish, and they feel that a son should obey his father. Well, I didn't do that. I ran away because I was tired of their rules and their boring lives. But now it seems to me that they do know what true love, and real family, can be."

"But I don't want to leave, Father! I want to be a Cheyenne. I *am* Cheyenne!" Yancy protested, his dark eyes glinting, his olive skin taking on an angry copper glow.

Daniel Tremayne sighed heavily, for this was as hard as he had known it would be. Yancy had known nothing his whole life but Indian ways. It was a life of freedom for young boys, and Yancy had reveled in it. The tribe didn't have much contact with whites, and Yancy knew very little about that world.

Daniel had been avoiding making a decision, but this incident with Hinto and White Buffalo settled the thing in his mind. His blue eyes looked into the distance, watching the scarlet sunset over the lake. He was quiet for a time, and Yancy, too, watched the sun as it seemed to be inextricably drawn down to the quiet red waters. "You know, Yancy, White Buffalo's people have been lucky," Daniel said thoughtfully. "We found a good place to settle, a fertile place, with a lake full of good fish, with woods and grass and herbs. There are deer, turkey, quail, dove, and wild hogs that make easy hunting here." He sighed deeply. "But it's destined not to last. The white men have pushed and shoved and maneuvered the Indians from everywhere in the West. I've told you that they made us move down here from the north, and many of the Cheyenne didn't find a place that was nearly as good to live as here, at Lake Essee." The Cheyenne had named the lake *E 'se'he,* which meant "sun," but the white men had corrupted it to *Lake Essee.* "And the day will come that they'll push the Cheyenne away from here. We can't stay with them. They are a dying people. And we are not of their own."

"They'll fight," Yancy said angrily.

"Yes, they will, courageously," Daniel agreed. "And they'll die."

Yancy stared at his father and saw that there was no point arguing, for when Daniel Tremayne's mind was made up, that was the end of it. It was part of his strength. "When will we leave?" asked Yancy, resigned.

"We'll leave right away, son." He rose and he put his hand on the boy's shoulder, saying gently, "One day when you're a man, you'll see I've made the right decision."

"When I'm grown up, I will come back to the Cheyenne!"

Daniel almost smiled, for the rebellion in his son was very familiar to him. It was exactly the way he had been when he was a young man. "That may very well be. But until then, you and I will be together. No matter what happens, you are my son, and I'm very proud of you. I will always love you, and I will never forsake you. So we'll see what comes — and even if we find no other people, we'll be a family always."

It took almost three months for Daniel and Yancy to travel from the Oklahoma plains to the Shenandoah Valley in Virginia. Even though Lake Essee had been like an oasis in the desert, in no way could it compare to the valley. To the west were the Allegheny Mountains, gentle and eternal, old mountains with tops rounded from the ages. To the east were the Blue Ridge Mountains, smoky, quiet, mysterious. Fertile, green, serene, even in the blazing heat of August, the Shenandoah Valley lay like a priceless emerald that stretched from southern Virginia to Maryland. Every view was scenic. Every scene was green. All the green was rich.

Daniel and Yancy stopped on a small rise

overlooking a large farm. The farmhouse was substantial, three stories, with gables in the attic and a wide veranda surrounding the house. There were several outbuildings — an enormous barn, stables, a housing for a huge windmill, two sheds for farm equipment, and a carriage house. Behind and to the west was a great pasture filled with fat cows, and to the east were horses feeding contentedly. Beyond were fields, rich with harvest; cornfields; hay; wheat; tobacco; barley; and soybeans. It all gave the impression of a great richness, though it was a richness that had nothing to do with money.

"This is my home," Daniel said softly. "This is where I grew up."

Throughout the entire journey, Yancy had grown more and more sullen. Now all he said was, "It's a big farm. Must be lots of hard work."

"It is," Daniel agreed. "But I think it might be worth it. And it's not just the farming. The valley is good hunting and good fishing, even in wintertime. I think you'll like it, Yancy."

"I dunno," he muttered. "I already miss home."

"But this is our home now," Daniel said. "We'll be fine." Daniel hoped this was true. He had sent a telegram to his parents from

Oklahoma City, saying that he was coming home and was bringing their grandson. He hoped they had received it. He knew they would never answer it, for the Amish wouldn't contemplate using something as modern and complicated as a telegraph.

As they rode toward the farmhouse, Daniel said rather uncertainly, "You'll find my parents are very religious. They are what's called Amish people."

"What does that mean? Amish?"

"They are people that sort of set themselves apart from others. They believe that they should live very simply and quietly. They are good Christian people, but their rules are much stricter than some others."

"Why didn't you tell me anything about this before?" Yancy demanded. "You've never said anything about God, or even about the Cheyenne gods!"

"I know," Daniel said with some discomfort. "It's because I'm still not sure where I am with the Lord, even now. But I do know that we need to come home." Daniel stopped in front of the house and slipped off his horse.

A woman came through the screened door and stood on the porch, watching him. She was a small woman but held herself so straight she seemed taller than she actually was. At the age of sixty-three, her hair was still black, but with one silver wing from her left temple back to the bun she wore. Her hair was thick and healthy. Since the Amish women never cut their hair, it reached below her waist when it was down. She had sharp features — a straight nose and a strong jaw, but her blue eyes were kind. She wore the dress of Amish women. They wore plain dark dresses with collarless high necks. Over their shoulders they wore a *holsz duch,* a triangular shawl pinned to their apron in front. All of their fastenings were straight pins, for buttons were forbidden. All Amish women wore prayer caps, usually made of white organza. "So you've finally come home, Daniel," she breathed. Then she held out her arms.

Daniel rushed to her, and they held each other for a long time. Then he held her out at arm's length and said, "You're looking well, Mother. I've missed you."

"I am well," she answered, "and I've missed you, too, Daniel. So this is Yancy?"

"Yes, this is your grandson. Yancy, this is your grandmother, Zemira."

"Hello, ma'am," Yancy said awkwardly, dismounting and taking off his slouch hat.

Zemira Tremayne smiled. "He favors you, Daniel."

"Maybe, but he favors his mother more." Daniel looked toward the house and asked, "Is Father inside?"

"No, son, he's over there." Zemira gestured toward a grove of oak trees, adding, "He went to be with the Lord two years ago."

Daniel glanced at the small cemetery then dropped his gaze, unable to meet his mother's eyes. He had left home because he'd been unable to live within the *Ordnung,* the set of rules and regulations that define the Amish lifestyle. He remembered how he had never fit into the strict confines demanded by the community. He remembered and regretted the heated arguments he had with his father, and now he burned with shame. "I'm so sorry about the way I treated you and Father. I wanted to ask his forgiveness for running away like I did."

"He forgave you without being asked," Zemira said. "Your father was never a man to hold a grudge. You hurt him badly when you left, saying hard words to him, Daniel. I was afraid he'd not be able to deal with it, but he did. He came to me one day about six months after you left and told me, 'If you ever see Daniel again and I'm not here, tell him I loved him even if we didn't agree.'"

"I was wrong to leave that way, Mother, and I want to make it up to you any way that I can. If you'll let us come back, I'll try and be a good son to you."

Zemira grasped both of his hands in hers, lifted her head, and looked straight into Daniel's eyes. "Of course you are welcome, Daniel. You are my son, and you are my family." Then she turned to Yancy, saying, "I expect you're hungry, Yancy. Come in the house, and I'll see what we've got to eat."

Daniel and Yancy followed her into the house, and Daniel ran his eyes over the front parlor as she led them through to the kitchen. "Nothing has changed, Mother. It's just like it was the day I left."

The Amish made all of their furniture, and like everything about them, it was simple and plain. Two settees, facing each other from either side of the fireplace, had straight backs with thin cushions. There were two straight chairs and two rocking chairs. One round table in the corner served as a tea table.

Daniel got a small lump in his throat when they passed through the dining room. The dining table was fine, made of maple, long enough to seat twelve. All of the chairs were handmade, ladder-back, and Daniel's father,

Jacob, had even indulged in a small scroll on the topmost crosspiece.

Daniel had helped him make this furniture. Or at least Jacob had pretended that Daniel was helping. He had been small, maybe five or six years old. Jacob had given him a piece of sandpaper and had told him to sand small pieces of wood. Now Daniel wondered if anything he had sanded was actually included in the furniture. In the crosspieces of the chairs, perhaps.

They went into the kitchen, where there was an oak worktable with four stools. "Here, Yancy, Daniel, you sit down. I have some leftovers from dinner today. Sol Raber and Shadrach Braun were here today, helping with the farm, and I fixed this for them."

"So how have you been managing the farm by yourself, Mother?" Daniel asked.

Zemira set down a platter of roast beef and a big bowl of mashed potatoes that had been kept on the woodstove, which still had coals enough to keep it warm. "You know this, Daniel," she answered matter-of-factly. "You are not my only family. This community is my family, too, and since your father died, everyone in the valley has helped me."

The Amish were indeed loyal to everyone in their community. Anytime anyone needed help — with money, with children, with work, with the farm — the entire community helped. The settlement in the Shenandoah Valley was relatively small, now with twenty-two family farms, though that number was growing as they married and bought more land. But when Jacob Tremayne had died, all of the able men of the twenty-two families took turns taking care of the Tremayne farm and holdings. Zemira was still strong, and she herself still tended to the milking, the cows, the horses, the kitchen garden, and the cornfield. But the men of the Amish community had helped with plowing, sowing, seeding, harvesting, selling the goods at market, and with firewood and tending the livestock in the bitter winters. Zemira told Daniel of all the men and boys who had helped her for the last two years since Jacob had died.

Yancy was quiet as he listened to his father and his grandmother. The roast beef and potatoes were delicious, and he ate hungrily.

As they were finishing up, Zemira asked, "What do you want to do, Daniel? Will you be going back to hunting and trapping?"

"No, Mother, I don't want to do that." Daniel hesitated, but he had rehearsed what he wanted to say, so he forged ahead. "I want to come back and join the community.

I want to work this farm. I want us to be a family."

Zemira gave Daniel a direct look. "Do you think so, Daniel? You never took discipline well. It will be difficult for you."

"I'll give it my best," Daniel said firmly.

"You'll have to prove yourself. You know what that will be like."

"It'll be hard, but if you'll have me, I'll be grateful."

"So be it then." Zemira turned to Yancy. "What about you, Yancy? What do you think of learning to live with us?"

Yancy shook his head. "I don't know. I don't really know much about you — about the Amish. But I'll tell you the truth, ma'am. It doesn't sound like I'll like it much."

"Call me Grandmother," Zemira said softly. "And I'll help you, Yancy. It'll be so good to have family here again."

"You'll have to help me, too, Mother," Daniel said. "I know I want to be here, but I'm still not sure where I stand with the Lord, and with Amish ways. It's been so long. . . ."

"It's never too long, or too late, with the Lord, Daniel," Zemira said. "You'll see."

Chapter Three

"Rebecca! What are you doing? Daydreaming about a husband?"

Shadrach Braun leaned up against the doorjamb and sipped his lemonade. It was August, and it was hot. He had been out working in the fields and had come in to cool off for a bit before they finished up and had to put the stock away. He was dressed as all Amish men dressed for work — dark trousers, plain white shirt, suspenders, straw hat. He was not a big man but was tightly muscled, with dark hair and dark blue eyes that sometimes looked like a muddy green.

In the parlor his three sisters sat on low hickory benches, and his mother sat in her favorite rocking chair. Lois, the youngest sister at thirteen, and her sister, Judith, who was one year older, were plying their needles industriously, sewing pillowcases. Their mother, Adah, was making a chair cushion.

Rebecca, the eldest sister, had dropped her pillowcase onto her lap and was staring out the window dreamily. She turned as Shad spoke. "Maybe I was just meditating on things of the Lord, Shad. That would be better than sewing another one of these dumb pillowcases."

Shad grinned. "I doubt very much that you were thinking of God. You don't meditate nearly as much as you should, at least according to the bishop." He came to sit by her. She was his favorite sister as he was her favorite brother, perhaps because the two of them were much alike.

Rebecca Braun was an attractive woman of twenty-eight. She wore the traditional unadorned garb of Amish women — a dark dress, white fichu, and white apron. Her devotional cap covered most of her coal black hair. Her eyes mirrored Shad's, a dark blue with a hazel green tint. She had an oval face with a mouth that was full and attractive but too broad for actual beauty.

"So did you leave the fields to come in here and see if I've magically produced a suitor this morning, Shad?" she asked pertly.

Shad shook his head in feigned disgust. "You're never going to get a husband, Becky. Look, Lois is only thirteen and she's got her hope chest full, and Judith's just a year older and her hope chest is packed full. Yours looks suspiciously empty, and you're years older than them."

Rebecca shrugged her trim shoulders. "I know. But if I should find a man that I would want to marry — which is highly unlikely, considering what I have to choose from — but anyway, if that happens I'll just steal my sisters' hope chests. I'm the eldest; I have the right, don't I?"

Both of her sisters protested loudly and shrilly.

Adah said, "Oh, do be quiet, girls. Can't you tell by now when your sister is teasing you?" Adah was a tiny woman, with red hair and green eyes. Though she was modest and quiet, she was fully capable of taking her children in hand.

Shad watched Rebecca. A mischievous grin played on her wide mouth as her sisters kept complaining to their mother. Rebecca was a self-sufficient, self-contained woman, but with a lively spirit. She had a temperament that could swing from hearty laughter to deep, honest anger. And she had a wry sense of humor that was sometimes embarrassing to her family.

"Don't worry, Judith, Lois. Becky's too picky. Your hope chests are safe." Shad told Rebecca, "You turned down Chris

Finebaum, and every girl in the community was after him. Dorcas Chupp stole him from right under your nose."

"He's boring." Rebecca yawned ostentatiously, patting her mouth. "I don't want to spend the rest of my life with a man that can't talk about anything but crops and the weather. I want a man who is entertaining."

"Oh, you want to be entertained? You should marry a juggler like that one that came with the medicine show last year."

"Father is put out with you," Judith said. She had red hair and green eyes, much like her mother. At fourteen she was already a serious young girl who was thinking forward to the time when her courtship would begin. "He says you're frivolous."

"That's right," Lois agreed piously. "Father has always told you to take the young men in the community more seriously, Becky."

"That's the trouble. They are too dead serious, deadly bore serious."

"Shad!" Judith said accusingly. "Tell her!"

"I do try," Shad replied with mock seriousness. "I've tried to teach my sister how to catch a husband. It doesn't take. Now she's twenty-eight years old and has run off three good men that I know of."

"Three." Adah sighed regretfully. "And

54

they were all so fond of you, Rebecca."

"Oh, they managed to get over me soon enough," Becky said cheerfully. "All three of them married only a few months after I ran them off."

"For shame, Becky. Shad has a point and you know it," Judith put in. "A good Amish girl marries early and has children."

Shad shrugged. "You all might as well face up to it. Becky isn't your typical Amish woman."

Lois was still naive in many ways. "Becky, don't you want to find a good man and get married?"

Becky picked up the pillowcase and put in two stitches, apparently thinking over the question. "I haven't so far. Perhaps God will send me a husband. He would have to, to make me want to get married."

"Becky, I just don't understand you," Judith exclaimed. "It seems like you *want* to be an old spinster!"

"Oh, don't worry about me. If all else fails I can always catch me an English." *English* was what the Amish called someone outside of the Amish community. "If that's what happens, just pray he is so weak I can persuade him to join our church." She got up and tossed the pillowcase in the cedar trunk that constituted as her hope chest which, truth to tell, was pitifully empty. "I'm going out to see the new baby goat. If a suitable man comes by, be sure to tell him my demands for a husband. He's got to be able to take orders from his wife; if he's an English, he's got to become Amish; and he's got to be entertaining." She winked at Shad and left the room.

"She'll never get a husband, Mother." Shad sighed. "You and Father will have her on your hands for the rest of your life."

The next day Rebecca decided to take her dog, Hank, into the woods to look for herbs. In spite of the fact that she was not really the ideal Amish woman — she was an indifferent cook, disliked putting up canned goods and preserves, cared little for sewing, and often went barefoot when it was considered scandalous — she was a very good nurse and was good at herbalism.

She had filled her basket and several sacks with black sage, which was good for tea to calm the nerves. She had also found a good bit of burdock that was good for purifying the blood. Some said it was also good for a rattlesnake bite, but Becky didn't hold too much with that and hoped she never had to test it in that way.

She sang softly as she made her way

home. The Amish didn't believe in using musical instruments. They thought they were frivolous. But they did sing, and Becky had a good voice. She sang a very old hymn from the traditional Amish hymnal, the *Ausbund*. It dated back to the 1700s, and all of the hymns were in German.

Suddenly Hank ran off barking, which he rarely did, so she became curious. "What have you stirred up, Hank?" She followed him and came to a wide creek that was covered with a log jam — the beginnings of a beaver dam. Hank stood on the bank, barking monotonously, at the beavers, Becky presumed. Looking across the stream, she saw a large growth of redroot, which made an excellent tea that was good for relaxation, tending to sleep. She had discovered that it was also good for excessive menstruation, diarrhea, and dysentery, and the leaves and the tender stems could be eaten raw in salads.

Carefully Becky started across the creek, stepping on one half-submerged log to another. She was a sure-footed woman, but one of the logs suddenly rolled over and threw her off balance and she fell into the creek. The log continued rolling until it came to rest across her thighs. It was heavy, and since the stream was shallow, it was only halfway in the water and there was no chance that it would float off. It seemed securely anchored right across her.

Becky knew she wouldn't drown, but it would be a long time before she was missed. Her family wouldn't know where to look, for she had just told them she was going to look for herbs, not the direction she was going. In fact, she hadn't planned that at all. She had merely wandered along and picked the herbs that she found.

Even though it was August and the heat was oppressive, the stream was cold. She knew that even in the blistering heat of summer a person could get chilled and shocked if they were submerged too long in cold water. She struggled and struggled, but the log didn't move at all.

The minutes passed slowly, and after almost an hour of trying desperately to free herself, her legs ached with the weight of the log, and she knew that she couldn't fight anymore. She was exhausted.

Becky began to pray with all the faith she had.

As the sun fell down into the deep woods to the west, Becky began to shiver, and at the same time she was growing drowsy. She knew this wasn't good, that it was a sign that she was slowly going into shock. She heard Hank, now somewhere in the distance, baying. He had a distinctive call, starting deep in his chest and ending up with a high howl. He bayed on and on, for a long time it seemed to Becky, and then suddenly he stopped.

Wonder what old Hank's doing. . . . He's too lazy to tree a raccoon. Barking at squirrels or something? she thought sleepily.

Then he bounded up, long ears flapping, tongue hanging out the side of his mouth. He splashed right into the water and started licking Becky's face.

She scratched his head, murmuring, "Dumb ol' dog."

"Not so dumb," a deep voice said somewhere behind her. "Came and got me. You've got yourself in a right predicament, haven't you, ma'am?" A man wearing buckskins and riding a bay mare came into her sight at the stream's edge. He dismounted, and she saw he was tall, with a sun-bronzed face and chiseled features.

"Hello," she said lamely. "And yes, I have gotten myself into a predicament. I was going to get" — she motioned weakly toward the other side of the stream — "that redroot. Can you get me out of this?"

He waded out into the stream. "I can.

When I lift the log, pull your legs out." He reached around the log that pinned her legs, grunted, and lifted one end.

Becky waited until the pressure eased, then she leaned back and pushed with her hands until her legs came free. When she was clear of the log, he dropped it heavily. Becky sat up and then tried to stand but found that her legs were numb; she could barely move them. So she just sat. "Just give me a minute," she said then shivered.

"Ma'am, you're already freezing. You don't need to sit in this cold water anymore. If you'll allow me . . . ?" He reached out both arms and she nodded with relief, reaching up to him.

He picked her up easily and then carried her to sit her sidesaddle on his horse. "It's so warm today that I didn't carry a coat with me. We need to get you home, ma'am. May I ask your name?" He led the horse through the woods toward the clearing.

"I'm Rebecca Braun," she answered weakly, clutching herself and rubbing her arms, trying to warm up. "H–hello, Mr. Tremayne."

"You know me?" he asked with surprise.

"I remember you. It's been a long time. Let's see . . . I was, I think, eleven years old when you left."

He looked her up and down. Then a light of recognition came into his eyes. "Oh, yes. Becky Braun. Black hair, skinny little girl."

"That was me. Still have the black hair, not so skinny."

"Still pretty hair," Daniel commented.

They came into the sunshine. Immediately Becky felt the welcome warmth of the afternoon August sun. Her cap had disappeared — into the stream, she guessed. Woefully she tried to wring out her long, dripping hair. "Thank you, but I must look like a drowned cat," she muttered.

He looked up at her and grinned crookedly. In the strong light she could clearly see the scar beside the right side of his mouth and the other on his neck. He looked well-worn and tough. "Mmm, you are kinda soggy, ma'am. You getting warmer?"

"Yes, the sun feels so good," she answered, but helplessly she shivered again.

Suddenly he gave a leap and got on the horse behind her. He reached around her and grabbed the reins, and she was very aware of the pressure of his body against hers as he embraced her to try to warm her.

She stiffened and started to protest, but then she reflected that he was the type of man that if he wanted to give her a bear hug, he would just do it. She stayed quiet and relaxed. "Why did you stay away so long, Mr. Tremayne?" she asked curiously.

"Nothing but foolishness."

"I see. My father says you're not a steady man."

"He's right. Or he *was* right. I've decided to become a solid, responsible man."

"Have you?" She turned to face him, and he met her with a steady gaze. "I heard that you have a son. Is your wife with you?"

He answered quietly, "I was married to a woman named Winona. She was half Cheyenne. She died two years ago."

"I'm sorry; that must be very difficult," she said softly. "What's your son's name?"

"Yancy. He's twelve now. So you're married, I suppose?"

Facing away from him, a small smile played on her lips. "Why do you suppose that?"

"It's been a long time, but if I remember right, most Amish girls get married young. Sometimes around fifteen, sixteen."

"And I'm older than that?"

"I think so."

"You think right," she said lightly. "It seems that I have never been able to find the right man for me."

The horse stumbled slightly and his grip tightened around her waist. Becky found herself enjoying it.

"No? Why not?"

"For two very good reasons, Mr. Tremayne. The first is that all of them seemed to be very boring."

Daniel found this amusing, and she felt him laugh slightly. "What's the other reason?" he asked.

"I haven't found a man I would like to share a bed with for the next fifty years."

Daniel did laugh aloud then. "Well, that's speaking right out! I like a woman that says what she means. What would you say if I asked to call on you?"

Becky twisted around to face him again to see if he was still laughing, but now he was serious. "I don't know. I don't know you well enough."

"Thought that was the point," Daniel said lightly. "How are you going to get to know how wonderful I am if you don't let me call on you?"

"I'll say one thing . . . you aren't boring, Mr. Tremayne," Becky said. "All right. You can come sit on the porch, and my whole family will sit with us, and they will watch every move you make and listen to every word you say. I'm sure you remember how the courting goes around here."

"I do, I'm sorry to say. But what about

the other thing — the bed thing?"

She answered primly, "We'll have to see about that."

"Yes, ma'am, we sure will," he agreed heartily.

Rebecca couldn't remember being more fascinated with a man like she was with Daniel Tremayne. There was a rough handsomeness about him and a strength that she recognized instantly. She also liked him for his plain speaking.

Finally they came up to her house. Daniel dismounted and then helped Becky down.

Simon Braun came out and exclaimed, "What in the world happened, daughter?"

"I fell in the creek, Father, and got trapped under a log. Mr. Tremayne heard Hank barking and came and got me out."

Simon stared at Daniel then said, "It's been a long time, Daniel. I remember you when you were just a boy."

"Yes, sir, I remember you and Mrs. Braun, too. She always had sugar cookies for us when we came to visit with Shadrach. And speaking of him — hello, Shad." The rest of the family had come outside. Daniel shook hands with Shadrach.

He said, "It's been a while, Daniel. We were glad to hear that you're back. And what's this? You had to rescue my sister from some scrape she'd gotten herself into?" He rolled his eyes at the sight of Becky.

Rebecca was in no hurry to go inside. She stood there, dripping and bedraggled, listening with interest to the men's conversation. Her mother had hurried back in to fetch her a towel, and slowly Rebecca folded her long hair into it and dabbed it.

"I'm real glad to be back, too," Daniel answered. "Especially just in time to rescue Miss Braun." He spoke to the entire family. "I want you all to know that I'm so grateful to you for helping my mother with the farm after my father died. Thank you, all of you. And I want you to know that I'm going to stay, and I'm going to take care of her and the farm now. I'm trying very hard to become a good, steady man."

"I told Mr. Tremayne that you wanted to find a steady man for me as a husband, Father, and he's assured me that he is now," Becky said lightly. "So I invited him to come sit on the porch and court me." She enjoyed the look of shock that came across her parents' and her sisters' faces. She saw that Shad was amused.

"So she has," Daniel agreed with equanimity. "But I know it'll take time for me to prove myself, both to you and to Miss Tremayne. I understand she has some high standards where a husband is concerned."

For a moment Rebecca was afraid he would mention her comment about sharing a bed with a man for fifty years. She was vastly relieved when he gave her a surreptitious wink and said no more about it.

Simon looked bemused. "Well — I suppose — if Becky wants to see you, then you're welcome, Daniel."

"Good. Thank you, sir. I'll be back. Probably before you really want me to." He mounted, nodded to the ladies, slapped his hat securely back on his head, then turned and dashed off.

"Well, I do declare," Adah breathed. "He's a man that knows what he wants, isn't he? Rebecca, have you been very forward?"

"No, ma'am," Becky replied, her eyes dancing. "He's the one who's forward."

"Better get used to his ways, Mother," Shad said, grinning. "Looks to me like he's hoping to be your son-in-law."

CHAPTER FOUR

August in the valley was hot, but it was nothing like the Oklahoma plains, Yancy reflected. Even though they had lived by a lake, surrounded by thick woods and rich grasses and herbs, it had still been scorching, dusty, and bone-dry from April to September. Yancy liked the Shenandoah Valley. Even on the hottest days it was cool in the deep shades of the woods and on the large veranda of the farmhouse, where he sat now, yawning in the first gentle light of dawn.

Zemira was cooking breakfast, but the kitchen and dining room did get steamy in the summertime, so Yancy's grandfather had built an oak table and chairs so they could have meals outside in the fresh breezes.

Although Yancy did like the valley, there wasn't much more about living here that he cared for. In the year since he and Daniel had returned, he had adjusted to farm life.

He didn't mind the hard work, for he wasn't lazy; and in some ways he had come to appreciate the verdant fields, the rich harvests, the satisfaction of making something out of one's own land. But the Amish were very strict in all things, and sometimes he felt as if he were suffocating.

He was thirteen years old — he had longings and desires for things he could barely name, and not all of them had to do with his newfound appreciation for girls. Sometimes he wished he could just be free again, not under scrutiny by an entire community, not have to go to Amish school, able to do what he wanted when he wanted . . . much like when they had lived with the Cheyenne.

Zemira came out onto the porch carrying a tray. It had a tin coffeepot, steaming, and cups and saucers and sugar and fresh cream on it. There was a basket, too, covered with a linen cloth. She set it on the table by Yancy and then put her hands on her hips. "Don't eat it all."

Yancy sniffed then grinned. "Friendship Bread." He lifted one corner of the cloth on the basket.

She slapped his hand lightly and then put her hands back on her hips. "Don't eat it all," she repeated sternly. "You'll ruin your breakfast that's good for you. It'll be ready in a minute or two, and when I come back with it, there had better be plenty of that bread left for me and your father."

Amish Friendship Bread was a rich bread that required a complicated starter, and then took ten days to make. It had milk, flour, sugar, heavy double cream, vanilla, cinammon, and nuts. The reason it was called Friendship Bread was because it was traditional, when one presented it as a gift to good friends, to include the starter along with a loaf of the bread.

She bustled back into the house. Yancy fixed himself a cup of coffee, very sweet with lots of cream, and ate two generous pieces of the mouthwatering bread. He sipped his coffee; then, with a guilty look around, he crammed another piece into his mouth, chewing quickly. Then he tried to rearrange the bread so it looked like it was piled up higher than after his raid. He was, after all, only thirteen.

Zemira returned with a very large tray that held plates, silverware, napkins, and four covered bowls with scrambled eggs, bacon, grits, and biscuits. She set three places then sat down with Yancy. "We'll go ahead and bless," she said. "Your father's milking, and I'm not sure when he'll be here." They both bowed their heads in silence. The Amish did not believe in praying aloud; they thought that it could induce pride.

Yancy watched her out of the corner of his eye until she raised her head. The first thing she did was look at the Friendship Bread. "You ate three pieces," she said accusingly. "The biggest ones."

"I can't help it, Grandmother. I love it more than anything," he said lightly, helping himself to large portions of all the breakfast dishes.

"Humph. Only Friendship Bread you've ever had, I guess."

"Still the best."

She shrugged a little. "I can see it hasn't ruined your appetite," she said begrudgingly. Although she grumbled at Yancy, she kept a batch of Friendship Bread, in different stages, going all the time now, so he wouldn't run out.

They ate in companionable silence for a while. Yancy was very comfortable with his grandmother; he liked her a lot and was still forming a growing attachment to her. They had lived with her for about a year, but Yancy's affections weren't easily given. This was a part of his mother's Cheyenne blood. The Cheyenne were extremely loyal to family but rarely formed affectionate attachments outside it. Zemira was his grandmother, but he was just now learning to love her.

She was watching him shrewdly as these thoughts flitted through his mind. Then she asked, "Yancy, are you very unhappy here?"

Carefully, slowly, he buttered a biscuit, his eyes downcast. He took a deliberate bite and chewed. Then he answered, "It's hard for me, Grandmother. It's so different, and a lot of times I just don't understand what the People are doing. I mean, what's the matter with buttons, for goodness' sake? And what's the matter with having a blue buggy, with blue cushions, instead of all black? And so what if my moccasins are beaded?"

"Yancy, I know you've been told that the Amish truly believe in simple living, plain dress, and keeping to the old ways," Zemira answered. "Those things separate us from the world, from the evils of the world. It helps to keep us pure in the eyes of the Lord."

"My mother made my moccasins," he said stubbornly. "There was nothing wrong with my mother. She wasn't evil. And neither am I."

Zemira sighed. "I hate to tell you this, Yancy, but you must understand — we all have the seed of sin in us. All of us. And that's why we need Jesus to save us from this evil that is born in us, that we have inherited from Adam and Eve, when sin first entered this world. And that is why we try to keep ourselves pure in these ways, to combat that evil that is in all of us."

Yancy answered steadily, "I know, I know, I've heard all that in church, Grandmother. It's just that I can't see that for me to wear a shirt with buttons and moccasins with beads makes me evil."

Zemira took a sip of coffee, eyeing him over the rim with her sharp blue eyes. "Is that why you're unhappy here, Yancy? Because you know, we've been very lenient. We've let you wear the clothes you want, let you hunt with your gun, though it's against our beliefs. We let you do whatever you want instead of doing chores, even let you skip the sing. I don't understand that; most young people look forward to that time of being together."

Yancy snorted. "Skip the sing? Singing in German, which I don't speak, with no instruments? Sitting across the tables from the girls and taking turns singing — which, again, I can't do — and then barely talking to a girl before her father and brothers swoop in like bobcats and hustle her off like I'm a criminal or something? Can't imagine why I'd miss all that."

"It is very different from the life you've known, Yancy, but it's a good life. It's a clean, orderly, rewarding life."

He shook his head. "Good life for some, I guess, but I don't think it's for me."

"Your father thought that, too, when he was your age, and was on *rumspringa*. He left because he thought this life wasn't for him. But he came back to us."

"I know, Grandmother. And I know he's happy now." Yancy played with some leftover eggs on his mostly empty plate then asked moodily, "So what did you mean? What's rumspringa?"

Zemira hesitated for a few moments, staring into her coffee cup. "We've debated about telling you this, because your father thought it might just — confuse you. But you're a smart young man, Yancy, and old for your years, so I think you should know." She lifted her head and continued. "The Amish realize that young people must have some leniency, some . . . leeway. And so we give them a time, called rumspringa, which means 'running around.' The church rules are relaxed, and it's understood that in these times there will be a certain amount of misbehavior. It's neither condoned nor overlooked, but it's understood at the end of this period, the young person will be baptized into the church, will marry, and will settle down in the community."

"So this is letting me run around?" Yancy asked with astonishment. "This is running wild? Seems to me like I'm watched like I'm a prisoner most of the time."

"We let you wear your own clothes, which violates the Ordnung," Zemira answered gently. "And as I said, we pretty much let you decide what you're going to do every day. We don't hold you to chores, and we let you ride around all day without questioning you if you wish to. In other words, we're letting you make your own decisions."

Yancy stared at her. "What if I decide to leave? To go back to the Cheyenne?"

"Would you do that? Leave your family?"

He dropped his gaze. "No, ma'am. I don't want to leave Father . . . or you. You're the only reason I haven't gone stark raving crazy."

She reached over and patted his hand. "I love you very much, Yancy, and you can't know how glad I am that you and your father are here. I've been very lonely since your grandfather died. To have family again is precious to me."

He kept his head low, his gaze averted, and Zemira could sense his discomfort. She withdrew her hand then asked lightly, "Has your father told you about our family? The Tremaynes?"

"Not much. He — I think he feels bad about leaving, about Grandfather and all."

"So he does. But he's making up for it now, and your grandfather loved him always. Anyway, his great-grandfather Tremayne, and my great-grandfather Fisher, along with the other families, came to the valley in the 1730s. They found a good land, a fruitful land, and established our community. All of the families here can trace their land back to that time. When they started, there were only eight families. Now there are twenty-two, and we're still growing. It was a good thing, to find this place," she said dreamily. "It's been a good home."

"It is a good home," Yancy agreed quietly. "I do like the valley, very much."

She smiled warmly at him. "When our great-grandfathers came here, there were several tribes of Indians. Mostly Kiowa, but also Iroquois, Shawnee, and Algonquin. And our great-grandfathers made fast friends with them. We traded with them, we sometimes cared for their sick, we attended their funerals, and we even broke bread with them. But then when the English — the *Long Knives,* the Kiowas called them —

began to come into the valley in greater numbers, the Indians slowly left, going west. And our forefathers regretted it. They felt that they had lost people that belonged in the valley, even though they regarded them as heathens. You see, Yancy, the Amish never judge others who are not of the People. We believe we should always show them God's love. So whatever you do, Yancy, we will love you. Always."

Yancy climbed up on the buggy, sitting beside Daniel on the driver's bench.

Zemira sat on one of the benches in the back.

"Can I drive, Father?"

"Sure, Yancy. You're a good hand with a buggy, just like you are at riding."

"We're going to the Keims' house, is that right?"

"That's right. That's where church this Sunday will be."

The Amish had church services every other Sunday. Each Sunday, services were at a different home in the community, for the Amish didn't believe in building church buildings. They took this from the verse Acts 17:24, "God that made the world and all things therein, seeing that he is Lord of heaven and earth, dwelleth not in temples made with hands."

Each congregation of the church owned community property in the form of tables, chairs, benches, and wagons to transport them from farm to farm as the services were held in each home. The men from the congregation moved them every other Sunday for services.

Yancy spoke to the mare, and she started out with a sassy little toss of her head. He liked the look of her and the way she high-stepped. She had spirit, so he had to keep her on a tight rein, but for Yancy that only made the driving better. He had no use for a plodding, slow-moving horse and kept the mare at a fast trot.

"Good mare," Daniel commented. "Now who is she?"

Yancy took care of the farm horses. "This is Fancy," Yancy answered. "I named her that 'cause there's nothing else around here that is," he added mischievously. "She's the one that has that fine little foal, Midnight. He's young, but I've already started training him. Grandmother says he's a showy horse, too showy for the Amish."

"Guess that's true," Daniel agreed. "The Amish have a simple life."

Yancy shook his head. "Their church services sure aren't. First a short sermon, then singing, then prayers, then a long sermon, then a longer sermon, then more singing, then the longest sermon. Last week over at the Beilers' house it lasted for over four hours. How are you supposed to stay awake for all that?"

Daniel said regretfully, "I had the same problem, son, when I was your age. Guess the sermons do get a little long-winded, and those benches are downright uncomfortable. The Methodists have seats with backs on them instead of those backless ones that the People like. For the life of me, I can't see that a comfortable seat would be a sin."

"I was just saying stuff like that to Grandmother, Father," Yancy said soberly. "Like, why can't I wear my own clothes to church? I hate these stupid breeches. They're itchy and too short. And these shoes are like wood blocks on your feet. They hurt."

"It's a matter of respect, Yancy. The Amish wear simple clothes. You notice all the men dress alike, and so do the women, pretty much. And we let you wear your clothes all the time, except for church."

After a rather awkward silence, Yancy said, "Yeah, I know. Grandmother told me about rumspringa today. You're letting me off easy for now."

Daniel studied his son's face. In profile,

he strongly showed his mother's heritage. He had a thin nose, very high cheekbones, the slight copper tint of the Cheyenne. His eyes were dark and penetrating. Even at thirteen, he was beginning to lose his childish awkwardness and fill out, lean and muscled. His hair was glossy black, and he wore it longer than the Amish, with the back brushing his collar and a lock that fell over his forehead. Sometimes Daniel thought that the only thing Yancy had inherited from him was the cleft in his chin. "You're so much like your mother . . ." he murmured absently. Then he roused and said, "Rumspringa, yes. But it's not just me and your grandmother, Yancy. It's the bishop, the deacon, the secretary, and the preachers. They all watch out for the young people in the community."

A redtail hawk suddenly crossed the road in front of them. Yancy watched it longingly until it disappeared. "Sometimes I wish I was a hawk. They don't have bishops watching them and don't have to go to sings and wear hard shoes that hurt their feet."

Daniel grinned and slapped Yancy on the shoulder. "Even hawks have their hard times, too."

"Guess so. Good hunters though."

"Yes, they are, but living by hunting is

hard, Yancy. You and I both know that."

Yancy was silent.

Daniel hesitated then said in a light tone, trying not to sound dictatorial, "I know it's hard, Yancy, but I'd like for you to try to be more friendly. There are some good young people here."

Yancy protested, "But all the girls think about is courting and getting ready to marry. Who wants to think about getting married when they're thirteen?"

"Girls do," Daniel said drily. "But you don't have to think about that right now. And the other young men are interested in the same things you are — fishing, riding, even racing."

"But no gambling," he said disdainfully. "I know the other fellows like to fish, and they're interested in horses. It's just that I'm used to doing all those things alone." It was the Cheyenne way.

Daniel decided to say no more. Actually, he was proud of the way that Yancy had surrendered such a free life for one of close confinement. Yancy hadn't complained much. In fact, he said very little at all about their circumstances. He kept to himself. Daniel didn't realize that that was something else Yancy had inherited from him.

So it was something of a surprise when

Yancy asked carelessly, "So, Father, are you going to marry that lady?"

Daniel replied steadily, "You know her name. It's Becky, and yes, I am."

"You've been sitting on the Brauns' porch for a year now, sipping lemonade and all of them watching you like that redtail hawk we just saw looking for a mouse. When are you going to ask her?"

"I had to take the time, son, to make the Brauns see that I'm a dependable man now, that I've settled down, and that I'll be a good husband," Daniel explained patiently. "When I feel the time is right, I'll ask her. So how do you feel about it?"

Yancy shrugged. "Okay, I guess. She's pretty nice. But she's not my mother."

"No, she's not," Daniel said quietly. "But she would be a good mother. I know she would."

Yancy drew the mare to a halt by the corral.

The lot before the barn was already crowded with buggies, and two men were working, unhitching the horses and turning them into the corral. Sunday services and dinner was an all-day thing.

Yancy helped his grandmother down and she immediately went to a group of women who were standing by the house, in the shade of great oak trees. Daniel and Yancy started unhitching Fancy from the buggy, who pranced and snorted as if to say, *I could go another twenty miles if I had to!* Yancy loved her, for she was also a good saddle horse.

A young boy Yancy knew came running up. "Hey, Yancy! Why weren't you at the sing last Sunday? So when are we going fishing? You promised to take me." The boy was Seth Glick, and he was twelve years old.

Seth had met Yancy at the Amish school, which was a one-room schoolhouse with children from six years old to fourteen, the age limit of Amish education. Seth tagged along after Yancy every chance he got.

Yancy shrugged. "Hi, Seth. Whenever we can get together. Not sure."

"That's what you said before," he said. "You promised, Yancy."

"I know, I know. We will . . . sometime."

The boy, his shoulders rounded and head drooping, went toward the barn. In the smaller houses the young boys often sat in the barn for services, and one of the preachers would go out there for the service. Yancy had sat in the barn once, but Daniel had found out that he had sneaked out, stolen Fancy, and gone riding. Since then Daniel made him sit in the house with him and the other men. The women were separated from the men, often in different rooms.

As they finished leading Fancy into the enclosure, Daniel said, "You ought to take the boy fishing, Yancy."

"He doesn't know the first thing about fishing. He talks too loud and too much. He'd scare away every fish in the stream."

"Then it'd be a chance for you to help him. You could teach him. He's looking for a friend, Yancy."

Yancy looked surprised. "I never thought of that."

Daniel clapped Yancy on the back. "Friends are good things to have. Everyone needs them, even you. Make some friends. You'll be happier here."

The congregation, which was about a hundred people including the children, moved toward the house. Many people spoke to Daniel. In the last year, he had established himself as a good man, a good neighbor, and a fine, upstanding member of the community.

Yancy usually spoke back to those who greeted him, but quietly and with few words.

Yancy was thinking about his clothing — mostly about his shoes that hurt his feet and wishing for his soft moccasins.

Carelessly his eyes roamed over the congregation. All the women, even the pretty young girls, looked alike in their dowdy clothing. He had learned that the manner of dress was set out by the Ordnung, which to Yancy was simply a list of too-strict rules that everyone in the local Amish community had to obey.

The men also wore identical clothing, almost like uniforms, which consisted of a long black collarless frock coat with no lapels and split tails, with hook-and-eye closings. All wore vests fastened with hooks and eyes. They wore trousers with no flies and wide front flaps that fastened along the side. In the winter, the men and boys wore wide-brimmed felt hats, but it was close enough to summer that most of the hats were straw.

Yancy had discovered the width of an Amish hat brim meant something. The broader the brim, the more conservative the wearer and the less willing he would be to change. Those who were more liberal and had wilder spirits trimmed their hats to make them at least a *little* different. But no matter what, they all had to conform to the Ordnung.

On Sundays, Yancy, too, conformed. He wore black homespun pants, a linsey-woolsey shirt with no buttons, and the hated heavy black shoes. He had, however, flatly refused to wear a straw hat. "They're girlie hats," he had complained.

"I wear one," Daniel had said mildly.

"And you look girlie," Yancy had retorted. "I'm not wearing one. I'll wear my old slouch hat. That covers my head good enough."

The men's congregation had been set up in the Keims' large parlor. The furniture had been removed, and backless benches had been brought in. The women were in the connecting dining room, with the young women. The young men were in the barn. The smallest children were with their mothers, but during the service they often wandered over to their fathers. As long as they were not disruptive, they were allowed to go back and forth as they would, since the service was so long and it was understood that small children grew restless.

As did Yancy. He studied the congregation with little interest or excitement. It was the same group that he had been meeting with for almost a year now. He knew their names but hadn't grown close to any of them.

The service began as usual with a relatively short sermon by one of the preachers. It was followed by scripture reading and silent prayer. Other preachers went to the barn.

Following this came a longer sermon by the bishop. The service always included hymns, without any musical instruments. Even harmony was not permitted.

Yancy sat silently as the sermon moved along tediously, struggling to keep from dozing off.

Finally the service ended. The men worked to put the benches and tables outside and to move the Keims' furniture back in. The women went to the kitchen and then outside to set the tables for Sunday dinner, as was customary. Hosting a Sunday service was demanding, but everyone in the congregation brought food, and they always made sure that any cleaning after services and dinner was done.

This was the one good thing about the services to Yancy — plenty of good food. Fried chicken, roast beef, all sorts of vegetables and casseroles, pies and cakes — all in plenty, enough to satisfy even ravenous teenagers. The men were all seated and the women began to serve them, replenishing their bread baskets; and the butter, tea, and lemonade cooled in the stream.

A young woman, Hannah Lapp, refilled Yancy's lemonade. She was thirteen and was in school with him. She was a pretty girl with sandy brown hair, dark brown eyes with perfect winging brows, and a beautiful complexion. She was a little shy, but she and Yancy had talked some, during lunches and recess. She tended to hover close by him at Sunday dinners. "Are you coming to the sing next Sunday, Yancy?" she asked softly.

"Hope not," he answered shortly.

"You should come. There'll be lots of games and good things to eat."

Yancy shrugged. "That doesn't make up for having to sit through a sing — when you can't sing and you don't even know what you're supposed to be singing."

"I could teach you some of them," Hannah said. "Not all of them are long and hard German words."

"If I cared," Yancy said harshly. "Which I don't."

Rebecca Braun was across from Yancy, serving up fresh bread. She gave him a stern look, but he ducked his head and ate steadily.

"Oh — I — of course not," Hannah said lamely. "I'm — sorry." Quickly she moved along to the next man, to refill his glass.

After the meal, when everyone was meeting and talking in companionable groups, Becky came to sit beside Yancy, as he was still sitting on the bench at the table by himself.

"You weren't very nice to Hannah, Yancy," she said quietly. "I thought you were more of a gentleman."

"Guess not," Yancy muttered. "But I don't see how it's any of your concern, ma'am."

"I think it is my business, Yancy, because I'm going to marry your father. I know I won't be like your mother. But I would like to look at you as my son. And so I would like to know that my son is a kind man, a man that I can be proud of."

Yancy stiffened. "You're right — you're not my mother. You'll never be my mother. And besides, my father hasn't asked you to marry him yet."

"No, he hasn't, but that's because of me. I wanted to wait until I could be sure that he was the kind of man I wanted to marry. A good man, an honorable man that could make a good home for me."

"And?" Yancy demanded.

"And he's that man," Becky said simply. "But there's something else I've been watching and waiting for."

"What's that?"

"I wanted to see if you would be a good older brother to my children."

This amused Yancy so much that despite himself, he smiled. This woman was the one person he saw of the Amish, besides his grandmother, who was different from the others. Becky Braun and Zemira Tremayne always spoke their minds directly, without hesitation or decoration. "So, do you think I'll be good with your children?"

"No. Not right now, I don't."

Her abruptness startled Yancy. "Why wouldn't I be a good brother? Is it because I'm part Indian?"

"No, that's not it."

"What is it then?"

"You haven't learned how to be kind." Becky paused and her eyes were fixed on Yancy with such an intensity that he couldn't turn his gaze away from hers. She had a way of drawing people's attention and keeping them fixed when she spoke. "You were short with Hannah, without need. You should be gentler with people, Yancy."

Yancy was irritated. "I guess you better not marry my father then, if I'm not what you want in a son."

"I know you could be." Becky smiled suddenly, reached out, and pushed a lock of Yancy's coal black hair from his forehead, where it had fallen. "I know you will be. I don't need to wait any longer. So come with me."

"Where are we going?"

"Just come with me and don't ask questions." Becky led Yancy through the crowd to the end of one of the tables, where Daniel sat with Becky's family. They all looked up as they approached, and Daniel got to his feet. "Hello, Becky. I see you've corralled my son. Won't you sit down?"

Becky stopped directly in front of Daniel and looked up at him. "Not just now, Mr. Tremayne. I need to know . . . do you still want to marry me?"

A silence fell over the group, and Yancy saw that his father was taken totally off guard. Astonishment marked Daniel's face and then he turned red. But he answered solidly, "I do want to marry you, Rebecca Braun."

"All right." Becky smiled. "We're engaged then, but I don't want to wait a year." A year was the common period most young couples waited before marriage. Now Becky turned to her father and said firmly, "Father, I know it's not the Amish way, but Daniel and I are older. He's proved himself to be a good man. We'd like your permission to get married in one month."

Simon Braun wasn't a man who was easily shocked, as he'd grown accustomed to Becky's "wild ways" as he called them. He frowned and said, "Daughter, I know when you've made up your mind, a whole string of plow mules couldn't drag you from it. But would you do me a favor, here and now? You know that we don't condone marriage except for November and December, because of the harvest. Won't you at least wait until then?"

Becky said stubbornly, "No, Father —"

Daniel took her hand, tucked it into his arm, and said, "Yes, Mr. Braun, we'll be glad to wait until harvest is over. November will be fine."

"But —" Becky began, looking up at him beseechingly.

Daniel put one finger on her lips. "Shush, bride. Let me win this one."

She took a deep breath then laughed. She had a good laugh, a rich laugh. "All right, groom. But you'd better count this one dear. You won't win many."

"You sure won't, Mr. Tremayne," Simon Braun said, sighing and shaking his hand. "You surely won't."

Chapter Five

July 1857 was a bountiful harvest, almost more than anyone could ask for. The Tremayne fields of hay, wheat, and corn were bursting. The pantry and the root cellar were overrun from the kitchen garden with peas, squash, tomatoes, carrots, and potatoes. Other women from the community came on Saturdays to help Becky and Zemira can them, as Becky and Zemira also went to their farms to help them with the riches of their lands.

Becky and Zemira sat on the veranda, sipping lemonade and shelling peas. The front veranda faced east, and often they could see the Blue Ridge Mountains, mostly just a grayish smoke on the horizon, but sometimes they could make out the dreamy peaks.

"I've never been there," Zemira murmured. "Jacob and I thought that we might go to the mountains once. But somehow home never let us go."

"Home is good," Becky said quietly. "Sometimes it's better just to stay close. At least, that's how I feel now. I couldn't ask for any other happiness."

Zemira glanced at her sharply. "Becky, daughter, are you with child?"

Becky's finely etched black eyebrows arched in surprise. "I — I think so. But it's so early, I haven't even told Daniel. How did you know, Grandmother?"

Zemira smiled. "I think the Lord tells me things. It's not like I hear His voice; it's just a *knowing*. So how far along are you?"

"I've been telling myself not to hope too much," Becky answered. "It would just be a couple of weeks. But like you, Grandmother, I feel like I just . . . *know.*"

"Women do." Zemira nodded. "Women generally do."

They shelled peas in silence for a while, their nimble fingers stripping the tough, stringy stems and separating them into bite-sized chunks.

"You and Daniel have been worried, haven't you?" Zemira asked softly.

Becky didn't answer; she ducked her head and shelled peas energetically.

"It's all right," Zemira continued. "I know you've wondered, though Daniel wouldn't say anything. You've been married eight months now, and I know it makes you anxious to wait. Jacob and I were married for almost forty years and had only one son. And Daniel didn't come along until we'd been married for fourteen years. I know you and he have thought about that." Zemira sighed deeply. She wouldn't tell of the two stillborn sisters Daniel had, one in 1818 and one in 1820. Daniel hadn't been born until 1823.

"It's — it's not just you, Grandmother," Becky said hesitantly. "It's my family, too. I mean, I was born, but then it was eight years until Shadrach was born, and then another six until Judith, and a year later Lois. Daniel and I — it's just that we both want children so badly, and we both want four, maybe five. I don't know if I'll — that is, if time — if we can —"

Zemira dropped her hands and gazed at her daughter-in-law sternly. "Child, you talk foolishness. My son has become a good man, a fine man, constant in the Lord and walking in His will. You are a good and faithful Christian woman. God will bless you. I've no doubt in my mind."

Becky ducked her head. "Yes. Yes, you're right, Grandmother, as always. I'm very proud of Daniel, and I'm so blessed to have him for a husband."

Zemira nodded emphatically. "I'm so proud of him, too. He's a good son, and a good husband, and a good father." She bent to her work again. "But he did have his wanderings. And I think that Yancy may, too. You wouldn't know it from the way Daniel is now, but Yancy is so much like him, when Daniel was in rumspringa."

"You see that in Yancy? That same rebelliousness?"

Zemira glanced at her. "Has Daniel ever told you about his time then? When he left home?"

"No, he hasn't, and I haven't wanted to intrude on him to ask. Whatever happened then, he's a different man now."

"That's the truth, daughter," Zemira agreed. "And I have to say that Yancy is much better behaved than Daniel was then. Maybe it's just a young man's restlessness. He does get into scuffles with the young men, and the girls say he's very forward with them."

Becky laughed. "The young men that he's bested say that, and I think the young girls that complain about him are the ones that don't get his attention. He's a very good-looking young man, you know, and he is strong and quick and probably very desirable to young women."

"I suppose so," Zemira said grumpily, "but the bishop is out here every week, it seems, complaining about another one of his scrapes. It's getting harder to find excuses for him."

Becky answered, "But you do find excuses for him, as I do. All we can do is pray, Grandmother. Pray that he stays with us and finds God. Until then, we must find more excuses."

It was a fruitful year and a bountiful harvest. Even the winter seemed benevolent. They had picturesque snows for Thanksgiving and Christmas and bright, brisk days for the New Year.

Becky and Zemira had been right. Becky was expecting, and though it was an easy winter in the valley, it was hard for her and Daniel. She was due in April and it seemed as if the baby — and the spring — would never come.

But the times of the seasons always come, and the spring of 1858 was glorious. The long days were delightfully warm and the nights refreshingly cool. Rain came just as and when it should. Even Yancy didn't mind working the fields; the days were so pleasant and the planting was easy.

Early in the evening of April 16, the family was gathered in the parlor. A small, comfortable fire crackled, and the last sweet rays of the sun shone strong through the large windows. Daniel and Yancy were playing checkers while Zemira and Becky quilted.

Becky had never before been a very good seamstress, but Zemira was very skilled. Once Becky had applied herself to quilting under Zemira's expert teaching, she had come to enjoy it.

Leaning back, she rubbed her eyes then sat motionless for a few moments, her eyes closed.

Zemira eyed her shrewdly. Once, when Zemira was young, she had been the best midwife in the community. But after her second stillborn daughter, she had refused to ever consider it again. Still, the founts of knowledge of men and women run deep and are hard to ignore.

Rebecca lifted her head with a small smile. "Daniel?"

"Yes, dearest?"

"I think it's time for you to go fetch Esther Raber."

Daniel jumped up, knocking the straight chair he was sitting in halfway across the room.

This made Yancy jump up in alarm, and his chair fell over.

"Stop!" Becky said, holding up one hand and laughing. "It's no emergency, you know. This little one has taken a sweet time coming, and for all we know it may be tomorrow or the next day before he or she decides to put in an appearance. It's fine, Daniel."

Zemira pursed her lips. "It's a girl, Daniel. And I do think you might step lively to get Mrs. Raber."

Daniel turned and bolted from the room, followed by Yancy.

"Just — wait! Don't kill your silly selves!" Becky called after them. "Grandmother, why did you scare them like that? How do you know?"

"Normally I don't say much about what's between a mother and her child and God. But you're precious to me, daughter, and I have to say that I think this little girl is going to be born before midnight, even though I see you're in real early light pains. Anyway, why don't we go on upstairs and get you fixed up in bed? And I'll have everything ready by the time Esther gets here. All I can say is" — she grunted a little, helping Becky rise from the straight-backed bench — "that I hope that silly, loud, little Leah Raber doesn't insist on following Yancy over here.

I declare right here and now, I think she'd kidnap him and hold him prisoner if she thought it would make him marry her."

"Can't blame her," Becky said, smiling. "He is a handsome young man."

"Doesn't excuse her. She's like a little gnat, always buzzing around him. So, daughter, what are you going to name her?"

"I'm going to be cautious and wait until we see what it is, Grandmother, even though I have faith in you. And anyway, I think I will let Daniel make the final decision when he sees her."

"Her?" Zemira repeated mischievously as they struggled up the stairs.

"Or him," Becky added quickly then bent over with a sudden sharp pain. "All right, all right, her," she whispered. Looking up at Zemira, she grinned. "Guess she's going to take after me."

It took about an hour for Daniel and Yancy to bring Esther back to the farm, and by that time Rebecca was already in hard labor, though it was perfectly natural and normal. After an examination, Esther, a kind, gentle woman with warm, dark eyes, came out into the hallway and said, "It looks like we're going to have a baby soon, Daniel. Please go downstairs . . . and don't worry. Both

Becky and the baby look very, very good."

"But how do you know? What do you mean? What — ?"

Esther was kind, but she could be firm when she had to be, particularly with wayward daughters like Leah and distraught fathers-to-be like Daniel. "You must trust me," she said firmly. "I know, and certainly Zemira knows. She was the best midwife in the community."

"Huh?" Daniel said, bewildered.

"Never mind. Just go downstairs, stay calm, and wait."

Yancy and his father went downstairs and waited, but they certainly were not calm. They paced in the parlor, they paced in the dining room, and finally they went out and paced on the veranda. The night was beautiful, with a full silver moon and a spangling of stars spanning the sky. They didn't notice. The only thing they noticed was when they accidentally ran into each other, and then they muttered distractedly, "Uh, sorry." They even ran into poor Hank a couple of times, who was sitting at the top of the steps, watching them blundering around with worried eyes.

In the still night, they heard a baby's cry. It was eleven minutes to eleven.

Esther's step sounded on the stairs, and

they rushed into the house like mad bulls.

"Come on up," she said, smiling widely. "They're fine."

They ran up the stairs and then, slowing down and almost tiptoeing, they went into the bedroom.

Rebecca sat up in bed. She looked tired, and her hair was dripping with sweat, but she smiled. "Look, Daniel! Just look! Isn't she beautiful?"

"She . . . she? It's a girl?" Daniel murmured, standing by the bed. "Thank the Lord! She's — all right?" he asked Esther anxiously.

Zemira soundlessly came up to stand beside him. She beamed down at the baby. "She's perfect, just perfect. She reminds me of — of —" She choked slightly, then finished in a low voice, "Of you, of course, Daniel. Of you."

The baby was awake and seemed to stare right up at her father. She had reddish blond hair and light blue eyes, just like Daniel. Most babies just look like babies, but Yancy thought that she did indeed resemble Father.

Becky held her up for Daniel to hold. He took her as if she were the most precious thing in the world. "A little girl . . . a girl . . . Oh, thank you, wife."

"Thank you, husband. So what shall we call her?"

"Well, we did talk about that. I know it's kind of a mouthful, but I still like it. Callie Josephine? Callie after my grandmother and Josephine after your grandfather Joseph?"

"Callie Josephine it is," Becky said, settling wearily back into her pillows. "What do you think about your new sister, Yancy?"

It gave Yancy a warm feeling for Becky to call the baby his sister instead of his half sister. Over the last two years he had come to love Becky, though he could never call her Mother. But this did give him a tie to the baby, for them to name her after his great-grandmother Callie. Grandmother had told him a lot about her mother. She had been a strong, loving woman.

Yancy answered, "Well, she's — uh, little. And she's all red. But she's got pretty-colored hair, like Father's."

Becky laughed. "The red will go away, and she'll have a beautiful complexion, just like her grandmother Zemira. And yes . . ." she finished softly, "she is very much like her father."

■ ■ ■ ■

PART TWO:
THE PRELUDE,
1858

■ ■ ■ ■

CHAPTER SIX

Three cadets scurried across the compound, headed for the classroom building. They were fifteen minutes late. They were students of Virginia Military Academy, better known as VMI. This institution was joined to Washington College in the small Virginia town of Lexington.

Sandy Owens, a tall, lanky boy of fifteen with hazel eyes and the sandy reddish hair that his nickname would indicate, led the three. Behind him was Charles Satterfield, a short, stocky fifteen-year-old with jet black hair and warm, brown eyes. Peyton Stevens, the third member of the group, was a handsome blond boy with china blue eyes and the look of aristocracy about him. He was sixteen but could have passed for eighteen. He wasn't as flustered as the other two boys, knowing he wouldn't be in a great deal of trouble since his father was a senator and had gotten him out of every trouble he had managed to get into.

Their awkward hurry was jarring with their splendid appearance. They wore the distinguished uniforms of the Virginia Military Institute, and with that uniform went the unbreakable rule that they be spotless and without fault. The cadets wore the gray tunic with tails. Finely embroidered "frogs" — so named for the three-lobed fleurs-de-lis — adorned the collar and the face of the tunics. At each frog was a button, a silver image of the seal of the state of Virginia. Their breeches were spotless white, and if they were not spotless, the cadet was immediately sent to the barracks to don acceptable pants. In formal dress, they wore snowy white crossbelts with a silver buckle. They proudly wore forage caps with thick silver cords around the brim.

The cadets' finery particularly troubled Sandy Owens; he was something of a ladies' man, and he despised his uniform getting spoiled. It was all too easy for the spotless white breeches to get soiled when riding, or in musket drill, or particularly in cannon drill. He avoided all contact with dirt and grime with great perseverance.

Charles, whom everyone affectionately called Chuckins, had a worried look on his face. He was a good-natured boy who took teasing very well, which was surprising considering he came from an extremely wealthy family. He showed no signs of the usually spoiled scion, however. Now he muttered nervously, "We're going to catch it, Sandy! You know what old Tom Fool will do to us for being so late!"

Sandy grunted. "Whatever happens, you better not let Major Jackson hear you call him Tom Fool. He knows more than we think he knows. I don't know who started calling him Tom Fool, but they're crazy, 'cause he ain't no fool."

"You're right about that," Peyton languidly agreed. He was breathing easily, and he kept his eye fixed on the great Gothic institute that rose before them. "They say that he ate those Mexicans alive during the war, with the artillery. He sure does know what he's doing with artillery pieces." In spite of his apparently languid and lazy appearance, Peyton Stevens dearly loved musket practice and artillery practice. He was very good with both rifles and cannons.

"We know, we know, his artillery class is the best," Chuckins agreed, breathing hard because he had been trotting to keep up with Sandy and Peyton. "It's just this natural and experimental philosophy class. He just recites it from memorization. Puts me to sleep every time, no matter how hard I pinch myself!"

"We have to stay awake, and we have to figure out a way to get into that classroom with a good excuse," Peyton said. "Otherwise we'll all get demerits." Suddenly he stopped walking.

Then Sandy stopped and Chuckins ran into him.

"What we need is a good, sound alibi," Peyton said thoughtfully. "What's the biggest lie you can think of, Sandy?"

"Uh — my grandmother died?"

"Your grandmothers have died four or five times," Peyton scoffed. "How about this? Chuckins, you ate too much dinner and it made you sick. Sandy and I had to take you to the infirmary."

Perplexed, Chuckins asked, "But what would I be doing coming to class if I was sick?"

"You weren't as sick as you thought," Peyton answered smoothly. "And you're so loyal to VMI that you insisted on coming to class, sick or not."

"Hey, that might work!" Chuckins exclaimed, his hazel eyes fixed on the forbidding gray sandstone building looming up before them. "I think I feel my sickness coming back on. Maybe you better help me in."

"That's it, Chuckins," Sandy said. "Here, Peyton, grab his arm. Poor boy is sicker than anybody knows."

Slowing their pace, the three cadets moved toward the classroom building. As they did, Sandy Owens said, "You know, I feel sorry for Major Jackson."

"Why would you feel sorry for him?" Peyton asked.

"You know he got married. Well, his first wife died along with his baby."

"Yeah, but he got married again right away," Peyton said. "He didn't let any grass grow under his feet. That woman he married, Elinor Junkin, she's the daughter of Dr. Junkin that was the president of Washington College. For sure she has money. I imagine she set up the Major pretty well."

Sandy looked at him with surprise. "But Peyton, didn't you hear? Last month Major and Mrs. Anna Jackson lost their baby. A little girl that they had named Mary Graham. She lived almost a month then died. I think maybe that's why he's been so much more stern this last month."

Peyton looked repentant. "No, I hadn't heard. That's — hard. That's hard for a man."

They marched on silently, but they were young, and the tragedies of life had not yet become real for them.

As they neared the classroom building, Chuckins said weakly, "I'm feeling sicker, boys. Let's go in."

The three, moving more slowly, entered the building and trudged down the hall until they came to a door that led into the classroom. They tried the door — but it was sturdily locked. They weren't too surprised, because Major Jackson often did this when he wasn't in a very good mood.

Soon the man himself opened the door and stepped out into the hallway. "Yes, gentlemen? I believe you are —" He ostentatiously pulled a watch from his pocket and stared at it, then looked up. "You are eighteen minutes late." He still wore his dusty major's uniform from the Mexican War. He had grown a fine mustache and beard, and right now they bristled. His eyes were as cold and icy blue as the darkest winter midnight.

"Yes . . . sir . . . Major . . . sir," Chuckins said weakly. "I was sick. Sandy and Peyton took me to the infirmary."

Major Jackson stared at him unforgivingly, raking him from head to toe.

"Uh — but —" Sandy started stuttering.

"Chuckins feels better now, though, Major Jackson," Peyton said smoothly. "He didn't want to miss class."

Jackson's blue-light gaze transferred to Peyton, and even he shifted uncomfortably. "Who is Chuckins?" Jackson demanded.

Charles Satterfield came to backbreaking attention and said stiffly, "It's me, sir. I'm Cadet Charles Satterfield."

"Well, Cadet, you are late for class, and being ill, you've also made your friends late for class. Two demerits for you, one for each of you, Cadet Owens, Cadet Stevens. If you don't want any further punishment, be on time for artillery tomorrow," Jackson said coldly. "Dismissed." He went back into the classroom and again locked the door firmly.

The three cadets stood still in shock for long moments. Then Sandy blew out a long, "Wheeew! We set him off this time, no fooling!"

They turned to walk back down the hall. "And I got two demerits," Chuckins wailed. "That's not fair! I didn't think of it. You did, Peyton!"

"Relax. I've already got four demerits," Peyton said carelessly. "It's not like they won't graduate you, Chuckins. You're a good little cadet. You'll be fine."

"Well, I'm never listening to you two

again," Chuckins grunted. "I'm gonna be right on time for artillery tomorrow."

"Me, too," Sandy agreed.

After a while, Peyton said, "Yeah, me, too."

Sandy Owens, Chuckins Satterfield, and Peyton Stevens were on time, even early, for artillery class the next day. With much self-righteousness, they sat in the front row, their eyes fixed, without wavering, on Major Jackson.

"Understand that learning to load and fire a cannon has no importance whatsoever if you don't learn to *aim* a cannon. . . . Any fool can fire a big gun, but it takes a smart man to hit what he's aiming for."

The cadets sat listening as Major Jackson lectured, and none of them wiggled, for they had learned that his eyes would glow dangerous blue fire if they did. Also, as unassuming as he was in his natural and experimental philosophy classes, he was the polar opposite in his artillery classes. He was authoritative, commanding, and knowledgeable to the point of being almost mystical. In the Mexican War, one of his sergeants had said that it was almost as if he had single-handedly invented artillery.

"Now, gentlemen, we will go out and take practice in the art of artillery. I will appreciate it that you understand that the cannon is an instrument. It is an *art* as much as a skill. Some of it has to be born in you, for it's not just the mathematics and the angle and the azimuth and the wind speed. You've got to have the eye. The eye, gentlemen! So let's go see if any of you boys are blessed with the eye." Jackson stepped off the podium and left the room.

In perfect order the cadets lined up two by two, marching behind him.

Before VMI was given the opportunity to obtain the services of the renowned Major Thomas Jackson, they had only conducted dumb-fire exercises of the cannons, relying on live-fire for the muskets. But former Lieutenant Thomas Jackson, of General Winfield Scott's army in Mexico fighting Santa Anna, had made quite a name for himself. He and one man, a sergeant of artillery, had managed to break down the great fortress of Chapultepec single-handedly, with one cannon. They held the line until reinforcements arrived from his commander, Captain John Magruder. General Winfield Scott had taken special notice of Lieutenant Jackson, and so because of conspicuous bravery, he had been brevetted to the rank of major.

Because Major Thomas Jackson had

gained quite a bit of fame and notoriety for his artillery work and he had persuaded the commandant of VMI that live fire of cannon was essential for the training of the cadets, he had been granted extremely special privileges for his artillery class. The college had, in effect, dug out a large trench, so that the cannons would fire into a hillside and not a fallible target. Four cannons had been purchased for the institute, and every month more powder and balls were bought for Major Thomas's enthusiastic students.

The low ground of open field was to the west of the classroom building. The cannons were placed into a twelve-foot gully that rose above them. Six-foot-tall bales of hay, with circles painted on them vaguely representing men advancing, served as targets. To the rear was a shed filled with ammunition and supplies. The targets were set up in the field, and the underclassmen among the cadets began to open the shed and bring out the powder and shells.

Major Jackson stood rigidly as they did this, staring at the targets as if they were an oncoming battalion.

Peyton Stevens, the only cadet that had ever dared to initiate a conversation with Jackson, stood close by him. "Sir," he asked speculatively, "do you think there will be a war? The papers all say so."

"I'm more interested in what God says than what the papers say, Cadet Stevens. But I pray daily that there will not be a war," Jackson answered.

The irrepressible Stevens would not be quiet and asked intently, "Would you fight with the Union, sir?" This was a constant question with Southern men — what would they do in case the South seceded?

"I ask God every day of my life to bring North and South together without shedding of blood. I love this country, Cadet Stevens, and it would break my heart to see brother fighting against brother on the field of battle."

And at that Peyton Stevens grew quiet.

Anna Jackson looked across the tea table at her sister Eugenia. Anna was pale, and there were dark shadows under her eyes. She had borne Thomas a daughter on April 30, and they had named her Mary Graham Jackson, but she was weak and ill and had died on May 25.

Eugenia had been here with her sister since the birth. It was the end of June, and Anna assured her that she was fine and Eugenia could return home. Eugenia herself had two healthy children, which, oddly, made her feel a little guilty. It didn't, however, diminish her true sorrow for her sister. Eugenia smiled a little. "You know, Anna, I never told you this, but I was absolutely astonished when you married Major Jackson."

"Why would you be astonished, Eugenia?"

"He's so *different* from you. You're so lively — and he seems so stately, I suppose you'd say."

Anna nodded a little. "He does appear that way. You were always prettier than I, and the young men were fighting to see who would squire you around. While you were doing that, I was spending time with Thomas."

"He's just so different from most men. Does he still worry about his health?"

Anna appeared somewhat disturbed with this. She hesitated before answering, "I'm afraid he's *too* concerned with his health. He seems to me to be absolutely strong and healthy, but he has some odd ideas. He stands straight up for long periods in order to keep perfect alignment of his organs, or so he believes. He will only study his books in the daytime, because he thinks that artificial light like candles harms his eyesight."

"My, that *is* strange."

"Yes, it is. I suppose you've noticed that he keeps a lemon with him at all times? Very rarely do you see him for a long period without his biting the end off and sucking the juices out."

"I don't see how he does that. I should think it would make his mouth pucker."

"He thinks it helps his health. He's really two men, Eugenia; it's almost as if he leads a double life."

"What do you mean?"

"I don't think you know him, and the people of Lexington have never really known my husband. He's so formal and stiff at times in public, but there are other times, especially when we're alone, when he is so gay and carefree no one would recognize him."

"I can't imagine him being gay and light-hearted."

"Oh yes! Why just yesterday he was talking to one of the little girls that belonged to one of the neighbors. He was saying a poem for her, and what poem do you guess it was?"

"I'd guess Wordsworth or Shakespeare."

"No indeed, it was quite different from their work." She smiled and quoted the small poem:

"I had a little pig,
I fed him on clover.
When he died,
He died all over."

"Oh, that's funny! Did he make it up himself?"

"He wouldn't admit it, but I'm sure he did. So as you see, he's really two men. The austere major and professor in the classroom, sometimes very stern and harsh. But when we're alone, it's a different story."

Eugenia said in a low voice, "I know you've grieved terribly over the loss of Mary Graham, sister. Yet Thomas, to a stranger, seems to be just as strong and sure as ever he was."

Anna put down her teacup and grasped her sister's hand in hers. "He suffers, Eugenia. He suffers as much or more than I do. You remember, he and Ellie lost a son."

"I know. I remember."

Anna's voice choked with tears. "Pray for us both, Eugenia. Thomas and I will forever grieve for the loss of our baby. Don't doubt Thomas. Just because he doesn't show it doesn't mean he doesn't feel it."

"Of course I will pray, sister. I'll pray without ceasing for you both."

"Thank you, my darling sister. And I'll

forever be grateful for your coming to me in this difficult time. God bless you on your journey home, and bless you and your husband and children."

When Thomas came in the door, Anna was there to meet him. He put his arms around her very gently. "Ah, my *esposita,* you're so much prettier than any of those ugly cadets I have to face all day!" He kissed her then held her at arm's length. "That's a new dress, isn't it?"

They had decided only to go into mourning for one month for their lost daughter. Jackson had not said much, but he had mourned for more than a year when he lost his first wife, Ellie, and their son. He didn't want to go down that dim gray road again for so long. Anna had tacitly agreed.

Now she looked down at the dress and touched the skirt. It was a pretty peach color, trimmed with green, with a wide hoop skirt. Since she had dressed for dinner, it was off the shoulder, and she wore a small gold pearl necklace and drop earrings. Sadly, she remembered that she hadn't worn the dress since before she had gotten pregnant. But she smiled a little and answered, "No, Thomas, you've seen it about a dozen times."

"I suppose I'm no expert on women's fashion," he said, taking off his jacket and hanging it on the hall tree.

"No, if something doesn't shoot bullets or a cannonball, you don't pay much attention."

He smiled. "I pay attention to you, dearest."

She took his arm. "Yes, you do, husband. Come along, dinner is on the table."

The two went into the dining room. The table was covered in fresh-baked bread, roasted beef, fresh corn off the cob, English peas, and pickled beets.

Thomas sat down across from Anna and they bowed their heads. He said, "Lord, we thank You for this food which is Your provision. I pray that You will bless it, and that You will give us wisdom and insight and will make us love You more each day. In the name of Jesus, Amen."

Thomas reached out and picked up the bowl of green peas. He filled his plate to overflowing. He had formed the habit of eating only one vegetable no matter how many were on the table.

Anna exclaimed, "Thomas, you're not going to fill up on those peas and eat nothing else!"

Jackson answered patiently, "Now, Anna,

you know that's the way I like to eat. I like to have one single kind of food, and I like to drink plain water."

"Thomas, you know I'm afraid that's not healthy for you. You should eat meat, vegetables, and bread at every meal."

"Foolish ideas! All of my ideas about health are sound."

"You mean even that you think one side of you is heavier than the other?"

"Sure enough, I figured it all out."

"How could you weigh just one side of yourself, Thomas?"

"I did."

"That's the reason you raise one hand up to arm's length?"

"Yes, it lets the blood flow down and lightens that arm."

Anna suddenly giggled. "Thomas — Thomas, my love! You do have interesting ideas."

Jackson grinned at her, which made him look a great deal younger. Indeed, if his cadets had seen him, they would've been astonished at how young he looked as he took his wife's hand. "That's the reason you fell in love with me, because I'm such an interesting fellow."

The two finished their meal and went for a walk in the garden, for Anna was very proud of her flowers. They waited until the daylight faded and then they went inside.

"I wish you would read to me tonight, Anna," Jackson said.

"All right, what would you like?"

"I would like to hear *Macbeth*."

"Oh, Thomas, that's a horrible play! It's full of blood and killing and horrible things."

"It's a work of genius. Mr. Shakespeare knew much of human nature. If you please, my dear, let's have *Macbeth*."

And so it was that they settled down in the drawing room. Thomas sat bolt upright in a straight-backed chair, but Anna curled up in a settee while reading the tragedy of *Macbeth*. She was a wonderful reader, and this to Thomas was the choice hour of his day. He dearly loved for Anna to read to him.

Anna sighed when she finished. "And so they all died. Some with honor, some not."

"Marvelous insight Shakespeare had," Jackson said thoughtfully. "Not a very godly man, though."

"You don't think Shakespeare was a Christian?"

"I can't think so. He didn't seem to have a very good idea of the goodness of the Lord God. But he did know humans, my dear. He did know the spirit of man."

"Perhaps you're right; he knew about men and women and their weaknesses and trials and tribulations."

Jackson came to sit by her and took her hand.

She closed the book and for a while they watched the dying fire. "Thomas?"

"Yes, my dear?"

"I've been meaning to ask something of you. Would you consider finding a young man to help me around the house?"

He turned to her then touched her face gently. "Is Hetty not enough help for you now, dearest?"

Since the death of the baby, Anna had very little interest in the housekeeping and especially the chores around the house, such as watering the garden, looking after her flower garden, and keeping the lawn. Hetty, her maid, kept house and cooked, but there was much more to maintaining a home than that.

"No, I think we need a young man. This old house often needs so many repairs, such as watching the well, making repairs on the outbuildings, and caring for the horses. You're so tired when you get home. I would like to have you to myself when you come home, instead of working so hard around here."

"I never gave it a thought, but I'm glad you mentioned it. I'll look around and find some young fellow who can help us out."

He reached out to her, and she came into his arms. Holding her tightly, he whispered in her ear, "I love you, *esposa!* The day I stop loving you will be the day I die."

"Oh, Thomas, my dearest. I wish everyone could see this side of the Iron Major. . . ."

CHAPTER SEVEN

As Daniel and Becky moved down the rows of the garden, the heat made a thin film in the windless air. The afternoon sun was warm, but all of summer's scorch was out of it. Now the deep haze of fall had come so that the land lay quietly, waiting for the harvest.

Daniel picked a large crimson tomato from the vine then took a big bite of it. The juice ran down his chin. He munched on the tomato. It was obvious he was at ease with the world.

"If you don't stop eating those tomatoes, we won't have any left for the table."

"Don't ever put off pleasures, wife," Daniel said cheerfully. He reached out and hugged her. She looked up at him, and he kissed her on the lips. "Becky, my love, you're sweeter than the tomatoes."

"You choose the strangest times to get romantic, Daniel."

125

"Anytime is a good time to find romance."

"Ah, yes. *Love among the Tomatoes.* That would make a good title of a dime novel."

Contentedly they picked tomatoes until their baskets were full. Then they returned to the house.

As they seated themselves on the veranda, through the open windows they could hear Zemira in the parlor, talking to Callie Jo. Zemira adored her granddaughter and begged Becky and Daniel to leave her in her care. Now, through the faint sounds, Daniel and Becky could hear that Zemira was reciting the alphabet to Callie Jo. "And *H* is for horse. We have five horses, and when you get bigger, your brother, Yancy, will teach you to ride just as fine as he does. . . ."

Becky and Daniel exchanged amused glances. "She's four months old, and already she's learning the alphabet," Becky said, laughing.

"And riding horses," Daniel added. In their chairs side by side, he reached out and took her hand.

"You know, Daniel," Becky said quietly, "I'm worried about Yancy."

Daniel sighed. "I know. He's not happy. I don't think he really hates being a farmer. I just think it's not for him."

"I think you have to grow up on a farm to like it."

"You may be right. I grew up on one and I hated it — until now, at least. But when I was young that was the real reason I ran away from home."

"Yes, and I wonder about Yancy. Sometimes I'm afraid we'll wake up one morning and *he'll* be gone."

"I know," Daniel said. "In some ways I know he does take after me. I guess I need to have a talk with him. The problem is you can talk *at* Yancy, but you can't really tell if you're talking *to* Yancy. He hardly ever says a word, and you can never tell what that boy's thinking. Gets that from his Indian mother, I guess. I have to go into town tomorrow, but maybe tomorrow evening Yancy and I can go for a ride and I'll see if I can get him to talk to me then."

They had time for a short ride after Daniel got back from town and Yancy had finished his chores. He had twice as much to do when his father went into town, but he never complained.

Daniel was riding a gelding named Reuben that doubled as a cart horse, and Yancy was riding Fancy. They went through the back of the property, into the pine woods that bordered the stream. Both of them were quiet. The only sounds were the jingles and creaks of the saddle and gear and the crickets cheeping and frogs calling. The air was crisp with the evergreen scent. It was gentle riding, just meandering along, enjoying the evening and the woods and the whisper of the stream.

Finally when the shadows grew long and longer, Daniel said, "We'd better be getting back. It'll be dark soon, and tonight's the new moon."

Yancy looked up. "So it is. I always thought it was funny that we call it the *new moon* when you can't see it at all. Wonder why that is?"

"I don't know, son. That is one thing that I regret, for you at least. The Amish education leaves much to be desired, I'm afraid, unless you're planning on farming for the rest of your life. And I don't think that's what you want to do, is it?"

Reluctantly Yancy answered, "No, sir. I just feel like I can't breathe. There are so many chores and rules, and everyone is watching you to make sure you don't do anything different from everybody else. Every day is packed full of work till nighttime and then there's nothing really to do even if you had time to do it. It's a hard life."

"It's not for everyone," Daniel agreed. "I didn't think it was for me when I was your age, either, so I can't blame you."

"Are you sorry you ran away?" Yancy asked curiously.

"Sorry? No, I'm not sorry, because then I never would have met your mother, and I wouldn't have you." They were riding side by side now, on the old bridle path that led from the stream up to the house. Daniel glanced at Yancy and saw the thoughtful look on his face. Then he added, "You know, Yancy, you've worked really hard on the farm, and I guess I've known all along that you didn't like it much. You're a hard worker, and a good worker, and I'm very proud of you."

"Thank you, sir." Yancy was quiet for a while, staring into the deepening twilight. Then he asked, "Do you think about Mother a lot?"

"Every day, son. Guess I always will."

"Did you love her in a different way than you love Becky?"

"Yes, I did. It was different. Just like I love you in a different way than I love Callie Jo. I think that's the way it's supposed to be. We have different kinds of love."

Yancy nodded.

Daniel said, "You know, Yancy, I was in town today, and I was thinking about what a good worker you are. I thought about maybe trying to find you a job in town. I was in Mason's Grocer and Dry Goods, and I asked him about any jobs around town. He told me something interesting. Major Thomas Jackson at VMI is looking for a boy to help his wife around the house. I think you'd do a real good job for Mrs. Jackson."

"Really?" Yancy asked with interest. "Who is Major Jackson? What does he do?"

"He's famous, in a way. He made quite a name for himself in the Mexican War. Evidently he is a very courageous, smart, and hardworking soldier. At VMI he's teaching natural and experimental philosophy, and also artillery, which I understand he is extremely good at."

"What kind of work would it be, do you think?"

"Taking care of the horses, helping in the garden, running errands, keeping the grounds. Mrs. Jackson lost a baby, you see, last May. I expect she doesn't feel like doing much of anything at all, so I assume you'd be responsible for driving the maid and cook into town for supplies, keeping the carriage and buggy up . . . things like that. Think you'd like to give it a try?"

"I sure would, sir," Yancy replied. "Don't think I want to get away from you and Becky and Grandmother, but I would like to get off the farm some, try something new."

Daniel nodded. "You'd still be living here, and under the Ordnung, but it would give you more freedom. Tomorrow you can take Fancy and go see Major Jackson."

It was the last week in August, and though the evenings had cooled down, the midday sun was still high and hot. But a fine breeze blew, ruffling Yancy's coal black hair and refreshing him as he rode onto the manicured grounds of Virginia Military Institute.

Straight ahead of him was the lofty edifice of the institute that served as classrooms, offices, and the cadets' barracks. A four-story building made of gray sandstone, it was designed in the Gothic tradition. On either side of the arched entryway were two tall turrets, topped by the institute's flag on one and the flag of the state of Virginia on the other. All of the windows were mullioned. The top of the fortresslike building was lined with mock battlements.

For a moment Yancy wondered how in the world he was going to find Major Jackson, but then he heard the sound of cannons firing and realized this must be Major Jackson's artillery class. He couldn't see the cannons or the men, but he did see faint trails of smoke rising from behind and to the left of the institute building, so he followed that trail.

It led down a gradual slope to a slight ravine. There, a large group of cadets were lined up behind four cannons, each of them with four recruits attending. Nearby, standing very erect, was a man in a blue uniform. Yancy realized he must be Major Jackson, but he didn't approach him; he was curious about the firing of the cannons.

They were still smoking, and the four cadets surrounding the big guns were watching Major Jackson attentively. He had lifted binoculars to his face to look at the targets, which were about three hundred yards away on the side of an earthen breastwork. "Not bad, men. Artillery up!" he shouted.

The four cadets that had been at the guns joined the ranks of the other cadets, and three new teams of four ran to each of the guns.

"Ready your guns!" Jackson shouted. He had a curious, high-pitched voice, though it didn't sound feminine, and it carried clearly on the air.

Two cadets stood in front at each side of the cannons, two at the rear. One of the boys in front took a long pole that had what looked like an enormous corkscrew on one end, rammed it down the barrel, twisted it, and slowly worked it all the way up the muzzle. This was called the "wormer." The other cadet took another long pole with a roll of canvas on the end, dipped it into a bucket of water, and swabbed the entire barrel, which was called "sponging." This was to kill any live sparks from the last charge.

Jackson called, "Advance the round!"

The cadet in the rear to the right of the gun picked up a burlap sack. In it was a twelve-pound ball and two and one-half pounds of black powder. He seated it in the barrel, and the sponger turned his pole around and jammed it down the barrel, all the way to the back. Then all four of the cadets stood at the rear of the gun.

Jackson ordered, "Come to the ready!"

One of the cadets inserted a brass spike into the hole for the fuse, puncturing the canvas bag. Then another inserted a wire fuse attached to a long lanyard. Each member of the crew moved back, the crew captain holding the lanyard and stepping carefully until there was tension on it.

"Clear, sir!" each captain shouted.

"Fire!" Jackson roared.

The explosion was extremely satisfying to Yancy, as it seemed to be to each boy there. All of them had bright eyes, and excitement was clear on their faces.

After Jackson checked the targets with his binoculars, his eyes were bright, burning blue, too. "Good men," he said. "Artillery up!"

And so they began again.

At the very back of the field, Yancy dismounted and stood, stroking Fancy, for she skittered a little at each round though she didn't panic or bolt. He watched the entire class, which lasted about another hour. He was fascinated.

Finally, Jackson walked back and forth at the front of the two rows of cadets, talking to them quietly enough that Yancy couldn't hear. Then they came to attention, and he called, "Dismissed." The group broke up and headed back toward the institute, Jackson several steps behind them.

Yancy took a deep breath then hurried over to Major Jackson, leading Fancy. "Sir?" he called when he got within earshot. "Sir? May I have a word with you?"

Jackson halted and turned his eyes toward Yancy. Yancy thought that he had never seen such a deep penetrating gaze in all of his life. "Yes, what is it, young man?" Jackson asked, not unkindly.

"I — sir — I heard you are looking for a young fellow to do some work for you?"

"So I am. Who told you about it?"

"My father. He heard it from Mr. Mason. From Mason's Grocery and Dry Goods."

"What's your name and who are your people?" Jackson demanded, stopping his stride and turning to look at Yancy attentively. Though Jackson was courteous, he still made Yancy very nervous. His gaze was so intent, and he had such a distant air.

"I'm — my name's Yancy Tremayne, Major. My father is Daniel Tremayne. We live in the Amish settlement just south of town."

Jackson nodded. "All right. Walk with me, and tell me about yourself."

Yancy fell into step with Major Jackson. He didn't tell his whole life story; he just told him that he and his father had returned to the Amish after his father had been away for many years. He told him that the Tremaynes had lived on the farm since the 1730s, and that though he didn't despise farmwork, he hoped to find a job in Lexington and work outside the community.

Jackson searched him, his eyes taking in his homespun trousers and his simple muslin pullover shirt, and then he looked at his feet. "You're wearing moccasins."

"Yes, sir. My mother was half Cheyenne. So I guess you know that means I'm one-fourth Indian," Yancy said evenly.

"Guess I do," Jackson said drily. "Nice moccasins. So I assume you know how to take care of horses?"

It took Yancy a scant moment to shift into the change in conversation, but then he answered eagerly, "Oh yes, sir, because that's what I love to do! I mean —"

"No, you said it, Yancy, a man does best that which he loves to do," Jackson said quickly. "And that is a fine mare you've got there, looks healthy and well cared for. But what about everything else? Other chores, hard work around a house?"

"I work hard at the farm, sir. I'm handy with tools, I'm strong, and usually I can — sort of figure out how to fix things. Like repairing a roof, or putting up a fence. And I've been to four barn raisings, so I've learned some carpentry."

"All right." Jackson nodded. "Then I want you to wait for me. I've got some things to do in my office. My horse is in the institute stables over there. The stable boy will show her to you. You go on over there, clean my tack, and brush her down and pretty her up, show me a little bit of what you can do. By the time you're through with that I'll be ready to go home. I'll take you and introduce you to my wife. As far as I'm concerned you can have a trial period. You can work for a week, and by that time we should know if we can get along with each other."

On 8 East Washington Street in Lexington was a modest two-story house that Jackson had bought. The front steps crowded up against the street, but as they rode up, Yancy could see a generous garden, stables, carriage house, and washhouse in the back.

Jackson went up the side street, where a path led right up to the stable.

"I'll take care of the horses, Major Jackson," Yancy said eagerly. "I know you'll want to talk to Mrs. Jackson before you introduce me."

"Good, good," Jackson murmured, nodding his head. The words and gesture were very familiar to those who knew him. He dismounted, handed the reins to Yancy, and hurried into the house.

Yancy hitched up Fancy, then began unsaddling Major Jackson's horse, which was an unassuming mare by the name of BeBe. In the stall next to her was a big gray gelding who whinnied in recognition when he led BeBe in and then poked his nose out of the stall to watch Yancy curiously. Yancy unsaddled the mare and brushed her down. It didn't take very long, for he had curried her very well at the institute and they hadn't ridden hard to Jackson's home, so he finished quickly. After that he petted the gelding and talked to both horses. He loved horses, and they loved him.

Yancy was standing at the gelding's stall, rubbing his soft nose and murmuring to him, when Jackson came to get him. "I see you've made Gordo's acquaintance," he said.

"That's his name? Gordo?"

"Actually, it's Cerro Gordo. Named after a place in Mexico, where I saw my first action," Jackson said. "This old goat" — he rubbed the horse's nose — "didn't have anything to do with it. I just liked the name, and I'll always remember it."

"I'd like to know about the Mexican War," Yancy said wistfully.

"Would you?" Jackson retorted, swiveling his shrewd gaze to Yancy's face.

"Yes, sir."

"I have two books, memoirs from men who were there," Jackson said. "Maybe you'd like to borrow them?"

"Oh yes, sir. I — I like to read, but the

Amish don't encourage it too much. Except the Bible, of course."

"Good of them. Everyone must study the Bible with great energy," Jackson said sternly. "But reading books is a good thing, Yancy. I'm glad you want to read. Shows me something of what you're made of. So, would you like to come meet my wife now?"

"Yes, sir."

Jackson led him into the house. It was modestly furnished, not spare but with good wool rugs, plenty of lamps, and comfortable, gently worn furniture in the parlor.

On a settee was seated a pretty lady, somewhat thin, with thick chestnut hair and warm brown eyes.

"My darling, this is Yancy," Jackson said. "Yancy, this is my wife, Anna."

Yancy did his best to make a sort of bow, not daring to extend his hand. "Ma'am," he murmured.

"I'm so glad to meet you, Yancy," she said in a soft voice. "Already I feel I know you a little, because Thomas has told me about you. Please, won't you be seated?"

Awkwardly Yancy perched on the edge of a straight chair by the fireplace.

"As I said, Yancy is reputed to be good with tools and on a farm, and I've already seen that he's very good with horses," Jackson said, seating himself by his wife. "And he's been working on an Amish farm, and I know that must be hard work."

"Yes, sir," Yancy said faintly.

Anna looked at him intently then smiled a little as she seemed to recognize his nervousness. "The Amish, you know . . . I've heard of them, but I know very little about them," she said. "Perhaps you and I can talk about them sometime."

"Yes, ma'am, even though I — I mean, I — it's kind of new to me, too, so I don't know much about it," Yancy said.

"Then perhaps we can learn together," she said lightly. "Now, you see, the most important thing to Thomas is if you can take good care of the horses and the cart and the carriage and make sure the pump and the drains are working properly. But the most important thing to me, Yancy, is my garden. I think it must be different from farming, but perhaps not so much. And so it doesn't really matter if you don't know much about the Amish, as long as you know about horses and gardening."

Suddenly Yancy smiled at her; he didn't smile very often, but she was so gentle and so obviously wanted him to be at ease that it made him want to reassure her. "Ma'am, I don't know much about flowers and things, but I can learn. And I'm not afraid of any hard work. I'll be glad to do anything around here that needs doing. If I don't know how to do it, I'll find someone who does, and I'll get him to teach me."

Anna and Jackson glanced at each other; and Yancy was surprised at the softness and the warmth with which the stern major looked at his wife.

Then Anna looked back at Yancy. "I think you'll do well, Yancy. I'm sure that we'll be glad that the Lord sent you here. I'll be glad to have the help, and it will be nice to have a young person around the house."

Suddenly Jackson reached out and took her hand.

Yancy saw the sadness in her then and remembered that Daniel had told him of their losing their daughter four months ago. "I will work hard, ma'am, Major," Yancy promised. "I don't know much about the Lord and all, but I do want you to be glad I'm here. I'll work hard to earn that."

Jackson called up, "How's it going, Yancy?"

Yancy was on the roof of the stable. It had a tin roof, and the seams had expanded and loosened during the hot summer. With cold rain and snow coming, Yancy wanted to make sure the roof was snug and secure, so

141

he was adding extra nails along the seams and sealing them with tar. It was hot work, and hard work, but he didn't mind. He wanted BeBe and Gordo to be comfortable this winter.

He looked down and smiled at the major. "Fine, sir, it's going very well. I think I can finish this by tomorrow."

Jackson nodded. "Come down here. I have something for you."

"Yes, sir."

Yancy climbed down the ladder, rubbing his dirty hands against his breeches.

"Here are your wages for the week." He held out two silver dollars.

With great pleasure Yancy took the coins and put them in his pocket. "Thank you, Major. It's been a good week. I like working for you and Mrs. Jackson," he said with a touch of uncharacteristic shyness.

"You have done a good job, Yancy. You are indeed a hard worker. What will you do with your money?"

"Give it to my family, sir."

"Good, good. Be back at eight o'clock on Monday, Yancy."

"Yes, sir, I'm looking forward to it."

"Carry on."

"Sir." Yancy climbed back up onto the roof of the stable.

CHAPTER EIGHT

One thing that Yancy loved about the Amish was their food. As he sat down to dinner with his family, his mouth watered. Zemira and Becky had prepared chicken and corn soup, biscuits, pork ribs and kraut, tomato fritters, and potato salad. Also, they had cheese cubes, pickles, and fresh, crunchy celery straight from the kitchen garden, the last of the season. Steaming on the sideboard for dessert was apple strudel, a jug of fresh cream standing by.

Daniel and Yancy took their seats, and then as was traditional for the Amish, the women seated themselves. Zemira sat down while Becky put Callie Jo in her high chair. Zemira had saved the well-made wooden tray chair for years, wrapped up carefully in an old quilt in the attic. It looked new, but her husband, Jacob, had made it more than thirty years ago for Daniel when he was a baby.

"Now we will bless," Daniel said.

They all bowed their heads for the silent blessing. As always, Yancy surreptitiously watched his father until he raised his head. Of course, most of the time Zemira caught him, but she didn't fuss. She merely gave him an amused, slightly conspiratorial look.

As soon as they began to eat, the conversation began. Dinnertime was usually lively, for the Amish worked hard all day at different tasks and it was a time for catching up on everything around the farm. Today, however, which was Saturday, they only wanted to hear from Yancy about Major and Mrs. Jackson. He had been working for them for more than a month now, and though the Amish considered themselves a separate people, they were always eager to hear about news from town and the outside world.

"So, Yancy, tell us all about Major Jackson and Mrs. Jackson and what has gone on this last week," Becky prodded him. "But first — how is Mrs. Jackson? I know you've told us that she still seems sad at times. It's been, um, six months since she lost the little girl? I can't imagine how long it would take to get over something like that. . . ." Her voice trailed off, and all eyes at the table went to Callie Jo.

As if she were aware of the attention, she grinned, her two top teeth and two bottom teeth shining. She had a bowl of creamed celery on her tray, and she buried one chubby hand in it, waved joyously, and smeared it all over her face.

Zemira, Becky, Yancy, and Daniel burst out laughing. Becky hurried to clean her face and spoon some of the celery properly into her mouth.

Yancy answered, "Mrs. Jackson is better. It seems like she gets a little better every week. Yesterday she even laughed. It's the first time I've heard her laugh."

"About what?" Becky asked curiously.

Yancy grinned. "We were out in the garden. I was down on my knees in one of the flower beds, turning the soil and mulching, and I guess Major Jackson didn't realize I was there. So he comes home and finds Mrs. Jackson, sitting on a bench, reading a book. He starts telling her about this new cadet; his name is Percy Smith. He's a distant cousin of Superintendent Smith's, and they're all under orders to sort of help him along. So during artillery class, Major Jackson lets him be a gun captain, but of course the other guys have to do all the worming and swabbing and priming and loading; all he's got to do is pull the lanyard when Major Thomas yells, 'Fire!'

"But it seems like this Percy Smith is kind of a muffin, 'cause on the first battery he pulls the lanyard, then jumps straight up in the air, covers his ears, and yells, 'Ooohh!' And Major Jackson acted it out, jumping up and screeching like a little girl. Mrs. Jackson laughed and laughed. And I did, too, but I was quiet about it, because I knew Major Jackson would be embarrassed if he knew I'd heard him and seen him."

The others were fascinated. Daniel said thoughtfully, "You know, I've never met Major Jackson, but his reputation seems to be of a rather stern, stiff military man of great dignity."

"So he is," Yancy agreed, "except with Mrs. Jackson. You wouldn't believe how different he is with her. Course, he's very gallant with all ladies, but with her he's kind and soft and smiles a lot and calls her pet names. He doesn't mind who sees, either. It's just that yesterday he was such a big clown that I figured he might mind me seeing that."

Becky nodded with understanding. "He sounds like a wonderful husband. And so the loss of his daughter hasn't affected his mind or his health too adversely?"

Yancy shrugged. "He never seems to be

really upset about anything, except his health."

"And so he is in bad health?" Zemira asked.

"I don't know about that. He doesn't really look sick, but he's always complaining of some kind of ailment. Last week he was complaining of an inflammation in his ear and in his throat. He also said he had neuralgia, whatever that is."

"I suppose he goes to the doctor quite often," Becky said sympathetically.

"No, I heard Mrs. Jackson urging him to go, but Major Jackson just said, 'I can prescribe medicine just as well as those fellows.' He showed me once what he was taking, a whole cabinet full of bottles. One was chloroform liniment, and the bottles were labeled — things like ammonia, glycerin, and nutritive silver."

"That sounds awful, and dangerous, too," Daniel said.

"He doesn't act sick, but he talks a lot about his ailments. I told you how he sucks on lemons all the time. Nobody knows where he gets them in the wintertime, but he always has a bunch of them. He thinks they help his digestion or something."

"But he is a Christian man, I heard," Daniel said cautiously.

"Yeah, he is. He talks about the Lord and the Bible all the time," Yancy answered. "And Mrs. Jackson, too. They're always quoting the Bible."

Zemira, Becky, and Daniel exchanged glances. The Amish didn't believe in quoting scripture excessively. As with vocal prayer, they considered it very forward and smacking of pride. Of course, Yancy didn't know this, and the adults had no intention of confusing him by explaining it to him now.

"He sounds like a good Christian man," Becky said generously. "One that I'm proud for you to work for."

Yancy ducked his head and murmured, "I'm proud to work for him, too."

Very early on Monday morning, Yancy left the farm for the Jackson home in Lexington. It was the second week in October, but they hadn't had a frost yet. It was chilly but not really cold. On this day he rode Fancy because his father had told him they wouldn't need her. He got there at about seven thirty, unsaddled Fancy and put her in her stall next to Gordo, and brushed her down good. Then he went in the back way to the kitchen.

Hetty, Mrs. Jackson's maid, was making

coffee. She was a good-natured but no-nonsense woman, chubby, with dark eyes that crinkled into tiny slits when she laughed. Hetty had been with Mary Anna Jackson for many years. " 'Bout time," she grumbled.

"I'm early," he countered. "Mmm, coffee smells good. Can I have some?"

"I don't know if we've got enough sugar and cream for you," she said, hands on hips. "You make such a syrup out of it."

"It's good for me." Yancy grinned. "A pretty girl told me at church yesterday that I'm a growing boy."

"Bet pretty girls tell you lots of things," Hetty said. "My daddy always told me don't believe everything you hear. He was a smart man."

"Bet he was. Bet his daughter is, too."

"Humph. What are you kissing me up for today?"

"Lunch, maybe?" Yancy suggested.

"Like I don't fix lunch for you every single time you're here," she said, sauntering out of the kitchen. "Dunno why I baby you, I truly don't. You're sure no baby. . . ."

Yancy finished his coffee quickly then went to the parlor.

It was the routine — Mrs. Jackson waited for him in the parlor to tell him his duties for the day. He knocked and she said softly, "Come in, Yancy."

He went in, where Mrs. Jackson sat by a small fire. To his surprise, she was wearing a plain skirt with no hoops and a plain white shirt.

Always before she had worn the elaborate dresses that were fashionable for ladies, with wide hoop skirts, lace trim, and lace caps topping full ringlets. Today Anna's hair was bound up tightly in a bun, and a wide-brimmed straw hat lay on the settee by her side. "Good morning," she said.

"Good morning, ma'am. What can I do for you today?"

She smiled. She had a sweet face and kind eyes. As Yancy had noted, she seemed to have overcome her grief for her lost baby slowly over the last month. "Today I want you to work on my flower garden, Yancy. And I'm feeling so well today that I'm going to work, too. My fall flowers are looking so wonderful that I know I'll enjoy working in the garden, as I did before — before."

"That's good, ma'am. I'll enjoy the company for a change."

Anna put on her hat and some leather work gloves, and they went out the back to the garden. Though the Jacksons had only owned the house for a short time, the garden had been created many years before by the previous owners. Anna Jackson loved gardening, so she was constantly making changes in the plantings and renewing the beds. There had also been a rather large kitchen garden in one corner. But Major Jackson had bought a farm just outside of Lexington, and as was everything else in the Shenandoah Valley, it was fruitful and grew all the fresh vegetables they could ever need.

Much of Yancy's time had been spent in this garden, uprooting the old vegetables and tilling and retilling the soil and fertilizing to prepare for flowers. Today, Anna pointed to six shallow crates full of colorful flowers. Yancy had seen them before — his grandmother had them in her front yard — but he didn't know what they were.

"Pansies," Anna said to his unspoken question. "I dearly love them." One crate held solid-colored orange flowers, one white, one yellow, one red, one purple with black markings around the center of the flower, and one with yellow petals and purple markings.

"They are pretty," Yancy agreed, stooping down to caress one of the showy yellow and purple ones. "It's funny; these two-colored ones have little faces."

"You're perceptive," Anna said. "That's

exactly what all of the expert botanists call it. They're wonderful flowers. If you have the soil conditioned just right, they bloom even in snow."

"Really?"

"Yes. They look fragile and delicate, but they're actually very strong."

"Mmm, like some ladies," Yancy said, rising and looking at her. He looked down at her, for she was a full foot shorter than he was.

Anna Jackson looked slightly surprised and then pleased. "I'd like to border the flower beds with them. Come, and I'll show you which color goes where and exactly how to plant them."

They worked steadily. Yancy, at the largest flower bed, worked carefully placing the tiny little plants closely around the border. Anna, down on her knees, worked at a small corner bed that had only three sides.

Yancy found himself humming a hymn, a doleful tune, as most of the Amish hymns were. He had no idea what the words said because it was in German, but it had been a hymn they had sung at church the day before.

Anna came to stand over him. "What is that tune, Yancy?" He looked up at her face. Her cheeks were rosy, though she didn't look hot; she looked happy. It was the first time he had seen a complete peaceful happiness on her face.

"I don't know, ma'am. Almost all of the Amish hymns are in German. For all I know, we're singing about sauerkraut and pretzels."

Anna laughed, a sweet, pleasing sound. "I rather doubt that, Yancy. It sounds much too sad for that. You're not sad, are you?"

"Oh no, ma'am. It's just the songs. They all sound sad, and the few that are in English are real sad."

Anna considered this. "So — are your people very somber and grave?"

Yancy thought for a few moments. "Not really, ma'am. I guess they're just like everyone else. Some of them are serious, some of them laugh a lot; sometimes anyone can be sad and serious and other times happy and light. They're just people. Except they dress funny."

"Yancy!" Anna chided him.

"Sorry," he said unrepentantly. "But they try to make me wear a hat that looks just like yours, Mrs. Jackson. It looks real pretty on you, but you're not going to catch me breathing and wearing a straw hat with a wide brim." Yancy wore leather slouch hats with a wide brim and beaded hatband that his mother had made.

"I suppose," she said, struggling to keep a straight face, "that I would feel such reluctance if someone tried to make me wear my husband's forage cap. It simply wouldn't do."

"No, ma'am," Yancy agreed heartily. "It would not do."

Anna knelt by him and they worked side by side for a while. The flower bed was the largest in the garden. Yancy had, in deference to Mrs. Jackson, memorized all the flowers that were blooming this fall — chrysanthemums, marigolds, nasturtiums, dahlias, and now they were adding pansies as a border.

After they had worked for a time, Anna sat up and pulled a heavy round yellow chrysanthemum bloom up to her face. "They're beautiful, but they have no scent. And you know, at Cottage Home in North Carolina we had a white chrysanthemum. It was so unusual. It looked just like a daisy. But it was hardy and fall-blooming. I wish I had one here, but I haven't seen one since I left home."

"You know, ma'am, I think my grandmother has some of those," he said thoughtfully. "There's three big bushes of them in the backyard by the kitchen garden that just

154

started blooming. I'll ask her. I'm sure she'd love for you to have some plants."

"Why, thank you, Yancy," Anna said with pleasure. "I would dearly love to have white daisy-mums in my garden."

They worked until noon, and then had a surprise. Major Jackson rode up and hurried through the backyard to embrace Anna. As Major Jackson and Anna had gotten more accustomed with Yancy, they had begun to show more affection in front of him. He always made a point to discreetly ignore them, and he knew this made them feel comfortable with him.

"Hello, sir," Yancy said, rising. "I'll go take care of BeBe."

"Don't unsaddle her," Jackson instructed him. "We're just going to have a quick lunch and then you and I are going back to the institute. So you go ahead and saddle up Fancy."

"Me, sir?" Yancy said with surprise. "But why?"

"You'll see," he said over his shoulder as he walked Anna into the house. "It's a special day."

CHAPTER NINE

The parade ground in front of the institute was filled with cadets, not wearing their dress uniforms but in trousers and shirts that looked like work clothes. They stood around in groups, laughing or kicking and throwing balls.

Major Jackson and Yancy rode in and stabled the horses.

"Bring your rifle," Jackson ordered Yancy.

Without question Yancy took his rifle out of the saddle holster, and they headed out to the field.

Jackson yelled, "Cadet Sims!"

Cadet Erwin Sims, at eighteen, was already tall and deep-chested. He had a voice like a foghorn. "Yes, sir!" he said, running up to the major.

"Assemble the men," Jackson said.

He turned and bellowed out, "All cadets, file in under Major Jackson!"

As the cadets came running toward them,

Yancy leaned his musket up against an unused hitching post. He saw that Major Jackson was looking at him with a direct expression. "Would you care to race with our cadets, Mr. Tremayne?"

"Yes, sir, I like to race."

"Fine, get in line there. Line them up, Mr. Sims, and I'll give the signal to start. You will be going to the other side of the institute, from this hitching post to that elm tree straight ahead and back. The winner gets a week off of all duties."

The cheer went up, and as Yancy took his place at the end of the line, he saw he was receiving some angry glances.

The cadet next to him said, "What are you doing here? You're not a cadet."

Yancy didn't answer, merely breathed deeply to prepare.

Jackson called, "Ready — set — go!"

Yancy broke into a burst of speed and ran with all of his might for the tree. It was a short race so he didn't have to worry about getting winded. He was the first one to arrive at the tree, and he whirled and ran back. He had learned in racing to give his very best at the last part of the race, and he outdid himself and crossed the line. He looked back to see the closest cadet was still thirty yards back.

The cadets all came in huffing from lack of breath.

Jackson had a slight smile. "Well, Mr. Tremayne, you're quite a runner."

"The Cheyenne boys race a lot," he said in a low voice. "It was something that the men thought helped us grow and learn."

"I don't know if you know it," Jackson addressed the cadets, "but Mr. Tremayne here lived with the Cheyenne Indians until he was twelve years old. The Indians are known to be great runners."

"Major Jackson, I don't think I ought to get any prize," Yancy said. "I'm not one of the cadets."

Jackson nodded with approval. "Very well. Mr. Hooper, you are the next in line and you're relieved of all duty for the next week. Now, we are going to see what kind of marksmen we have. Go down to the artillery field and get your muskets."

The small arms were stored in the same shed that held the cannon armaments. The boys, whooping and yelling, ran down to the gully that housed the shed and the cannons.

Jackson nodded for Yancy to get his musket. Together they walked down to the artillery field. "That's a fine rifle, Mr. Tremayne."

"Thank you, sir. My father gave it to me. It's an Enfield rifle musket."

"I see you take good care of it, too. You have your cartridges and rounds and caps?"

"Yes, sir."

"Want to try your hand against my cadets?"

"Well — but . . . they might not like it, sir. I don't think they much liked that I won the race."

"Then they need to grow up and act like men and improve themselves and not worry what the man next to them is doing," Jackson snapped impatiently. "Take the second team, so you can see how we drill."

"Yes, sir."

"Teams of five!" Jackson roared. "Step up, men!"

The cadets started jostling around, ranging themselves in fives.

Yancy quickly joined three of the cadets in the second line, and then Cadet Sims joined the four. To Yancy's surprise, both he and the cadet on his other side grinned at him.

On his left was a rather chubby cadet, with a good-natured smile. "Can you shoot as good as you can run?" he asked.

"I dunno," Yancy answered honestly. "Never thought about it much."

"Silence in the ranks!" Jackson ordered, and both boys fell silent, staring straight ahead.

There were twenty-three cadets, and the five targets had been set up at fifty yards.

Jackson waited until all of the cadets were assembled in their teams. When they were all quiet, he called out, "Company! Loading nine times!"

Yancy watched and listened carefully and realized that this meant nine commands required to load and fire the muskets. Jackson barked them out quickly, and Yancy observed the first team, memorizing each movement and each command.

Finally Jackson yelled, "Fire!"

Five loud explosions sounded, then the cadets held their muskets upright by their sides.

Jackson took his binoculars out and surveyed the targets in silence. He nodded briskly. "Not bad, men. Hart, Preston, bull's-eye. Manning, Bridges, and Rogers in the red. Team one, ready for battle command?"

"Yes, sir!" the first five cadets called.

"One minute!" Jackson announced. He took out his pocket-watch, glanced at it, waited a few seconds, then commanded, "Load and fire at will!"

A good rifleman was supposed to be able to load and fire in twenty seconds, and get off three rounds in a minute. The speed was important, but so was the repetition of the drill. Many greenhorns, in the excitement of battle, would shoot while their rammers were still in the barrel. The rammer would travel yards away — and then the rifleman had no way to reload his weapon.

Major Jackson drilled the cadets as much as he could with live rounds, begging and scraping the institute for ammunition. If they didn't have it, he dumb-show drilled them. Almost all of his cadets could fire three rounds in a minute. As could the five cadets on the firing line.

At one minute Jackson called, "Cease fire!" and they had all loaded and shot three times. Jackson ordered Cadet Hart to collect the targets and reset with new ones.

This took a little time, so the friendly cadet next to Yancy spoke to him again in a low voice. "Hi, I'm Charles Satterfield."

"Yancy Tremayne."

"How do you know Major Jackson?"

"I work for him and Mrs. Jackson at their house."

Satterfield's brown eyes widened. "You work for him? On purpose?"

Yancy nodded his head. "He's not like this

at home, with Mrs. Jackson. He's different."

"Different? But —"

"Cadet Satterfield, if I catch you making noise on my field just once more you're going to be cleaning every cadet's musket tonight!" Jackson barked.

Satterfield shot to attention. "Yes, sir! No, sir! It won't happen again, sir!"

"Next team, get ready for commands!" Jackson ordered.

Yancy and the four cadets put their muskets upright next to their sides.

Although Yancy had only observed the "Company! Loading nine times!" routine, he was very quick and picked it up easily. He was even quicker than the cadets. His shot was dead bull's-eye.

The four cadets were in the red.

In battle drill, Yancy just managed to fire four times in a minute, with every shot a bull's-eye.

Jackson studied his target carefully then handed it to Yancy. "Here, you ought to take this and show it to your father," he said in a low voice.

Yancy took the target and said slowly, "No, Major. This isn't the kind of thing my family is proud of. Amish, you know."

Jackson nodded with understanding. "Still, you should be proud. Would you like

162

to try a big gun when we get through with muskets?"

Yancy grinned up at him. "I surely would, sir. They look like even more fun."

Jackson smiled one of his rare, short smiles. "Oh, they are, Mr. Tremayne. They are."

As soon as all of the cadets had done their musket drills, they started bringing out the ammunition and supplies for the four cannons.

Yancy watched three teams shoot three rounds each this time. Firing a cannon didn't have any more steps than firing a musket, but it was a good deal more dangerous. He especially observed how careful the cadets were never to step in front of the muzzle and how far they stood back when the gun captain pulled the long lanyard that fired the piece.

Once again he teamed up with the four cadets he had shot the muskets with. The four seemed to just naturally team up together, and they had sort of hung around Yancy when forming the cannon teams. He was relieved; the cadet that had gotten so mad at him at the race was a big, arrogant eighteen-year-old named Franklin Hart, and his dark eye had lit on Yancy more than once during their drills.

Yancy got to be the wormer, then the sponger/rammer, then the primer on their three shots. Cadet Sims was the gun captain; evidently this was a position that was earned and not automatically rotated. Yancy did all right; he was slightly slower than the others, and once he stepped in front of the muzzle when he was sponging.

One of the other cadets — he later found out it was Peyton Stevens — ducked under the gun and pushed Yancy hard. Then he stood up and with a charming smile said, "Don't want to be standing there, Cheyenne. Sorry about the shove."

"It's all right. Better than getting shoved by a six-pound ball," Yancy said. His gun crew did well, hitting the target with all three rounds.

When the drills were finished and the cadets were returning to the barracks, the four young men he had been shooting with introduced themselves. Cadet Sims was senior, at eighteen, Peyton Stevens was sixteen, and Sandy Owens and Charles Satterfield were fifteen. They shook hands all around.

"Thanks for helping me out today," Yancy told them.

"No, you helped us out in the musket drill," Satterfield said.

"Right, Chuckins," Stevens said lazily. "At least today you didn't fire your rammer."

"Oh I only did that once, the second time we drilled," Chuckins grumbled. "Old Blue Light was yelling at me and made me nervous."

"Old Blue Light? Is that what you call him?" Yancy asked, glancing at Major Jackson.

"Among other things," Cadet Sims said. "So are you coming to VMI, Yancy?"

Yancy shook his head. "No, I couldn't do that. No, I just work for Major Jackson, and I guess he just wanted to bring me today to have some fun."

"Hard to think of races and gun drills as fun," Sandy Owens grumbled. He couldn't run very fast, and he hated the dirt and grime and noise and smell of the musket drills. He secretly, however, did love artillery drill, even if it did get his breeches dirty. He was the best in his class at it.

"Really?" Yancy said in surprise. "I thought it was great." He saw Major Jackson motioning to him, and he hurriedly said, "I've gotta go now. Thanks again, cadets, for the day."

He joined Major Jackson and they went to the stables and saddled up. Jackson didn't say anything, and Yancy didn't either.

They had ridden awhile before Major

Jackson said, "That was quite a show you put on there, Mr. Tremayne."

"I didn't mean to show off, sir. It's just that from about the time Indian boys can walk, they race, and their fathers teach them to use a rifle. That's the kind of life I had. It just comes natural, I guess. And you know, I didn't do so good with the cannon."

Jackson answered, "You did real well for your first time. Better than most all of those boys did on their first times. So your father is the one who taught you to shoot like that?"

"Yes, sir."

"But it takes a lot of practice, and a lot of discipline, to get that accurate and that fast."

Yancy shrugged a little. "It doesn't seem like a discipline to me, sir. I love it. Not just hunting, but as you say, target practice and speed practice. My father and I used to compete. He always won. Course we don't do that anymore," he added with a touch of sadness.

"But don't you stop, Mr. Tremayne," Jackson said sternly. "Don't you stop. You're young and tough and good at what you do. You'd make a good soldier."

Yancy was pleased and relished a rare compliment from a man he admired. Then he sighed. "You know, Major Jackson, that

166

the Amish are against any kind of violence. They won't fight in a war."

"Yes, I've heard that."

"I've wondered about that myself sometimes," Yancy said hesitantly. "The Bible says, 'Thou shalt not kill.' "

"I've read that many times. I have a friend who is a scholar in the Hebrew language. I asked him about that commandment. He told me that the word used in our Bible for *kill* is literally *murder* in the original Hebrew text. 'Thou shalt not murder.' "

"What's the difference, sir?"

"You murder someone out of gain, or anger, or jealousy. You take the life to serve yourself. But those who serve as soldiers, they are giving their lives for their country, to preserve it. In most cases they are fighting to save their people from godless armies. So, I tell myself I will not murder, but I will defend my country."

"Yes, sir," Yancy said quietly, thinking, *And I would, too.*

Every Amish community had a bishop, a deacon, and a secretary. When all three of them showed up at a house, it was generally a grave situation. Daniel wasn't very surprised when he opened the door and invited them in.

The bishop was Gideon Lambright, who had performed Daniel and Becky's marriage ceremony. Today, in constrast to that day, he seemed tall and stern, his beard and white hair bristling. He had come along with Joshua Middleton, the short, forty-four-year-old deacon, who was normally a jolly man but today was somber. Also accompanying them was Sol Raber, another deacon. He and Daniel had become good friends, but now he seemed distant.

Daniel led them into the parlor where Becky and Zemira waited. "Will you sit down, gentlemen?" he said.

"Thank you, Mr. Tremayne," Lambright answered. He took a chair and the other two flanked him.

"Would you like for us to leave, Bishop?" Becky asked, motioning to herself and Zemira.

Daniel stood by Becky's chair.

"I would like for the whole family to be here." Bishop Lambright took a deep breath and continued, "This isn't a pleasant task that we have, I'm afraid. But it must be done. There is some serious difficulty concerning your son, Yancy."

"Is there a charge being brought against him?" Daniel asked at once. He was facing the men squarely, and there was a light of challenge in his eyes. He had been expecting a visit such as this and forced himself to show no signs of temper.

Bishop Lambright shook his head. "There are no charges against him at this time, Mr. Tremayne, nothing like that. It's just that we have decided that it is highly unseemly for your son to work for Major Jackson. You know well our stand on war and that none of our men are allowed to serve as soldiers."

"But Yancy isn't serving as a soldier. He is just working for the major."

"We understand that he is also taking part in military exercises, using the musket, firing the cannon."

"I fail to see any harm in that," Daniel said firmly.

"But we do see the harm. It wasn't so bad when all your son was doing was working at Major Jackson's home. But now he is mingling with the soldiers at the institute, and he is shooting cannons. I understand he is even learning to use the saber. Please, Mr. Tremayne, you must bring the boy home, here, to work on the farm. Or to find a trade for him."

Daniel was angry, and he knew it wouldn't be good for him to speak what was on his heart.

Becky, however, spoke up. "You must

understand, Bishop, that Yancy led a completely different life with the Indians — a life that included hunting, fishing, and using guns. And after all, he is still in rumspringa. He's only fifteen years old."

"I'm well aware of this, Mrs. Tremayne," Bishop Lambright said, not unkindly. "But the fact remains that Yancy is not hunting and fishing. He is learning the tools and the ways of war. And that we cannot allow."

Becky, Zemira, and Daniel all exchanged glances. Daniel took up the argument. "But most of the time he is working at Major Jackson's home, helping Mrs. Jackson. Surely you can find no fault in this?"

"Major Jackson has exposed him to these weapons of war and has influenced his conduct for the worse," Lambright said. "Yancy needs to be here, with the People."

"Major Thomas Jackson is an honorable, Christian —" Daniel began angrily.

Becky laid her hand on his arm, and he was silent. "Do I understand," Becky said in a quiet voice, "that you want us to make Yancy quit this job he loves and bring him back here? And if we don't, will the three of us be punished?"

"Mrs. Tremayne, you and your husband, and of course you, Zemira, have done nothing wrong. But surely you understand the consequences for the boy, if he persists in this course."

That ended the conversation and the three left.

After they were gone, Daniel turned and the expression on his face was bleak. "I can't do this to Yancy, make him leave the Jacksons and come back here," he said. "I think if I did, he'd just take off and leave us. Like I did," he said bitterly.

"Of course we won't do that!" Becky said. "I know we shouldn't disagree with the bishop, but it's not right. It's just not right. You shouldn't *force* people into the community. That's just another form of aggression. You must let them decide for themselves. Yancy has a right to do what he wants, whether it is the Amish way or the English. You know, Daniel, that we don't shun the members of our families who have gone the way of the English. Look at your cousins, Caleb Tremayne's family. Sol Raber is still good friends with him."

Daniel nodded. "I know. I agree. But — Mother? Are you afraid that the leadership may order us to shun Yancy if we don't make him stay home?"

Zemira said firmly, "I don't know, and I don't care. Yancy is a good boy. If I would have had this choice with you, Daniel, I never would have tried to force you into our ways, as Becky said. I think that we must let Yancy do whatever seems right to him, and never in this life will I turn my back on him."

And that settled the matter for the three of them.

When Yancy came home from work, Daniel called him aside and related what Bishop Lambright had said. Then he told him what he, Becky, and Zemira thought.

"What do you think I should do?" Yancy asked worriedly.

"Whatever your heart tells you, as long as it's honorable," Daniel answered, patting Yancy's shoulder. "And I know it will be. We trust you. Follow your heart, and whatever you decide your family will be with you."

The next day Yancy went to work at the Jacksons' home. He and Mrs. Jackson worked more out in the garden, planting the new daisy-mum that he had brought her from Zemira's yard. Anna had been delighted. And they were busy weeding and turning over the soil and mulching, preparing the beds for the long winter.

After a while Anna took a break, getting lemonade for them from the kitchen. She invited Yancy to sit down in the shade for a few minutes. Even though it was the middle of October, the midafternoon was still warm for gardening work.

They sat in silence, as Yancy had very little to say all day. He was tired, as he hadn't really slept.

Finally Anna put her head to one side and asked, "Yancy, what's wrong? Are you not feeling well today?"

"No, ma'am, it's not that," he said, ducking his head. "It's — it's a problem. At home."

"Is it something you can tell me about?" she asked softly.

He hesitated for a long time then looked up at her. His dark eyes were troubled. "I don't know, ma'am. I wouldn't want to trouble you."

"Nonsense," she said. "I would like to help, if I could."

Slowly he explained to her his dilemma. "And so, I'm certain to be shunned if I don't go back and just stay on the farm."

"What do your parents say?" Anna asked.

"They told me to do whatever I feel is right," he answered. "Even my grandmother says I should pray and ask God for what is right for me. Even *she's* not trying to force me to be Amish."

"She sounds like a very wise woman."

"She is. I wish I was as close to God as she is. But I'm still not sure about Him, either."

"You're young," Anna said sturdily, "and you'll find Him. In the meantime, I will pray for you, Yancy. So you'll know in your heart what you must do."

That night, again, he lay awake at home, staring at the faint starlight on the ceiling. His father had told him that he could take as long as he needed to think about his decision. Yancy didn't pray much, and when he did, he felt like he was talking to the ceiling. And so it was on this night.

But close to the dawn, he finally made his decision in his heart and knew his course was set. He dozed for a while then rose early, as always, to go to the Jacksons' house.

When he arrived and took Fancy into the stables, he saw that the new hay for the stall beds had been delivered. He decided to go ahead and muck out the stalls and replace the hay before he checked in with Mrs. Jackson. He had arrived early, anyway.

He started shoveling out the soiled hay bed in the first stall, working energetically. He even started whistling. Since he had made his decision, his heart felt lighter. He knew he had chosen the right course.

Yancy wasn't really surprised to see Major

Jackson come into the stable, for both of the Jacksons' horses were still there, so he knew the major hadn't yet gone to VMI.

"Hello, Yancy," Jackson said pleasantly.

"Good morning, Major Jackson. Want me to saddle Bebe or Gordo for you?"

"Not just yet. I'd like to speak with you for a few minutes. Will you come into the kitchen? Hetty has made fresh coffee for us."

"Yes, sir," Yancy said, a little mystified. He and Mrs. Jackson often had coffee or tea or lemonade for a little break, but Major Jackson had never sought him out for a break in work.

Yancy followed Major Jackson into the kitchen, where they seated themselves comfortably on the high stools at the work-table. Yancy almost always had lunch in here, talking with Hetty. Although the Jacksons had made no specific provisions for Yancy's meals — in fact, he almost always brought food from home — more often than not Hetty would fix him lunch, usually leftovers from breakfast and last night's dinner. Sometimes Yancy wondered whether Major and Mrs. Jackson knew this, but then he decided that they were generous people and probably didn't mind.

They sipped their fresh hot coffee for a

few moments, and then Jackson said, "My wife tells me that you've had some trouble at home with the Amish leadership."

Yancy shifted uncomfortably on his stool but didn't drop his gaze. The blue glare of Jackson's stare hardly allowed one to look away. "I'm sorry if I bothered Mrs. Jackson," he said. "I didn't mean to, sir."

Jackson gave a dismissive wave. "You didn't bother her, Mr. Tremayne. She told me out of concern for you and your welfare. And I have an interest in that, too."

"You do?" Yancy gulped. "Well — thank you, sir."

"And so, have you been able to come to any conclusions about the course you should follow?" Jackson asked.

"Yes, sir, I have," Yancy answered. "I'd like — I'd like to keep working for you, sir. There's just one thing I'd like to ask. It's kind of a big favor, but I was hoping you might understand."

Jackson nodded. "And what is that?"

"You see, sir, if I keep working for you and disobey the bishop, it — it puts my family in a bad way. They support my decision, sir, but the bishop could still sort of put them in disgrace. They wouldn't be shunned." He grinned unevenly. "Guess that's what's going to happen to me. But still, they would be out of favor with the leadership of the community. So what I was going to ask is if maybe there's a room for me out at your farm, sir. Even if it's just in the loft of the barn or in the carriage house, I could make do. It would just be so much better for my family if I wasn't actually living at the farm."

Jackson leaned back, crossed his arms, and studied Yancy for a long time.

Yancy didn't flinch at his scrutiny; he met his icy gaze solidly.

"That's a hard decision for a boy of fifteen, Yancy. Are you sure this is what you want to do?"

"Yes, sir. And it's not really so hard," he added. "There's no law that says I can't go back and visit them anytime I want. Even if I'm supposed to be shunned, if they decide not to do it, no one's going to go tell on them to the bishop."

"I see. All right, Mr. Tremayne, now let me tell you of something that I think the Lord is leading me to do. You see, Anna and I prayed last night for you, to see if there was something we might do to help you. I believe you're an honest, hardworking, gifted young man, and that is something that I believe should be encouraged always. So I have a proposition that I'd like you to consider."

"What's that, sir?"

Jackson leaned across the table. "How would you like to attend VMI?"

Yancy's eyes widened. "Me? Go to VMI? But — how?"

"One of the alumni has established a charity scholarship program for promising young men who can't afford to attend the institute," Jackson answered. "I believe that if I submit you as a candidate, with my recommendation, you'll be accepted. It would pay for your tuition and your uniforms, provide a small allowance for food and other necessaries, and you would live in the barracks."

Yancy was stunned. "But — you really think I can qualify? I've had very little education, sir."

"Very little formal education, I know," Jackson agreed. "But I've observed that you're very quick, you're intelligent, and you pay attention. I know it will be difficult, but" — he sighed dramatically — "it couldn't possibly be harder for you than it was for me at West Point, Mr. Tremayne. I did it. I have every confidence that you can do it."

Yancy jumped off the stool and reached across the table. Jackson took his hand, and

Yancy pumped it enthusiastically. "Yes, sir! I can! I will! And how can I ever thank you, sir?"

"Don't thank me, Mr. Tremayne," Jackson said. "It will be all to my satisfaction to see you become the soldier I know you will be. And the time is coming, I think, that it will be good soldiers that we need."

■ ■ ■ ■

Part Three:
The Foundation
1859–1860

■ ■ ■ ■

CHAPTER TEN

Broad bands of yellow sunlight streamed through the window, illuminating the snowy white tablecloth on the modest four-seater dining room table at Major Thomas Jackson's house. Anna put the good Blue Willow china on the table; she liked to have a fine table setting when Thomas was home. She looked over the two table settings with satisfaction, with Thomas at the head and her sitting at his right hand. They always sat close together when they dined alone.

Hetty brought in scrambled eggs, grits, and bacon, and then fresh bread and marmalade. She sighed. "I know Major Jackson is only going to eat one thing. Wonder what it'll be today? All the biscuits, or all the bacon, or all the eggs?"

Hetty also served as the Jacksons' cook, but sometimes Anna Jackson cooked, too. She enjoyed it, although ladies such as those in the Morrison family rarely did any cooking. But this morning she had done the scrambled eggs all by herself, and it lent a rosy hue to her normally pale cheeks.

"I'll tell him I cooked everything," Anna said with a touch of amusement. "Maybe then I can make him feel guilty enough to eat a little of everything."

"You can try it, Miss Anna," Hetty said resignedly. "But he'll likely outfox you." She huffed back into the kitchen.

Anna poured two cups of hot coffee, then put sugar in one and set that one in Jackson's place. Then she went down the hall to her husband's study. Politely she knocked — she would never burst in on him uninvited — and called, "Thomas, Thomas, time for breakfast." She returned to the dining room.

In a few moments he appeared at the door, buttoning up his uniform tunic.

She smiled at him. Just then Anna wanted to tell him how happy she was just to see him in the morning, but somehow she could never form that in feeling or proper words. *How do I tell this man that when he isn't here I'm lonely and have a great emptiness? How do I tell him the minute I see him coming I feel safe and secure?*

For so long Anna Jackson had buried her feelings for Thomas Jackson, as she had when he had married Eleanor Junkin. Then, she could never admit to herself that she was in love with a man who was betrothed to another woman; and she could never, would never, entertain the thought that it was through that woman's death that she had married Thomas Jackson. In a way it held her back from expressing her deepest, most secret feelings. But Thomas Jackson was such an affectionate, loving husband that she thought he probably wouldn't profit from her confessions anyway. He knew she loved him.

When he came into the dining room, he put his arms out and she went to him. He held her tightly for a moment, neither of them speaking. He kissed her cheek. "You're better than any breakfast."

Anna said, "I know you, Thomas Jackson. You have eating on your mind, no matter how pretty your words. Let's sit down and eat this food before it gets cold."

They sat down and bowed their heads, and Jackson prayed a simple prayer of thanksgiving. Anna knew that he prayed about everything. Once he told her that he prayed over a glass of water when someone gave him one. Anna knew when he was offered any kind of help he always thanked God for it.

"Now, that bad habit you have of only eating one thing off the table won't work today," Anna said firmly. "I made everything this morning, and I want you to eat some of all of it."

"Why, I could fill up on these good biscuits you made. Look, you made eight of them. I can eat seven and you can eat one. Then you can fill up on all the eggs and grits."

Anna smiled and reached out and took two of the biscuits off the platter, put them on Jackson's plate, then said, "Eat those with your eggs."

She watched as he scraped some eggs on his plate then gave her the rest. He flatly refused the grits, insisting his plate was full, much more than he could eat. They ate in silence for a few moments, and in spite of Anna's best intentions, Jackson ate his two biscuits, got two more, and ignored his eggs. Anna gave up.

Then she said, "Thomas, the news about the North and their antislavery program threatening our cotton states has gotten so heated. What will we do if the South secedes?"

Jackson said quietly, "God hasn't told me, esposa. But He doesn't need to tell me until the problem comes. "Take therefore no thought for the morrow," the scripture says. "Sufficient unto the day is the evil thereof."

"I can't help thinking about it. All these riots all over the country! It frightens me. I would like to know I have the courage to face a war."

Jackson reached over and took her hand. "I was talking to young Mr. Murphy just last week. After Sunday school he came up to me and said he'd like to talk to me for a few moments, so I took him aside into the church office. 'Major Jackson, I have a problem.' Of course I asked what it was. He said, 'I hear of people who die so easily it is like going from one room to another. If we go to war, I don't think I can face death like that. I just don't have dying grace.'"

Anna asked, "What did you tell him, Thomas?"

"I told him that he didn't need dying grace, and he asked me why that was. I said, 'Because you're not dying. When it comes your time to die or my time to die, that's when God will give us dying grace. Until that time comes, don't worry about it.' So, my dear, don't worry about it."

Anna always marveled at how her husband could simplify theological problems. He loved nothing better than talking about the deep, profound, and often mysterious things of the Bible. Basically he saw things in a very simplistic manner that she envied. To him the scripture was very clear and very personal.

"I had a dream last night of having a baby," Anna said dreamily. "But then I worried that it might be too hard to bring a child into this world when it seems there is such trouble ahead."

"Why, Anna, don't you know that Adam might have said something like that to Eve when they were driven out of the garden of Eden? 'Eve, let's not have any children, for it might be too difficult.' " He took a bite of the last biscuit and chewed it thoughtfully. "There never was a time free of trouble. People are afraid of what might happen, but we must trust the Lord, and we must be wise." He smiled. "If God wants to send us another child, He will do so." He rose then and said, "It is time to go to church. Let's go hear what the Lord will teach us this morning."

Yancy rode up to the farmhouse and dismounted. With satisfaction he petted Midnight. He was three years old this month. Grandmother, muttering about "showy, proud horses," had given Yancy the foal after he had been at the farm for only a month.

Yancy had trained him for two years now, and it had been difficult, for Midnight was a high-spirited, proud horse. But when Yancy had been a young boy, the Cheyenne had taught him to train shaggy wild mustangs, and he had developed a special knack for turning them into superb saddle horses. And so he had done with Midnight. But he would tolerate no rider except Yancy.

Before he went in he wanted to savor the cool October afternoon, the dry fall scent of the grass and fields, and the high pale sun set in a light blue sky. Hank, coming from the shade of the oak trees in the back of the house and alerted to his presence, bayed once, then loped up in welcome, ears flopping and tongue lolling. Yancy bent to pet him, scratching his ears and murmuring, "Dumb ol' dog. How are you doing, dumb ol' dog. Huh?"

Now he stood for a moment, absolutely still, remembering the richness of the farm. He was alive to the world that was about him, whether well-known or strange. He was sixteen years old now and one inch over six feet, and weighed one hundred and eighty pounds. He was one inch taller than his father, and this amazed him each time he thought of it.

Yancy hadn't worn his VMI uniform

home, though it had been the proudest thing he had ever done to have worn it for a year. It wouldn't have been suitable to the Amish, however, for they seemed to freeze every time they saw any man in uniform. So every time he visited home, he wore his old work clothes, this time a pair of heavy wool brown pants and a dark blue wool shirt. He had the sleeves rolled up, and it showed his forearms, which were now strong and thickly corded with muscle. He had given up his silver-trimmed VMI forage cap for his old wide-brimmed slouch hat. In deference to the Amish he had even taken off the bead-trimmed band his mother had made.

Hearing Hank's welcome bark, Becky came out onto the veranda. Holding out her arms, she cried, "Yancy! Yancy, come in! We've missed you so much!"

He went into the parlor, where Becky and Zemira had their quilting rack down.

Zemira looked up to him, her bright dark eyes glowing with pleasure. "You've come back again! I suppose you got hungry."

"I'm always hungry for your cooking, Grandmother." He went to her, bent over, and kissed her smooth cheek. "You're getting prettier every time I see you," he teased.

"Go away from here with that nonsense!" She waved him away with a little laugh.

"Becky, are you all right? You look big as a house."

Becky laughed. "Yes, I'm well. But you have an odd way of framing a compliment, Yancy."

"But that's the way mothers-to-be are supposed to look, aren't they? And you're glowing, you look so pretty. So, Grandmother, are you going to feed me or what? I'm starved!"

"You can have some leftovers, but save an appetite," Zemira said sternly. "For supper I'm going to cook a meal that will make your hair curly."

"I always wanted curly hair." Yancy drew up a chair and sat down. He was soon eating heartily of lunch — cold ham, fresh white bread, jacket potatoes, pickles, and cabbage slaw. "This is wonderful!" Yancy said. "I don't get anything like this at VMI."

"Of course you don't. You're not supposed to get home cooking anywhere but at home," Zemira said. "Now, tell us everything you have been doing."

"It would bore you to death." Yancy smiled. "I get up in the morning, and I have to make sure my bed is made and everything is put away. I have to be sure that all the younger cadets get their rooms clean and their beds made. We then all go out to eat breakfast. Then we have classes, and then lunch. Then we go back to classes, and then supper. Nothing good like this, though."

Becky asked earnestly, "And how are your classes going, Yancy?"

He chewed thoughtfully. "It's hard. They're hard. Stuff I don't know, and stuff I have to work on real hard to catch up. But Major Jackson has helped me. He said he was like me when he went to West Point. He was behind and he had to study extra all the time. He doesn't favor me in class — it would be against his sense of honor to do that — but he helps me figure out how to study. He even talked Peyton Stevens into being my tutor, and he helps me a lot."

"Who's Peyton Stevens?" Zemira asked curiously. "I think I've heard that name before."

"Maybe so," Yancy said. "His father is Virginia Senator Peyton Stevens, Sr. Peyton is Jr. But he's not pompous or anything. He's real smart. He's just kinda lazy, I guess. But Major Jackson talked him into helping me with my studies, and he's helped me with everything, from English literature, to mathematics, to European history. . . ."

They heard a soft call from upstairs, and Zemira stood up. "That's Callie Jo waking up from her nap. I'll go get her."

"I'll get her," Becky offered.

"No ma'am, I'm not too old to climb those stairs and get my granddaughter," Zemira said over her shoulder as she left the room.

"You'll never be old, Grandmother," Yancy called after her. He told Becky, "I've never known anyone like her. She's sure not what I expected when we came here. I was afraid she was going to be this mean old Amish woman that never smiled."

"Nice surprise for you. She's very fond of you, Yancy. I think it's been good for her — and me, too — that you are here."

"You sure?" he asked gravely. "Even though you're supposed to be shunning me, and all of you are not exactly in the good graces of Bishop Lambright?"

Becky smiled warmly at him. "Well, you know, Yancy, shunning is not necessarily absolutely ignoring a person. Of course no one expects you to attend church or the sing, but neither are they angry with you or are they going to openly shame you. I don't think anyone in the community would refuse to speak to you, and certainly no one thinks that we shouldn't still be your family."

Callie Jo came toddling through the door, pulling Zemira by the apron. "Nance!

Nance!" she cried, holding up her arms and running to Yancy.

He stood up, hoisted her high over his head, and turned around in circles. She squealed with delight. Then he sat back down with her on his lap.

"Hi, Nance," she lisped.

Yancy looked up at Zemira and Becky. "No one here had better ever tell my nickname to anyone at VMI," he said darkly. "Ever."

"Okay, Nance," Becky said. "It'll be our secret."

Yancy kissed Callie Jo's flushed cheeks. She was two years old now, with thick strawberry blond hair and light blue eyes like Daniel. "Hello, Jo-Jo. Did you know that I brought you a present?"

"Present?" she said, her eyes lighting up.

"Yep. It's out in my saddlebag. Wanna come with me to get it?"

"Yep."

He picked her up and went outside, where Midnight was still hitched to the post in the front yard. He snorted and danced a little when he came out.

"Minnite," Callie Jo said and pointed.

"That's right. You're a very smart little girl."

He pulled a book out of the saddlebag.

"See here? This is for you."

"Book!" she announced. "My book! Read me!"

It was a picture book of Bible stories. Yancy sat with Becky and Zemira in the parlor and went through the entire book with her.

Then she said, "Froo with book. Go ride Minnite?"

"You're a mighty little girl for such a big horse."

"Pleez, Nance?" she begged, her blue eyes big and round as saucers. Yancy had been taking her for rides since she turned one year old.

Yancy told Becky, "You heard her. I'm under orders."

Becky smiled. "Be careful. Hold her tight."

"Always," Yancy said. He left the house carrying Callie Jo and headed toward Midnight. He stepped into the saddle and put her in front of him, letting her hold the reins. The beautiful black stallion galloped away lightly, and Yancy reveled in the thrill of the moment.

It was riotous fall in the valley, with the leaves of the hardwoods turned all the warm shades of red, orange, and yellow imaginable. As always, the evergreens cast their emerald glow over the land.

The three young men made their way through the thick forest just behind the Tremayne farm.

Suddenly, Yancy stopped, threw his rifle up, and pulled the trigger.

"You got him!" Clay Tremayne said. "I didn't even see that little beast."

"I didn't see him either!" Clay's brother Morgan exclaimed. He picked up the squirrel. "You got him right through the head, Yancy. Don't you ever miss?"

Yancy shrugged. "Not much. Well — no. I don't."

"Liar," Morgan scoffed.

"Have you seen me miss?"

"No. But that doesn't mean that you don't, when no one is watching."

They all laughed.

"We've got about enough of these things, haven't we?" Morgan said, holding up his game bag. "Let's go back and get Aunt Zemira to cook us up a great big supper of squirrel and dumplings."

They shouldered their rifles and started back to the farmhouse.

There were two families of Tremaynes in the Shenandoah Valley: The Enoch Tremaynes, as they were called, were the Amish Tremaynes. The Luther Tremaynes were

English and lived in Lexington.

In the 1730s the Tremayne family moved to the Shenandoah Valley from Pennsylvania. There were two brothers, Enoch Tremayne, the eldest, and Luther Tremayne, who was the younger. Enoch stayed with the Amish and was Yancy's great-great-great-grandfather. Luther fell in love with an English, became a Methodist, and left the Amish. Luther was Clay's and Morgan's great-great-great grandfather. Basically the Tremaynes were somewhat distant cousins by now, but the two families had stayed close. They all called each other "Cousin" or "Aunt" or "Uncle," whatever seemed appropriate to their respective ages. Clay and Morgan called Yancy "Cousin," and Zemira "Aunt," and Daniel "Uncle."

In the golden afternoon glow, Clay suddenly straightened, pointed, and yelled, "Look, Yancy! There's one!"

Like lightning Yancy shouldered his rifle and sighted. Then he lowered it and muttered, "No, there was not one. What are you playing at, Clay?"

Clay laughed. "Told you you'd miss when no one's watching."

"Idiot," Morgan grumbled as they trudged on, but his tone was unmistakably affectionate.

He and Clay were brothers but were different in almost all aspects. Clay was twenty-three, two years younger than his brother, as tall as Morgan and more lightly built. Morgan had auburn hair and blue eyes, while Clay had dark-colored hair and gray eyes. Clay was high-spirited, a prankster, sometimes loud and boisterous. Morgan was thoughtful, quiet, serious. Since they had been old enough to stand, they had fought each other, verbally and physically. Though Clay seemed the more vigorous of the two, Morgan had always had a quiet, intent strength, while Clay was more suited to fighting like a windmill. Somehow Morgan had always managed to keep his rowdy young brother in check, but now that they were older, Morgan sometimes lost his grip on what Clay was doing. Clay was sly.

"Say, Yancy," Clay said, "Now that you're such a big VMI man and all, swaggering around with Major Thomas Jackson, we ought to go out and celebrate."

"Celebrate what?"

"You, man! It's time you put your pretty-boy uniform away and have a good time for a change!"

"Clay," Morgan said, "you don't want to be teaching him any bad manners."

Clay grinned mischievously. "Don't pay

any attention to him. He's just an old milksop. I know a young girl about your age, Yancy. We'll go out and I'll teach you how to handle women."

Morgan warned, "He'll just get you into trouble, Yancy. I'm telling you, I don't care what he says, you'll just get into trouble."

Clay slapped Morgan on the shoulder so hard it almost staggered him. "You know, you're the good brother and I'm the bad one. I guess we're like Isaac and Ishmael. I always like what the Bible said about Ishmael, that he'd be a wild man. That's in Genesis 16:12." He glanced at Yancy and said, "That's my favorite scripture, because that's me." He turned back to his brother and said, "You're the good man and I'm the wild man, Morgan. Nothing you can do to change it."

"Of course there is, dummy. You say that all the time and you know you can change anytime you want to," Morgan insisted. He told Yancy, "If you want to do something, we'll go hunting or fishing. My sister plays the piano beautifully, too. You can come for supper and a concert. But don't go with Clay because he'll lead you astray."

"If I possibly can, I will." Clay laughed. "You better watch out for me. I'm a wild man, Yancy Tremayne!"

The next day was Sunday, so after his father and Becky and Zemira had left for church, Yancy headed back to VMI. About halfway to town he saw a buggy pulled over on the side of the road. He looked closer and saw that it was the Lapps' carriage. Almost all of the Amish buggies looked alike — black with unpainted and unadorned wooden wheels — but Yancy's powers of observation were sharp, and he also knew the gelding pulling the buggy. It was a big bay named Acer, and he belonged to Hannah Lapp's family.

The buggy was pulled to the side of the road, leaning precariously. One of the wheels was awry. The wheel lock had obviously come off, and the wheel tilted drunkenly to one side.

There were two horses hitched to the rear of the buggy and two men standing in the front. Between their thick shoulders, Yancy could see a white Amish prayer cap.

Quickly Yancy cantered up to them, dismounted, and said, "So, is there some trouble here?"

The two men turned, and Yancy recognized Boone Williams and Henry Cousins.

They were both tall men, older than Yancy. The two worked at the sawmill in town, where Yancy had met them when fetching lumber for the farm. He had also seen them loitering on the street corners in town, spitting tobacco and furtively watching women who walked by.

Boone sneered at him. He was a burly man with thick, coarse brown hair and muddy brown eyes to match. "Go on your way, Tremayne. There's nothing here that you need to worry about."

Cousins laughed coarsely. He was a thick-set man with bulging muscles and had obviously been drinking. "You heard him. Move on, Injun. We saw this squaw first."

They were standing too close to Hannah; Cousins's shoulder almost touched her face. She had her eyes downcast, but Yancy could see her hands, twisting nervously, and the way she cringed backward away from them.

Instantly Yancy made a decision. One of the tactics he learned from Major Jackson was to hit your enemy quick and hard and put him out if you can with the first blow.

Yancy kicked out and his boot caught Cousins in the ankle, which drove the big man off balance. He yelled as he went down, and immediately Boone roared and threw himself toward Yancy.

Yancy whipped out the knife he always carried and held it steadily pointed at Boone's barrel chest. "On your way, Boone. You, too, Cousins. You're not hurt. But if you two stick around you will be."

Cousins got up and snarled, "You won't always have that knife, Tremayne!"

"You're wrong. I'll always have it," Yancy said evenly. "Now get out of here before I use it on you."

The two glared at Yancy, then mounted and rode off, cursing him.

Yancy turned back around and said rather uncomfortably, "Hello, Hannah."

With a sob she threw herself into his arms.

He jerked with surprise but then patted her awkwardly and said, "It's okay. It's okay. They're gone now."

She clung to him desperately and cried, "That's — they scared me. I don't know what they wanted. Probably nothing . . . but — my brother went for a new wheel lock, and I stayed, and I shouldn't have, it was so stupid of me. . . ."

He held her out at arm's length. "It's not your fault, Hannah. Never think that this happened because of anything you did. It was their fault, not yours."

Woefully she gazed into his eyes, and he noticed that she was still just as pretty as she had ever been. Her ash brown hair had come loose in soft ringlets from her prayer cap. Her cheeks, though tear-stained, were still soft, and she had a flawless complexion. Her long lashes were wet with tears. Gently he reached out and smoothed one ringlet away from her face.

The gesture seemed to bring her back to the present. She straightened and pulled away from him, almost imperceptibly. Then she calmly folded her hands and composed her distraught features. The change in her attitude was subtle but unmistakable. She was distancing herself from him.

With a sigh, he stepped back. "So you said your brother was with you?"

"Yes, he was driving. When the wheel lock came off, he decided to walk to the Keim farm and see if they have another one."

"I'm sure they do. Mr. Keim has a good carpentry shop there," Yancy said lamely.

"Yes, he does."

"How — how have you been?" Yancy hadn't seen Hannah for almost a year, because of course he stopped going to church when he joined VMI and the bishop decreed that he must be shunned. He reflected that she hadn't changed at all; she still looked frail and vulnerable and naive. He knew, however, that he had hardened and toughened, and it showed on his face.

"I've been very well," Hannah answered softly. "You look fine, Yancy. You're very tan, I see. Were you out in the sun much this summer? Um — shooting, or drilling or something?"

"Something," he agreed. "But you know. Indian."

"Yes. Of course."

"Yes. Okay, well, I'll just hitch up Midnight and wait with you until your brother gets here."

"Thank you."

Yancy led Midnight to the back of the buggy and tied him up. Then, his hands stuck in his pockets, he went back to the front of the buggy where Hannah silently waited. As she regarded him, he saw that she had completely regained her composure. Her gaze was not hostile, but neither was it welcoming. She just seemed placid and sure of herself.

Yancy swallowed hard and decided to plunge in. "You know, Hannah, I've thought about you a lot. I thought — I thought that we were becoming good friends." Hannah had always shown particular interest in Yancy at Sunday dinners, constantly serving him more lemonade, more biscuits, more butter.

She sighed. "It's been a long time, you know, Yancy. A lot has happened. You're very different now than you were then."

He nodded. "Guess I am." He looked up and squinted in the afternoon sun. "I hear a wagon. Maybe it's your brother."

It was Amos Lapp, Hannah's oldest brother. He was a tall, muscular man with straw blond hair and a stern jaw. He reined the wagon up and nodded at Yancy.

"Hello, Amos," Yancy said. "I happened by and thought I'd wait with Hannah until you got back."

"That was very good of you, Yancy. Thank you. The Keims had a wheel block and also let me bring an extra wheel in case it's warped." He jumped out of the wagon.

Yancy looked closely at the wheel on the buggy. "It looks true, though. Can I help you fix it?"

"It would be easier with two."

"Glad to help."

"I'll pick up the wagon if you just slip the wheel back on the axle, Yancy. Then we'll see if the new block will hold it."

"Sure." Yancy noticed that Amos picked the wheel up as if it was made of feathers. Yancy straightened the wheel over the axle and then Amos let it down. Together they fit the wheel lock over it and hammered it in until the wheel was secure.

After they were finished, Amos said, "Thank you, neighbor. I appreciate the help, and for staying with my sister while I was gone."

"Glad to do it," Yancy said, holding out his hand.

Amos looked down at it then looked up at Yancy gravely. "I'm sorry," he said.

Some of the arbitrary rules of the Ordnung dictated certain conditions of shunning. The Amish could offer help to those who were shunned and could accept help from them. But they couldn't, for example, offer them rides or accept any from them. And they couldn't shake hands with them.

"It's all right. I understand," Yancy said hastily. He turned to Hannah. "Hannah, I was wondering — that is, I thought —"

"I'm sorry, too, Yancy, but no," she said so softly he could barely hear her. And then she turned her back.

Yancy didn't go home the next weekend. He stayed at the institute, doing some extra studies — he always had to work twice as hard as the other boys because of his lack of education when he was young. He washed all his clothes and cleaned the barracks room — twice — and busied himself with other work so that he wouldn't think too much about Hannah Lapp. Seeing her again had sharply reminded him that he had begun to develop feelings for her. In the last year since he had joined VMI, he had been so busy that he was able to block most things out of his mind except his classes and training. But when he had seen her in such awful circumstances, it had awakened all those emotions that he had with such determination put aside.

He had awakened before dawn on Sunday morning, ventured out in the bitterly cold gray predawn, and went for a short ride on Midnight. He found no joy in it though. He and Midnight both got chilled, and there was an icy fog that lay around the grounds of the institute, turning everything in sight a dull gray. He led Midnight back to the stables and began to give him a thorough brushing-down. After that, on the livery potbellied stove, he heated up a pot of hot mash. It was a mixture of oats, grits, and barley soup. It was Midnight's favorite treat.

Major Jackson came into the livery and came right to Midnight's stall. "That smells as good as my breakfast did this morning," he said, stroking Midnight's velvety nose. "This is a fine horse, Cadet Tremayne. No wonder you spoil him."

"Thank you, sir," Yancy said listlessly.

Jackson eyed him shrewdly. "You have anything planned for this morning, Cadet?"

"No, sir."

"Good, good. I want to ask you a question. Are you a Christian, sir?"

Yancy looked up, directly into his burning blue gaze. "I don't rightly know, Major. I pray, but it doesn't seem to do much good, for me or anything else. So I'm just not sure."

"Good answer, Cadet," Jackson said briskly. "Honest and to the point. One day you'll be able to answer with one word — yes. But for now, I'd like you to come with me this morning."

"Where to, Major Jackson?"

"To Sunday school."

"Yes, sir." Yancy was puzzled. Normally no one at the institute saw Major Jackson on weekends. Of course, since Yancy had worked for him and Mrs. Jackson, he was a little more familiar with them than the other cadets. But during the time Yancy had worked for the family, Major Jackson had never asked him to go to church. He wondered now if the major had noticed how low he had been for the past week.

Quickly Yancy saddled Midnight up again and they went into town, into the fine First

Presbyterian Church of Lexington. Between the sanctuary and a private residence was the "Lecture Room." Major Jackson and Yancy dismounted and hitched there, a modest one-room addition to the church.

"Here we are, Cadet Tremayne," Jackson said. "I started this Sunday school in 1851, when I first came to Lexington and to the institute. We've had a wonderful time in the last eight years."

He opened the door. Yancy followed him and stopped suddenly as he saw that the room was filled with black people. Many of them were children, some of them young people, but there were also several adults.

Jackson went to the podium at the front of the room. "We have a guest today. This is Yancy Tremayne, one of our cadets from the institute. I thought you might want to meet one of our fine young men."

Yancy was speechless, for he had never dreamed of such a thing. He had remembered hearing Mrs. Jackson speak of a Sunday school, but it had never occurred to him that it was for black people. He took a seat and listened as Jackson taught the lesson. Yancy was once again amazed at how complex this man was. When he had heard of Jackson's fighting ability in Mexico, he pictured him being a man with a murderous spirit in battle. Here he was speaking gently, and one could see the affection that the children had for him, which he returned. After the lesson, they questioned him with spirit and intelligence about the lesson. They called him "Marse Major."

After the lesson and the singing were over, Jackson and Yancy left.

"That's a very fine thing, Major. I didn't know you did it."

"It was something the Lord told me to do. It gives me a great deal of pleasure. I feel sorry for these people because they have a hard way, and I believe the children should be taught just as well as white people, in all things. Ignorant people are sad people, and it's a waste."

Yancy asked hesitantly, "Major, do you think that slavery is wrong?"

Jackson sighed deeply. "I believe that all men should love God and His son, Jesus Christ. I believe that all men should be treated with dignity and respect and courtesy."

Yancy waited for Major Jackson to expand on this equivocal answer but he did not.

They rode on silently. At the cross street that led to Major Jackson's house, he bade Yancy farewell and turned toward home, and Anna.

CHAPTER ELEVEN

Late at night on May 24, 1856, armed raiders went into men's homes and took them to a dark place, and eventually, to their deaths. The condemned men were proslavery settlers in Pottawatomie, Kansas, and their names were James Doyle, William Doyle, Drury Doyle, Allen Wilkinson, and William Sherman. The killers who kidnapped them followed an antislavery crusader named John Brown. They hacked the five men to death with sabers. Later John Brown claimed to have no part in the killings, though he observed them. And he did say that he approved of them.

John Brown's long journey from the Pottawatomie Massacre to Harpers Ferry, Virginia, was a long and convoluted one. Along the way he went from Kansas to Missouri and all over New Engand and to Canada and the Midwest and finally back to Kansas.

He met such notable sympathizers as William Lloyd Garrison, Henry David Thoreau, Ralph Waldo Emerson, Harriet Tubman, and Frederick Douglass. However, none of these stalwart men and women were with him on October 16, 1859, when he led eighteen of his followers in the attack on the Harpers Ferry Armory. He had two hundred .52 caliber Sharp's rifles and nine hundred and fifty pikes contributed by Northern abolitionists. It was his feverish dream that all the slaves in Virginia would join them in the uprising and no blood would be shed except in self-defense.

At first they met no resistance. They cut the telegraph wires and easily captured the armory, which was only defended by one watchman. Then they spread out and took hostage slaveowners from nearby farms, including Colonel Lewis Washington, great-grandnephew of George Washington. Along the way they spread the news to the local slaves that their liberation was at hand.

But then a Baltimore & Ohio train came to the station. The train's baggage master, Hayward Shepherd, tried to warn the passengers that the station had been taken by gunmen. Brown's men called for him to halt and then opened fire. He was shot in the belly, and he spent the next twelve hours begging for water . . . until he died. He was a free black man and had a good reputation in Harpers Ferry. His death was much mourned, by black and white alike.

By 7:00 a.m. on October 17, John Brown's dream had become a nightmare. Local farmers, shopkeepers, and militia pinned down the raiders by firing from the heights behind the town. Some local men were killed by Brown's men. The raid became a pitched battle, with Brown outgunned and outnumbered. Brown was trapped in the arsenal.

By the morning of October 18, Harpers Ferry Armory was surrounded by United States Marines. In command was Colonel Robert E. Lee of the army. A young army lieutenant by his side was J. E. B. "Jeb" Stuart.

Colonel Lee turned to him. "Lieutenant Stuart, take the message in to Brown, if you please."

Stuart, a heavy-set, muscular young man with a full beard and piercing eyes, jumped off his horse, saluted smartly, and said, "Yes, sir!" Waving a white handkerchief, he reached the door of the arsenal and called out, "Surrender now, sir! If you surrender now, your lives will be spared!"

Brown shouted, "No! No, I prefer to die here!"

The Marines used sledgehammers and a battering ram to break down the door. In three minutes Brown was captured, along with his captives.

In those three days, Brown had killed four men and had wounded nine. Ten of Brown's men were killed, including two of his sons.

With the last week in November, winter had come to the Shenandoah Valley. The days were bright and cold, the nights frosty and starry. There was no hint of snow in the air yet, but the wise longtime inhabitants of the valley felt it coming, smelled it coming, in the biting morning air.

Yancy was in Major Jackson's office. The two of them were going over plans for an overnight out in the woods to toughen up the cadets.

A knock sounded on the door.

"Come in," Jackson ordered.

The door opened.

"Lieutenant Stuart," Jackson said, "it's good to see you." He stood up, smiling one of his rare shy smiles.

Jeb Stuart stepped inside in his blue uniform, the uniform of the United States Army. He came over immediately to shake hands with Jackson. The two men knew each other slightly and had a mutual admiration for each other. "This is Cadet Yancy Tremayne. Cadet Tremayne, this is Lieutenant Jeb Stuart."

Yancy took his hand, and Stuart clapped down on him like a vice and spoke the words expected. He had taken off his hat and had jauntily tucked it under his arm. His full head of auburn hair was a mass of curls, as was his beard.

He turned back to Jackson. "I have orders for you, Major Jackson." Stuart reached in his pocket and pulled out an envelope.

Jackson opened it, read it, and looked up. "Do you know what these orders say?"

"Yes, sir, I do. You and a number of your cadets are ordered to go to the execution of John Brown."

Jackson nodded, pointing toward a chair. Stuart took his seat and Jackson resumed his, sitting bolt upright as always. Yancy deferentially stayed behind Jackson's chair, hoping he wouldn't send him out.

"I see these orders come from Governor Wise to Commander Smith," Jackson said. Francis Smith was the superintendent of VMI.

Stuart replied, "The governor decided it was the politic thing to do. This whole John

215

Brown uprising has become a powder keg. And the pride of Old Dominion is the Virginia Military Institute. Since Southerners believe Brown incited slave insurrection in the South, but particularly in Virginia, the governor thinks that it would be better for the superintendent of VMI to be in charge of the execution, rather than the army."

"It's hard to believe that responsible men and women in the North actually helped this madman," Jackson said disdainfully. "The situation between North and South was bad enough as it is. Armed insurrection against Harpers Ferry, and all those senseless deaths . . . No good can come of it, no good at all."

"I agree, Major Jackson. Brown's trial was nothing short of a circus sideshow, with all the newspapers, North and South, competing against each other to see who could shout loudest and longest about who's right and who's wrong," Stuart grunted. "Makes me very proud that I'm a soldier and not a politician and not a journalist."

Jackson nodded agreement. "What is it like, with Brown?"

Stuart shrugged. "He's quiet. He glares with those fiery eyes of his. The old man doesn't have any nerves, I'll give him that."

John Brown's futile attempt to free the slaves had been in October, lasting for three days, the sixteenth through the eighteenth. He had been imprisoned in Charles Town since then.

Stuart continued, "Anyway, as you see there, Major Jackson, his execution is slated for December 2, so you've got some preparations to make." He rose and the two men enthusiastically shook hands again.

Stuart turned to Yancy, his blue eyes alight. "When I was in the livery I saw a fine black stallion, and one of the cadets told me that it belonged to a young man named Tremayne. Are you that lucky young man by any chance?"

Yancy smiled. "Yes, sir, I am. His name is Midnight."

"That horse is the only horse I've ever seen that I think someone riding him might beat me in a race."

"Midnight would beat you, sir, on any mount."

Stuart laughed, a hearty, rich sound. "I like a man who believes in his horse. Maybe we'll have a chance to try that out sometime, Cadet Tremayne." He turned back to Jackson. "I assume Cadet Tremayne will be accompanying you to Charles Town, Major?"

"He will. He's proven to be a very good

aide," Jackson answered.

"Then I will see you there, Cadet," Stuart said, holding his hand out to give his usual bone-crushing handshake again. "Though I fear it will not be such a pleasant day as this."

Jackson and twenty-one VMI cadets arrived in Charles Town on November 28. Although Jackson had never made any official appointments, the two cadets whom he depended on most were Yancy Tremayne and Peyton Stevens.

Stevens, in spite of his languid ways, was a good and conscientous cadet and would make a good soldier. He rode a magnificent gold Palomino with a blond mane and tail named, appropriately, Senator. Yancy rode high-stepping Midnight, and between them Major Jackson slouched along on Cerro Gordo. They were an unlikely trio, with Peyton and Yancy in their fine, showy VMI gray and white uniforms and Jackson tightly wound up in his dusty blue coat. There could be, however, no question of who was in command.

The streets were crowded with people talking loudly, groups of men arguing on the street corners, paperboys shouting the latest penny press. The troop rode slowly through and kept in wonderful trim until they reached the town square.

"Courthouse," Jackson said succinctly.

Immediately Yancy held up his hand and shouted, "Company, halt!"

The mounted cadets stopped immediately with barely a sound.

Jackson, with Yancy and Peyton behind him, rode to a hitching post in front of the courthouse and dismounted. They stopped to survey this shabby building that had come to the center of attention of an entire nation.

It was a coupled courthouse, old, with gray and white pillars with the paint flecking off. The windows were of thick, wavy glass, and they were forlorn and dusty. The United States flag on the pole in front was faded and tattered.

Next door was a jail with worn, uneven bricks, with moss growing in between. It, too, was old and dismal looking, the last home John Brown would ever know. As they watched, they saw a plump man, who was evidently the jail master, holding court outside, his thumbs stuck in his suspenders self-importantly. He was talking to some journalists and some others who were obviously just curious.

"He's having his day in the sun," Jackson

muttered. "I tell you, cadets, this whole thing has been shameful from beginning to end. I'm going in to see the sheriff about our accomodations. You wait, and don't let any of the boys wander over there to listen to that fool."

That night Jackson wrote to Anna:

Charles Town, Nov. 28, 1859

I reached here last night in good health and spirits. Seven of us slept in the same room. I am much more pleased than I expected to be; the people here appear to be very kind. There are about one thousand troops here, and everything is quiet so far. We don't expect any trouble. The excitement is confined to more distant points. Do not give yourself any concern about me. I am comfortable, for a temporary military post.

The gallows had been erected on a hill just outside of Charles Town. Facing it squarely were two artillery pieces, each manned by seven VMI cadets. Behind them, mounted, were the seven remaining cadets. Yancy and Peyton again flanked Major Jackson. They waited in perfect silence, the gunners at the ready. It was feared by the governor that Brown's fanatical followers might make a last-ditch attempt to rescue him. Charles Town and Execution Hill were ringed with militiamen.

Below them one thousand militiamen waited to escort John Brown to his execution. They led him out of the jail. His steel gray hair and beard bristled aggessively, yet he shufffled slowly in ugly carpet slippers, for he had been injured when he was captured and he was ill. A jail was no place to get healthy and gain strength. Although his step was tentative, his face showed no weakness. He handed a piece of paper to the plump jailer, who took it and started to read it, but Brown spoke in a low tone to him and he folded it and put it in his pocket.

Brown stared around at the soldiers surrounding him and the others waiting in the roadway beyond. He blinked a little, for the sun was incongruously bright and cheerful. It was a cold, crisp day. "I had no idea Governor Wise thought my murder was so important," he said bitterly.

With his jailer on one arm and the sheriff on the other, he went to the waiting wagon. They helped him up into it, and calmly he seated himself on the coffin between the seats. The driver cracked a whip over two white farm horses, and slowly they crawled out of the town and up the hill to the waiting gallows. The wagon finally reached the hollow square of troops, one thousand of them. It filed past the artillery and the VMI cadets.

In a low voice Yancy called, "Attention!"

The standing cadets stood at a perfect formal stance.

The old man lifted his head and gazed at the distant hills, sweet and blue and faraway, and the meeting place of the Shenandoah and Potomac rivers. Yancy heard him say, "This is a beautiful country. I never truly had the pleasure of seeing it before."

"None like it," the sheriff answered.

The prisoner mounted the scaffold first. He turned and stared straight at the cadets and the artillery pieces. Yancy thought his eyes glinted fiercely as he gazed into the gaping mouths of the cannons. Two men fitted a white hood over his face while another adjusted the rope.

One man gently nudged him in the direction of the rope, and in a muffled but calm voice he said, "I can't see, gentlemen. You must lead me."

The sheriff and a guard led him to the trap, where he stood in his carpet slippers and waited. The militia that had accompanied him from the jail traipsed about below, a confusion of stamping feet and muffled commands.

The sheriff asked Brown, "You want a private signal, now, just before?"

"It's no matter to me. If only they would not keep me waiting so long."

The militia went on and on, trying to get themselves into order, and the minutes, it seemed to Yancy, went on endlessly. He felt slightly sick. But some of the younger cadets glanced at each other in secret amusement at the citizen soldiers' stumbling.

Although they had made no sound, Jackson growled, "Gentlemen."

Every cadet immediately became perfectly motionless and expressionless.

Finally the militia were arrayed, and Execution Hill became quiet.

John Brown murmured to his jailer, "Be quick, Avis."

The noose was tightened, the ax parted the rope, the hatch swung open, and John Brown was dead.

Still the field was quiet.

Then Major J. T. L. Preston of VMI shouted loudly, "So perish all such enemies of Virginia! All such enemies of the Union! All such enemies of the human race!"

The soldiers were ordered at ease. Men went forward and took his body down. Nails sounded in the coffin.

The jailer took out the piece of paper that John Brown had handed him, his last words:

I, John Brown, am now quite certain that the crimes of this guilty land will never be purged away, but with blood. . . .

The cadets were very quiet as they returned to their rooms in town. The citizens of Charles Town had been very generous, taking them into their homes and feeding them and making sure they were as comfortable as they could be under the circumstances.

Yancy, Peyton Stevens, Charles Satterfield, and Sandy Owens rode together after the company was dismissed. Chuckins and Sandy had attended the cannons. They had all been very close to the scaffold, close enough to hear everything that had been said and see all the inner workings of a hanging.

Chuckins said in a tired voice, "I didn't know it was going to be like that. It wasn't what I thought it was going to be at all."

Sandy asked, "What did you think it was going to be, Chuckins?"

"I don't know. Not so — sad. I think the man was crazy, and I think he was wrong, wrong, wrong in what he did, and I know

224

that he's massacred people here and in Kansas. But somehow this — this cold, bloodless . . ." His voice petered out.

"I know what you mean, Chuckins," Peyton said quietly. "No guts, no glory, no thrill of battle or ringing trumpets or great men shouting commands or fiery martyrdom. Just a kind of whimper."

Sandy sighed. "I've seen dead people before, but that's the first time I've seen an execution. And you're right, Peyton, I've no stomach for it at all. I'm glad it's over."

After a few moments Yancy muttered, "I don't think anything is over. I don't think anything ended today except John Brown's life. I think because of it, the trouble has just begun."

CHAPTER TWELVE

On this unrestful year of 1859, Christmas came on the last Sunday of the month, so the Virginia Military Institute let classes out on Friday, December 23. Yancy hurried home early that morning, anxious to see his family. At about noon it began snowing, a soft swirl of big flakes that slowly covered the landscape in a delicate fluffy white quilt. Midnight's steps puffed up big pillows of snow as he turned up the road to the farm.

Hurriedly Yancy hitched Midnight up to the post at the front porch and jumped the steps up onto the veranda. He heard Hank howling, and before he could knock, Daniel came out onto the porch.

"Son! You made it for Christmas!" He held out his arms and gave Yancy a suffocating bear hug.

Zemira, Becky, and Callie Jo came out on the porch, hugging Yancy over and over. Hank blundered out and jumped on everyone. Becky was now so big that Yancy could barely put his arms around her. He bent over and kissed her on both cheeks. Grinning, he said, "You still look beautiful."

Sassily she replied, "I suppose if I'm as big as a barn I'd better still look pretty."

Daniel laughed. "And you do, Beck. Come on, let's get into the parlor. We've got a big warm fire and lots of food."

"That sounds good, Father, but I don't want to leave Midnight out in the snow. I'll stable him and be right back," Yancy said.

Zemira said, "That's good, Yancy. Everything's fresh in the kitchen, but it'll take us a few minutes to set the table."

Daniel went with Yancy. Together they led Midnight to the stables, unsaddled him, and brushed him down. It went quickly with the both of them.

"We'll fix him some of his special mash after we eat," Daniel said. "And since it's Christmastime maybe we'll treat the other horses, too."

"That we will," Yancy murmured. He went to each of the stalls — Fancy, Reuben, Stamper, and Reddie — petted them all and murmured nonsense horse talk to them.

They went back to the house. Yancy noticed that the table and chairs from the veranda were now in the parlor so they could eat by the immense fire. Becky and Zemira had prepared a plain homey meal, for the feasts would commence on Christmas Day, and the following day, December 26, which was for family visiting. On this night they had an immense beef potpie, corn fritters, pickled beets and onions, and fried turnips with greens. For dessert Becky had prepared apple cake, a complicated recipe that she had perfected. For a woman who had never cared much about cooking, Zemira had taught her so well that she now loved it.

As they ate they talked about the farm, the livestock, and the horses.

Zemira said, "Becky's father has offered to exchange a billy goat and a nanny goat for one of our roosters and two sitting hens. I think it's a good trade. Callie Jo likes goat milk. Maybe the new one will, too."

"I like goat cheese, too," Yancy offered.

"You like everything," Daniel scoffed.

"Like his father," Becky said indignantly. "I think you'd eat grass if Mother Zemira cooked it for you."

"When he was six years old he ate it without me cooking it," Zemira said airily. "He saw the horses grazing and decided it might be good."

"Did he get sick?" Becky asked incredulously.

"No, not at all. That's why I don't bother to cook it for him," Zemira answered.

"Well for me, if I'm ever reduced to eating grass, I'm going to hurry home from the war and have some Friendship Bread," Yancy grunted.

A silence descended on them for a moment. The only sound was Callie Jo in her high chair, chewing noisily on a piece of beef from the potpie.

Finally Yancy broke the awkward silence and said, "I know, I know, we don't talk about war. But at the institute that's just about all we talk about. You know that the Southern states are going to secede from the Union. It's going to happen."

Daniel sighed deeply, almost a groan. "We know, and you're wrong, son, we do talk about it. We think about it all the time, because we love you and we understand what will happen if there's a war. I don't suppose that maybe you'd think about coming back to us? Neither the North nor the South will bother the Plain People. They leave us to ourselves and leave our lands to us."

With slow deliberation Yancy put down his knife and fork, wiped his mouth with his napkin, and pushed his plate away. "I can't do that. I've chosen my way. I love you all" — he looked at everyone clearly — "but this is my life. This is the life I want. I want to be a soldier."

"But son, this is a big mistake, in these days and times," Daniel blustered. "You're so young. You're only sixteen! You can come back to us before there's some kind of awful war and then, afterwards, see what you want to do! There's no need for you to —"

Zemira reached over and took Daniel's hand in hers. "Don't make a mistake with him, Daniel," she said quietly. "The boy's a man, and he's decided his way, for the time being. All we can do is love him and offer him a home, no matter what."

For a few moments Daniel's square jaw tightened, but then he closed his eyes and nodded. "I know, Mother. I know. All right then, Yancy. So, what are the English saying out there?"

"Ah, us English talk too much," Yancy said, grinning. "The North says we're a bunch of devils because we own slaves. The South says the North is a bunch of devils because they just want to take us over and steal our lands and our rights."

"I still read the newspapers, in spite of what my mother says," Daniel said mischievously. Zemira made a face at him. "I read where the North has conferred a sort of sainthood on John Brown, and the South has made him out to be the devil incarnate." He studied Yancy's face, which was expressionless, and then he added, "You haven't said anything about him and his execution, Yancy. What did you and all the cadets think about him?"

Yancy replied, "We didn't think about him much at all, you know. We didn't know him. We didn't know anything about him. We only witnessed his execution."

"That must have been very hard," Becky said sympathetically.

"It was, in one way," Yancy said thoughtfully. "In another way it made us all want to — to — fight, to offer our lives in a meaningful way, to want our lives to count for something. John Brown was a sick old man that died a sorry death. Even though we knew he stood for something, we all believe that we would rather die fighting for a noble cause, standing up for our beliefs and dying a death with glory."

"There is no death with glory in war," Zemira said solidly. "There is only death, bloody and unnecessary death."

"I understand you, Grandmother," Yancy said quietly. "But I would much rather take the chance of a death with honor, facing it with courage, so that it means something to my country."

After supper Yancy and Daniel made sure the livestock were warm, dry, and well fed in the barn and stables. They banked the fires in the bedrooms and kitchen stove and brought in plenty of firewood for the morning fires. By 7:00 they were tired, and everyone went to bed.

Yancy was having a confused dream in which he and Hannah Lapp were frantically running up and down stairs . . . when he realized that people were running up and down the stairs. He jumped out of bed and pulled on his clothes, murkily realizing that when people were running about in the middle of the night it must be an emergency.

When he stepped outside of his bedroom, he saw that his father was indeed running up the stairs with a basin of hot water and several white cloths over his arm. "It's the baby," Daniel said breathlessly.

"But I thought it wasn't due till the second week of January," Yancy said anxiously.

"So we all thought, but it seems the baby thinks otherwise," Daniel answered, heading toward his bedroom, balancing the steamy basin carefully.

"Should I go get Esther Raber?" Yancy asked.

"Mother says there isn't time," Daniel replied tensely. "Go down to the kitchen and make sure there's more boiling water. And watch Callie Jo if she wakes up." He went into the master bedroom, kicking the door shut behind him.

Yancy hurried downstairs and built up the fire in the kitchen iron stove. He filled up two copper pots and set them on the stove to start them boiling. Then he ran upstairs to the nursery, where Callie Jo was sleeping. Silently he slipped in and watched her in the crib that he and his father had built for her. She slept soundly, peacefully.

He hurried back downstairs to stare at the pots of water. Hank was in the kitchen, and even he was anxious, sitting and staring at Yancy and then going around and around in circles before lying down on his rag rug in front of the stove. Then he got up and started circling the kitchen again.

Clearly this was a fruitless occupation for both of them, so Yancy went upstairs, grabbed his boots, coat, and warm felt slouch hat and went back down. He took Hank out to pace on the veranda.

It was a beautiful December night. The

sky was so thick with stars that it seemed like a mirror to the snow-spangled earth. The air was clear and biting, with a clean, brisk scent to it. Yancy inhaled deeply.

Then began an odd, seemingly aimless round in the silent snowy December night. He paced with Hank; he went to the kitchen to check on pots of water that eventually boiled; he went upstairs to check on Callie Jo, who slept peacefully on.

Once, on one of these roundabouts, he couldn't stand it any longer. He tiptoed to the master bedroom and pressed his ear to the door. He could hear, through the thick oak, his grandmother's soft murmur and his father's low mutterings. No sound came from Becky.

Yancy had much experience with childbearing — or of hearing it, at least. In the Cheyenne camp any woman who was bearing a child was the concern of the entire community. In the tepees their cries were clearly heard. Men bore them with no sign of distress; they accepted it as a part of giving life.

Now Yancy remembered that he'd heard nothing when Becky gave birth to Callie Jo, until she uttered her first baby cries. But now the silence seemed to be ominous, as was this entire night. He wondered if things were going terribly wrong.

Slowly he went back downstairs and led Hank out onto the veranda. There he stood at the head of the steps, staring across to the east. Comically, Hank sat down beside him, sighing a doggy sigh and sorrowfully looking out.

Yancy took off his hat and held it to his heart. He spoke out loud. "Father God, I know I'm not a — a — oh, I don't know what I am. But I know what You are, and I know that my father and Grandmother and Becky are Your protected and beloved children. I pray for Becky right now, and for that baby. You love them, I know You do. Save them. Make them well. Make them strong. Thank You."

As always, Yancy felt nothing at all, but he was glad he had prayed anyway. He resumed pacing.

At one minute after midnight he heard loud raucous stomping on the stairs, and his father rushed out onto the veranda. He hugged Yancy so hard he thought he'd suffocate. Hank started howling. "It's a boy, a boy, a big fine boy, and Becky's fine, just fine," Daniel shouted. "C'mon, you have to see your new brother, Yancy. In fact, he kinda looks like you! Hurry, hurry, Becky's got to go to sleep and the baby's tired, too.

They had a hard time, but they're both fine. . . ."

They ran upstairs, taking them two at a time, now uncaring that their stout boots made such a rowdy man's noise. Yancy followed his father into the bedroom.

Becky was soaked with sweat, with purple shadows etched under her eyes. But she looked happy, and her smile was beatific. "Your brother, Yancy. We've decided to name him David." She held him up.

Yancy took the tiny bundle into his arms. His face was red and wrinkled, like an old man's. But he had a great thatch of black hair, and his eyes were dark as he sighted around his new world. He was colored like Becky, of course, with a fine complexion, not darkened like Yancy's, but Yancy was still proud. "David," Yancy repeated softly. "Does he have a middle name?"

Becky and Daniel glanced at each other. "Yancy," Becky said. "Yancy is his middle name."

In spite of the growing dark clouds on the horizon that separated North and South, that Christmas holiday at the Tremayne farm was joyous.

All day, Christmas Eve had been a sort of catch-as-catch-can day, for Becky was still very weak, and the baby, though he was healthy, demanded constant attention for the first critical hours.

But that night, all of the Tremaynes, David Yancy included, slept soundly. Just before dawn, Zemira woke up and, after checking on Becky and the baby, started Christmas cooking. Now the family was reaping those riches at Christmas Day dinner.

"Mother, you've outdone yourself," Daniel said enthusiastically. "I think this is the best, biggest, and most wonderful feast I've ever had. How in the world did you do it?"

"Humph," Zemira grunted. "Didn't you know that Yancy helped me cook almost all of it?"

"What!" Daniel said in surprise. "But he's been doing all the chores and taking care of the livestock. How could he have possibly helped you?"

Since the birth of David had been of some difficulty to Becky, she had stayed in bed until joining the family for Christmas dinner. Yancy had assured Daniel that he would take care of the farm, while he took care of Becky and the baby. Daniel had stayed almost continually in their room, bringing Becky broth and cool water and fresh milk and continually changing the baby and bathing him so that he'd be clean and comfortable.

But on Christmas Eve and Christmas Day, Yancy had indeed found time to help Zemira in the kitchen. The Amish didn't believe in a conspicuous, tawdry celebration of Christmas — to them it was a time to meditate upon the birth of the Christ child and of scripture. But they did believe in celebrating the riches of their heritage, which included the wonderful and tasteful foods of the Amish.

Now Yancy grinned crookedly. "I've chopped vegetables. I've kneaded dough. I've tenderized meat. I've timed boiling pots of vegetables. I've worked flour and salt and pepper and spices and vegetables into gravy. I've stuffed a turkey. I've made four batches of corn bread. Take my word for it, Father. I thought studying and classes and artillery and gunnery and marksmanship and mathematics and history and philosophy were hard. They're nothing compared to helping in Grandmother's kitchen."

David Tremayne was a robust, bawling, demanding baby, exactly the opposite of Callie Jo. Sitting in her high chair at the Christmas feast, she pointed to him with her spoon. "He loud," she said plaintively. "He loud."

Becky was holding him, and discreetly she put the squalling child under her shawl to nurse him. He immediately grew silent. "Now he's quiet, Callie Jo," she said soothingly. "Eat your porridge."

"Porrith," she repeated happily and began to, somewhat messily, spoon it into her mouth. She loved oatmeal with cream and brown sugar.

"Good Christmas," Yancy said happily. "Never thought I'd get a present of a little brother. Thought the Amish didn't go in for gifts and such for Christmas."

"So they don't," Daniel said. "But David was a surprise. Showy gift for the Plain People, he is."

"Maybe we should name him Christmas," Yancy said mischievously.

"I think not," Becky said sturdily. "I'd just as soon name him Tinsel or Holly or Plum Pudding."

"Hmm . . . Plum Pudding Tremayne," Daniel said meditatively. "There's a thought."

"No, it's not," Zemira said sternly. "That is what I would call no thought at all."

As they continued the easy banter while finishing up the sumptious meal, Yancy could only be thankful for this special time with his family and hope the coming war —

for he was certain it was coming — would not take this all away.

The Amish considered Decmber 26 a day of feasting, of celebrating and visiting among families and the community. At dawn that day, Daniel had ridden around to all of the Amish farms to spread the joyous news of his son David and also to let them know that Becky was still unable to travel around visiting.

By two o'clock that afternoon, the Tremayne farm had received representatives of eighteen families of the community. The food that they had brought overran the kitchen and was starting to crowd even the roomy root cellar.

Every family had been joyous at the arrival of David Yancy, hugging Daniel and shaking his hand vigorously, kissing Becky gently, kissing Zemira . . . and nodding politely to Yancy. Finally he had seen that his being there, and being shunned, was paining his parents and Grandmother, and he decided to go for a long ride on Midnight. He disappeared at about three o'clock.

They wandered aimlessly along the stream, seeing deer and raccoons and opossums and squirrels scurrying along on their errands. Yancy was amazed at all of the tracks in the snow. For once, Yancy wasn't zeroing in on a single track to hunt; he was merely observing all the wildlife. Now he saw that they, too, had purpose and family life and homes. It affected him oddly. Never before had he seen prey as anything but animals to be killed and eaten — or merely to be killed as nuisances. Now he saw that they had an intrinsic design to their lives, with mates and children and an urge to hunt for food and shelter.

"Aw, c'mon, Midnight, I must be getting tired and crazy. I'm feeling sorry for that last nasty 'possum we saw that had six babies on her back. Let's go on home. If we're still overrun with Amish, I'll sleep in the stable with you." Yancy turned him toward home, and Midnight knew the way. Midnight huffed great icy clouds of breath, while Yancy's was a thin stream of mist. He was bone-tired and bent and yawned over the saddle.

It was actually about eight o'clock, three hours after dark, when Yancy and Midnight returned to the stables at the Tremayne farm. Midnight led the way into the stables and stopped before his stall. Sleepily Yancy jumped off and, by an automatic mechanism stemming from hundreds of repetititons, unsaddled him and brushed him down. Gratefully he saw that his father had left a pot of hot mash on the stove, and he fed all five horses on this frosty night.

He went into the farmhouse through the back door, through the kitchen, into the back hall. To his dismay he heard people — men — laughing . . . but then he recognized the raucous roar of his cousin Clay. He hurried into the parlor.

The Caleb Tremayne family had all come to welcome the newest Tremayne. Caleb Tremayne was now forty-seven years old, as was his wife, Bethany. Caleb was a burly man, with dark hair and intense dark brown eyes. Clay had inherited his father's looks. But Morgan took after his mother; she had auburn hair, with light blue eyes, and was of a slender frame, tall and willowy. Clay was as tall as Morgan but more muscular.

And then, to their everlasting surprise, Caleb and Bethany had a "late-in-life" baby, but then, adding more to their surprise, they were late-in-life twins. They called them Brenda and Belinda, and they were born in the spring of 1854. Now just over five years old, they seemed to be foundlings that all the Tremaynes were both delighted and bemused by. They looked like picture-book angels, with strawberry blond curls and heaven blue eyes and perfect little faces. Only their mother and father could tell them apart; even Clay and Morgan got them confused. But then, because of the difference in their ages, it wasn't too surprising that they had spent very little time with their sisters. Clay had dubbed them Bree and Belle, but most of the time he just called both of them Bluebell.

Yancy greeted them all happily. He loved the Caleb Tremayne family. They seemed to be a very happy, stable, loving family, in spite of Clay's mischievousness. He sat down and took Belinda on one knee and Brenda on the other.

Clay was standing, leaning against the mantelpiece and sipping coffee. "Where have you been, Yancy? Hiding?"

"Yes," he answered expressionlessly.

There was a tense silence that Caleb Tremayne finally broke, with a covert glance at Daniel. "Being shunned must be hard — on everyone."

Zemira, seated by Becky, dropped her head and sighed. But Becky straightened her shoulders and said sturdily, "Yancy is strong, and he makes good decisions. Daniel and Grandmother and I have decided to respect that, and him, no matter what."

"I admire you all," Bethany Tremayne said

softly. "But still it must be hard. Is it not, Yancy?"

He shrugged carelessly, but his words were not. "What I'm wondering is when — or if — I'm just going to be accepted as an English. As you all are. I know, Uncle Caleb, that the Amish do business with you, that your family is respected, that you're recognized as a leader of the Lexington community by the Amish and the English alike. How — how long will it take before I'm accepted just for who I am?"

Caleb and Daniel exchanged dark glances. Slowly Caleb answered, "Our family has been English for three generations now. Times change, and people change. Who knows? Next year you may be regarded as just one of the English members of the Amish family. We're not the only ones, you know. There are English Rabers, Fishers, and even an English Lambright, a distant relative of Bishop Lambright. One day you will be treated with affection and respect, Yancy, if you earn it as an honorable man."

"I will," Yancy said. "I have to."

The twins were staring at him, trying to fathom this serious grown-up conversation, when at this moment Callie Jo grew jealous and decided to object to their sitting on her brother's lap. She toddled over and yanked on Belinda's bright curls. "My bruvver," she pouted.

The twins' eyes grew round but they said nothing.

"Here now, none of that," Daniel said, hurrying over to pick her up and settle her into his lap. "You have to learn to share. Especially now that you've got a new baby brother."

"Why?" Callie Jo demanded.

"Because it's the right thing to do."

"Why?"

"Because the Bible tells us to do unto others as you would have them do unto you. So you must love everyone and share with them."

"Why?"

Daniel frowned. "Because I think it's past your bedtime, and so we must save this Bible lesson for later." He stood up, holding Callie Jo, who looked as if she were going to rebel, but then she threw her head onto Daniel's shoulder and closed her eyes.

"I'm too tiwed," she lisped.

"I thought so. If you would all excuse me," Daniel said.

Belinda and Brenda looked at each other in the most uncanny way, perfect echoes of the other's expressions. "Callie Jo's tired," Belinda said.

"Yes, she's tired," Brenda agreed. Solemnly they watched Daniel carry her to the stairs.

Clay, standing propped against the mantel, observed idly, "Does anyone else think that's scary?"

Belinda's and Brenda's heads swiveled to him. Belinda said, "What do you mean, Clay? Who's scary?"

Brenda echoed, "Who's scary?"

"Never mind, Bluebells. Forget I said anything."

"Yes, forget it, girls. Sometimes your brother Clay speaks out of turn," Bethany Tremayne said. "As in, since you were born," she added pointedly to him. "Clay cried all the time, Morgan never cried, and it seemed as if Belinda and Brenda began talking the day after they were born and haven't stopped since. And that brings me to your darling David. He seems to be a very good baby."

"He wasn't at first, but he's beginning to settle into his routine now, I think," Becky said, looking down and rocking the brand-new cradle very gently. David's dark eyes were open, and he seemed to stare up at her as if assessing his mother. "He hasn't cried or fussed all day, and he's definitely been a very busy boy."

Caleb Tremayne rose. "Forgive us, Becky; we've stayed far too long. But the hospitality of your house, Zemira" — he bowed in her direction — "makes us so comfortable. As soon as you're feeling stronger, Becky, you and your family have an open invitation to dinner at our home."

They all rose, and Yancy kissed the girls on their cheeks before setting them down. "Thank you, Uncle Yancy," they echoed.

Clay shook Yancy's hand. "Next Saturday is the New Year, cousin. If you're going to be an English, you'd better come to town and celebrate like one."

"Better not," Morgan grumbled, shaking Yancy's hand in his turn. "Every New Year since he turned fourteen has been nothing but trouble."

Clay clapped Morgan on the back. "Come with us, Morgan, and act your age for once, instead of like a seventy-year-old man! So meet us at Mason's Grocer and Dry Goods. You can't come to the house. Mother would probably chain us to chairs. How about it?"

Slowly Yancy nodded. "Might do me some good, to have some fun for a change. I'll be there. If you're coming, Morgan," he added. "I know there's no way I can handle this wild man by myself."

"I'll come," Morgan agreed. "I wouldn't

mind celebrating a little. But I'll keep a close watch on you, Clay. You're not going to get either me or Yancy in trouble. I'll promise you that."

"We'll see," Clay said with a mischievous grin.

The trouble was that Morgan wasn't there. When Yancy went into Mason's to find the two, he found Clay sitting in a straight chair by the iron stove.

His feet propped against an upturned bucket, Clay was eating a pickle and had a handful of crackers and cheese. "Have some of these crackers and cheese, Yancy. They make the pickle go down really good."

"Think I will." Yancy fished a pickle out of the barrel then took a hunk of cheese and some crackers out of a jar. "You buying?"

Clay answered, "Sure. I know you boys at VMI don't make much money, marching around so pretty and shooting at dirt." Clay's great-grandfather had, wisely, decided to spin cotton instead of grow it. He had built a cotton mill, which had been built up until it was the largest in the valley. By this time the Caleb Tremaynes didn't actually work; they were presidents and vice presidents of the mill, gentlemen with the income of merchants, but that didn't actually sully their hands with manual labor. And the Caleb Tremaynes were very well off indeed.

Yancy bristled. "You don't want to insult me about the institute, Clay. I'm not going to take kindly to it."

Clay laughed. "Calm down, cousin. I've lived here all my life. I know how all the institute boys take offense at the least little thing. And they say I make trouble for myself? You boys growl at one wrong syllable."

"Right. Don't make a wrong syllable," Yancy grunted. "Even though I'm not wearing it, I still revere the uniform."

Yancy was wearing his buckskin breeches, moccasins, an undyed, rough linsey-woolsey shirt, and a vest that had been intricately beaded by his mother. He had a canvas rainproof overcoat that his father had given him.

Clay, in contrast to Yancy, was wearing the typical well-bred gentlemen's clothes — a black suit, white linen finely-ruffled shirt with silk tie, and black boots. He looked immaculate, with his black hair combed back and curling over his collar. His chiseled features, his mouth shaped by good humor, and his sparkling dark eyes all added to his fine looks.

"Yes, suh, Cadet, I heah you," Clay finally said after giving him a careful once-over. Then he gave Yancy a mock salute. "And by the way, don't you have any gentlemen's clothes?"

"These are Cheyenne clothes. They're better than gentlemen's clothes. Except for VMI uniforms," Yancy said succinctly. "Anyway, where's Morgan?"

Clay shook his head in mock shame. "Mama Morgan had to go home. He got word one of his favorite cows is about to have a calf. It's out of season, and she's having trouble with it. You know Morgan, he's more worried about cows and horses and dogs and cats than he is with people."

"Well then, why don't we wait till tomorrow, when we can celebrate with Morgan?" Yancy asked diffidently.

"No, no! You know what the Bible says, 'Don't put off tomorrow what you can do today.'"

"I don't believe it says that," Yancy scoffed.

Clay shrugged. "Then it ought to. Come on, let's settle up with these pickles and crackers." Rising, he went up to the counter, tapped on it, and called, "Mr. Mason! Mrs. Mason! Hello?"

A large, round woman came through the curtains from the back of the store and chugged along to the money drawer. "There is no need," she huffed, "for calling out so sharp and yelling like a wild Indian." When she caught sight of Yancy, her big blue eyes widened in surprise. "Oh, I do beg your pardon. Are you, sir, a wild Indian?"

"No, I'm a tame one," Yancy said with a smile. He came forward, his hand held out. "How do you do, ma'am. I'm Yancy Tremayne."

She stepped back and primly folded her hands in front of her apron. "How do you do, sir. I am Mrs. Mason, and it is my pleasure to meet you. I'm aware that you are being shunned by the Amish. However, that is not why I refuse to shake your hand. You, Mr. Tremayne, and you, Clay Tremayne, smell like pickles, and I don't wish to smell like pickles or to take money that smells like pickles. I insist you come back to the kitchen and wash your hands and face before I take your money . . . or your hands."

"Aw, come on, Delilah, I'll buy some of that rum bay cologne so you'll let me kiss your hand," Clay teased as they headed back toward the curtained kitchen.

"I have not given you leave to call me by me first name, sir, and certainly you're not going to kiss my hand. And if I did sell you

251

the bay rum you would simply smell like bay rum and pickles. Now, wash up and put the money in the cash drawer. Also, I suggest that you freshen your breath, so that everyone you meet won't think you've been putting up pickles. I'm going out back to pick the fresh herbs for the afternoon customers," she said and majestically sailed out the back door.

"What a woman," Yancy said admiringly.

"Maybe if you get lucky we can find you a Delilah tonight," Clay said, grinning.

Just east of the township of Lexington was an old road that ran from north to south. The Indians that had originally colonized the Shenandoah Valley called it the Great Warriors Trail. Then the Quakers and Amish had come in, and they called it the Valley Pike. The other colonists — the Long Knives, the English — called it the Great Wagon Road. They had come to the verdant valley from Pennsylvania and northern Virginia. Finally the state of Virginia had macadamized it, which made it the quickest and most comfortable road in the state, and then it was called the Valley Turnpike. It ran the length of the valley from Tennnessee to Maryland.

Although Yancy had traveled many miles across America, he had never ventured east of Lexington. Virginia Military Institute was north and slightly west of town, and that had been the border of his wanderings beyond the Tremayne farm. Now as they rode the turnpike he saw that there were outposts and stores and farms as they rode northeast. "Where are we going, anyway?"

"We're riding the Great Valley Road," Clay answered grandly. "Been here more than one hundred and fifty years."

"History's not my favorite subject," Yancy grumbled. "Might as well go back to the institute and read a book."

"Ahh, but one thing you're never going to find in your history book," Clay retorted, "and that would be Star's Starlight Saloon. Right up ahead."

Yancy looked ahead, then, as he was accustomed, he sniffed. He could see faint points of light ahead, and his sensitive hearing picked out noise — nothing of definition, just cacaphonic sounds that did not fit the night — and a very slight man-scent. He looked at Clay and repeated, "Star's Starlight Saloon? Kind of redundant, isn't it?"

Clay stared at him, one sardonic eyebrow raised. "Redundant? So you're such a grand gentleman after all?"

Yancy blushed, though Clay couldn't see

it in the dark, and his voice sounded proud. *"Grammar for the Southern Gentleman —* 'redundant: superfluous repetition.' "

Clay laughed long and heartily. "I congratulate you, cousin. You've become an interesting man. You look like a savage Indian and converse like a gentleman. The women are going to eat you alive."

They proceeded to Star's Starlight Saloon, hitched their horses, and went through the double oak-and-glass doors.

Yancy stopped inside to look around and let his senses take everything in. The first of his senses that was assaulted was the most sensitive, as always — his sense of smell. The place smelled of unwashed men, horse manure mixed with mud, strong acrid cigar smoke, cheap perfume, and whiskey. He heard a tinny piano playing "Camptown Races." Underneath the murmur of the crowd, he heard men placing bets and calling hands. His sharp gaze swept across the room, taking in the hard men and half-dressed women, and he saw that Clay had already crossed to the bar, ordered a drink, and was embracing a full-figured blond lady who giggled and embraced him with obvious recognition.

Yancy moved to join him, and then his gaze, stunned, was fixed on a young woman standing at the piano, who was obviously getting ready to sing. She looked like Hannah Lapp. Or rather she looked like a somewhat vulgar copy of Hannah Lapp, but she still gave Yancy a small shock. She was small-boned, with ash brown hair streaked with blond. She had dark eyes and the same narrow shoulders as Hannah, with an erect bearing. She wore a very low-cut dress, and her hair was mussed, with tousles of curls hanging over her shoulders. But primly she crossed her hands and nodded to the pianist. He began a reedy "Ben Bolt."

Oh don't you remember sweet Alice, Ben
    Bolt
Sweet Alice whose hair was so brown . . .

She sang earnestly, but her voice was drowned out by the din in the saloon, which did not lessen. Still, Yancy could hear her high fluted voice clearly.

Who wept with delight when you gave her
    a smile,
And trembled with fear at your frown. . . .

The rest of the song was so sad and dreary that Yancy blocked it out, but he listened and watched the girl until she finished. Men crowded around her.

Then Clay appeared in front of him with his blowsy blond woman. "This is the famous Star," he said, his eyes glinting. "Star can make any man happy. Including you, Yancy. Here you go."

He handed Yancy a bottle, but Yancy hesitated. "Here, handsome," Star said, tipping the bottle toward him. "It's smooth, it'll make you happy, and it's on the house," she said silkily.

"Like you," Clay said, planting a kiss on her reddened lips.

"Only for you, Clay, my young devil," she replied. "Just for you."

"You should be so lucky, Yancy," he leered. "Maybe when you're old enough to be a real man."

Star looked him up and down. "Indian, ain't ya? Handsome Indian, too. Some places don't welcome Indians 'cause the drink makes 'em crazy. But Clay here speaks for you, so I know you'll behave."

"Thank you, ma'am," Yancy said and took another swig. "And thanks for the good whiskey. It's smooth and it makes me happy, 'specially since it's on the house."

"Good manners, too, just like a real gentleman, even if he is a savage," Star said admiringly.

"You got that all wrong, Star," Clay said.

"I'm the savage." He started kissing her passionately, and Yancy politely looked away. He took another swig of the whiskey then decided that he wanted to meet the pretty singer.

"Miss Star, ma'am?" he interrupted, slightly nudging Clay on the arm.

"What, cuz?" Clay asked lazily, looking up.

"Who is that lady that was singing just now?" Yancy asked.

Star looked around. "Oh, her? She's one of my very best girls. Here, just wait a minute. . . ." She disentangled herself from Clay and sashayed through the crowd. Pushing aside the men that surrounded the girl, she took her by the arm, whispered, and pointed.

The girl nodded and followed Star back to where Clay and Yancy stood at the bar. Star grabbed Clay's arm again, and the girl stopped and looked Yancy up and down. Then, as elegantly as any well-bred young woman, she curtsied.

Instinctively, as Major Thomas Jackson had taught him to do with ladies, he bowed. "How do you do, ma'am," he said. "May I introduce myself? I am Yancy Tremayne, at your service."

She smiled up at him and put one delicate

hand to her half-exposed breast. "Well then, Mr. Yancy Tremayne, suh," she said with an exaggerated Virginia accent, "muh name is whatevuh you would like it to be." She curtsied low again.

Star, Clay, and the girl burst into raucous laughter. "Don't take it amiss, cousin," Clay said with amusement. "These *ladies* are playful, and sometimes as gentlemen we don't quite get the joke."

"I don't get the joke," Yancy said darkly.

The girl took his arm gently and stared up into his eyes. She really was much like Hannah Lapp, except for her blatant worldliness. Her lips were reddened; her eyes were lined with kohl, and now that he was close to her, he could see the coldness in them. She looked hard, and he was sure she looked older than she really was. The skin of her throat and breast was smooth, but she already had tough lines around her eyes and mouth.

"What is your name, ma'am?" he asked with all the gentleness he could muster.

"Hmm. Let's see . . . Your name is Yancy? Then my name is Nancy," she said with cold amusement.

Clay laughed drunkenly. "And he's riding a horse named Fancy! Oh, this is rich!"

They all laughed for a ridiculously long

period of time over this poor joke. Yancy had forgotten that he was riding Midnight, not Fancy. He took another drink, sat down on a barstool, and pulled Nancy — or whatever her name was — down on his lap. He kissed her . . . a lot.

Time melted; time meant nothing. His sense of smell, and hearing, and sight, and even feeling was dulled.

Drunkenly he looked up at a loud and annoying ruckus and saw Clay on the floor. Three men were working him over, one holding his arms and the other two landing blows on his chest and face. Yancy shoved Nancy aside, stood up on a barstool, and jumped into the melee. He felt his right fist connect with someone's cheekbone, and then he kicked and felt a shinbone shatter. With his left fist he grabbed someone's throat and squeezed, feeling the life slowly leaking out in short, frantic breaths.

The last thing he heard was, "That's enough! You're all under arrest!"

He felt a stunning blow against his forehead, and everything went night black.

CHAPTER THIRTEEN

Yancy woke up, to his very great sorrow. His head felt like a busted melon; his eyes felt like there were great thumping hammers behind them. His mouth tasted like he had eaten cow dung, and his lips were dry and cracking and felt oddly fat. His body ached, from his fingertips to his toes. He tried very hard to go back to sleep, but such succor evaded him.

He sat up, groaning like an old man. He saw a roughhewn ceiling very close to his head, and he saw that he was on a top bunk. Though the world swirled around him, he bent over to look into the bottom bunk.

His cousin Clay lay there, one knee-booted leg hung over the side negligently. He snored.

Very, very slowly and with much care, Yancy turned so that his legs hung off the bunk. Then, holding his breath, he jumped to the floor. He felt that he landed on steel spikes, from the pain that shot from his feet all the way up to, it seemed, the tips of his hair. Then the nausea hit him, and barely registering that the chamber pot was right by a row of steel bars, he bent over it and was horribly sick. Finally, shakily he stood up, wiped his sore mouth, and mumbled, "So this is jail. I don't like it much."

He started to try to climb back into his bunk, when his cousin's voice sounded, remote and reedy, "Not jail that made you sick, cousin. Sorry 'bout that."

"But what happened?" Yancy asked, bewildered. "I remember that girl named Nancy, and I remember you arguing with three big ol' guys."

"I dunno," Clay answered, "but I think the three big ol' guys won."

A deputy came down the hall and banged on the bars.

Yancy winced at the clanging noise that seemed to burst his eardrums.

"Clay Tremayne, Yancy Tremayne, let's go. You've been bailed out. Come on with me before I change my mind."

Even though Daniel Tremayne and Morgan Tremayne had only the remotest family connection, they looked oddly alike as they stood in the sheriff's office. Both of them stood, their legs planted far apart, their arms crossed, their faces severe. Daniel, of course, was eleven years older and his face was more chiseled and worn. Morgan had fair, fine features and coloring, but his demeanor was so dignified and offended as to seem like the most righteous of preachers.

As they entered, Yancy was as low as low, but Clay seemed airy and unconcerned, even though he pressed his right hand hard to his abdomen. "Hello, brother," he said. "The good news is that they didn't break my nose. The bad news is that I think they broke one of my ribs."

Morgan frowned darkly. "I ought to leave you here. Clay, that boy is sixteen years old. How could you do this? Are you ever going to grow up?"

"Sixteen?" Clay was genuinely surprised. "He doesn't look sixteen, and he sure doesn't fight like he's sixteen. Didn't realize it. Sorry, cousin. I don't think I would have led you into the den of iniquity if I'd known it."

"I may be sixteen, but I still make my own decisions," Yancy grunted. "It's not your fault, Clay. I made up my own mind."

Daniel uncrossed his arms and lifted Yancy's face with one finger. "Not very pretty, son. Black eye and busted lip. Anything else hurt?"

"Everything else," Yancy answered sullenly, "but especially my shin." He pulled up his breeches leg and pulled down his moccasins. There was a big black bruise on his right leg. "Someone kicked me."

"Probably one of those evil women," Clay said, grinning, but then he grimaced and grabbed his ribs again.

"Shut up, Clay," Morgan said. "Don't you ever get tired of this every year?"

"Yes," Clay answered smartly. "But by the time next December rolls around I'll probably forget how tired I am of it."

Morgan rolled his eyes and muttered something unintelligible. Then he took his brother's arm very gently. "C'mon, dummy. No, no, I'm not going to take you home for Mother to work you over. I'll take you to your place and get the doctor." Morgan looked over his shoulder as he helped his brother out the door. "Are you two all right, Uncle Daniel? Is there anything else I can do?"

Daniel shook his head. "No, thank you, Morgan. I'm indebted to you for coming to get me."

"No, sir, there is no debt," Morgan said firmly. "We're family. Call on me and mine anytime for anything."

They went out the door and Yancy's sharp ears caught the low sound of Clay still grumbling.

Yancy pulled himself up straight and gazed into his father's stern blue eyes. "Sir? Are you going to punish me?"

"Before I answer, I need to ask you some questions."

"Yes, sir," Yancy answered solidly.

Daniel narrowed his eyes and studied Yancy's fractured face carefully. "So, did you have fun?"

Yancy hesitated for long moments then answered, "It seemed like fun last night. But it's no fun now, no sir."

"I see. But was it worth it?"

Again Yancy thought carefully. "No sir, it was not. Now that I realize I have to face you, and Becky, and Grandmother, and — and — Major Jackson, I know it wasn't worth it. Not at all. I'm so very sorry, Father."

Daniel nodded. "It's good for a man to take responsibility for his actions."

Yancy looked up at his father with appealing, vulnerable dark eyes. "Sir, will you forgive me?"

Daniel laid his hands on his son's shoulders. " 'Neither do I condemn thee.' Just don't do it again, for my sake and your sake and Becky's sake and Grandmother's sake."

"Don't worry, I'm going to find some other way that doesn't hurt so much to have fun. But sir, what do you mean about not condemning me? What was that?"

Daniel answered, "It's a Bible verse, and it means that I can't condemn you for anything that you've done, son. I've made my own mistakes, and I've seen my own sins. I can't condemn you or anyone else. I just want to protect you and try to help you to have a good life. That's all. And I'm hoping that a black eye and a fat lip will help you learn that lesson."

"Do you think my nose is broken?" Yancy asked anxiously.

Daniel chuckled. "No, I think your pride is, which may be a very good thing. Just remember always, son, 'Pride goeth before destruction, and an haughty spirit before a fall.' And that's even worse than a broken nose."

Slowly they rode home, Yancy dreading every hoofbeat that brought him closer. It was a dreary day, with the sun hidden behind looming snow clouds. He shivered in the biting air, and it seemed as if every inch of his body ached. His left eye was swollen shut, and his lips felt like raw meat.

He fully expected Becky and Grandmother to be very angry with him, but he was wrong.

Becky met them on the veranda and threw her arms around him to hug him. "Oh, Yancy, you look awful! And with you so handsome, too!"

They went in and then Zemira hugged him. "You are your father's son, that's sure enough," she said drily. "Come on in. Lie down on the sofa in the parlor. Daniel, take a rag and go get some icicles to put on that eye. Otherwise it'll be swollen for days." She bustled around, getting quilts to put over Yancy and pillows for his head.

Becky said, "I'll go heat up some soup. I know you're probably starving, Yancy, but I doubt you'll be able to chew anything much for a day or two."

Zemira finished making Yancy comfortable then pulled up a straight chair close to the sofa. "Looks like you and Clay had quite a party," she said with a glimmer in her dark blue eyes.

"Seems like I remember something about a party," he sighed, speaking with difficulty because of his sore mouth. "But then it seems like it wasn't very much fun, for a party." He looked up at her woefully. "Grandmother — I'm so, so sorry. I know

I've disappointed everyone so much. I can't tell you how sorry I am. And I thought — I thought that you'd be really mad at me."

She smiled and gently smoothed back the lock of his hair that always seemed to fall over his forehead. "Being angry with you is not going to teach you anything. If you were younger, Daniel would probably feel obliged to punish you in some way. But in spite of the fact that you're only sixteen, in the last year you've taken on a man's job and a man's burdens. And since you have a repentant attitude, we see that you're taking responsibility for your actions. So there is no need for us to be angry with you, Yancy. I suspect you're angry enough at yourself."

"You're right about that, Grandmother," he agreed caustically. "Talk about acting like a fool. I know you're not supposed to swear to things, but right here and now I'm telling you I'm going to try very hard not to get myself in such a stupid position again."

"Good boy," she said softly.

Daniel came in with a rag with crushed icicles in it. "Here, Yancy, lay that down on your eye. Maybe after a while the swelling will go down and it'll open back up."

"Thanks." Gingerly he put it on his eye. "Father? Would you sit down for a minute? I want to ask you both something."

"Sure," Daniel said. He stoked up the fire to a comfortable roar then pulled another straight chair up by Zemira's.

"Father, I've been thinking about what you said, about not condemning me because — maybe because you've seen — you've been in some — kind of —"

Daniel put up his hand and then winked at his mother. "Son, I've been there, and worse. Your grandmother may not know the details, but she knows me, always has. So don't worry you're going to surprise her with some dark secret about my past."

"I should say not," Zemira grumbled. "Just come out with it, Yancy. I got over being shocked by what men do a long, long time ago."

"Okay," he said and took a deep breath. "I can understand, Father, that you may have been like me when you were younger and feel like you can't be angry with me because of that. But Grandmother, I know you've never done stupid, wrong things like I've done. So — so what did you mean? About teaching me something by not getting mad at me? It seems like you'd have the right to, if you get my meaning."

Zemira shook her head. "Jesus said, 'He that is without sin among you, let him first cast a stone. . . .' I'm not without sin. No one is, except Jesus. Only He has the right to condemn anyone for sin. And as far as teaching you, Yancy, we only want you to learn one thing from us. That's Christ's love. In the scriptures it's called charity. 'Charity suffereth long, and is kind; charity envieth not; charity vaunteth not itself, is not puffed up. . . .' All of that means that when you love a person with Christ's love, you seek out and do what's best for them. For me to be angry with you would not be Christlike. For me to show you love and be kind is like our Jesus Christ. And that you will remember a long time, Yancy, much longer than any selfish anger. I love you, and I forgive you, and Jesus loves you and will forgive you."

Uneasily Yancy shifted then turned the compress on his eye. Already some of the swelling was going down. "I understand, Grandmother. But I have one big worry left. I know Major Jackson is a good Christian man, and I know he knows a lot about the Bible and Jesus and all that. But I don't think that in his position he's going to be able to forgive me. I'm so afraid I'll get expelled."

Zemira reached over and took his hand. Softly she said, "Yancy, no one ever said there are no consequences for sin; there always are. And you're right. Major Jackson's position regarding you, under the circumstances, is very different from your family's position. But why don't we, right now, get Becky, and all of us will pray for you, that God might spare you and allow you to stay on the path you have chosen? It may be that in His great mercy and understanding, He will spare you this shame."

"Knowing how you feel about soldiers, you'd do that for me, Grandmother?" Yancy asked.

"Of course, because I have the Lord's charity in my heart, and the Lord is kind and merciful and understanding," she answered firmly. "And will you pray with us, Yancy?"

He closed his eyes and a single tear rolled down his cheek. "I can't. Right now I would feel like the worst kind of hypocrite and like a liar. But please — please — do pray for me."

"Always," Daniel said. "Always, son."

Major Thomas Jackson's classes at VMI always began at 8:00 a.m., and as he was always a punctual man, he always arrived at his office at 7:30 a.m. to prepare. On this Monday, January 2, 1860, Yancy Tremayne was waiting for him in the hallway. When

Major Jackson came up the stairs, Yancy came to strict attention.

Because of his shame, he hadn't worn his VMI uniform; he was dressed in plain brown wool trousers and a cream-colored linsey-woolsey shirt. He clutched his plain wide-brimmed hat in his hand, turning the brim over and over nervously.

When Major Jackson reached him, Yancy saluted and muttered, "Major Jackson, sir! Cadet Tremayne at your service."

Jackson looked him up and down sternly, and Major Thomas Jackson's severe once-over was stern indeed. "You are out of uniform, Cadet, and you are also out of countenance."

"Yes, sir!"

"Come into my office."

He unlocked the door, led Yancy in, and seated himself behind his desk. Yancy stood at attention, and Jackson did not put him at ease.

"What have you done?" Jackson asked abruptly.

Yancy took a deep breath, his back as stiff as a board, his arms aching at attention at his sides. He sighted somewhere beyond Jackson's right shoulder. His eye was still swollen but had opened, and his lip had gone down somewhat, but his speech was still slurred. As clearly as he could speak, he said, "Sir! I got drunk, running with the wrong crowd. Then I got into a fight and got arrested. My father bailed me out, sir."

Jackson's blue-light eyes glowed balefully. "I see. And so this wrong crowd, they got you into this trouble, and you couldn't help yourself?"

"No, sir. I — I misspoke, sir. I made my own decisions, went my own way, and chose to do the things I did. The — the wrong things."

"You see that now, do you?" Jackson asked sharply.

"Yes, sir."

"And how do you propose to undo the wrong things you did?"

Yancy dropped his head wearily. "I can't, sir. I know that now. It's done. All I can do is apologize. I've gone to my family and begged their forgiveness. And now, sir, I ask you to forgive me and give me another chance. I want to redeem myself."

"How will you do that?"

Yancy lifted his head and stood at strict attention again. "I will be a better cadet, sir. I will work harder, I will study harder, and whatever punishment you feel is appropriate, I will bear. I will regain my honor and my integrity, sir."

Jackson rose and looked out the window, out at the parade ground of the institute. "This is a proud and honorable school, sir, and you have a charitable scholarship here. You have betrayed that trust."

Yancy almost choked but managed to say, "Yes, sir, I know that, all too well. Please, if you will give me another chance, I promise you I will make you proud. I will make the institute proud. I know I have it in me, sir. I know I can achieve, and achieve excellence."

For long moments Jackson stood at the window, staring out. Finally he turned around. "Cadet Tremayne," he said quietly.

Yancy met his ice blue gaze.

"All of us fail," he said firmly, "but the test of our faith and our military life is when we fail, do we just lie there or do we get up and start over again? Do we fight much harder so as to regain the ground we have lost? I'll be watching you, Cadet Tremayne. You know everyone here at the institute has heard about this disgrace. You'll have to work much harder, and longer, to regain your honor and the respect of the faculty and staff and that of your fellow cadets. If you can do it, you will indeed be a fine addition to the institute and a fine soldier."

"I will, sir," Yancy said with a lump in his throat. "I will fight hard."

Jackson nodded. "Then go get into your uniform and go to class." He turned back to the window.

As Yancy left he thought, *I won't quit! No matter how hard it gets, I will never quit!*

■ ■ ■ ■

Part Four:
The Beginning
1860–1861

■ ■ ■ ■

CHAPTER FOURTEEN

Yancy kept the promise he made to himself on that dreary January day. He didn't quit, no matter how hard it got and how many long hours he had to work. For the next year he was the model cadet. He never missed a class. His rifle skills could hardly be improved, but he still practiced every chance he got. Since his artillery skills needed to be honed, he worked with the cannons every spare minute he had. Of course the only time he had live fire was during artillery class, so he practiced all by himself in dumb show, mouthing the commands, from worming, to sponging, to loading, to priming, to the complicated geometry in aiming, to inserting the fuse, then to firing.

Night had almost taken over the artillery field, but Yancy told himself he had one, maybe two more drills he could do before full dark. Muttering to himself, he went through the repetitive motions as fast and as thoroughly as he could manage. Finally he ordered himself to fire and pulled on an invisible lanyard.

Behind him he heard single, slow applause and a low chuckle. He turned to see Major Jackson smiling and clapping.

It was such an unusual sight that Yancy was speechless for a moment, but then he dropped his head and blushed. "Guess I look pretty silly, huh, Major?"

"Not at all, not at all, Cadet," he said. He came forward and held out his hand for Yancy to shake. "I'm very proud of you, Cadet Tremayne. I might wish all the cadets have the dedication that you show."

"Not all the cadets have to make up for the mistakes I've made, sir."

"One mistake is all that I know of, Yancy," he said gruffly. "And you've more than made up for it. Look, here it is Saturday night and I think you're the only cadet here at the institute. And working at artillery skills at that."

"Yes, sir. Believe me, I've stayed out of saloons and away from — from — ladies — er —"

"I'm not that old, Cadet. I think I know what you mean. Sometimes some ladies can get us gentlemen into trouble. We must

278

always mind the ladies."

Yancy grinned. "You know, that's exactly what my father always says — to mind the ladies."

"Your father sounds like a wise man," Jackson said. "So it's almost too dark to see the targets. Are you going in now?"

"Sir, if you'll excuse me, I'd like to go through just one more drill. Just one more," he answered anxiously.

Jackson asked curiously, "Why? Why is one more so important?"

"Well, sir, it's like this. Today is September 1, 1860."

"Yes," Jackson agreed, puzzled.

"And so tomorrow is my birthday. I'm going to be seventeen."

Jackson nodded. "You seem older. I forget you're so young."

"Most people do, I think. Maybe it's because I'm so tall. Anyway, last January, when I got myself into so much trouble, one of the things I decided was that I was going to get in one hundred artillery drills, all by myself, before my birthday."

"Yes?"

"And sir, that last one was ninety-nine."

"I see," Jackson said gravely. "Well, Cadet Tremayne, it's so dark now I'm not sure I could sight a target with eagle eyes. But why don't we do just one more drill. You're the gun captain. I'll worm, sponge, and prime."

"Sir? You — you want me to be your gun captain?"

"Said so, didn't I? Let's go!" They went through a perfect drill, with Major Jackson worming, sponging, and priming.

Yancy aimed, set the fuse, and instead of mouthing the words, stood tall and shouted, "Fire!" then pulled his invisible lanyard.

"One hundred," Jackson said with satisfaction.

"Yes, one hundred, sir. And thank you, sir."

"My pleasure. And by the way, Cadet Tremayne . . ."

"Yes, sir?"

"On Monday I'll make you a gun captain. Think about the crew you want."

"Sir! Yes, sir! Thank you, sir!"

"Good, good. You've earned it, Cadet."

Yancy picked up the "worm" and the sponge and started toward the storage shed. To his surprise Major Jackson walked with him. "You know, Cadet, I've been watching you carefully this year. I wanted to make sure that I didn't make a mistake in recommending you for your charity scholarship."

"You didn't, sir," Yancy said firmly.

"I'm sure of that now. It takes time to earn trust once it's been broken. You have done that. Not only with rifles and artillery but with your studies. You're nineteenth in a class of one hundred and forty-two. That's quite an accomplishment, Cadet Tremayne, because I know you had no formal education before you came here."

"No, sir," Yancy said. "But my barracks mates have helped me a lot. Especially Cadet Stevens."

Jackson said, "He's a good man, a good soldier. He looks like the worst kind of fop but he's solid. He kind of reminds me of . . ." His voice faded out.

"Lieutenant Jeb Stuart," Yancy supplied. "In fact, Peyton met Lieutenant Stuart in Charles Town before John Brown's execution. He's sort of Peyton's hero."

Jackson said drily, "I can see how he would be. Lieutenant Stuart is a very interesting man."

"Interesting, yes," Yancy agreed. "And by the way, sir, I already know three men I want on my gun crew. My barracks mates — Peyton Stevens, Charles Satterfield, and Sandy Owens."

Jackson nodded. "Very good, Cadet Tremayne. You'll need three more. Any ideas on that?"

"Not yet, sir, but I'll know by Monday." Yancy shut the door to the storage shed, and they walked up through the parade grounds to the stables.

Yancy looked up. The Milky Way was like a diamond shawl thrown across the sky. In this luminous starlight they could see their way. There was no moon. "Major Jackson?" Yancy murmured, staring overhead.

"Yes?"

"Do you know why, when there's no moon, it's called the new moon?"

Jackson looked up and studied the sky. "Cadet, you just happened to ask me something that I know. After the full, the moon gets positioned between the earth and the sun, and the dark side is toward the earth. So after the fullest moon, there's a time when it's born again that we can't see. It's brand-new, and we won't see it until the earth has turned just right to catch the tiniest glimpse of it."

"Born again, and then a glimpse," Yancy repeated softly.

"That's right. Just like life, and love, and learning to live in God's will," Jackson said. "It's not something that just happens. It takes time and dedication." He glanced at Yancy. "Just like you've shown this year, Cadet. Think about that."

282

"Yes, sir, I will," Yancy said soberly. "I will."

Peyton Stevens lay on his bunk with his forage cap upside down between his booted feet. Negligently he held a deck of cards and with two fingers flipped one into the cap. "Fourteen," he said.

"Shut up," Sandy Owens said irritably. He was on the other lower bunk, frowning over a book.

Stevens flipped another card, perfectly sailing through the air and settling neatly into his cap. "Fifteen."

"Stevens, we all know you're so brilliant you don't have to study, but not all of us are as smart as you are," Yancy said from the bunk above him. He was diligently memorizing from his physics textbook. "Why don't you go outside to the parade ground to show off your card skills? Or go to town and call on one of those girls who is always chasing you around?"

"Boring. And boring," Stevens said lazily. He flipped another card. "Sixteen."

"Shut up," Charles Satterfield grumbled from above Sandy Owens's bunk.

"Whoa, Chuckins, getting kind of bossy, aren't you?" Stevens said, grinning. "What are you trying to study anyway?"

"History of the Founding Fathers," he answered. "But all that's going through my head is your dumb 'fourteen, fifteen, sixteen.' "

"Take my word for it, Chuckins, what's going on today is going to make more history than all the Founding Fathers put together," Stevens said. It was November 6, 1860, and it was the day of the presidential election.

Abruptly Yancy shut his book and turned over on his back. Putting his hands behind his head, he stared at the blank ceiling. "So what do you think this election means, Peyton? What do you think will happen?"

Peyton flicked another card into his cap but didn't count it. "I don't know everything, you know. Just what my father says." His father was a United States senator from Virginia.

"So? What does he say?" Sandy asked impatiently.

Apparently carelessly Peyton replied, "The Democrats have three weak candidates that will split the Southern vote. Abraham Lincoln will probably win. He is undoubtedly antislavery and altogether against secession. If he wins, there will most likely be a war."

And so Abraham Lincoln did win, and the

rumblings of war did sound in the air of the United States of America. Between his election in November and the first of February 1861, the cotton states held conventions and voted to secede — South Carolina, Mississippi, Florida, Alabama, Georgia, Louisiana, and Texas. That month delegates from those states met at Montgomery, Alabama, and voted to found a new nation. They called it the Confederate States of America. Its first president was Jefferson Davis.

Secession and war were the topics at VMI — except in Major Thomas Jackson's classes. He flatly refused to allow any discussion other than the class texts. Even during artillery practice he sternly corrected any cadet that mentioned Virginia's possible involvement in the growing hostilities.

But then April came, and it seemed to Yancy as if everyone, both North and South, had gone mad.

In the first week of April, Abraham Lincoln decided to send a naval relief expedition to Fort Sumter in Charleston, South Carolina, and, carefully avoiding dealing with the Confederacy, notified the state authorities. The fort was a federal naval base and always had been. The problem was that now the Confederacy regarded it as the property of the Confederate States of

America, and that government gave the order for the North to immediately surrender the fort. If they did not surrender, Montgomery ordered the dashing Creole commander, General P. G. T. Beauregard, to reduce the fort by arms — to, in fact, start a war.

On April 12, 1861, Beauregard made his demand to Major Robert Anderson and his seventy-five men. He rejected the demand. The Confederate guns opened on the fort, firing all that day and into the night. The next day the garrison yielded.

Responding to the frenzy of outrage in the North, on the fifteenth, the president called for seventy-five thousand volunteers to subdue the rebellious South. This resulted in a fury of patriotism in the Confederate states.

On April 17, Virginia seceded from the Union. Within three weeks, three other states of the Upper South had seceded: Arkansas, Tennessee, and North Carolina. The eleven states of the Confederate States of America was complete.

Major Thomas Jackson was in his element, for a Presbyterian synod was meeting in Lexington. It was Saturday, April 20, and the Jackson home was packed with ministers. The sound of their voices speaking and laughing was meat to Jackson.

Anna came to him once and whispered, "You're in your element, Thomas. You love nothing more than to argue over the Bible with ministers."

"We're not arguing. We're discussing. It is edifying. You know, esposita, at one point in my life I wished desperately that God would call me to be a minister, but the call never came. So here I am a poor soldier. I can at least give comfort and hospitality to those who are."

Anna smiled. She put her hand on Thomas's arm and said, "In your own way, my dear, you are a minister of the Word, too. Remember one of my favorite chapters in the scripture?"

"Second Corinthians, chapter five," Jackson answered.

"Verse twenty: 'Now then we are ambassadors for Christ. . . .' " Anna said confidently. "You are not only an ambassador, you are a minister. Not only do you teach your cadets, you minister to them, too. Now, please excuse me and I'll go to the kitchen to see about my ministry — providing enough coffee and tea to these gentlemen. It's like trying to keep a battalion supplied," she said with a smile.

■ ■ ■ ■

In the hot kitchen, Hetty was boiling two big pots of water when Yancy came in the door with three pounds of coffee, a pound of Indian tea, and a pound of chamomile tea. "Hello, Mrs. Jackson. More coffee and tea for the gentlemen." Sometimes on weekends he still helped Anna at the house with her garden and with repairs and with the horses.

"And just in time, too," she sighed. "I think both the coffee samovar and the teapots are empty. Yancy, you look splendid in your uniform. And let me see . . ." She stepped up to him and looked up into his face. "You have, I think, grown another inch or two."

"Guess so, ma'am," he agreed. "I'm a couple of inches taller than my father now, and he's right at six feet."

"And is he as handsome as you are?" Anna asked innocently.

At the stove, Hetty's broad face broke out in a smile.

Yancy replied, "Yes, ma'am — I mean, no, ma'am — wait, that's not right —"

Anna took pity at the woeful confusion on Yancy's face. "I'm sorry, Yancy, that was not a fair question, and I didn't mean to trick you. Well, perhaps I did, but anyway, I was going to ask you to go into the parlor and bring in the samovar and the tea wagon. It's too hot in this kitchen, and I don't want you to wilt in your uniform. It looks so very crisp and clean and fresh."

"Yes, ma'am. Thank you ma'am," Yancy said, still with some confusion, and hurried out of the kitchen.

Indeed, the house was buzzing with activity. Ministers gathered in groups of two or three in spirited discussions; sometimes one man would hold forth to a large group of men in the parlor, sitting and standing — and all of them sipping coffee or tea. Yancy counted them; there were twenty-three men crowded into the Jacksons' modest home. He was kept busy refreshing the coffee samovar and the teapots.

Once, on one of his countless trips from the kitchen to the parlor, he heard the knocker at the front door. He answered it to see a tall man, distinguished looking, wearing a somber black suit and a tall top hat. "Good afternooon, sir, may I help you?" Yancy asked, thinking that he was another minister.

The man looked him up and down in an assessing way.

Yancy was not in full uniform dress with his crossbelts and sword, but he was wearing his gray tunic, and his white trousers were — as Anna had noticed — spotless and flawlessly pressed with a knife-edge crease.

Yancy must have passed muster, because the man removed his hat and made a slight bow. "You are, I believe, one of our excellent cadets from Virginia Military Institute."

Yancy, having learned much etiquette from Peyton Stevens, returned his own cool bow. "Yes, sir. I am Cadet Tremayne, sir."

"My name is Evans, Henry Evans. I am from Governor Letcher's office." Solemnly they shook hands. "May I have an audience with Major Jackson, Cadet Tremayne? It is a matter of some importance and of a private nature." His glance wandered toward the parlor, where the spirited discussions and some laughter sounded.

Yancy stepped back and extended his white-gloved hand for Mr. Evans to come in. "Please wait here, Mr. Evans. I'll tell Major Jackson that you're here."

Yancy found Jackson listening to a minister who was holding forth to a group of six men concerning dispensations. Discreetly he went up to Jackson and whispered, "Sir, there is a Mr. Henry Evans who would like a private word with you. He's from Governor Letcher's office."

A shadow passed over Jackson's face, and he nodded. He had told Yancy he had been expecting a summons of some kind ever since the seventeenth when Virginia had seceded. "Very well. Where is he?"

"In the foyer, sir."

"Good, good," Jackson said absently, and slipped out of the parlor.

Major Jackson and Evans made their introductions and niceties. Then Evans commented, "It sounds as if you're having a party, Major."

"No, it is a group of Presbyterian ministers."

"A group of ministers? They sound like men at a prize fight."

Jackson smiled briefly. "Perhaps so, but I can assure you we are much less inclined to hostility than just honest debate."

Evans nodded. "There is a sad lack of honest debate these days, sir. Which brings me to the governor's business with you." Evans reached into his inner pocket and brought out an envelope. "Orders for you, Major."

Jackson took the envelope and read it, then nodded. "Thank you, Mr. Evans. Am I to understand that these orders are effective immediately?"

"Yes, sir. You'll go into active duty at once."

"Sir, please tell Governor Letcher that his orders will be obeyed to the letter."

"God bless you, sir." After a few more polite words, Evans took his leave.

Jackson went back into the house. Anna wasn't in the parlor or the dining room where the ministers were, so he went into the kitchen where he found her there with Hetty, still boiling water and making more coffee and tea. He went to her and said softly, "Let's go out in the garden for a few minutes."

She looked surprised. "With all our guests?"

"Yes, my dearest."

Anna grew sober. She followed him out to a stone bench in her garden, and they sat down together.

He put his arm around her. "I just got my orders from Governor Letcher, esposa."

She stiffened slightly, but her voice was calm and even. "And what are your orders, Thomas?"

"The best cadets from the institute are called to duty in Richmond. I am to command them."

She nodded. "When are you to go?"

Somewhat sadly he replied, "Tomorrow, I'm afraid. I had hoped to have the Sabbath for church affairs and some rest, but Governor Letcher has ordered us to muster and go to Richmond immediately."

She leaned against him and rested her head on his shoulder.

He lightly kissed her cheek and whispered, "I hate to leave you! God knows I do!"

Anna couldn't answer. His arms tightened on her and they rested together in silence for a few moments.

Finally he said, "I must go dismiss our guests. There is much to do. I'm going to send Yancy to the institute to alert the cadets, and then I'll go talk to them."

Yancy rode to the institute, and for an hour rousted everybody out. Most of them were wearing their uniforms, but the ones who weren't started to change. "Don't bother with uniforms right now. The major just wants to talk to you."

Finally all the cadets were turned out on the parade ground, and Major Jackson walked up. He spoke loudly, "Attention!" and the line stiffened and fell silent.

Yancy kept his eyes on Jackson's face, and he could see that there was some sort of a portent in the major's expression. His features were usually mild and benign, but not now. There was something hard, almost harsh in it.

He stopped in front of the cadets and said, "I have received orders from Governor Letcher. All of the cadets seventeen and older will march to Richmond tomorrow to serve with the Army of Virginia. I'll be your commanding officer. I want you to be ready to march at 1:00. You know what field packs are. Be sure and bring your rifles and plenty of ammunition. Write letters to your families tonight, and I'll arrange a special mail pickup tomorrow. I'll be back early in the morning to see how you're proceeding, and all of our institute officers will be available to help you in any way we can. That's all for now. Dismissed."

Yancy went up to Jackson and said, "Sir, since my family is so close, may I go tonight and tell them good-bye? I'll be back in plenty of time to make up my field pack and for muster tomorrow."

"You may, Cadet Tremayne," Jackson answered. "Give them my best wishes."

It was almost nine o'clock at night before Yancy got to the farm. He was afraid that everyone might be asleep, and waking them up to tell them his news would make it seem so much more melodramatic than it really was. After all, it wasn't as if Richmond was a battle zone. The capital of the Confederate States of America had been moved from Montgomery to Richmond, and so it was the center of the government. Yancy was a little unclear as to what exactly the cadets would be doing, but it seemed unlikely that they would be marching to war.

For now, at least.

As he rode up he was relieved to see the lamps lit in the parlor. Someone was up, at least. He dismounted and tied Midnight to the hitching post. "I'm not going to unsaddle you, boy," he said, rubbing his nose. "We can't stay long."

He went up on the veranda and knocked lightly on the door then stuck his head in. Hank gave one long bay then came galloping out to meet him. "It's just me," he called. "Yancy." He gave Hank a friendly ear rub then went into the parlor.

His father had risen, but Becky and Zemira were still sitting on the settees by a small friendly fire.

"Of course we knew it was you," Zemira said drily. "Who else would it be gallivanting around in the middle of a Saturday night?"

"Not me . . . not for a long time anyway,"

Yancy replied, kissing her on one smooth cheek. "And I'm not gallivanting. I came out because I have some news."

Slowly Daniel sat back down. All three of them suddenly looked grave.

Yancy sat down by Zemira. He knew there was no way to soften it or sugarcoat it, so he just said it. "The top cadets at VMI have been detached to Richmond to serve with the Army of Northern Virginia. Major Jackson is our commander."

There was a long heavy silence, finally broken by Becky. "I suppose we all knew something like this would happen, considering what's been going on in the last few months. I just suppose we didn't expect it quite so soon. And somehow I thought that maybe the cadets at the institute might be spared unless it was some kind of last resort."

Yancy merely looked at her, a tinge of regret shadowing his feelings.

Daniel said in a low voice, "You would volunteer, wouldn't you? If you hadn't been called up?"

"Yes, sir," he answered without hesitation. "And depending on the nature of our duty in Richmond — and what Major Jackson does — I still may."

Zemira sighed heavily, almost a moan. "I

could see it in you, Yancy. I knew. I saw that you'd decided to be a soldier. And we always told you that we would respect your decisions, and we do. But I have to tell you that it grieves me, it truly does."

"I'm sorry," Yancy said lamely.

"Don't be sorry," Becky said, though she sounded sad. "Of course no one wants loved ones in a war. But as your grandmother said, Yancy, we respect your decisions. And I for one am very proud of you. You've grown to be a strong man this last year. You made a promise to us and yourself and you've kept it. The Lord honors those who keep their word and turn from their mistakes. I'll pray that He will bless you, watch over you, protect you, and bring you back to us safe and sound."

"Please, all of you pray for me, every day," Yancy said slowly. "I know I'm going to need it."

"We will, son," Daniel said. "Always."

Yancy nodded and rose. "I can't stay. We all have a lot to do. We're moving out tomorrow afternoon. Can I go say good night to Callie Jo and David? I won't wake them."

"Of course, you must," Becky said. "Go on up."

Quietly Yancy went up to the nursery. Callie Jo looked like a little doll as she slept with her thumb stuck in her mouth. He bent over and kissed her forehead. She stirred just a little but didn't wake up.

David had turned one last Christmas Eve. Yancy took one of his tiny fists, and in his sleep David wrapped his hand around one finger. "Be good, brother," Yancy whispered.

Then he hesitated, because he realized that what he had really been doing was telling his brother and sister good-bye. It hit him then that he may not see them again, and he drew in a sharp breath. For a moment he felt a deep searing fear. But then he bowed his head and prayed silently. *Lord, help me overcome this fear. Please help me to know the right thing to do. Help me find courage. And help me find You.*

Major Jackson went to the institute before dawn to help with the preparations, to prepare his cadets for their first march. It was still early morning when he rode back home, but he stopped at First Presbyterian Church and sent his pastor, Dr. White, to the barracks to pray for his young soldiers. Then he went home and had a late breakfast with Anna.

After breakfast he and Anna went into the parlor and sat close together on the settee. "Let's read the fifth chapter of Second

Corinthians," he said.

It was one of Anna's favorite passages. Together, from memory, they said in unison, " 'For we know that if our earthly house of this tabernacle were dissolved, we have a building of God, an house not made with hands, eternal in the heavens.' "

Thomas read the entire chapter aloud, and then he prayed. Humbly he entreated God for peace, for his country and countrymen and cadets, for Anna and their home and the servants.

And then, as soldiers must do, he left to go to war.

CHAPTER FIFTEEN

Jackson led his cadets into Richmond. Wearing his old dusty blue uniform, he rode into town on his shambling gray gelding, Cerro Gordo. Following him as color bearers, Yancy rode Midnight and Peyton Stevens rode his showy palomino, Senator. The contrast between Jackson's humble appearance and his sharp-dressed and trim cadets was striking, but as always, Jackson had a marshal air of authority and competence, so there was no doubt who was in command.

Jackson installed the cadets into a small camp at the fairgrounds, about a mile from the center of the city. Then he called Yancy and Peyton aside. "Until we get settled in and find out exactly what is required of us here, I want you two to be my aides-de-camp and couriers. Right now I'm going to the capitol to speak with Governor Letcher, and you'll accompany me."

"Yes, sir!" they answered, at stiff attention.

They rode back into town, to the Virgina State capitol, situated on Shockoe Hill, overlooking the James River. It was a graceful building, said to be designed by Thomas Jefferson. Modeled after a simplified Roman temple, with soaring columns and an airy porch, it was dignified and stately.

But on this day it more resembled a kicked-over anthill than a peaceful temple. Horses and carriages surrounded the building on all sides. Men, some dressed as gentlemen and some dressed as soldiers and some dressed as laborers, hurried in and out. More groups of men crowded the front in groups of threes and fours and more, and the timbre of their loud conversations could be said to be almost frantic. Young boys, presumably couriers, ran to and fro, weaving nimbly among the crowds, their piping voices calling for their addressees.

The milling crowd of wagons, carriages, and horses around the building made it impossible for them to tether the horses anywhere. Jackson dismounted and told Yancy, "Just stay out of the way as much as you can. I'm going to try to wade through all this to-do and see if I can get an audience with Governor Letcher. Wait here, and try not to get stampeded."

Yancy's Midnight and Peyton's Senator were big, spirited horses and could easily make their own way through a crowd, because other horses shied away from their high-stepping, aggressive gaits. "Let's put old Gordo between them," Yancy said, almost shouting at Peyton in the din of the throng. "Then I think we can get them to crowd out those two carts and those saddle horses and get them hitched up there by the watering trough."

Peyton didn't even try to answer. He just nodded.

They maneuvered the horses around with some trouble, but once Midnight and Senator picked up the scent of the water, they practically shoved everyone and everything aside to get to the trough. They were thirsty, and all three horses had good, long drinks. There was about one foot left of a hitching post, and they tethered the horses. Then Peyton and Yancy went to stand in the shade of the capitol, keeping in sight of the horses.

Though it was April, the sun was hot and bright, and they were very warm in their formal uniforms. They watched the crowds coming and going. All of the streets of Richmond had been just as busy and buzzing.

Peyton finally commented, "This city looks like bedlam."

Yancy agreed. "So far everywhere we've seen has been like everyone's gone mad. The only difference here at the capitol is that there's no ladies. I couldn't believe the way the ladies were crowding the streets talking. I've never seen that before." It was extremely rare to see Southern women gathered together on the streets.

Peyton smiled, a lazy, thoroughly charming, boyish grin. "I was glad to see that, you know. There are some very beautiful ladies in Richmond." Peyton's family owned an enormous mansion on the banks of the James River.

Slyly Yancy said, "Might know you'd have noticed that, Peyton. But you better be a proper gentleman or Old Blue Light will tan your hide, no mistake."

"Don't I know it, and there's no way I'd take that chance. I'm not missing out on this war for anything," Peyton said with uncharacteristic passion. "And I'm going to do whatever it takes to stay with Major Jackson, even if I have to get my father to pull some strings and appoint me personally to him."

Yancy considered this. "You know they're going to activate him, probably soon. So you're saying you'd resign your commission to the institute and join the army?"

"Yes, I will," Peyton answered sturdily. "What about you, Yancy? Have you thought about it?"

"No, this month has been so crazy that I guess I hadn't looked that far in the future. But I'm sure going to think about it."

Peyton sighed and wiped sweat from his aristocratic brow. "You might have plenty of time to do that now. There's no telling how long Major Jackson may have to wait to see the governor."

But he was wrong. Jackson returned just a few minutes later. Wordlessly he mounted up and motioned Yancy and Preston to do the same. They made their way through the city and back to the fairgrounds. Jackson didn't speak until they reached the camp, and then he ordered them to muster the men.

When they were assembled, he addressed them with his typical lack of drama. But he was an intense man, and Yancy could sense his purpose and will and drive as a soldier. The cadets didn't make a sound as he spoke.

"Cadets, I've just met with Governor Letcher. The Virginia Volunteers are men and boys from all walks of life. They are dedicated and loyal and want to serve Virginia and the Confederacy, but they have no training. Some of the commanding officers assigned to them have a military background; some have not. It's been decided that you men have the best training available, so you will be assigned as drill masters. You will teach them the orders, the march, the formations, and the small-arms drill."

There was some murmuring then among the cadets, most of them smiling with satisfaction. Yancy knew, indeed, that they had received the best education and training available in the South.

Jackson allowed them a few minutes to digest this, and then he continued, "Tomorrow you will receive your assignments. I know that all of you will do your duty to the utmost of your abilities; and I know that the men you train will benefit to a great extent from your knowledge." He made a half turn, his hands behind his back as if to leave, but then he turned, and even the cadets in the back rows could surely see the unearthly light in his fiery blue eyes. "I'm proud of you all. Very proud. Dismissed."

Basically, the cadets were snatched up. In two days they were drilling men in every vacant lot and little-used back street in

Richmond. This left Major Jackson with very little to do, because the cadets were so expert and so disciplined that they had no need of oversight. Still, he visited each drill team every day. And though he was staying with friends in town, he came to the camp at the fairgrounds every night to get updates on the status of the volunteers the cadets were training. Each drill team had been assigned a captain, and each captain gave Jackson a daily report.

Yancy had been appointed captain of a drill team which included his friends, Peyton Stevens, Sandy Owens, and Charles Satterfield. On the second night he reported to Major Jackson in his officer's tent which had been established, though he was staying in town. Standing at strict attention he said, "Sir, I have learned more about the company that I have been assigned to, Raphine Company. Almost all of the men are from that little town in Rockbridge County. They were recruited and organized by Captain Reese Gilmer, whom you met yesterday. Since he formed the company, sir, they elected him as their captain, and he was confirmed by Secretary of War Walker when they reported for duty."

Jackson, seated at his camp desk with a single candle for light, nodded and muttered, "Good, good. And how do you find Captain Gilmer?"

"Sir?" Yancy asked, mystified.

"How do you find him? As a man, as a soldier, as an officer?"

"But sir, I don't know the man. I only met him yesterday. And — and — he is my superior officer. He's a captain."

Jackson gave Yancy a cold, appraising look, and those ice blue eyes made him straighten and stand even more stiffly. "You, sir, are a drill team captain, and even though this does not outrank an army captain, in this peculiar situation you are his teacher and he is your student. And, Cadet, you are going to have to learn to be a judge of men. Not to judge them for their sins — no, no, no man ever has that right — but to see them, to instinctively know if they are honest and true and men of their word, and to try and estimate their intentions and abilities. In war, this is not only important, but it is crucial, both in summing up your allies and your enemies. And so give me your first impressions of Captain Gilmer."

Yancy swallowed hard. "Major Jackson, I believe he is an honorable man, anxious to serve Virginia and the Confederacy. He is humble enough to know that he hasn't had the training that we have had, and so he eagerly learns all of our drills. But he still maintains a dignified control over his men and has an officer-like demeanor. He is anxious both for himself and his men to prove themselves brave and unwavering soldiers in this war."

"Good, good," Jackson said, scribbling notes. "And, Cadet Tremayne, take notice of any particular men who distinguish themselves, whether in zeal or determination or marksmanship. I shall expect that in your further reports."

"Yes, sir."

Jackson looked up at him in the dim candle glow. "Cadet Tremayne, did you know that Robert E. Lee was appointed general of all forces in Virginia?"

Yancy's face lit up. "No, sir, we had not heard. This is good news, sir."

"Good news indeed. I had the privilege of serving under him in Mexico, and he has proved himself to be a good friend to me ever since then. And this means that things will change and quickly."

Yancy hesitated, for Major Jackson was a private man who always kept his counsel to himself. But then he reflected that the major had offered him this information, and therefore this opening. Summoning his courage, he asked, "Sir, please explain to me what you mean. Will the Virginia Volunteers be called up soon? Maybe immediately?"

Somewhat to Yancy's surprise, Jackson didn't reprimanded him for his impertinence, and he did not hesitate. "Yes, they will. I'm certain. So drill them hard, Cadet Tremayne. Train them on orders and formations and the march, but especially drill them on small-arms battle and the bayonet. Soon even these young men will be facing battle, and I know that with the training of the institute, they will give a good accounting and serve out the enemy with all fury."

Major Thomas Jackson was not a man to be content babysitting raw recruits when the Confederacy was at war. Governor John Letcher was a Rockbridge County man and knew Jackson well. Jackson had come to the attention of Robert E. Lee when serving under him in Mexico, and several years earlier Lee had highly recommended him for a position at the University of Virginia. Jackson had also met other influential friends in Richmond, and he diligently sought his friends' backings to get a position and a post in the army.

His strategy worked. A mere six days after he had arrived in Richmond, Governor

Letcher proposed Jackson for the rank of colonel to command the Virginia Infantry. The state convention promptly approved it.

Jackson was sent to Lee, who was very glad indeed to see him and eager to put him to work. They had a meeting, and General Lee assigned him to his new post — Harpers Ferry.

That night, Jackson went to the fairgrounds. Diligent to the last, he wanted his status reports, which he turned in daily to the secretary of war. And he wanted to say good-bye to his cadets.

He was somewhat surprised to see about a dozen cadets waiting for him outside his tent. When he rode up they formed into two rows and came to attention.

Yancy stepped forward. "Colonel Jackson, sir, our drill captains have their reports ready. And also, these men would like to speak to you."

Jackson nodded curtly. "Come in, Cadet Tremayne."

Yancy went into the tent with Jackson, standing at attention as he settled himself behind the camp desk with the candle on it.

"At ease, Cadet. Now, what's all this about?"

Yancy relaxed a bit, took a moment to frame his words, and then said, "Colonel

Jackson, I would like to join the Virginia Volunteers. In particular, I hope to join you. We've heard that you're going to form the 1st Brigade, and I would like to enlist."

"Good, good," Jackson murmured under his breath. Then he looked up at Yancy, his eyes sparkling with an inner light. "And is that what all of the cadets out there wish to speak to me about? To join up?"

"Yes, sir."

"Very well then. I'm going to swear you in, Cadet Tremayne. And from now on, you will be Sergeant Tremayne, assigned to my staff as my aide and courier."

"Sir! Thank you, sir!"

"And as my staff assistant you will swear in any such able-bodied cadets as wish to join the 1st Virginia Brigade, and you will document their inductions."

"Yes, sir!"

"Good, good. Now I'll swear you in. Attention!"

Yancy snapped back to attention.

"Repeat after me, cadet:

" 'I, Yancy Tremayne, of the county of Rockbridge, state of Virginia, do solemnly swear that I will support, protect, and defend the Constitution and the government of the Confederate States of America against all enemies, whether domestic or foreign; that I will bear true faith, allegiance, and loyalty to the same, any ordinance, resolution, or laws of any state, convention or legislature to the contrary notwithstanding; and further, that I will faithfully perform all the duties which may be required of me by the laws of the Confederate States of America; and I take this oath freely and voluntarily without any mental reservations or evasions whatsoever.' "

The remainder of the document read:

Subscribed and sworn to me
In duplicate this 28th day of April, 1861.

The above named has dark complexion, black hair and black eyes, and is six feet, two inches high.
Colonel Thomas J. Jackson, C.S.A.

When Yancy and Colonel Jackson finished dutifully filling out the solemn document, Jackson said, "I'm going to make out your certificate of induction. Pay attention."

"Yes, sir."

Again by hand Jackson filled out the form:

The Fairgrounds
Richmond, Virginia
April 28th, 1861

This is to certify that I have this day sworn Yancy Tremayne into the service of the Confederate States of America as a volunteer in the 1st Brigade, Virginia Infantry serving in the Army of Virginia.

Thomas J. Jackson
Colonel, C.S.A.

"You got all that, Sergeant?" Jackson demanded.

Yancy swelled until he thought he would burst. "Yes, sir!"

"Then for your first duty as my aide, you're going to have to copy these two documents fair. Then you're going to have to swear in all those recruits out there and make two copies of each document. Meanwhile, direct each drill captain to me to make a daily report on our Virginian Volunteers here in Richmond. After that, report back to me and I will brief you on our upcoming posting. And after I brief you, then you will brief each new member of the 1st Brigade of our first mission."

"Yes, sir!" Yancy said snappily.

Jackson regarded him shrewdly. "You know, Sergeant Tremayne, that the 1st Brigade is going to be formed from the 2nd, 4th, 5th, 27th, and 33rd Virginia Infantry Regiments."

"Yes, sir?" Yancy answered curiously.

"But you're the first volunteer for the 1st Brigade."

"I'm proud to be, sir. And thank you again for my promotion. I won't let you down."

Yancy immediately returned to the cadets and organized the drill team captains to report to Colonel Jackson. Then he set up a camp table outside Jackson's tent and began the tedious task of swearing in the cadets who were joining the Virginia Volunteers, although all of them wished to request the 1st Virginia Brigade.

The first cadet he signed in was Charles Satterfield. Chuckins signed the handwritten forms and watched as Yancy painstakingly made out duplicate forms. Penmanship was not Yancy's strong point and his spelling was not stellar, so he kept having to refer back to the originals that Colonel Jackson had made out for him.

"There's no printed forms for this?" Chuckins asked.

"There were plenty when the call went out for volunteers," Yancy answered, "but they were almost all used up. Colonel Jackson has a few left, but he wants to keep them in case it takes any time to get new printed forms to us. He told me to make handwritten copies for us, the cadets that are signing up."

"I could help you with those forms," Chuckins said.

"Yeah, you're the best in penmanship, I know," Yancy replied thoughtfully.

"And you know, I've already memorized those forms," Chuckins said diffidently.

"What?"

Chuckins shrugged. "Memorized them. I dunno. It's just something I can do."

Gladly Yancy said, "Go find a chair, report back here, and help me out. I'll take their oaths and induct them, and you can write them in."

It was almost one o'clock in the morning when Yancy reported back to Colonel Jackson. Of the fourteen cadets that had volunteered, Jackson called in Yancy, Peyton Stevens, Sandy Owens, and Charles Satterfield. They stood at uncomfortable attention in his tent.

"At ease," Jackson said.

They assumed the at ease position, relaxing their postures and holding their hands behind their backs.

Jackson, seated at his desk, frowned darkly. There was no seating for the cadets, which seemed to dissatisfy him. He rose and started pacing, his hands clasped behind him. "Gentlemen, I am not in the habit of addressing men in a personal manner. However, I have found that you four cadets have been exemplary, both in scholastics and in the military disciplines. Therefore I have made decisions concerning your positions, especially regarding the 1st Virginia Brigade, for which you have volunteered."

The four cadets nodded solemnly but did not speak.

Jackson paced. "Sergeant Tremayne, I've already given you your posting. Since you have such a magnificent horse, we're also inducting Midnight into the 1st Brigade. And, Stevens, I'm giving you a promotion to sergeant, as aide-de-camp and courier. But this is provisional if your horse, Senator, also joins the 1st Brigade."

Yancy had rarely seen Jackson's humor at home, but no other VMI cadet had probably ever witnessed it.

Peyton Stevens appeared nervous. "Sir, yes, sir. I'm — I'm — my horse is happy — that is, we volunteer."

"Mr. Owens," Jackson continued.

"Yes, sir!"

"I know that getting gunpowder and grease on your breeches causes you great distress. But you are one of the best gunners in the institute. The Rockbridge Artillery has been assigned to the 1st Brigade, and it is my wish that you would serve with them."

It was true that Sandy Owens was something of a dandy, and he hated for his dynamic VMI uniform to get soiled or wrinkled. But that was for the carefree days when he was a cadet in the finest military school in the South, and these were days of war. He was best at artillery, and he loved artillery best. "Thank you, Colonel Jackson," he said quietly. "I would be honored to serve with Reverend Pendleton." Colonel W. N. Pendleton was the commanding officer of the Rockbridge Artillery, and he was also an Episcopal rector. Sandy attended his church.

"So that brings us to you, Mr. Satterfield," Jackson said. He sat down at the desk and shuffled through the pile of papers there.

Chuckins was obviously so nervous he could barely talk. "Y–yes, sir. Me. Th–that brings us to m–me."

Jackson's eyes sparked blue ice, and his set mouth had a slight tinge of amusement. He looked down and went through two more pages then looked up. "These documents are written in a fine hand."

"Th–thank you, sir."

"And there are no errors in the copy, none

at all. That's very unusual."

Chuckins swallowed hard. "I — I had them memorized, sir. The forms."

"I see. It seems to me, Mr. Satterfield, that you would make a fine clerk. As it happens, I need a clerk on my staff."

"Sir! May I volunteer for your staff?" Chuckins asked anxiously.

"You may, and I accept. I'm promoting you to sergeant, and I'm appointing you as my chief clerk."

"Colonel, thank you, sir, thank you!"

"You may not thank me when you see the paperwork it takes to sustain a brigade," Jackson said drily. "All right, men, now I want to brief you on our posting. Please keep in mind that the regiments that will form the 1st Brigade have not been briefed yet. I prefer to keep my counsel to myself, for the most part, until I know I have a staff I can trust. I've known you men for a few years, and I feel I can trust you as I already know that you're capable of discretion."

Yancy knew Jackson thoroughly believed that the fewer people that knew the movements of his men, the fewer chances the enemy had to learn them.

Jackson continued, "General Lee has assigned us to Harpers Ferry."

The cadets exchanged puzzled looks.

"Yes, the same Harpers Ferry that John Brown took," Jackson said somberly. "We all witnessed his execution. The reason he took Harpers Ferry is that it is both a strategic and tactical target. Tactical because it's a United States arsenal. The arsenal, with its ordnance manufacture, consists in a complex of government buildings, including an armory, an arsenal, and an enginehouse. And it's a strategic target because a main stem of the Baltimore & Ohio railroad runs right through the town. In fact, it has double tracks, running east-west and west-east. Tons and tons of coal from the Appalachian mines in the Midwest run through that line to the East. And there's a bridge across the Potomac at Harpers Ferry that runs through Maryland on its way to Baltimore and Washington. And that means supplies going to the Federal army."

Owens, Stevens, and Satterfield all looked at Yancy. He seemed to have been elected the speaker for them, since he was in some ways closer to Colonel Jackson because he had worked for the Jacksons. "Sir, if I may ask, what will be the 1st Brigade's responsibility there? What is our mission?"

Jackson didn't grin, but his habitually stern expression lightened to one of amusement. "We're going to kidnap a railroad."

■ ■ ■ ■

Colonel Thomas Jackson, commanding officer of the Confederate troops stationed at Harpers Ferry, Virginia, lodged a formal complaint with the president of the B & O Railroad, John W. Garrett of Baltimore. The trains disturbed his men at night, and Colonel Jackson demanded that they come through Harpers Ferry at about noon. Mr. John W. Garrett was hardly in a position to to argue with the Confederate officer who held the major railroad bridge over the Potomac. The loaded trains began running west-east from 11:00 a.m. to 1:00 p.m.

But then there were the empties returning east-west at night, and again Colonel Jackson complained and demanded that the dual tracks be scheduled so that the trains ran only around the noon hour. Again he was accommodated, and for two hours a day Harpers Ferry was the busiest railroad hub in America.

At noon on May 23, less than a month after he and his brigade had arrived in Harpers Ferry, Jackson ordered his troops to seal off each end of the thirty-two-mile-long sector that he held. The trains were trapped. By the time the final tally was done, Colonel

Jackson had kidnapped fifty-six locomotives and more than three hundred cars.

Another hostage was kidnapped during this raid — a nondescript, rather small reddish mare with soft brown eyes and a coltish gait. Colonel Jackson determined to give her as a gift to Anna, but he grew so fond of her that he kept her for his own mount, conscientiously paying the quartermaster for her value. Little Sorrel she was called, and somehow Colonel Jackson sensed she would be with him to the very end of the road.

CHAPTER SIXTEEN

Colonel Thomas Jackson's "kidnapping" of a railroad resounded throughout the South, and he enjoyed some good publicity. However, a few days after this famous exploit was completed, Jackson was abruptly replaced. Brigadier General Joseph E. Johnston arrived at Harpers Ferry to take command. Jackson quietly stepped aside. General Johnston did give him command over the 1st Virginia Brigade that he had formed and had so carefully and ceaselessly trained.

In the middle of June, Federal troops began amassing on the Maryland side of the river, a force of about eighteen thousand under United States General Robert Patterson, a rather elderly and slow-moving, cautious officer. Still, General Johnston felt threatened that the superior force might outflank his 6,500 troops, so he withdrew to Winchester, about thirty miles southwest of Harpers Ferry. Jackson and his 1st Brigade were dispatched to Martinsburg, about twenty miles north. Colonel Jeb Stuart and his cavalry were ordered to observe the Federals and immediately give word if they showed any signs of crossing the Potomac.

In his position, Jackson saw nothing of the enemy and no activity was reported to him. But one thing did happen that reduced the difficulty of being relieved of his command . . . and of his boredom in Martinsburg. On June 17, he received his commission as brigadier general in the army of the Confederate States of America.

As it happened, Chuckins Satterfield was in Jackson's camp tent transcribing some of Jackson's dictation when the courier from Richmond arrived with the orders for Jackson's promotion. He witnessed the courier deliver the papers and swear Jackson in. After the courier left, Chuckins jumped to attention and said, "Sir! May I be the first to congratulate you, sir, on your commission, General Jackson, sir!"

"You may. Thank you," he answered succinctly. "Sit down, Sergeant Satterfield, and continue your work."

"Yes, sir!" Chuckins sat back down to his

dreary paperwork.

Surreptitiously he watched the brand-new general, but Jackson showed no outward signs of excitement or elation at his promotion. He sat calmly at his desk, his pen endlessly scratching across paper.

Finally Chuckins could stand it no longer. "Sir? General Jackson? Would it be all right if I took a short break to have a cup of coffee, sir?"

Jackson didn't look up; his pen scratched and scritched. "Dismissed."

Chuckins ran out, grabbed the first soldier he saw, and told the news.

Soon everyone in the 1st Brigade had heard that they were now commanded by a brigadier general. And they were proud. Though Jackson had none of the glad-handing, backslapping ways of many powerful men, he carried with him an unmistakable air of authority, of sure and certain knowledge and understanding, and of honor and integrity. To a man and to the utmost they respected him and trusted him. It may even be said that they loved him.

When Jackson heard Colonel Jeb Stuart was riding into the camp, just outside of Martinsburg, with the usual drama, he came hurrying out of his tent to greet his friend.

Stuart galloped full speed through the camp, coming to a stop by abruptly reining in his magnificent mount, who skidded to a stop, threw his head up, reared and pawed the air, and came to a furious stamping halt. Jeb Stuart jumped off, throwing the reins to one of his escorts. As usual, he was greeted by the soldier's whoops and calls.

Stuart stopped before Jackson, came to a parade attention, and then saluted beautifully. "May I congratulate you, General Jackson, on your well-deserved promotion. It is an honor to serve under you, sir."

Jackson returned his salute and said quietly, "You serve with me, Colonel Stuart. We serve God and the Confederacy."

They went into Jackson's tent where they stayed for about an hour. Then Colonel Stuart and his escorts left, as dashing and daring as they had arrived.

Jackson then called in Yancy and Peyton. "You two men go to all the commanders of the regiments and tell them we'll be marching within the hour. Light field packs. Sergeant Stevens, tell General Pendleton to get the guns ready to move into Martinsburg."

They saluted and ran off to alert the command that they were moving to battle, the first fighting that they had seen.

Tethered by his tent was Midnight, and when Yancy ran to saddle him up, he saw that a private from Lexington named Henry Birdwell was visiting Midnight, stroking his nose and feeding him some dried corn.

When he saw Yancy, he snapped to attention and saluted.

"At ease, Birdie," Yancy said, returning a careless salute.

Henry Birdwell had joined Captain Reese Gilmer's Raphine Company, of the 33rd Virginia Regiment, the unit that Yancy had trained in Richmond. Now they were part of the 1st Brigade.

Captain Reese Gilmer was the ultimate Southern gentleman. He owned a cotton plantation, about thirty slaves, and his family could be traced back to the Mayflower. He was a good soldier and a good leader, and he had managed to recruit about one hundred men from his small central village of Raphine and the farms and plantations beyond. Henry Birdwell had been employed as a stable boy at Raphine Plantation, and he had immediately signed up for Reese Gilmer's company.

Henry Birdwell was one year older than

Yancy, but he seemed much younger, with his open face, mild brown eyes, and short brown hair with a pronounced cowlick. He loved horses, though his family had always been too poor to buy saddle horses. He especially loved Midnight, for the high-bred stallion responded to him with a friendliness and glad whinny that was rare, except for Yancy and his family.

"Go get ready, Birdie," Yancy told him. "We're going to march out soon."

Birdwell blinked in the bright morning sunlight. "Are we going to fight, Sergeant Tremayne?"

"General Jackson doesn't confide in the likes of me," Yancy replied lightly. "All I know is that we're marching out. Here, you want to help me saddle him up?"

"Yes, sir." Quickly the private gave Midnight's back a brush-down then laid one of Yancy's fine soft Indian blankets on his back.

As they were saddling Midnight, Yancy asked, "Why are you here, Birdie? Why are you fighting?"

"They called us. And I wanted to fight for Captain Reese and General Jackson," he answered simply. "We all knew General Jackson in Lexington. We all wanted to fight with him."

Yancy nodded. "I know what you mean."

Birdie continued, "I still want to fight, but . . . I sure hope the war's over soon, like the newspapers say. I've got a girlfriend, Ellen Mae Simpkins. She's a maid at Raphine Plantation. When I get home we're going to get married."

"That's good, Birdie," Yancy said quietly. "I know you'll be happy. Now, go on. Go get ready to march."

He saluted. "Yes, sir!" he said snappily and turned and ran off like a boy on his way to his favorite fishing hole.

Within an hour, the brigade was ready to march. General Jackson rode forward and, without a word, led the way out of camp. They pushed hard all morning long. It was late in the afternoon before Jackson ordered the brigade to halt. He called all his aides and commanding officers together.

"You see that church over there?" he asked, pointing. "That is the church in Falling Waters. The Federals are just on the other side of it. They are advancing. Now, we are going to move just past the treeline of that glade over there and we're going to wait for them to advance into this open field. And then we'll take them. Position your men in three stances: first volley, from a prone position; second volley, kneeling position; and third volley, standing. Then, gentlemen, we will charge and give them the bayonet. Ride out."

Yancy caught up to him and said, "General, sir? Permission to join Raphine Company?"

Jackson frowned. "Is that the company you've been training and drilling, Sergeant Tremayne?"

"Yes, sir. I'd very much like to be with them in their first battle, sir."

"Permission granted."

Yancy saluted and turned to ride away.

Jackson called after him, "Sergeant Tremayne?"

"Yes, sir?"

"Fight hard, Sergeant Tremayne. This is for Virginia, for our homes, for our families. No matter what they think about this war, this is for them."

"Yes, sir!" Yancy said, wheeling Midnight and hurrying to the front.

As Jackson planned, the enemy came marching across open fields, and they met deadly musket fire. Jackson and his three regiments charged them.

Captain Reese Gilmer drew his sword, thrust it forward, and yelled, "Charge!"

Yancy, on Midnight, charged right behind

him, sword drawn.

From then on, all was a confusion of harsh glaring light — for it was a blistering July afternoon — hot gulping breaths, the smell of blood and gunpowder, and the echoing screams of men fighting and firing and dying. Yancy saw, as if in magnification, a man fall just beside him. The soldier was on his back and the lower part of his jaw had been shot away and he clutched at the wound, his heels kicking into the ground.

A tall soldier named Ed Tompkins was beside Yancy, and he yelled and drove his bayonet into the chest of the wounded soldier. "Here's one Yankee who won't give us no trouble, Lieutenant!" he screamed. He then raced forward, yelling at the top of his lungs.

Yancy carried his rifle. Midnight carried him, directed by the pressure of his knees, and he never wavered. Yancy shot three men that he saw aiming a rifle at him, but he didn't stop to see the results. He kept riding, reloading, and shooting at the Federals in blue.

"We've got them!" Jackson shouted. "Drive them with the bayonet!"

The battle turned into a foot race. The Union soldiers turned and fled away from the advancing Confederates, but before they had gone very far, a Union artillery of hidden guns fired and shells began exploding around the Confederates. One of them hit so close it rocked Yancy and he almost lost his balance. His eyes were full of dirt, so he pulled Midnight to a halt so he could clean out his eyes.

When he finally could see, Yancy started to signal Midnight forward, but he looked up and saw a single blue-clad soldier that had a rifle aimed right at him. Yancy threw up his pistol and fired. The shot struck the Federal soldier and drove him backward. His finger was still on the trigger and he shot at the blue sky above. Yancy slowly eased Midnight forward then stopped to peer down at the soldier.

Around them was still the chaos and thunder and maddening yells of a battlefield, but for a moment Yancy was encased in quiet as he saw the first man he had ever killed. He was an older man with a russet beard, and his eyes were open. His uniform was dyed scarlet with his blood. His final expression was one of surprise as if to say, *What? This can't be happening to me!*

Yancy stared at him for a moment, but the blood of battle was still thrumming in his veins, and Midnight was spoiling to run. He reloaded his rifle, took it in his right hand and his pistol in his left, and spurred Midnight forward, yelling like fury.

But Jackson called them back.

The Reverend Colonel Pendleton then activated his big guns across the road, decimating the column moving along it. He raised his head and cried, "Lord, have mercy on their souls."

The Battle of Fallen Waters was over. As Yancy withdrew with Captain Gilmer's company, he saw a Confederate body lying in a crumpled way as if it had fallen from a great height. He dismounted and turned the body over and saw it was Private Birdwell. "Birdie," he whispered, "you'll never get back to marry Ellen Mae now." Yancy thought of how she would cry when she learned of her lover's death. *And his mother and father will weep, and his friends — all will suffer an awful loss.*

For the first time Yancy realized just what a sacrifice war was — not just for the men fighting, but for their families, their loved ones, their friends, their countrymen. *General Jackson said it,* he thought sadly: *"War is the sum of all evil."*

He hurried to report back to Jackson's headquarters, and General Jackson greeted him immediately. "Sergeant Tremayne, are you and your horse fresh or are you battle weary, sir?" he asked sternly.

"We are ready and waiting for our duty, sir," Yancy answered.

"Good, good. I have dispatches for Richmond, so you can ride?"

"Yes, sir."

"And Sergeant Tremayne —"

"Sir?"

"The sooner Richmond knows of all of our movements, the better they can direct this war and give us timely orders. Your horse is fastest in the Confederate Army, I imagine, except for maybe Colonel Stuart's. Ride hard. Don't stop."

Yancy and Midnight headed for Richmond.

Abraham Lincoln stared at the men of his cabinet gathered in the room with him. He had listened to their arguments, but basically what was being said was summed up by the blunt secretary of war, Edwin Stanton. "Mr. President, we must give the people something to see. We need a military victory."

Lincoln had been opposed to bringing on action, but finally he was convinced. "Very well, then, we shall have it."

The commander chosen to lead the army in this first campaign was General Irvin

McDowell, a well-regarded graduate and instructor at West Point. Until the war, he had served in the adjutant general's office in Washington.

As the days of preparation took place, there was no secret about what was going to happen. It seemed that every man on the street knew the army was preparing to do battle, and most of them knew where the first field of battle was to be. It was near a creek called Bull Run, which was adjacent to a small town called Manassas.

There was almost a holiday air as the army was sent to war with marshal music, stirring tunes by marching bands, cakes and doughnuts by the thousands baked by the ladies of the land. In fact, the North was so certain of an easy victory that many families in their carriages went to the site of the impending battle and had picnics and visited with each other on a hillside overlooking the picturesque creek of Bull Run and the Manassas Crossroads.

As the Army of the Potomac marched out of Washington headed southwest, Lincoln's face grew sad, and he whispered, "Some of those young men will die. How can I bear it?"

General McDowell listened to the cries of "Forward to Richmond!" fill the air, but he moved his army slowly. He was an experienced soldier but not a brilliant strategist; nor was he the man to inspire troops.

The Confederates were well aware of both the strategic and tactical moves of the Federals, because there were spies in Washington that kept close tabs on the movement of the Union army. Commanding generals Joe Johnston and P. G. T. Beauregard knew the movements of the Federals almost as well as they themselves did.

On Friday, July 19, the 1st Brigade, led by General Jackson, arrived at Manassas Junction. He had given few orders, and Yancy had stuck close to his side acting as a courier. Now the men were placed in a line along Bull Run Creek and were ordered to stay in reserve. At this time there were arguments among the top-ranking Confederate generals of where the Union charge would be made.

On a blistering Sunday, July 21, it was obvious that the Federals were advancing. Yancy was by his commander's side during the whole time, except when he was assigned to dispatch messages. Midnight was the fastest horse on the Confederate side, and he never seemed to tire.

Finally, the attack came, as McDowell

threw his army forward. The Confederates stiffened and General Jackson took his stand on a small rise. Still ordered to hold in reserve, he watched calmly as the battle raged on back and forth. Jackson was clearly outlined against the sky on the knoll; though, of course, it was doubtful that anyone would take him for a general from his nondescript uniform and awkward, small Little Sorrel. Still, he carried a certain authority as he watched, occasionally through his field glasses, the battle raging just below. Shrapnel from Union shells sometimes showered about him. He never even flinched. At one point it seemed a sharpshooter targeted him. A bullet came so close between him and Yancy that Yancy could feel the hot air as it whined by. Then another, so close to Yancy's hair that it stirred it a bit, and convulsively Yancy ducked. Jackson didn't blink.

Uncertainly Yancy said, "Sir? Don't you think you might take cover from that sharpshooter that's firing at you?"

Jackson turned to him. His face was grim, his mouth a tight, hard line. His eyes were like the very core of blue flame, sparking dangerously. At that moment Yancy realized that General Thomas Jackson was, indeed, a dangerous man. "How do you know he's not aiming for you?" Jackson said drily and turned back to view the field through his glasses.

One more bullet came close, but not as close as the other two, whistling a few feet alongside Yancy's knees. With a self-control he had no idea he possessed, he managed not to jerk away and sat tall and straight in the saddle. It seemed that Jackson could bring out this quality of bravery in men.

The Federals advanced and were driven back by fierce Confederate forces, but the Union troops seemed to be coming from all sides. The Confederates were hard pressed all along the front.

Jackson pointed and stated, "Look, General Bee is being pushed back. They've been shot to pieces."

Yancy saw General Bee turn, the agony of defeat on his face. He had lost his hat and his sword was bent. Then General Bee saw Jackson, and he called out so all could hear him, "Look, men, there stands Jackson like a stone wall! Rally behind the Virginians!"

Jackson could stand it no longer; though he had been given no orders, he shouted the command, "Charge, brigade! Drive them from the field!" He spurred forward, and Yancy stayed by his side.

The rest of the day was a time of thunder

and confusion, a time of blood and fear. More battle, more death, and after a while Yancy's mind rebelled against seeing the faces of the men, the horrors inflicted on both sides, the carnage.

Slowly, almost imperceptibly, the battle began to turn against the North. A charge by Jackson's 33rd Virginia regiment and by Stuart's cavalry were pivotal points in the battle that made the Northern troops retreat, and then that retreat became an insane rout. Soldiers threw down their arms and ran on foot; teamsters driving carts stampeded the crowds; the road was packed with retreating cavalry, sutlers, civilians, companies, even whole regiments of men running back toward Washington. They left their arms, their supplies, their carts and horses, their wounded, and their dead.

As the Union army fled, Jackson tried to convince his superior officers that this was the time to strike Washington, but no one would listen. He turned to Yancy in despair and said, "Now is the time to win this war, but no one sees it."

Yancy said, "Our men are pretty tired, sir."

"We'll never be in a better position to strike Washington than we are now. Go find General Johnston; I've written this note. But you tell him that the 1st Virginia Brigade will attack Washington alone if we have to!"

Yancy said, "Yes, sir!" He wheeled Midnight around and took off across the broken battlefield.

He delivered the message to General Johnston who said, "No, we're too weak and they'll be behind the barricades. Tell Jackson we have won the victory."

Dispiritedly Yancy rode back and gave Jackson the message.

Jackson just replied, "Very well. Here, Sergeant. I have written a report for the president. Take it to Richmond. Remain there until you get an audience with him."

Yancy rode Midnight south toward Richmond, believing that the battle was over and he was safe, paralleling the Confederate lines to the east. But he had not ridden more than a mile when he suddenly saw that part of the battle was still raging. A small group of Federals were engaged in a desperate fight with a force of Confederates. The Confederates appeared to be winning because they outnumbered the opposing force, but Yancy was a soldier, and he had to fight.

He tied Midnight to a scrub oak then ran forward, loading his rifle as he ran. But by the time he reached the line of battle, the men in blue had fled with the Confederates in full pursuit. Yancy considered them and realized that the Federals were sure to be taken prisoner.

He remembered his first duty was to carry out General Jackson's orders. He turned back . . . then suddenly stopped dead still.

Not ten feet away was a wounded Union officer, a lieutenant, sitting with his back against a tree. His hat was on the ground. Locks of his sandy brown hair, fine and caked with sweat and battle grime, had fallen down over his forehead. His tunic was covered with blood. He had a pistol in his hand that was aimed directly at Yancy. The lieutenant's eyes were clear enough, and the pistol in his hand was steady.

Yancy stopped dead still then threw up his rifle, but he knew that he had not finished loading it. There was no charge in the barrel, so helplessly he lowered it again.

At that moment, as he saw the officer's finger tighten on the trigger, Yancy Tremayne understood with a shock that he was only a few seconds from death. He would be facing a God whom he had never served. Strangely enough, he felt little fear, only regret that he'd never found God. A cry leaped unbidden from his lips: "God, forgive me!"

He then waited for the shot that would send him to eternity.

CHAPTER SEVENTEEN

As Yancy stared into the barrel of the pistol aimed directly at his heart, he was very aware of all of his surroundings. He could still hear the faint cries of the Confederates, chasing the company that this Union lieutenant belonged to, or so he supposed. The chilling Rebel yell carried on the still air. He could feel each great drop of sweat that rolled off his forehead and down his nose and cheeks. He could smell burning gunpowder in his nostrils.

Yancy's hands were trembling. He was intensely aware of the details of the wounded lieutenant, even noticing that he had a gold ring on his finger on his right hand, the hand that held the pistol that was aimed at his heart.

But now, even as he took these inconsequential details into his mind, he was very aware of his overall state of mind. Since he had cried out to God, he was amazed to find that the fear that had burned in him was gone. Calmly he waited for the lieutenant to fire, even standing up straight and turning slightly to face him full front. As the seconds ticked off, he couldn't understand why the end didn't come.

He shifted his gaze from the round muzzle of the pistol upward until he focused on the face of the officer. Oddly, he thought, *He looks like a good man.* He didn't expect to find goodness in a man trying to kill him, and he was unsure of what quality in the man's face made him think such a thing.

The gray eyes of the soldier stared at him steadily.

Yancy stared back, expressionlessly, and then he leaned forward, unconsciously anticipating the force of the bullet that would kill him. But no shot came.

Abruptly the officer dropped the gun into his lap. A deadly weariness washed over his face. He was pale and his lips were moving unsteadily as he spoke. "I'll be in the presence of God soon, and I don't want the blood of a helpless man on my hands." He slumped forward, his chin falling on his chest.

With somewhat of a shock Yancy realized that he was still alive and that he wasn't going to die, in the next few minutes anyway.

He fell to his knees, bowed his head, and cried, "Oh, God, I believe that Jesus is the Son of the living God, and I believe He died for my sins. I put my faith in Him and I ask You, God, to save me from my sins and make me into the man You want me to be!"

He knelt there for only a few moments, and a strange peace descended upon him. Slowly he got to his feet and found that his hands were now steady.

Yancy went to the wounded man, knelt down beside him, and took the pistol that lay on the man's lap. As he did, he saw that there was a wound in his leg that was bleeding. But it was just a graze, on the outside of his thigh. He opened the officer's tunic and saw an entry wound just down and on the left of his chest. He thought that probably the ball had missed the lung, but when he eased him forward, he realized that the bullet hadn't come out.

Gently he propped the man back against the tree. Running to where Midnight waited, he grabbed an old muslin shirt out of his saddlebag. After he returned to the wounded man, he ripped the shirt into shreds and removed the man's coat. He tied the strips of the shirt together and took a larger piece and placed it over the wound that was bleeding. He used the strips to tie

343

the rough bandage in place. Then he cut the man's trousers off and bandaged the wound in his thigh.

Yancy was just finishing up bandaging his leg when the man's dull gray eyes opened and he murmured, "Do you have any water?"

"Yes, I'll get my canteen." He once again rose and went to Midnight and got his canteen. He took the cap off and held it to the man's lips.

The soldier grabbed the canteen and looked as if he was going to gulp it down.

Yancy pulled it away and said, "Don't drink too much right now, because of your wound. Just sip it. After we get you fixed up you can have more."

The soldier's eyes were steady now, and he was lucid. He nodded and took only three small sips. "Thanks for the water."

Yancy, kneeling beside him, asked, "Why didn't you kill me?"

The lieutenant managed to smile. "For the same reason you're not killing me. We didn't want blood on our hands. Blood of unarmed men, anyway."

"What's your name, Lieutenant?"

"Leslie, Leslie Hayden." The young man closed his eyes and Yancy thought he was losing consciousness. But he opened them again to regard Yancy gravely. His voice was faint, but Yancy could clearly hear him. "I'm going to ask you a favor, Sergeant. I think I've lost too much blood. Would you carry a message to my family?"

Yancy answered, "I don't think you're going to die, but I'll do what you ask."

"My father lives just outside of Richmond, just south of the Episcopalian church. His name is Dr. Jesse Hayden. If I don't make it, will you go and tell him and my mother that I died trusting in the Lord? And tell them that I'm not afraid. I'm not afraid at all anymore."

Suddenly Yancy knew what he had to do. This man in one sense was the enemy, and Yancy had sworn to defend his homeland from men like this soldier; but now he was no longer a soldier. He was now a noncombatant, and he had shown Yancy mercy.

Yancy made a hard decision. "I'll take you to your family, Lieutenant Hayden, and your father can treat your wounds."

Surprise washed over Hayden's bloodless face. "But if we get caught, you could be executed for giving aid and comfort to the enemy."

"Then we won't get caught. I'll be back. You just hang on."

The roadside was littered with field packs

and even weapons that the Federals had thrown away in their disorganized rout. Yancy had passed a wagon about a quarter of a mile back, a supply wagon with blankets and tents. Someone had taken the horse and run. Yancy rode Midnight to it, hitched him up, and hurried back to Lieutenant Hayden. He jumped out of the wagon and said, "This should get us back to Richmond with you as comfortable as can be, under the circumstances."

"My uniform . . ." Hayden said weakly.

"I've got some work clothes in my pack. We're about the same size." He pulled his extra shirt and a pair of work pants that he wore sometimes in camp when doing rough work. Being as careful as he could, he took off Hayden's tunic and redressed him. He had fine officer's boots, so Yancy took those and, wrapping the uniform and boots together, threw them to the side of the road. He had seen some dead soldiers in the field where they had been skirmishing, but somehow Yancy didn't think he could stoop to stripping them of their shoes. He had one pair of extra socks, and he put those on the wounded man and thought that would have to do.

"All right, Lieutenant Hayden, it's going to hurt, but I've got to get you in that wagon." Leaning down, Yancy put his arm around Hayden and pulled him to his feet. He heard the man sigh heavily, but he didn't cry out. They staggered over to the back of the wagon. Hayden was almost dead weight, and for a few moments Yancy wondered if he would be able to bodily lift him into it, but somehow Hayden managed to summon some strength and drew himself up to get up onto the tailgate. He then fell heavily on the bed of blankets.

Yancy jumped up into the bed and managed to pull him into a more comfortable position. "If anybody stops us, let me do the talking."

Hayden was lying flat on his back, staring up at him. "Why are you doing this?"

Yancy thought for a moment, then he smiled slightly. "Lieutenant, I think that God is telling me to help you." His own words surprised him. He hesitated then went on, "This is the first time I've ever heard from God, so I guess I'd better do what He says."

He jumped to the ground and put the tailgate up on the wagon. Quickly he climbed into the seat, snapped the reins, and muttered, "Come on, Midnight, we have long miles to go."

■ ■ ■ ■

It was a smoky, sultry night in Richmond. Thinking hard, Yancy remembered having seen the Episcopal church just south of the heart of town. He skirted around the city. There were few people stirring, but he suspected that downtown and around the capitol would be one great buzzing hive of activity. But it was quiet, with very few home lights glowing, in this gracious residential section.

The moonlight was brilliant; its silver light bathed the street in argent beams. Before they had ridden out, he had asked Lieutenant Hayden what his father's house looked like, and the Lieutenant had described it as "a large two-story house with four gables in the front and framed by two enormous walnut trees."

The description was accurate enough, and Yancy pulled Midnight to a halt. Quickly, he tied the lines off and jumped into the back of the wagon. He hadn't wanted to waste time stopping to check on his passenger. Hayden had been very quiet, and by the time Yancy found his family home, he was afraid he might have died. He checked him and saw that he still had a faint pulse and his breathing was very shallow; he was unconscious, but he lived.

Yancy jumped out of the wagon and looked up and down the street. It was an elegant street, with two-story family homes, great live oak trees, magnolias, elms, and walnut and pecan trees. Few of the windows were lit. Yancy didn't know what time it was, but it was late.

At the Hayden residence there was only one small light in an upstairs window, and the home had a private, reserved air that made Yancy wonder exactly how he would approach this family of Union sympathizers. He still wore his Confederate gray uniform and forage cap. Undoubtedly this family would not exactly welcome him with open arms. Still, he knew he had to get Hayden to his father.

He went up the steps onto the wooden veranda, and his boots seemed to make a lot of noise. He knocked on the door, quietly and softly. There was no answer. Sighing, he turned to go back to check on Hayden.

Then suddenly behind him was a sharp wedge of light, a quiet tread on the porch, abrupt darkness, and then a woman's voice. "Stop right where you are, Johnny Reb. Be very still, or I'll shoot you. Put your hands up over your head."

Yancy froze, put his hands up over his head, and said in a voice as calm as he could manage, "I'm looking for Dr. Hayden."

"What for? What do you want with him?"

"I'm going to turn around now. Please don't shoot me." He turned around with his hands lifted high.

There in the shimmery moonlight, he saw a young woman who was indeed holding a pistol in each hand. Both of them were cocked and both of them were pointed at his chest. She had slipped out of the front door and stood in the shadows in the corner of the entryway.

Yancy swallowed hard. "I have the doctor's son in that wagon. He's been shot and he'll die if he doesn't get medical attention."

The pistols wavered just a bit. "You wouldn't have Leslie in that wagon. He's a lieutenant in the 2nd Division, United States Army."

"Yes, ma'am, I know."

"And you're a Confederate soldier."

"Yes, ma'am."

She stared at him. She was wearing night-clothes, with a thick robe. Her eyes were great dark pools in a white, heart-shaped face. Her hair cascaded over one shoulder and reached almost to her waist. Moonlight made everything look colorless, only gradations of white and black, but he had the idea that her hair was light-colored, though not blond. She was tiny, her shoulders narrow, her hands small. In them the pistols looked gigantic, but with a sort of oddball humor, Yancy reflected that from this end they would probably look huge to anyone, no matter who held them.

"Ma'am —" Yancy began.

That moment the front door opened and Yancy saw it was an older man, tall but stoop-shouldered, wearing a robe. "What is it, Lorena?"

"I don't know, Father. Some soldier that says he wants you," she answered disdainfully. The pistols, once again, were steady.

"Are you Dr. Hayden?" Yancy asked.

"I am. And you are?"

"My name is Yancy Tremayne, doctor."

"He's a Confederate soldier," the woman said harshly.

"So I see," the older man said quietly. "How can I help you, Sergeant Tremayne?"

"Dr. Hayden, I found your son on the battlefield at Manassas Crossroads. He told me where you live and I brought him to you."

Dr. Hayden started and asked alertly, "What? Where is he?"

351

"He's in the wagon."

"Lorena, go get that lantern," Dr. Hayden said, pulling his night robe closer about him.

Still the woman pointed the pistols at Yancy, staring at him unblinkingly.

"Please lower those pistols, miss. They could go off."

"They will go off if you're lying," she said fiercely.

"Nonsense, Lorena, what do you think? That this man has come to lure me outside and assassinate me? Go back in and get that lantern, girl, and put those things away before someone gets shot," Dr. Hayden insisted.

She lowered the pistols, but slowly and reluctantly. Her look at Yancy was still hard, cold, and suspicious.

"Ma'am, here's my pistol, in the holster at my side. You can take it if you wish."

"Give it to me."

Wordlessly he unsnapped the flap, took his service pistol out, and handed it to her. Silently she took all three guns inside. Immediately she came back out with a lantern.

The three of them now hurried to the wagon and looked over the side. The woman held the lantern high, and in the lurid light they could clearly see the paper white face of the wounded man.

She whispered, "Leslie . . . Oh no, it *is* Leslie. . . ."

With a swift movement, she shoved the lantern into Yancy's hands, lowered the endgate, and jumped into the wagon. She laid two fingers by his throat. "He's alive, Father. Breathing shallow, pulse shallow, but he's alive."

"We must get him inside," Dr. Hayden said. "I'll get Elijah to help us carry him in." He moved quickly to the house, night robe flapping behind him.

Gently she touched Leslie's face then looked up. "Who did you say you were?"

"My name is Yancy Tremayne. My family lives outside of Lexington. Who are you, miss?"

"I'm Lorena Hayden, Leslie's sister. You're a Confederate soldier. . . . My brother is a Union officer. . . ."

"Yes, ma'am," Yancy said patiently. "I took off his uniform and put some of my clothes on him."

"Why are you helping him?"

Yancy had no time to answer for the doctor was back, and beside him was a black man, perhaps six-five and massive. "Elijah, we need to get Leslie in. Do you think you can carry him?"

"I 'spect I can, sir."

"Here, I'll help." Yancy leaped up into the wagon and lifted Hayden's shoulders while Elijah lifted his legs. Together they eased him to the back of the wagon. Then Elijah picked him up as easily as he would a child.

"Put him in his room, Elijah," Dr. Hayden ordered.

"Yes, sir."

They followed him into the house, Yancy behind Lorena Hayden. A pretty black woman with huge dark eyes was lighting candles and lanterns. As they entered the now well-lit foyer, Yancy saw that his hunch was right. Lorena had light brown hair with lighter golden streaks in it. She was small — she might only come up to his chest — but she held herself ruler-straight, and she walked proudly. The stiff, uncompromising line of her spine showed him that she still was not happy to turn her back on him.

Yancy was sitting in the Haydens' kitchen. The maid servant, Missy, had fixed him what would normally be called a breakfast, though it was about ten o'clock at night. But it was fresh and hot and delicious, and Yancy ate heartily. Seated at Missy's work counter by the stove, she had put before him ham and eggs and biscuits and grits.

Oddly, Elijah and Missy stood by the

stove, silently watching him eat. Missy's hands were clasped in front of her apron, while Elijah stood silently, his hands clasped behind his back. Yancy wondered if they were slaves, but then he thought that surely they must not be, since it appeared that the Haydens were obviously Northern sympathizers. Of course, not all Southerners held slaves. Anna Jackson's maid, Hetty, was a free woman, a paid servant.

Yancy realized that they probably wouldn't speak unless spoken to, so he said, "This is mighty fine cooking, Missy. Thank you."

"Why, you're welcome, Mr. Tremayne. Maybe you want some molasses and some butter to put on them biscuits?"

"I would appreciate that, Missy."

As she was fetching it for him, Lorena and her father came in.

Yancy got to his feet at once, almost standing at attention. "How is he?"

"Sleeping, but very weak," Dr. Hayden said. "Luckily the bullet was lodged very close under the skin in his back, and I was able to remove it fairly easily. I think he has a broken rib, but at least the bullet didn't hit any vital organs. Elijah, please go sit with him and call me if he stirs in the slightest. Missy, my wife is with Leslie right now, but she's exhausted. Please see if you can get her to go back to bed."

"Yes, sir," they murmured and slipped out.

Dr. Hayden turned back to Yancy, who studied the man. He was tall, as Leslie Hayden was, over six feet, though he had a slight stoop. They were slender men, with classic features, and Dr. Hayden had bequeathed to both his son and daughter his fine light brown hair with golden streaks. Dr. Hayden had a thick sweeping mustache. "Please, Sergeant Tremayne. Sit down and finish your meal."

Missy had made a pot of coffee. Lorena fixed cups for herself and her father, and then they sat on two of the high stools in the kitchen.

Yancy felt somewhat awkward, but he was still hungry. He sat down and finished his last biscuit and the final bites of eggs and grits. Carefully he wiped his mouth with a fine linen napkin that, somehow, he found incongruous in the circumstances. Finally he said, "I know you're wondering about all of this."

"I know it was a good thing that you got Leslie here when you did, Sergeant Tremayne. Much longer, and my son likely wouldn't have survived without you."

Lorena's eyes narrowed. Now he could see that she had very dark blue eyes, almost black. Her mouth was well-shaped, her lips rather full but not vulgarly so. She asked in an even voice, "Can you tell us exactly why you brought him here? What could possibly have happened between you, who are obviously sworn enemies?"

Yancy murmured, "It's a strange story and I don't understand some of it myself yet."

Lorena and Dr. Hayden watched him intently.

He was silent for long moments. Narrowing his eyes, he lifted his head and stared into space, trying desperately to think what to tell these people, how little or how much. Regardless of the fact that he had given aid to Leslie Hayden, he had no intention of telling these Union sympathizers anything that could be construed as information about the war. He knew very well that the newspapers would all have accounts about the battle in the morning, but still he felt it wouldn't be right for him to tell them. And he certainly wasn't going to tell them that he was a courier for General Jackson. Jackson was secretive to the point of paranoia anyway, and besides that, it wouldn't be right to let them know of his position and his mission.

His mission . . .

Though he had been, for the past several

hours, concerned about Leslie Hayden, he now realized that he was on a mission. He was in possession of important — and secret — dispatches to the president of the Confederate States of America from one of his top commanders. Suddenly his heart beat faster and unevenly, a raw and uncomfortable feeling. Those dispatches were still out in his saddlebag in the wagon, unguarded . . . and almost forgotten.

Yancy jumped up so quickly that he knocked over his stool. "I–I'm sorry, but I have to go."

"What?" Dr. Hayden said in astonishment. "But — but surely you can stay and at least tell us who you are and explain to us how it came about that we should be in such great debt to you!"

"No, no, sir, I'm very sorry but I really must leave now," Yancy said, striding to the foyer to retrieve his forage cap. "Ma'am, may I please have my pistol back?" Dr. Hayden and Lorena had followed him.

Her eyes narrowed and her face grew dark with suspicion. "And why is it that you should have to leave in such a hurry, sir? Who are you going to report to, and to whom are you going to tell of my brother, and —"

"No, Lorena, no," Dr. Hayden said with

sudden understanding. "Sergeant Tremayne surely has his own way to make. He would never betray us after he has gone to such trouble, and he has without doubt saved your brother's life. Leave him be, and let him go."

After hesitating a few moments, with obvious reluctance Lorena pulled Yancy's pistol out of a drawer in a side table in the foyer. She handed it to him without meeting his eyes.

"I'm sorry, Dr. Hayden, Miss Hayden. But I know that in the next few days you'll know — more — about this day, and what has happened between us. Between the North and the South. With your permission I would like to return and see Leslie, and then perhaps I may be able to speak more freely."

Dr. Hayden gave him his hand. "You will always be welcome in my home, Sergeant Tremayne, regardless of what happens out there in the fields of battle. Please do come back as soon as you possibly can."

"Thank you, sir. I will." Yancy turned to Lorena and searched her face, but there was nothing there except doubt and suspicion. As Yancy hurried to Midnight, Lorena and Dr. Hayden followed him to their porch. Their conversation carried to his ears, obviously unknown to the pair.

Lorena turned to her father. "I don't trust him. It just doesn't make sense."

"We will need to hear his story before we decide if it makes sense or not, Lorena," Dr. Hayden said mildly. He turned and gently put his hand on his daughter's shoulder to walk with him toward the stairs. "I think it's a miracle. This young man, I believe, has a good heart, honorable and true. I don't know how I know it, and I don't know why, but I believe the Lord touched him, and then he saved your brother. I know you're suspicious of all men, Lorena, but I think you can trust this one."

Without any reaction to their words as to give away that he had heard, Yancy mounted and rode away.

As was to be expected, Richmond was like a boiling cauldron after the victory at Manassas. In particular, the capitol had great swirling crowds of men at all hours, running in and out, shouting to each other, disappearing into offices and then coming back out on other urgent war business.

Of course the Department of War offices were insanely busy. That night, on July 22, Yancy reported there at about ten o'clock.

He was seated in an anteroom and watched men come and go, their faces by turn fiercely delighted or grievously worried, until about seven a.m. the next morning.

Yancy recognized one of the secretaries, a dry, threadbare little man with a bald pate, thick glasses, and ink-stained fingers, when he came out of one of the offices. All night long Yancy had seen the secretary call one man in, escort another man out, take papers from that one, deliver them to another. "Dispatches!" he called, as the secretaries did when they were ready to take the messages the couriers brought in. "Dispatches from the 1st Virginia Brigade — the Stonewall Brigade!" Wild cheers and calls sounded throughout the hall. General Jackson's new nickname was already famous.

Grinning like an idiot, Yancy stood and held up his hand. "Here, sir! Dispatches from the — the Stonewall Brigade!"

Men gathered around him, clapping him on the back and shaking his hand, until he was almost dizzy. "There he stood, like a stone wall!" they kept repeating. Yancy duly delivered his dispatches, and the secretary told him to wait. He was besieged by the men who demanded detailed accounts not only of the action, but of every gesture, every word, every expression of Brigadier General "Stonewall" Jackson's. Yancy talked until he was hoarse.

But eventually the men got back to their own peculiar business, and Yancy was left to sit on the hard bench again, waiting. It was a long, grueling day, sitting on a hard bench. Yancy once went out to water Midnight and retrieve his own canteen, but he was worried he might miss his summons so he hurried back inside. From time to time he dozed, even though he was uncomfortable. He was exhausted.

At about seven o'clock that night a report circulated from the war office. In the Battle of Manassas, the Federals had 3,000 dead and wounded, and they lost more than 1,400 as prisoners. These were paraded through the streets of Richmond where crowds yelled, "Live Yankees! Live Yankees!" The Confederates had lost 2,000 men of which 1,500 were wounded; only a scant dozen had been taken prisoner. Yancy did learn that General Beauregard had taken treasures also, including six thousand small arms, fifty-four field guns and five hundred rounds of ammunition.

Poignantly Yancy thought, *And one supply cart that brought a wounded Yankee home.* He had been thinking a lot about Leslie

Hayden. He didn't regret his actions. Even though some might regard his sheltering the enemy as traitorous, Yancy knew, without a doubt, that the Lord had told him to be a good Samaritan to the wounded man who had so mercifully spared his life.

Eventually the secretary returned and told Yancy, "Sir, we will have messages to return with you, but they won't be ready until tomorrow. Do you have a place to stay? I'm certain we can find room for one of Stonewall's boys!"

Yancy stood and shook his hand for the third time. "Thank you, sir, but I have some friends in town. I'll go visit them."

Yancy was glad to leave behind the roiling and boiling at the capitol. He rode slowly on Midnight, savoring the quiet after he got out of the center of town. It was a mild night, for July, with a light breeze that sometimes, as he came into the residential sections, carried on it the sweet, fresh scent of jasmine. After the stench of blood and guns and death, it was like a sweet shower to Yancy. His clothes and hair still stank of gunpowder.

He reached the Hayden home and was glad to see that there were still warm lights on both upstairs and downstairs. Although it was only about eight o'clock, he had realized that Dr. Hayden seemed frail, and he had been afraid that the household regularly retired early. Gently he tapped the front door knocker twice. He saw the curtains move in the parlor, and then Lorena Hayden opened the door.

"Hello, Sergeant Tremayne," she said. "Won't you come in?" She turned and led him into the sitting room. Although she was polite, Lorena's tone had a chilly quality about it, and her entire demeanor was distant.

Yancy wondered what had hardened this woman so, or if she simply still didn't trust him. He supposed if that was it, it would just take time to gain her trust, and Yancy was vaguely surprised at how important that suddenly seemed to be to him.

Dr. Hayden rose to greet him. Beside him was a small woman with chestnut hair who was modestly pretty, watching him with warm brown eyes.

"This is Sergeant Yancy Tremayne. He brought Leslie home, my dear. Sergeant, this is my wife, Lily."

The woman came forward at once and held out both her hands. Yancy was surprised, but he took them in his, noticing that her bones were almost birdlike in their fragility. Suddenly her kind eyes filled with tears and she said softly, "We can never thank you enough, Sergeant Tremayne, for bringing our son home."

"I — I had to do it, ma'am. It was the right — the only thing to do."

She nodded with complete understanding. "Please, sit down. If you'll excuse me, I'll go have Missy make tea. Or perhaps you prefer coffee, Sergeant?"

"Actually I do, if it's not too much trouble, ma'am," Yancy answered, taking his seat in a wing chair across from the sofa where Dr. and Mrs. Hayden had been seated. "Especially Missy's coffee. It was very good."

She nodded and left the room. Lorena sat in a matching chair next to him, her back perfectly straight, her hands folded in her lap. He saw that she was wearing a blue dress with a white lace collar. She would have looked beautiful if she were more poised, but the set of her head was so defiant and her posture so stiff that it detracted from her china doll looks.

"So how is Lieutenant Hayden?" Yancy asked Dr. Hayden.

"He's doing fairly well," he answered. "Thankfully neither bullet hit any vital organs, though he did lose a lot of blood. Actually, the wound in his leg may give him the most trouble. It tore some muscles and ligaments, and it's possible he may have a slight limp, or at least may have to walk with a cane. But he's resting comfortably, and Leslie is strong. I believe he'll recover quickly."

"Thank the Lord," Lily said, coming back in and sitting down by her husband.

"Amen," Yancy said quietly. "And that is, by the way, the message that Leslie wanted me to give you, in case . . . in case. He said he wanted you to know that he was trusting in the Lord, and that he wasn't afraid."

"The Lord has mightily blessed us, Sergeant Tremayne," Lily said, "by sparing Leslie and sending you to him."

Dr. Hayden said gravely, "We understand, Sergeant Tremayne, the position you so willingly put yourself in, and because of that I would like to explain something about our family. We — Lily, Lorena, and I — are actually what might be called neutrals in this war, although that is somewhat unrealistic under the circumstances. We love Virginia. Richmond is our home. But we could not bring ourselves to agree with secession, and we think this war is tragically, utterly wrong on both sides. I will let Leslie explain his decision to join the Union army, if he chooses to. But I wish you to know that, as a doctor, I am attending injured soldiers from the North and the South, without discrimination, and I pray every day for the end of this war and blessings and peace for all of the men who are in it."

Yancy sighed. "Thank you, sir. That does help me to understand a little. You've been caught between two forces that seem to be inescapable, just as Leslie and I were in the battle. I assume you've heard the news?" he asked hesitantly.

"Yes, we understand that the Confederate forces had a great victory," Dr. Hayden answered. "There were many, many wounded."

"Chimborazo Hospital is filled to overflowing," Lorena said sadly. "Father has worked very hard to help."

"As you said, Sergeant Tremayne, I have to. It's the right thing to do," Dr. Hayden said with a small smile.

Missy came in then with tea and coffee service, and they took a few minutes in the homey, comfortable ritual of taking refreshment.

After Missy left, Dr. Hayden continued, "And so, now that we have given you some idea of our views on the war, I hope you will see that we would never ask you to betray any confidential or sensitive information to us. But we would very much like to hear how it happened that you found Leslie and brought him home to us."

Yancy told them the story, although he didn't say what his mission was, and he downplayed the horribly tense moments when Leslie was pointing his pistol at him and Yancy was sure he was going to kill him.

"So there I was, looking down the barrel of a Yankee lieutenant's pistol, and at the time all I remember thinking is, *I don't know the Lord. I may be facing Him in the next few minutes, and I don't know Him.* So I asked God to forgive me, and I waited. But Leslie laid the pistol down in his lap and just sort of sighed. And then I prayed, hard, and asked the Lord to save me and lead me, and then I knew. I had to help Leslie," he finished.

Lily smiled and her voice was soft and glad. "I'm so glad you found the Lord, Sergeant Tremayne. Even when we are facing death, to know Him is to know life."

"My grandmother has told me that and many other things about the Lord," Yancy said. "And they're only just now starting to make sense." He smiled. "And I can tell you that I think I have a pretty good understanding of the situation you are in, about the war and struggling to stay neutral. You see, my people are Amish."

"Are they?" Lorena asked with an abrupt interest that surprised Yancy.

"Yes, they are. At least, my father and stepmother and grandmother are. My mother, my father's first wife, was half Cheyenne Indian. She died, and we came back here, to my father's family."

"Cheyenne Indian," Lorena repeated in a half whisper, her eyes wide and dark as she looked at him. "So that's it. . . . They must be handsome people. . . ."

"I beg your pardon?" Yancy said blankly. He thought he had misunderstood her.

A quick, amused smile came over Lily Hayden's gentle features, and she said, "Your countenance shows your heritage, Sergeant Tremayne, and you should be proud."

"Yes, I learned their ways and I know them," he said simply. "My mother was a wonderful woman, and I am proud of her. So my father and I returned to Lexington, to his home, and he rejoined the Amish community. He married a fine woman. She's been as good to me as my own mother. They have two children now, and my grandmother lives with them."

With some difficulty Lorena asked, "So —

so you, you obviously aren't — don't completely agree with their beliefs."

"Not all of them," he said. "They are fine Christian people, but they're extremely strict, you know."

"I admire their willingness to pay a high price for their beliefs," Dr. Hayden said. "But I understand that living that way of life is just not possible for everyone."

Missy came back in and said, "Dr. Hayden? Leslie's awake now, and I told him the sergeant was here. He'd like to see him."

"Please, by all means, Sergeant Tremayne, let Missy take you up to his room," Dr. Hayden said. "I know he has been wanting to see you and talk to you."

Missy led him upstairs to Leslie's bedroom, a rather spartan room with a big four-poster bed and armoire. With something of a start, Yancy saw that the armoire was partially open, and he saw four blue uniforms with gold braid hanging inside.

Leslie Hayden was slightly propped up, his face still almost as pale as the white bed linens. But his voice was much stronger and steady. He held out his hand, and Yancy shook it. "I'm glad you came back, Sergeant Tremayne."

"Good to see you looking so well, Lieutenant Hayden," Yancy answered. "You sure look much better than the last time I saw you."

"Since I was near dead, I hope I do look some better," Leslie said drily. "And that's thanks to you."

Yancy grinned. "And thanks to you that I'm not all the way dead."

Suddenly Leslie grew grave. "You took an enormous chance, bringing me here. I still don't understand how you expected to get by with it."

Yancy met his gaze soberly. "I've told your parents, and I want you to know, too. There are three things that happened on that bloody field that I'm sure of. I found the Lord because I thought I was going to die, and because of that my soul has been saved. Another is that I believe the Lord directed you to spare me. And lastly and most certainly, I know that the Lord told me to bring you here. I may not have heard a voice, but I knew then and I know now that it was His will that we met at that moment and in that way."

Leslie nodded thoughtfully. "I was in pain, and the battle — you know how you kind of go crazy in battle? How it's awful and horrible but all you can think of is to keep going, never to stop, to keep fighting?"

"I know that," Yancy said. "I've felt it."

"That's still how my mind was fixed when I saw you. But then — but then, after a few minutes, it's like my vision cleared, and my mind grew quiet. I knew the Lord had given me peace, and that no matter what happened, I could not and would not shoot you."

"And so it seems that this isn't a one-sided deal," Yancy said quietly. "You spared my life, and I thank you."

"And you saved mine, and I thank you," Leslie said. "And may God deliver us from ever facing each other over a battlefield again."

Yancy shifted. "About that. I'm afraid I have some fairly bad news, Lieutenant Hayden, about your outfit. I found out that those men of your company that were with you in that last little skirmish were taken prisoner. There were nine of them, right? Part of Walcott Company of the 8th Battalion?"

"How did you know that?" Leslie demanded. Then his face fell. "No, no, don't answer that. Of course I know you can't tell me. If the roles were reversed, I wouldn't tell you."

Uncomfortably Yancy shifted again. He had seen the detailed lists of the dead, wounded, missing, and those taken prisoner.

"But I do have to tell you this. You're listed as missing."

Leslie lifted his head. "Missing. Guess I'd better lay low."

"I don't know how you'll be able to rejoin your unit, Lieutenant Hayden," Yancy said.

"I'll worry about that when the time comes. By the way, it's Leslie."

"Yancy."

"There's just one more thing I'd like to tell you, Yancy," Leslie said quietly. "I love Virginia; it's been my father's home and my home our whole lives. I can't imagine living anywhere else, and that's why I took the chance of staying here when I decided to join the Union. I couldn't face moving somewhere in the North, and I know that my family would have insisted on coming with me."

"I believe they would," Yancy agreed. "You have a good, strong family."

"But I love the United States of America, too," Leslie went on steadily. "I hate the thought of this country divided, torn apart. I want Virginia to always be a part of the United States of America. It's just that simple."

"I understand," Yancy said. "Believe me, I understand."

Lorena slipped in then and came to her

brother's bedside. He reached out and took her hand. "Don't fuss. I feel fine."

She scoffed. "I didn't come up here to fuss at you like some nanny. I just wanted to tell Sergeant Tremayne that Missy has laid out a cold supper for him. After witnessing him devouring one meal, I think it's safe to think that he may be hungry." She gave Yancy a sidelong glance.

"Isn't it annoying when people talk about you like you're not in the room?" Leslie asked, his gray eyes twinkling.

"It is," Yancy answered him. "But I do have to admit that I'm hungry. I'm not surprised that Miss Hayden noticed that."

"Silly boys," Lorena grumbled, turning and marching out of the room.

Yancy watched her leave then turned back to Leslie and sighed. "She hates me."

Leslie managed a weak laugh. "She likes you. If she didn't, she wouldn't tease you."

"Really?" Yancy asked. "You think so?"

"I know so," Leslie answered. "It's when she starts getting all frosty polite that you have to watch out."

"Mmm. I'll remember that," Yancy said thoughtfully.

"See that you do," Leslie warned him. "For your own good."

Yancy moved toward the door. "You do

look tired, and I'm going to leave before your sister comes back and bodily throws me out. Good night, Leslie."

"We'll see you again, right?"

"Hope so, my friend. Hope so."

Yancy made his way back downstairs to the parlor, where Dr. Hayden and Lorena waited for him. Dr. Hayden said, "My wife has gone on to bed; she's not well. But she made me soundly promise to invite you to stay the night, Sergeant Tremayne, if you haven't made other arrangements."

"That's very kind of you, sir, but I wouldn't want to impose."

"Nonsense," Dr. Hayden said briskly, rising. "After what you have done for this family, it's as I said before, you will always be welcome in my home. Now I'm tired and I'm going to go to bed, but Missy will see to your late supper and then show you to your room."

"I'll take care of it, Father," Lorena said, rising to stand on very tiptoe to give her father a kiss on his cheek. "And I'll check on Leslie before I retire. Please don't worry. Just get some rest."

He did look tired; his shoulders were a little more stooped, and his gait was slow as he left the parlor. "I think I will be able to rest tonight. Good night, daughter. Good night, Sergeant Tremayne."

"Good night, sir."

Lorena turned to Yancy and said, "Missy's got your supper all laid out." She led him to the kitchen, where there was a fine spread of ham, potato salad, bread, and sliced apples.

Yancy bowed his head and said a short blessing in silence, in the traditional Amish way, and then ate ravenously. He hadn't had anything to eat since he had sat in this kitchen before. Even though Lorena was watching him, he was so hungry he didn't mind. Too much.

She poured him coffee and refilled his plate when he got low. When he showed signs of having enough, she said slowly, "Sergeant Tremayne, I know that I was very harsh to you when you first arrived. I'm sorry that I doubted you, but surely you can understand my feelings now that you know our story."

"I do," Yancy agreed. "It was a strange thing, what happened to me and your brother. I could hardly expect you to jump right into it and know how things were, with me being a Johnny Reb and all."

She didn't blush, but she did look slightly amused. "Well, you are, you know."

"Yes, I know," he agreed.

"Are you going to accept my apology or not?" she demanded.

"Begging your pardon, ma'am, but I don't believe I heard an apology anywhere in there."

"There wasn't?" She seemed genuinely surprised, so surprised that Yancy laughed. At first Lorena glowered at him, but then she smiled, too. "Perhaps there wasn't. So I apologize."

"Accepted."

She began to gather up the dishes and cover them with linens.

Yancy helped her. As they finished up, she showed the first sign of true discomfort with him that he had seen yet, and it secretly amused him.

"So, Sergeant Tremayne, would you like me to show you to your room now?" she asked with artificial brightness.

"That would be nice, ma'am. I have to admit that I'm tired, and I have a long ride tomorrow."

She led him toward his room and said, "Oh? Where are you — oh, no, no, never mind. Here's your room."

It was a bedroom next to Leslie's, with a bed fully long enough to accommodate Yancy's six-plus feet. It had clean linens, and the fresh smell floated in the room. On

377

a washstand was a pitcher of water, a basin, soap, hand towels, and a razor and soap-brush. Yancy smiled a little; he still didn't have to shave — his Indian legacy. "This looks wonderful, Miss Hayden," he said, and in a grateful gesture he reached out and took her hand.

She stared up at him for a few moments, still and silent, her hand warm in his. Then abruptly she pulled free and said hurriedly, "Good night, Sergeant Tremayne," and almost ran down the hall.

Softly he called after her, "Good night, Miss Hayden."

He washed, and slept, and for six hours heard no echoes of battle and knew no fear or pain.

CHAPTER EIGHTEEN

At dawn the next morning, Yancy went to the capitol. His dispatches were waiting for him, so he rode out. It was ninety miles back to the camp at Manassas Junction; since both Yancy and Midnight had been rested, they were able to make it in less than twenty-four hours, with only brief stops for rest and food and water.

On the outskirts of the camp, Yancy saw General Jackson sitting on a split-rail fence, nodding a little in the early sunlight. Beside him, Little Sorrel grazed, her reins trailing in the verdant high grass. Yancy came to a stop, and Midnight stamped and whinnied a little, as he was accustomed to do, but the general didn't stir.

Yancy watched him affectionately. No one would ever take him for a general, much less for the mighty Stonewall Jackson. Still he wore his old, dusty, threadbare major's tunic, grimy and wrinkled. As always, his beat-up forage cap sat with the bill right down to his nose. Although he sat ruler straight, as he always did even in his five-minute naps, he still looked rumpled and awkward, like a nondescript meager clerk.

So different on the battlefield, Yancy thought in wonder. He remembered his cool courage when the sharpshooter had targeted them at the Battle of Manassas. He recalled that when Jackson rode up and down the battle lines, shouting to his 1st Brigade, it stirred the blood and gave the men courage and a sense of fierce honor and grim determination to fight for Virginia and the Confederacy — and for Stonewall Jackson.

The object of Yancy Tremayne's admiring reverie jerked a little, stirred, muttered something under his breath, then looked around. "Good morning, Sergeant Tremayne."

"Good morning, sir." Yancy saluted sharply.

Slowly, with deliberation, Jackson took a lemon out of one pocket, a small paring knife out of another, cut the top off the lemon, lifted it to his lips, and began to suck out the juice. "You have my dispatches?"

"Yes, sir."

Jackson motioned to him with a peremptory wave. "Bring them here."

Yancy dismounted and handed him the courier's bag.

"Wait," he ordered.

Yancy tied Midnight to the fence then stood at parade attention.

Jackson took out his spectacles that he needed for reading. But his eyes were not weak. He could see a battlefield well enough. As he sucked on the lemon and perused his orders, the frown on his face grew darker and darker. "If they would just give me ten thousand men, I would be in Washington tomorrow," he growled. "What a waste, what a criminal waste of time and opportunity."

Yancy knew that he spoke to himself, as he often did when they were alone. Around other officers and men Jackson spoke succinctly and without giving away any indication of his feelings. Certainly he never spoke aloud to himself. But Yancy knew that because of his prior relationship with Jackson when he was just a servant, basically, and because of Anna Jackson's closeness to Yancy, General Jackson somehow trusted Yancy more and was able to let his iron guard down. Somewhat and sometimes, at least.

After another guttural grumble of exasperation, Jackson took off his glasses, tucked them away, and looked back up at Yancy. "At ease, at ease, Sergeant. Don't stand there posing like a popinjay. Sit down and tell me about Richmond."

Yancy sat on a fence rail, took off his cap, and mopped his forehead. The July sun was climbing higher in the sky. It was going to be another scorching day. "I brought the papers, sir. They're in my saddlebag. They're full of the battle, of course — and of you."

"Me?" Jackson grunted.

"Yes, sir." Yancy grinned. "They're all raving about the famous General 'Stonewall' Jackson."

"Stonewall," Jackson mused. "What General Bee said . . ."

"Yes, sir. That's your new name, sir. And they're calling us the Stonewall Brigade."

"Good, good," he murmured. "The credit should go to the noble men who fought and to God. Not to me. All that nonsense aside, Sergeant, what is the mood in Richmond? And at the capitol?"

Yancy told him about the tumult at the capitol, centered mostly around the Department of War. He described the crowds in the streets, excitedly talking and milling about, apparently only to go over and over any small detail or gossip about the battle, and related the sight of the Federal prisoners with the crowds jeering at them. And he told Jackson of Chimborazo Hospital, which Yancy had briefly toured on his way into town to get the dispatches. "Of ours, almost 1,600 wounded, sir," he finished in a low voice.

Jackson nodded. "Brave and courageous men, God will they be healed to return to stand with us once more." He jumped off the fence and mounted Little Sorrel, still working on his lemon. "Back to my headquarters, Sergeant Tremayne. I want you to brief my aides, then you can eat and rest. Rode all day and night, did you?"

Yancy untied Midnight and mounted up. "Twenty-two hours, sir, with only two short breaks for food and water," he said proudly.

Jackson reached over and patted Midnight's sleek neck approvingly. "Fastest horse in the Confederacy, I guess, and never seems to tire. No wonder Colonel Stuart keeps trying to buy him from you. And if I know that rascal, you might better keep him on a tight rein when Stuart's around. Rogue cavalrymen been known to steal what they can't buy." Jackson spurred ahead and Yancy followed, grinning.

Anna Jackson came north by train to the camp in Manassas. On the last lap of the journey, the train was absolutely packed with soldiers. They were boisterous, exuberant. Anna sat quiet and still in her seat, her gaze downcast, but it was to no avail. She noted in her writing, *"A lady seemed to be a great curiosity to the soldiers, scores of whom filed through the car to take a look."*

Finally she arrived at Manassas Junction, where an awkward young corporal with his right arm in a sling met her and told her he was to take her to a hospital to wait for the general. She sat in a tiny, dusty, deserted office beside the front entrance.

Across the street, squads of soldiers were making coffins for their fallen companions. The sight made her deeply sad. She remembered the rowdy young boys on the train and wondered how many of them would die in the battles that must surely come. She wondered if her husband would join them. And as the thought crept into her mind for perhaps the thousandth time, she turned her eyes away from the bitter sight, bowed her head and whispered, " 'But they that wait upon the Lord shall renew their strength; they shall mount up with wings as eagles; they shall run, and not be weary; and they shall walk, and not faint.' Only in You, Lord, do I find strength."

Peace settled on her like soft satin, and

she waited calmly until Jackson came driving up in an ambulance to rescue her. He jumped out and the corporal led him in.

When Jackson saw Anna, his eyes brightened, he ran to her, enveloped her in his arms, kissed her sweetly, and held her to him. He whispered, "Esposita, my darling wife, how I have missed you! How grateful I am to the Lord for bringing you to me!" As always, Jackson was oblivious to others when he was with Anna. With her, no matter who stood by or overheard or observed, he was the tender and boyishly adoring husband.

"I've missed you, my darling Thomas," she said, clinging to him. "Every day, every hour."

"Here's the buggy the Kyles have been kind enough to loan me. We're going to go to my headquarters," he said, entwining her arm with his. "Such a grand name for a tent in the Kyles' yard." He smiled down at her, for she was so tiny that she barely reached his chest. He smiled often with Anna . . . but almost never without her.

She squeezed his arm and said, "It doesn't matter, Thomas. You are my home, and wherever and whatever it is, it is a joyous home indeed to me."

Jackson, disdaining a driver, drove the buggy himself. Theodorus Kyle's farm was about two miles from the Manassas railroad junction, and the brigade had encamped around the farm.

Theodorus and Deidre Kyle had a large boisterous family. Their own four daughters lived with them — for their husbands were serving in the 1st Brigade — and between them they had nine children. The Kyle farmhouse was large and spacious, of two floors, with two wings that had been added over time as sleeping porches. The Kyles had begged Jackson to stay with them, but with his customary humility — in some matters — he declined, insisting that he would be much more comfortable in a command tent, with his long hours and men constantly coming and going. He never realized what an honor and a boost of reputation it would have been for the Kyles to have him as a houseguest, for his fame had spread throughout the South. Without doubt he was the the most revered and admired commander in the Confederate Army.

Anna confided her discomfort on the train

to her husband, though softening the effect to a mild embarrassment.

On later trips Jackson promised to send her an escort. However, he knew, even this soon after Manassas, if the soldiers would have known Anna to be Stonewall Jackson's wife, she would never have suffered the slightest disquiet. Indeed, the 1st Brigade regarded her with true reverence, believing she was a saint walking on earth. It wouldn't be long before the entire army believed it, too.

They passed the first camp tents, with two men sitting outside playing cards. As the buggy went by, one of them jumped up and called out the now-famous Rebel yell, and men flooded out of the tents and to the roadside. They hoorahed and called and whistled and cheered. The Stonewall Brigade did this every single time Jackson rode through the camp, even if they were in drill formation. The officers, grinning, allowed it.

For his part, Jackson gave no sign of recognition at all, driving and looking straight ahead. It had become his habit when he was on horseback to ride around the camp for precisely this reason, but in the buggy he had to take the farm road right down the middle of the brigade's tents. As they passed, the wild chorus went on and on, with men crowding to the very sides of the buggy, waving their hats and grinning.

Anna pinched his arm lightly. "Impressive, Stonewall."

"Don't tease, my darling," he said awkwardly. "They're a bunch of holloing fools, is all."

Finally they went up the private lane to the Kyle farmhouse, and there in the shady side yard was Jackson's spacious command tent. Lined up in precise rows outside were his staff officers and aides. Slightly to the side were Yancy, Chuckins Satterfield, Peyton Stevens, and Sandy Owens. Every single man in attendance was grinning like the village idiot. There was very little time for levity on Stonewall Jackson's staff, but he had been so excited about Anna's arrival that they all were in a lighthearted mood.

Jackson helped Anna down from the buggy, and to the colonel's and major's bemusement, the first person he introduced her to was his manservant Jim, who had come to take the buggy to the farm's stables. He was a tall handsome mulatto with a flashing toothy smile, and he bowed as deeply as any courtier when Jackson said, "My dear, this is Jim, who came to me after the Battle of Falling Waters. Jim, I have the pleasure and honor to introduce you to my wife, Mrs. Jackson."

Anna smiled at him and inclined her head, as ladies do when introduced to gentlemen.

A smile of pleasure lit Jim's face. "It's a right honor to meet you, ma'am. And I want you to know that I takes good care of the general, I surely do."

"I'm so glad," Anna said kindly. "I shall rest better now, knowing that he is in such capable hands."

Now Jackson escorted her to meet his staff, and she greeted each one of them, from colonel to waterboy, with the same warmth and grace. When she came to Yancy, she held out both her hands for him to hold. Then, to the envy of every man present, she said with obvious delight, "Oh Yancy, how good it is to see you again! Hetty and I have missed you so much. You were always so very helpful to us. And especially this summer I have missed you in the garden. I believe you have a gift for gardening, for everything you did for me has prospered amazingly."

Still holding her hands in his, Yancy said somewhat shyly, "Thank you, ma'am, but it's not me that the plants and flowers love. It's you and your tender care."

"Perhaps, but I must share the glory of

the daisy-mums with you and your grandmother," she said lightly. "Tell me, how is your family?"

"Very well, ma'am. We write regularly, and it seems they are having a peaceful and prosperous year," he answered somewhat wistfully.

"I'm glad," Anna said. Finally she withdrew her hands from his and finished, "I hope while I am here that you may take me to see Midnight. I should like to see him again, such a glorious horse."

"I hope so, too, ma'am," Yancy said gratefully.

She moved on to Chuckins Satterfield, and the general introduced him. Despite Anna's best efforts at making him feel at ease, Chuckins's round chubby face turned scarlet, and he could only bow and gulp and mumble.

Next was the sophisticated, aristocratic Peyton Stevens. Jackson introduced him, and he swept off his dashing hat, a wide-brimmed gray felt with one side pinned up with a gold pin and sporting two small red feathers. He bent one knee, crossed one arm over, and bowed deeply, an old-fashioned court obeisance. "Mrs. Jackson, if I may say, I thought this day to be beautiful, but it is nothing compared to you."

General Jackson growled, "Impertinent young pup."

Anna gave him a mischievous sidelong glance. "Why, Thomas, I did not know that you had such chivalrous young gentlemen on your staff. I am very pleased to meet you, Sergeant Stevens."

Next she met Sandy Owens, who also was something of a ladies' man but who didn't have the panache of Peyton Stevens. "Mrs. Jackson, all I can say is that now I can see that indeed our general is a fortunate man," he said with obvious sincerity.

"Thomas and I are both blessed that the Lord led us to each other," she said.

And this began a brief holiday for General Jackson.

Anna had a sweet voice, both in speech and song. Jackson enjoyed when she read aloud, but he especially loved for her to sing to him. She sang "Dixie" for him; it was the first time he had heard it. He loved the song and made her sing the lively ditty over and over until they were both giggling like children.

Anna met the officers of the army and seemed especially impressed by General Joe Johnston, the commanding officer of what had come to be called the Army of the Valley. He spoke highly of Jackson, which, though Thomas was characteristically a modest man, was certainly gratifying to him.

Nearly every officer spoke of his valor and steadfastness at the Battle of Manassas. One officer commented, "If it hadn't been for your husband, I think we might have lost the battle."

Jackson said, with a reply that was to become characteristic, "No, Major, you must give credit to God and to the noble men who did the fighting."

It was a wonderful visit for Anna and Jackson, but of course it had to come to an end. He took her back to the train station at Manassas Crossing, this time with an escort of two slightly wounded men — one of them the shy corporal, who was almost beside himself with the sense of honor — who would accompany her all the way to their home in Lexington. She found herself struggling not to cry, for it upset Thomas very much when she wept.

He clasped her to him. "Sometimes I think the hardest thing about this war is being separated from you. I'll have you come again when I can, esposita."

"Soon, God willing, Thomas, my dear. I pray that it will be soon."

The sweltering July melted into a sizzling

August. Oddly, as if the seasons were to be separated by the stroke of a sharp knife, the first week of September 1861 suddenly turned into autumn, with cool dewy mornings, fine freshening breezes in the afternoon, and evenings just chilly enough to really enjoy sitting around a fire, one of the few pleasures of camp life. These two months passed idyllically, with only a few very minor skirmishes, usually caused by Federals lurking around the lines, getting lost, and blundering into Confederate territory. The casualties were light and the skies were clear of the smoke of cannons and thousands of rounds of musket fire.

But idleness in a soldier's camp can become very monotonous and boring. Yancy and Peyton were glad that they were couriers, because at least they kept busy, mostly riding back and forth to the different commands of the Army of the Shenandoah that were still ranged up and down northern Virginia.

Yancy only went to Richmond once in August and twice in September, when he got to visit the Haydens. Leslie had been on a steady mend, and though he and Yancy didn't directly speak of it, Yancy knew he was planning on rejoining the Army of the Potomac soon.

As September wore on, the weather got steadily colder, and in the first week of October, the camp at Manassas had their first hard frost. The Kyle family had donated an unused cast-iron stove to General Jackson. On Monday, October 7, Jim and Yancy were struggling to install the stove in Jackson's tent. Yancy often still did chores like this for General Jackson, much as he did when he worked at the Jackson home in Lexington.

The struggle to install the stove was because General Jackson was supervising them. Inactivity irritated Yancy, but it made Thomas Jackson as grouchy and touchy as a wounded bear. Now he barked, "No, I don't want it that close to my cot. I'll be too hot trying to sleep! And not too close to my prayer bench, either. If that should get scorched I'd have the hide of both of you. Go on, put it over there by the aide's desk."

At this desk sat Chuckins, scribbling fanatically. He didn't dare look up or make a sound.

"But, sir," Jim said placatingly, "that there desk is right by the tent flap. Sure enough all the heat would go out that hole every time there's all the comin's and the goin's."

"Then put it —" Jackson began.

But he was interrupted when a voice from

outside the said tent flap called, "Sir? Orders from Secretary Benjamin, General Jackson."

"What? Come in, come in," Jackson ordered quickly.

The courier came in, a young bespectacled captain in the uniform of the War Department Army Staff.

Yancy recognized him; in fact, he had handed over a couple of dispatch bags to this man.

The captain came to strict attention and saluted. "Captain Monroe Hillyard, sir, of Secretary of War Benjamin's staff."

Jackson returned the salute and bid him, "Come here, come here." He took the courier's knapsack and took out a bundle of four thick envelopes. Opening the first one, he frowned, took out his spectacles, read it again, then looked up. "You men are dismissed," he said, now calmly and quietly, to Jim, Yancy, and Chuckins.

They fled. But Yancy loitered around outside the tent with Chuckins, for he was almost certain he had seen a glance of recognition from Captain Hillyard. Couriers, of course, rarely knew the contents of their dispatches, but for a captain on Secretary Judah Benjamin's staff to act as a courier meant that likely he knew very well the messages he was carrying. The chances of his telling Yancy or anyone else about them was extremely remote, but Yancy was so feverishly curious that he wanted to take the chance. He and Chuckins manifestly had nothing to do outside the tent, but they drew away a discreet distance and paced up and down anyway.

Jim fetched a pail of water and went to the captain's horse to give him a drink. Then, as if he had strictly been assigned the job, he began brushing the horse down, whistling softly between his teeth.

It was about an hour before Captain Hillyard came out, pausing at the tent opening to pull on his gloves and replace his hat.

Boldly Yancy came to stand next to him. Yancy stopped, came to attention, gave him a snappy salute, and stared straight ahead without saying a word.

Languidly Captain Hillyard returned his salute. "You're one of his couriers, aren't you?" he asked, speaking in low tones so that, inside the tent, General Jackson couldn't hear.

"Yes, sir," Yancy answered in the same quiet voice.

"Thought I recognized you." Captain Hillyard finished pulling on his fine white leather gauntlets, pulled his wide-brimmed hat from under his arm, flicked an imaginary speck off of it, and settled it firmly on his head. Taking a firm grasp on the scabbard of his sword, he murmured, "Major General." Then he walked briskly to his horse, took the reins from Jim with a nod of thanks, and galloped briskly off.

Yancy kept his stance until the man was out of sight, watched curiously by Chuckins and Jim, who came to stand close to him. Then Yancy, with Jim following, ran over to Chuckins, gave him a friendly punch to the shoulder that almost knocked him down, and whispered to them, "Major General."

"Yep," Jim said with satisfaction, crossing his arms over his broad chest.

Incautiously Chuckins began to whoop, but he quickly clasped his hand over his mouth and stifled himself. Without another word, he turned and lumbered off for the nearest tent.

Yancy opened his mouth to say something, but at that moment the tent flap whipped open and Jackson leaned out. "Sergeant! Jim! What about this infernal stove?" But now he sounded almost jaunty instead of testy. As they hurried into the tent, Jackson asked, "Where did Satterfield go?"

Yancy started then stuttered, "Well, sir, he — he — I think there was something —

maybe he forgot —" Then he swallowed and pointed. "He went that way."

Jackson looked at him, his bright blue eyes fired with intelligence. "He did, did he? If he's not back in fifteen minutes, he's going to work all night tonight and all day tomorrow and maybe tomorrow night, too, if I'm of a mind."

"Yes, sir," Yancy said.

It was an hour before Chuckins came back. But Major General Stonewall Jackson said nothing.

After the enforced inactivity of the previous two months, the month of October took on feverish activity. Jackson ordered full and complete rolls of each company of each regiment, with status of wounded included. Complete inventories of arms and material were taken and retaken; every week new orders went to Richmond.

Yancy and Peyton took turns on the Richmond run, for often Jackson had new dispatches as soon as one of them returned from a run. On these trips Yancy did pay very short visits to the Haydens. Often Jackson's orders required no reply, but still Yancy and Midnight required some rest before beginning the trip back.

The Haydens knew better than to urge him to stay, so they fell into a comfortable routine. Elijah tended to Midnight and Missy would fix Yancy a meal and usually some food to take back with him. Lorena would put clean linens on the guest room bed while Yancy visited with Leslie for a few minutes. Then he would nap for two hours, when Lorena would quietly awaken him. He and Midnight would ride hard back to the camp.

In the middle of the month, Yancy was, to his surprise, given dispatches to Winchester, the town in the northern Shenandoah Valley that was only lightly invested. As usual, none of General Jackson's staff or even officers knew anything about Jackson's plans, no matter how hard they tried to discern them. Jackson made no comment whatsoever about the contents of the courier's bag.

Yancy arrived in Winchester two days later, and it took three days for the aged, rheumatic colonel in command to prepare his answering dispatches. Finally Yancy returned to Manassas and delivered them to Jackson, who took them without a word.

It was the last week of October before Yancy learned that General Jackson had been assigned to command the army in western Virginia. He would be returning to the Shenandoah Valley that he so deeply loved.

■ ■ ■ ■

Monday, October 28, was a fine, crisp, biting day. At noon a pale white sun glowed faintly in the sky. To the north was a bank of faint gray clouds, moving slowly south, and Yancy thought they may have an early first snow in them. He knocked on the now-familiar door of the Hayden home.

Light footsteps sounded, and Lorena threw open the door, her face alight. "Yancy! Mother and I were just talking about you. Come in, please."

Yancy came in and companionably she threaded her arm through his as she led him into the parlor. Lily was there, sewing, and Yancy saw Lorena's sewing basket beside her familiar wing chair next to the fireplace. After greeting Lily, he took what was now considered his chair, next to Lorena.

"We've missed you, Yancy dear," Lily said, for now he was on such familiar terms with Dr. and Mrs. Hayden. "It's so difficult because we never know when we are to see you again. Of course, there are thousands and thousands of families all over the States that are in the same predicament."

Her words warmed him, both because she included him as if he were family and because she so tactfully said "States" instead of "United States." The family was always careful not to draw any lines between them and him.

"I surely never know when I'm going to be here, either," he said good-naturedly, "which, as you say, is exactly the same predicament of everyone in my command."

After the Battle of Falling Waters, Yancy had come to trust the Haydens enough to tell them that he was in the Stonewall Brigade. Of course he had not told them his capacity, but they weren't fools, and he was sure they knew exactly why he popped up in Richmond so often, considering the different camps the Stonewall Brigade had occupied. He also knew that they would never question him about it and would never say anything to anyone about him.

"How's Leslie?" Yancy asked.

"He's doing very well indeed," Lily answered. "As a matter of fact, he's out marching around the garden. He's grown so weary of being inside that he spends hours, sometimes, walking in circles. But the exercise and fresh air have done him a world of good. Lorena? Why don't you go tell Missy to make coffee for Yancy and go tell Leslie that he's here. I know he'll want to come in to visit with him." The Haydens' back garden was a generous square of almost a quarter of an acre, and it was walled in, so prying eyes couldn't see the Haydens' Union soldier son.

"Yes, he will," Lorena agreed, already on her way out.

Lily rose to pull the drapes at the front windows and continued, "Jesse is at Chimborazo, although, thank the Lord, there are only a few men left. His duties are very light now. They closed the emergency field hospital at the old Shockoe railroad station, you know."

"Yes, ma'am, I heard that."

They talked desultorily about the lack of wartime activity for the last three months until Lorena and Leslie returned.

Yancy stood to shake his hand. "You look better every time I'm here. That's good. And barely a limp, I see."

"Only now when I'm very tired. Of course, it's hard to get tired out there trotting around the garden like some demented fairy," Leslie grumbled. "I'll be so glad to get back on a horse, to ride, to be of use, to work again."

"I know you feel better because you're so ill-tempered," Lorena said, taking up her sewing. "You were much sweeter when you were weak and in pain."

"Didn't have the energy to complain, Rena," Leslie said good-naturedly. He turned to Yancy. "So how long can you stay? Can you stay the night?"

"Yes, I have to leave early in the morning, but I can stay the night."

"Good," Lorena said happily then tempered it with, "Father said he may be late, and he would hate to miss you."

"Oh, yes, *Father* really wants to see you, Yancy. *Father* really misses you a lot," Leslie teased, winking broadly at Lorena, who made a face at him.

But these niceties were lost on Yancy. When he was younger he had always been very aware of feminine attentions and had been sensitive to the signals they sent him. Now he had grown to be a man so handsome, so striking, that women he met or even passed in the street would stare wide-eyed at him until they caught themselves and, blushing, dropped their gazes.

He was now six feet, three inches tall. His shoulders were broad, his arms and legs muscular from his eternal horseback riding. His thick night black hair had grown somewhat, brushing his collar, the errant lock always falling rakishly over his forehead. In the outdoors his skin had deepened to a rich burnished bronze. As he had grown into a man, he had lost all traces of childhood in his face. His forehead was broad and fine, and with his dark, slightly slanted eyes and his high chiseled cheekbones, he looked exotic and mysterious.

But for the last two years he had been at VMI and then in the army and had been much bereft of female company. He had lost that instinctive insight into women that he had formerly had. Now he was slightly puzzled at Leslie's sally but shrugged it off. Lorena and Leslie often had exchanges he didn't understand, and he assumed it usually was some private family joke.

Missy came in with coffee then, and they talked and laughed, the lively conversation never wavering. Yancy amused them with Chuckins's antics and with stories of odd, often funny things that happened in camp. Leslie had stories, too. Both of them kept the details of when and where very vague, and the characters were unnamed but always vivid.

At about four o'clock, the late editions of the newspapers came out, and the Haydens had every newspaper within a thirty-mile radius of Richmond delivered to them. Yancy, Lily, Lorena, and Leslie all spent a companionable two hours reading in silence, sipping more tea and coffee. Occasionally

Elijah came in with more firewood and stoked the fire. The room was warm and comfortable and inviting, and Yancy reflected that he felt more at home here than anywhere, except at Grandmother's.

Dr. Hayden came home about six o'clock, and at seven Missy served them a wonderful meal, as usual.

When they finished, they were all getting ready to go back to the parlor and their newspapers, but Yancy stood, handed Lorena out of her chair, and asked very formally, "Miss Hayden, would you care to come sit in the garden with me for a while? I need some fresh air, and I would appreciate the company."

Hesitantly Lorena glanced at her father, who smiled and nodded slightly. "I'll go get my cloak," she said.

Yancy pulled on his caped greatcoat and Lorena returned with a beautiful dark blue wool mantle trimmed with black piping. She pulled up the hood, and the color made her eyes look like the deepest midnight. They went out the kitchen door to the back garden.

The Haydens' garden was not so manicured as some, for Lily Hayden preferred a more natural woodland look. Cobbled paths wandered here and there, screened by large shrubs and small sculpted pear and dog-wood trees. In the center was an enormous live oak tree, and underneath it was a stone garden bench that had been put there in Jesse Hayden's father's time.

Arm in arm, Yancy and Lorena strolled slowly and sat down there. Most of the leaves had fallen, but occasionally, carried on the lightest air, a leaf fluttered down, dancing its final dance in the cold moon-light.

They sat in silence for a while, looking up at the hard, brilliant stars. In a restless movement, Yancy took Lorena's hand in his. He rarely touched her, although they had lately come to give each other very brief, tightly controlled hugs when he left. Now he felt Lorena stiffen slightly, but she left her hand in his.

He turned to her. "I — I may not be see-ing you for a while. I can't tell how long it may be, but I expect it will be some time."

"You're leaving Manassas, aren't you?" she asked slowly, looking up as if she were speaking to the uncaring moon. It was com-mon knowledge that the army was in the north. "General Jackson is moving, and you can't tell me where."

"I'll miss you so much, Lorena," he said in a low tone. "I know we haven't known each other for very long, but somehow that doesn't matter to me. I think about you all the time, and the more time that goes by between my visits, the harder it is to be away from you."

She turned to him. Her white, perfectly shaped face and the great pools of dark eyes made her look unworldly, like a creature of secret streams and soft mists. "I have to tell you something. It's — very difficult for me, a cruel memory of a bitter time in my life. But perhaps you may understand me a little better . . ."

To Yancy's surprise she took both of his hands in hers and turned so that she was very close to him. In an even voice she said, "When I was seventeen, I met a man, a gentleman from a good Richmond family. I was so much in love with him, and I thought he was the most wonderful man in the world. We decided to marry when I turned eighteen. My birthday is in January, so we decided to marry that very month. I ordered my dress. My mother and father and I planned a wonderful wedding in that very Episcopal church right over there. I was so happy. I thought that my life was, and always would be, perfect." She stopped and dropped her gaze, and her hands grew unrestful.

Yancy stroked them and said quietly, "He left you, didn't he?"

She nodded, and when she spoke her voice was slightly choked. "Yes, he left me. The weekend before the wedding he said he wanted to visit some family in New Orleans. As it turned out, he had found out about a woman he had known for several years, and she had just become widowed. He stayed in New Orleans, and within two months he had married her."

She looked back up at him, and her lips trembled. Tears stood in her eyes. "He didn't even send me word. After he had been gone for four days, my father made inquiries with some friends he has in New Orleans. They found out about it. And that's the only way I knew that my engagement, my trust, and my heart had been broken." Now a single silver tear rolled down her smooth cheek.

Gently Yancy brushed it away and then drew her to him, holding her close. He pulled the hood down so he could kiss her hair. It was soft and warm and smelled of flowers.

She clung to him, and he could tell that she wept, but it was a gentle thing, not at all convulsive or wracking. For a long time they stayed that way, with Lorena's face buried in his shoulder, him murmuring soothing things against her hair.

After a while she moved slightly away and pulled a handkerchief from her pocket. "I've cried all over you," she said in a slightly shaken voice as she wiped her eyes.

"I'm glad," he said.

She took a deep, trembling breath. "Now you see that I have a very hard time trusting men."

He nodded. "With good reason. But Lorena, I must know. Do you trust me?"

She looked at him for a very long time, studying his face. He met her gaze squarely. Finally she answered him. "Yes. Yes, I do trust you, Yancy."

He put his arms around her and pulled her to him again. This time she looked up at him. He kissed her, gently, her lips warm and vulnerable on his. She slipped her hands behind his neck and caressed him. It was a long, sweet, poignant kiss.

They stayed in each other's arms, contentedly. Then Yancy said, "You know what I'm telling you, Lorena. I'm falling in love with you."

"I know," she whispered. "And right now I don't quite know how I feel. I've been afraid for so long, and I've smothered my emotions for so long that I feel a little dazed. Like — like when your arm goes to sleep, and when it wakes up, it prickles and feels like it doesn't belong to your body, quite."

"I understand," Yancy said. "And I don't mind. But please, Lorena, can you tell me this?" He pulled back to look at her face. "Will you wait for me? Will you wait long enough to give me a chance?"

She smiled. "I will, Yancy. Gladly, I will."

Yancy could only pray that she would wait for him and that she would remain the same sweet girl he had come to love in the meantime. He knew that only time would tell. . . .

■ ■ ■ ■

PART FIVE:
THE BATTLES
1861–1862

■ ■ ■ ■

CHAPTER NINETEEN

The next morning Yancy collected his dispatches to General Jackson from the War Department and hurried out of Richmond. On the entire journey back to the camp at Manassas, Yancy could scarcely think of anything but Lorena Hayden. She had allowed him to give her a modest good-bye kiss that morning, and it had elated him.

I think she does care for me. She's just afraid, he thought, *after what that dog did to her — no, that's an insult to dogs. I'd like to meet that joker sometime, like in a dark alley so he couldn't see me coming. Leaving a girl at eighteen —*

Suddenly Yancy laughed to himself. *She must be . . . let's see . . . she said two years ago, and her birthday is in January . . . She must be twenty now and turning twenty-one in a couple of months! She's so proper sometimes — she's going to have one hissy fit!* Yancy, in the previous September, had just turned eighteen years old.

Yancy didn't mark birthdays, because the Cheyenne Indians didn't mark birthdays. They observed and judged people according to where they stood in their journeys from childhood to adulthood. No numbering system figured in their assessment and acceptance of either boys or girls; they were simply recognized when they reached different stages of life. Of course the Cheyenne marked the passage of time, but no single day or even month was recognized as a landmark in a person's life.

Yancy, like his father, was very mature for his age. At sixteen years old, Daniel Tremayne had struck out on his own, hunting and trapping, and along the way he had met many coarse and hard-bitten men. And he had earned their respect. Yancy was the same. He had reflected a man's sense of duty and responsibility by the time he had reached sixteen and had gone to work for Thomas Jackson. He was, indeed, older than his years.

I'm going to tease her about being an older woman, he reflected with amusement. *The next time I see her . . .*

He hoped against hope that it would be soon.

■ ■ ■ ■

Major General Jackson had actually received his orders in the middle of October. United States Commanding General George McClellan was massing his sixty thousand men across the Potomac, intending to overtake Richmond. The plan was for General Irvin McDowell, with his forty thousand troops stationed north of McClellan, to join him at Richmond. This would mean the death of the Confederacy.

General Robert E. Lee saw that only too well. His only hope, and it was a slim one, was Stonewall Jackson. If Jackson could defeat and chase the Federals out of the valley, and perhaps even draw some of McDowell's forces across the Potomac to reinforce them, then Lee thought that he might be able to outfight McClellan. Lee's were delicately worded orders, for naturally Lee could not state the case so baldly and place such a burden upon one single general.

But Robert E. Lee and Stonewall Jackson had a most peculiar understanding. Lee took special care of his temperamental and eccentric general and had immediately recognized him as one of the most capable men, so obviously born to command, that he had ever known. And Stonewall Jackson understood Lee's aristocratic, gracious orders, always worded with the greatest courtesy and generally ending in some rather vague suggestions that left Jackson to interpret what Lee wanted, not what he said. And so he did; and so he readied himself to fight, and fight hard, in the Shenandoah Valley.

On November 4, 1861, General Jackson gave a stirring goodbye speech to his beloved Stonewall Brigade. But as it turned out, all the high emotion and regret was wasted, because by November 12, they had joined him in Winchester. Jackson had been appalled at the troops stationed in the Shenandoah Valley.

There were three little brigades numbering about 1,600, and they were dotted around the northern part of the valley. There were four hundred and eighty-five wild cavalrymen under the doubtful command of old Colonel Angus McDonald, a sixty-year-old Southern gentleman with rheumatism who had absolutely no control over the undisciplined boys that galloped around the valley at will.

All this to fight General N. P. Banks, who was holding western Maryland directly across the Potomac with 18,000 men, and they were moving east. In addition, more than 22,000 Yankees were just across the Alleghenies in western Virginia, under General William S. Rosecrans. And worst of all, on Jackson's western flank, General Benjamin F. Kelley and his 5,000 men had captured the village of Romney. It was only forty miles away from Jackson's headquarters.

As soon as Jackson understood his position, he had sent Yancy on a wild trip to Richmond demanding reinforcements. "Tell them," he growled at Yancy, "that the Shenandoah Valley has almost no defenses."

Even before Yancy arrived, Secretary of War Benjamin had decided to send Jackson's old brigade to the valley. He greeted Yancy with this happy news and promptly turned him right around to ride to Manassas with his orders.

Yancy was happy to be reunited with the Stonewall Brigade, but he regretted that he didn't have time to see Lorena.

The Army of the Valley wintered in Winchester. Anna joined Jackson in December in his pleasant headquarters, the Tilghman home. She stayed December, January, and February, and wrote about that winter being one of the happiest times of their lives. All through those short winter days and long nights, Jackson made his plans and drilled his troops, ever the vigilant and disciplined general. At home with Anna he was, as always, happy and even jolly.

In March, the general turned back to war, and he sent Anna home. On March 22, he began what was known as the Valley Campaign. And this campaign — it was understood in the Army of Northern Virginia and throughout the South — saved Richmond. Stonewall Jackson had understood General Lee's orders, and like the extraordinary soldier that he was, he had followed them to the utmost.

Basically, the Valley Campaign was a complicated series of maneuvers orchestrated by Stonewall Jackson, and by him alone. His staff never knew his plans. His officers never knew who they were attacking. His men never knew where they were marching to. Of course, this meant that the enemy never knew anything about the elusive Stonewall, either — until the day came that they, thunderstruck, were looking at the Army of the Valley — who were themselves often bemused, they had traveled so fast and so victoriously — from the field of defeat. Before they could decide which direction to run, forward or backward, the army, and Stonewall, was gone, and again they knew not where. In the Valley Campaign this was to happen to armies in places that were forever attached to Stonewall Jackson's laurels — Front Royal, First Winchester, Cross Keys, and Port Republic.

With 17,000 men, Stonewall Jackson had, from start to finish, faced about 62,000 Federals. The Federal defeats in the valley had so stunned Washington that they had frozen McDowell's forces so he couldn't join McClellan in the Peninsular Campaign against Richmond. So it may even be said that just the fear of Stonewall Jackson had stopped a force of 40,000 men.

When it ended on June 9, 1862, there had been forty-eight marching days. The Army of the Shenandoah Valley had marched a total of 676 miles, an average of 14 miles a day. After this they were known as Jackson's Foot Cavalry. They had fought six formal skirmishing actions and five pitched battles. They had taken 3,500 prisoners, and 3,500 Federals lay dead or were wounded in the valley. Considering the relative numbers of the armies, Confederate losses were low indeed — 2,500 dead or wounded and 600 prisoners.

Jackson had also added precious supplies and arms to the needy Confederate armies. He had captured over 10,000 muskets and rifles and nine cannons. He had burned or destroyed countless tons of Federal supplies.

The Valley Campaign had succeeded without costly battles. Outnumbered by more than three to one, Jackson's superb tactics had soundly beaten a far superior force, although they were much more poorly led. In addition, his Army of the Shenandoah Valley had paralyzed McDowell's forces. Stonewall Jackson's name was now worth an army.

Senator Blake Stevens of Virginia, Peyton Stevens's father, was so proud of his son being in the famous Stonewall Brigade that he regularly sent special couriers with gifts for him. When the brigade had gone into winter quarters at Winchester, a wagon had arrived with a tent almost as large as General Jackson's, a camp stove, a padded cot, six new uniforms, two pairs of boots, six pairs of wool socks, four blankets, and two crates crammed with tins of food.

Peyton asked his old VMI roommates, Yancy and Chuckins and Sandy Owens, to share his tent with him. Yancy and Chuckins gladly did, though Sandy had to tent with the artillery. Still, whenever he got a chance he came and stayed with them.

But on Monday, June 16, 1862, all of that finery had been packed away on the brigade wagon train, and the four of them were as humbly bivouacked as though they weren't Stonewall's Boys, which they called themselves though they kept it a supreme secret. They had built a campfire and were lying in a circle around it. On the ground was an oilcloth. They lay on that and covered themselves with one blanket and an oilcloth on top of that to guard against the dew.

Sandy and Chuckins were asleep, but both Peyton and Yancy lay awake, hands behind their heads, staring up at the night sky. Yancy was thinking forlornly that he hadn't seen Lorena for almost eight months. He was surprised at how deeply he missed her.

"Can't believe we're marching tomorrow," Peyton said, interrupting Yancy's melancholy musings. "After the last few months we've had. And the battle in Port Republic was just what — yesterday?"

"Feels like it," Yancy answered, "but it was a week ago. And no wonder we don't know what day it is or what month it is or what time it is. You and I both have made two runs to Richmond in the last week, haven't we?"

"Guess so," Peyton said. "Yancy? Do you know where we're going and what we're gonna do?"

As usual, Jackson had kept his orders and plans a strict secret from everyone, even the field commanders, which drove them utterly insane. Yancy was quiet for a while. He generally did know more than almost anyone else in the command, except for maybe Jim. It was because Jackson relaxed a little more with Yancy and even held conversations with him, which was unusual for the taciturn general. Yancy knew him and understood him, and so it gave him some advantage in reading him. He had never said anything else to anyone, and he hesitated now, though he knew Peyton would never let on.

"You do know, don't you?" Peyton asked quietly.

"Well, I don't *know*. It's not like he tells me anything."

"But you know. Can't you just tell me if it's north, south, east, or west?"

Finally Yancy lifted his arm and pointed. "That way." He pointed southeast, toward Richmond.

■ ■ ■ ■

General Lee was planning a counterattack on the Army of the Potomac, led by General McClellan, and he needed Stonewall Jackson's Army of the Valley desperately. Jackson planned to march them double-quick to Lee's aid.

They left at dawn, a bleak foggy morning that made it difficult to even see the man, or the horse, in front of them. Yancy, Peyton, and Chuckins rode in the general's train, behind the general staff. Even Midnight and Peyton's great stallion, Senator, seemed sluggish and bleary. Only Chuckins's plump mare, Brownie, seemed to plod along cheerfully as she usually did. But then, Brownie was not a Stonewall Jackson courier's horse, and in the Valley Campaign she had not ridden many reckless miles, day after day.

Midmorning the fog lifted and the day became pleasant. Some of the staff officers ranged up and down the lines of marching men, checking with the regimental officers and trying to discourage the men from straggling, for they were riding through orchard country. Yancy, Peyton, and Chuckins found themselves just behind General Jackson and had the good fortune to witness a delightful little scene.

General Jackson had given strict orders that no soldier was to say, in any manner whatsoever, anything about the plans of the army. This afforded the army a lot of mirth, for they had no clue about the plans of the army anyway, but it amused them when General Jackson showed his penchant for mystery.

Now they came upon a soldier that had stepped off the side of the road, for a cherry tree was temptingly close to it. He had climbed the tree, where he was sitting contentedly, gobbling.

Jackson stopped and stared up at him. "Where are you going, soldier?" he asked.

"I don't know."

"What command are you in?"

"I don't know."

"Well, what state are you from?"

"I don't know."

With some exasperation, Jackson demanded, "What's the meaning of this?"

He answered, chewing thoughtfully, "Well, Old Jack and Old Hood passed orders yesterday that we didn't know a thing till after the next fight, and we're keeping our mouths shut."

Jackson threw back his head and laughed, a rare sight indeed, and rode on.

Jackson marched them a roundabout way, instead of the straightaway that the couriers took, for he and General Lee hoped to deceive McClellan into thinking that Jackson was still in the valley. In fact, General Lee had even sent General Winder and his 10,000 men, ostensibly, to Jackson in Winchester. General Winder had made it there, camped a couple of nights, then had turned around and was now following Jackson back.

But this deception was hard, for the country was not made for brigades of men walking through. There were enemy pickets, skirmishes, impenetrable thickets, and creeks sometimes six feet deep to be forded. Moving the cannons was like a nightmare for man and beast alike. No trails were marked, of course, and their maps were very poor indeed. Jackson had two new guides he didn't know.

On Tuesday the twenty-fourth it rained, long and heavily. They had been passing through one of the thick woods with almost impossible thickets, and now they found that the enemy had cut so many new roads in the tangle that one of the new guides lost his way and led them astray.

But finally on the twenty-sixth the exhausted army had reached their goal, a small crossroads call Old Cold Harbor, just above Gaines' Mill, where Lee planned to concentrate his forces and attack the Federals massed there. On the twenty-seventh they moved in. Jackson was on the Confederate left, Longstreet's army on the Confederate right. There were 88,000 Confederates in the field.

Yancy had asked General Jackson to fight with his old unit from his days of training in Richmond when he was still a VMI cadet, Raphine Company.

Jackson had shaken his head wearily. "We've got more than two dozen outfits out there, with three Army headquarters — me, Longstreet, and General Lee. I'm going to need every courier I've got. I especially need you and Sergeant Stevens, for you two have the best horses. You two stick close by me."

"Yes, sir," Yancy said.

And so they followed him, from the swampy bog below Old Cold Harbor to the little hills and wooded fields around Gaines' Mill. Lee had opened fire at daybreak, but it was afternoon before Jackson reached his command post, a knoll just northeast of the Confederate center. The fighting was, and already had been, savage. General A. P. Hill in the center had attacked too soon, before he could be reinforced, and the Confederates had taken heavy casualties. The Confederates charged and would gain ground; then the Federals would countercharge, and the Confederates were forced back again. The lines stubbornly stayed stagnant, with very little ground gained nor lost for either side, but with both sides losing dozens of men by the hour.

Almost as soon as they arrived at Jackson's command post, he called for Peyton. "Ride to General D. H. Hill's command and instruct him to send in Rodes, Anderson, and Garland, and to keep Ripley and Colquitt in reserve," he ordered brusquely. Stonewall Jackson wasted no words in battle.

General A. P. Hill was badly beaten down, but the brigades that had arrived with Jackson's command were fully engaged. Finally, at about four thirty that afternoon, three of his trailing brigades under General Richard Ewell topped the hill at Old Cold Harbor. Jackson sighted them immediately and sent orders to them by Peyton.

He then turned to Yancy. "You've got to go down to General A. P. Hill, down on the battle line. He must be made aware that General Ewell is on the way to support him with three brigades. And then ride to General Lee's headquarters and assure him that we can relieve General Hill."

"Yes, sir!" Yancy said then started to turn away.

But Jackson pulled Little Sorrel up close to Midnight and Yancy stopped. Jackson said in a low voice, "You're the fastest. It's going to be hot and heavy down there, Sergeant. Ride hard, as fast as you can, and no need to linger on the line. It's just as important for you to notify General Lee as it is for you to notify General Hill. Understood?"

"Understood, sir."

"Good, good." Jackson turned away, and Yancy galloped off at Midnight's top speed, which was fast indeed.

Midnight had been around battles, of course, and had been in the line of fire before, but neither he nor Yancy had seen the savagery at the line of the Battle of Gaines' Mill. General A. P. Hill, a red-headed, brave, hot-tempered, experienced soldier was on his third horse of the day only about fifty yards back from the front lines. He wore his bright red flannel shirt, as he always did in battle, thumbing his nose to enemy sharpshooters. As Yancy approached, even over the thunderous din of battle, he could hear General Hill's scratchy voice screeching orders at the top of his lungs, liberally laced with curses.

Midnight was in tearing high spirits, foaming at the mouth, eyes wild. He wasn't spooked; he was battle ready. As Yancy tore up to the general, Midnight lowered his backside and skidded to a stop on his back legs, reared, threw his head up, and screamed.

Even General Hill turned to see this magnificent spectacle, and he recognized Midnight and Yancy. "Ho, you, boy! Looks like that crazy beast is ready to down a few Yankees himself!" he shouted.

Yancy grinned and Midnight skittered up to the general. "He would, sir, but General Jackson gave Midnight his orders along with mine."

"Orders from Stonewall, huh? What? Attack the North Pole?"

Even with bullets whistling by him and shells exploding all around him, Yancy was feeling the irrational exuberance of battle, and he laughed. "Better news than that, sir. General Jackson sends his compliments and wants to make you aware that General Ewell is on his way to support you with three brigades."

General Hill let loose with a string of happy profanity. He finished with, "Good news from Stonewall, good news. Now you and your big black monster better be running along, little boy."

Yancy saluted. "Yes, sir, I am ordered to General Lee. Not the North Pole."

He pulled Midnight's reins to the left and felt a curious thumping blow on his right arm. Puzzled, he looked down. There was a slowly spreading red stain on his gray sleeve. He looked back up at General Hill, who was looking down at Yancy's arm. "Sir . . . ?" Yancy began.

He felt his head whip to the side, as if he had been struck sharply on his right forehead. And then, curiously, slowly, his vision faded to black, and he knew no more.

CHAPTER TWENTY

"Matthews, give him more chloroform. He's stirring a bit and I need about two more minutes to close this up," Dr. Jesse Hayden ordered the steward assisting him. Dr. Hayden waited for Matthews to apply another two drops of chloroform to the cloth covering the patient's face then resumed stitching up the stump of the man's right leg. As he bent over, his back and shoulders burned with an ache that felt like it went right down to his bones. It was the nineteenth amputation Dr. Hayden had done that day.

He finished stitching and slowly straightened up. His whole back felt like it was on fire. "Done." He looked at the tag on the soldier's clothes that were neatly folded at the foot of the operating table. "He's Thirteenth Virginia. Check with Matron to see which building we're putting them in," he told the two orderlies who were transporting men to the buildings where they would receive nursing care. Chimborazo Hospital had forty buildings. Even when receiving patients in a steady stream after a battle, the efficient and compassionate administrator, Dr. James McCaw, stipulated that every effort be made to keep the soldiers together with others in their units.

In this, one of two buildings set up to receive the soldiers coming in from the battles raging just to the east of them, ten operating tables had been set up, with a team of anesthetist and surgical assistant assigned to each table, though they had only eighteen doctors in all, rotating as they could. In both buildings, doctors performed surgery after surgery. In the building next to them was the non-emergency care receiving, and the orderlies were steadily stitching, medicating, and treating wounds — and sicknesses — as quickly as possible.

Two ambulance attendants brought a stretcher up to Dr. Hayden's operating table, a groaning man with severe shrapnel injuries on the right side of his body. He was groaning, his eyes wide and frightened and unseeing, his left hand clenching and unclenching spasmodically. Wearily Dr. Hayden saw that most likely both his right arm and right leg would require amputation.

Just then Dr. McCaw came up to Dr. Hayden and laid his hand on his arm. Dr. McCaw was a man of medium stature, with light brown hair and a mustache that was turning prematurely gray. His features were nondescript, except for the warmth and kindness of his expression. Now he said firmly, "Dr. Hayden, I believe I must insist that you stop and rest for a bit. You have been working steadily for hours on end, and I know that last month you were unwell. I don't want you to fall ill, please. We need you too much."

"But —" Dr. Hayden gestured toward the moaning soldier on his table.

Dr. McCaw shook his head. "I insist, Jesse. I'll take this table myself. You go rest, get something to eat, have some coffee, and don't come back for an hour."

"Very well," Hayden said. "I must admit that sounds very inviting. Thank you, Dr. McCaw."

"Of course." He turned to Matthews and started giving instructions for anesthesia.

Dr. Hayden went outside, stopped just outside the double entry doors, closed his eyes, and took several deep breaths. Inside, the emergency ward smelled like blood and sweat and fear, and over it all hung the distinct acrid fumes of chloroform. Outside it was warm and humid, but high up on "Hospital Hill" no stench of battle drifted on the heavy night air. He opened his eyes and sighed when he saw the ambulances coming from the east, lined up along Thirty-fourth Street.

The attendants returned to the ambulance that sat in front of the building. The driver snapped the traces, and the horses started trotting to the west, returning to the field of battle to reap another grim harvest.

Behind it another ambulance pulled up. The orderlies jumped down, climbed in the back, and brought the first man out on a stretcher. He was unconscious, mercifully, Dr. Hayden thought, for his right side and the right side of his head and face were blood-soaked. Bandages had been wrapped around the man's right arm and forehead, but if they had once been the standard white bandages, they were now the deep crimson of blood. Dr. Hayden glanced at his face as the orderlies hustled to the doors then did a sharp double-take. "Wait!" he ordered, striding quickly to the stretcher. Surprised, the orderlies halted at this unmistakable authoritative command.

Lanterns were lit outside but the light was uncertain. Dr. Hayden bent over the unconscious man and smoothed his dark hair back from his forehead. Quickly he straightened and said, "Follow me."

He hurried inside, followed by the medics. Dr. McCaw was still at the table that Dr. Hayden had occupied, but the one right next to it was empty, and it still had an anesthetist and assistant standing by. Dr. Hayden directed the men to put the stretcher there. Dr. McCaw was right in the middle of amputating his patient's right arm, but these surgeons had so much experience with that type of surgery lately that now they could do amputations with hardly a second thought. Dr. Hayden stepped close to him and said, "Elijah, this young man is a friend of my family's. He saved my son's life. I want to treat him."

Dr. McCaw nodded without looking up. "All right then, go ahead, Jesse."

Dr. Hayden turned back to the assistants. "Get those bandages off, and get his clothes off. I'll be right back."

He hurried back outside. There were always boys loitering around the hospital, begging for errands to run for a penny. He collared a promising-looking boy of about twelve that was fairly clean and neat, took a pencil and notepaper out of his pocket, and talked as he wrote. "I want you to run to the Richmond Episcopal Church on Myrtle

Street. Do you know it? Excellent. Next to it is a two-story house with two big walnut trees in front. Give this note to them, and a man named Elijah is going to be coming back to the hospital with a wagon. You may ride back with him, and when you return I'll give you two pennies. A nickel if you hurry as fast as you can."

"Yes, sir," he said over his shoulder, already taking off at a dead run.

Dr. Hayden hurried back inside to his patient.

Almost a year before, Elijah had picked up a pale and limp Leslie Hayden from Yancy's wagon and carried him upstairs as if he were a young child. Now Elijah picked up Yancy Tremayne from the wagon and gently carried him upstairs to the guest room. Yancy was wrapped in a sheet from the waist down. His face and right side were still covered in dried blood, and his thick hair was caked with it. With his dark complexion, Yancy could not be said to be pale, but his face was a rather sickly tan. His right eye was swollen and blue beneath the thick bandage on his forehead. His upper right arm was bandaged from shoulder to elbow, and it was secured in a sling.

Her face as pale as the moon, her eyes as

wide and dark as drowning pools, Lorena followed.

Elijah laid him down on Leslie's bed.

Lily appeared at the door, almost as pale as Lorena. "How is he? Is he badly hurt?" she asked anxiously.

Lorena went to her and took her arm. "I'm sure he isn't critical, or Father would have come home with him. Please, Mother, try not to worry. Go on to bed. I'll bring you a cup of chamomile tea."

Lily said, "I think I will sit up in bed and try to read my Bible. And thank you, my dear, but Missy has already made chamomile tea for me. Please come let me know how he is. I don't think I'll be able to sleep until we know he will be all right."

"Of course, Mother," Lorena said and went back to Yancy's bedside.

Elijah pulled some papers from his pocket. "Miss Lorena, Dr. Hayden tole me to give these to you. It'll tell us how to take care of Mr. Yancy. Why don't you go on down to the kitchen where it's good light and read it while I tend to him."

Lorena started to object — she didn't want to leave Yancy, not for a moment — but then she realized that of course Elijah would be attending to Yancy's personal needs. Just then Missy came in with a

437

steaming copper water pot, thick tendrils of vapor rising and filling the room with the soothing scent of rosemary. Lorena inhaled gratefully. Some of the confused panic retreated, and she felt her mind cleared somewhat. "Missy, do you know where Leslie's nightshirts are?"

"Yes ma'am, when the boy comes with the news that Mr. Yancy was hurt, I took one of 'em out and steamed it to freshen it up. It's hanging in the cupboard," she said kindly.

Missy does the laundry and ironing. Of course she knows where all of our clothes are. She must feel that sometimes the gentry thinks these things get done by magic. "Yes, of course, of course," Lorena said, turning to the door. "Please let me know when you've finished."

Lorena went down to the kitchen and sat down at the oak counter where she and Yancy had sat so many times before. Pulling a lamp close, she read her father's notes.

Lorena,

First of all, please do not be too distressed. Yancy has two injuries, but at this juncture I don't believe either of them are life threatening. Clear your mind and be calm. It won't help Yancy if you are troubled.

First, his head wound: He has a scalp laceration, I believe a graze from a bullet. He sustained a simple linear skull fracture (it's just a thin line about three inches long), and the skull is not splintered or depressed or in any way distorted. This is good news; but all skull fractures are serious injuries, and he will require constant monitoring for the next twenty-four hours. The scalp laceration required eleven stitches, but the wound and the edges were clean.

For care: Wrap ice chips in a clean white towel and apply to his forehead and eye every hour for about fifteen minutes. Head wounds bleed profusely, and even with the stitches he may bleed through the bandage. Rebandage as necessary, gently cleaning any dried blood at the laceration site if necessary.

As for his mental condition, I do not believe he is in a coma. I think he is unconscious, but in a very light state as he goes back and forth into a deep sleep. He drifted into consciousness as I was stitching his arm, and he seemed to be lucid. He knew his name and could see me very well. But he was in pain, so I gave him some morphia and he slept again. Don't attempt to rouse him, but if he does wake up just ask him some simple questions: his name, if he knows where he is, if his vision is clear, if he is in pain. You may give him twenty drops of laudanum as often as every four hours if needed.

Head injury patients generally have a sensitivity to bright light and noise, so keep the room dimly lit (I suggest with candles only, and keep the drapes drawn) and speak and move as softly as possible. Also, it is best that he be propped up to a half-sitting position; he will be much more comfortable than lying flat.

I must caution you, daughter, that when people receive the shock of head wounds, they usually evidence some distressing symptoms, but in actuality they are the norm. He will likely be confused as to time; he won't know what day it is, and it will mean nothing to him when you tell him. He will have lost the instinctive sense we have of knowing whether it is day or night, and this usually results in increased anxiety. I'm sure this will be magnified for Yancy, as he does seem to have sharper senses than most men. Perhaps it is the Indian in him. At any rate, if he wakes up and seems to be alert enough to want to talk, first gently let him know where he is, what day it is, and what time it is, for he very well may not know where he is.

It is common for victims of skull fractures to have amnesia to one degree or another. They rarely remember the incident that caused the injury, and the amnesia may evidence itself in many ways. He will almost certainly have holes in his memory, both short-term and long-term. Do not be alarmed, for it's natural that he will have trouble with his memory for a while.

As I said, I don't believe the head injury is too severe, but there are a few symptoms that would indicate a graver prognosis, and I wish you would send for me immediately should they occur. They are: convulsions, slurred speech, stiff neck, visual disturbances, or clear fluid leaking from his ears or nose.

As for his right arm, he was shot and the bullet lodged just at the edge of the humerus. I removed the bullet without trouble, but the bone is slightly chipped and it sustained a hairline crack, which is not even considered a break. We will need to keep it bandaged tightly and tied securely into the sling to keep it immobilized for a few days, but I think he will regain full use soon. He may suffer pain at the incision site, and you can administer laudanum for that, too.

The hospital is extremely busy. Men are pouring in from Gaines' Mill just east of town, where the battle was today. Dr. McCaw kindly let me take an hour's break, and I ate and even napped a little, and so I feel refreshed enough to keep working on. I am going to try to stay tonight as there are so very many emergency surgeries to perform. And you may take that as a measure of what I would term only moderate concern for Yancy. Certainly if I was worried to a great degree I would have come home with him, for as you well know in the last year, your mother and I have come to regard him almost as a son.

Keep hope in your mind, Lorena. Trust my judgment and trust yourself. You're an excellent nurse, and as you know, Missy and Elijah are wonderful with sick or injured people. Yancy could not have better care. And of course, we will all "pray without ceasing" for Yancy.

With my great love,
Father

Lorena read it all again, slowly. But she felt a tremendous burden and fear both for Yancy and herself. She was frightened that Yancy might actually be much more severely injured than even her father, who had practiced medicine for almost thirty years, could know. And she was frightened that she might make some horrible mistake with his care; with misjudging his state, either physical or mental; some stupid mistake with his medication . . . An ugly picture of Yancy in bone-jarring convulsions grew large in her mind. Tears welled up in her eyes, and she buried her face in her hands. She was on the verge of panic.

But Lorena knew she was a strong woman who knew where her true strength came from, and with a supreme effort, she suppressed the paralyzing dread and banished the desolate visions in her mind. She bowed her head and quoted softly, " 'Come unto me, all ye that labour and are heavy laden, and I will give you rest. Take my yoke upon you, and learn of me; for I am meek and lowly in heart: and ye shall find rest unto your souls. For my yoke is easy, and my burden is light.' " She felt a great calm and clarity of mind and strength of will flow over her and through her, and she thanked the Lord for it.

Gathering her father's notes, she went upstairs to reassure her mother that Yancy was going to be just fine. She had every confidence that she could take care of him.

■ ■ ■ ■

Lorena stayed by Yancy's side all night, except when Elijah came to attend to him. He stirred lightly when she applied the ice chips to his forehead and eye, but he didn't seem to be in distress. Once he opened his eye — his left eye, for his right was swollen shut — and looked at her. Even with one eye, she could see that his gaze was direct and clear. But his lids were heavy, and after just a few seconds he slept again.

Her father came home at dawn, his shoulders heavily stooped, his eyes shadowed. "Hello, my dear. How is our patient?" he asked, laying his hands on Lorena's shoulders.

"He just seems to be resting quietly," she answered. "He opened his eyes once, but he slipped right back to sleep."

"You know, dear, Elijah and Missy are perfectly capable of watching him. They would let us know if there was any change at all."

"I know," Lorena agreed. "But I don't want to leave him. I want to be here if — when he wakes up."

"I understand," he said, moving to Yancy's bedside. He bent over, gently lifted his left eyelid, and nodded with satisfaction. "But you should have Elijah bring up your favorite chair from the parlor. You could rest easier in it."

She had been sitting in a side chair with a padded seat. It wasn't uncomfortable, but neither could one lounge in it. "Wonderful idea, Father," Lorena said appreciatively. "As always, your prescriptives are just perfect."

He smiled. "Also, as your physician, I'm going to insist that you rest later today. I'm going to sleep for a while. Later this afternoon, before I go back to the hospital, I'll stay with Yancy. I need to do an overall assessment of him and cleanse the arm incision and scalp laceration anyway. While I'm doing that, you can have something to eat and sleep for an hour or two. Oh no, young lady, don't you make that face at me. I insist. If Yancy wakes up, I promise I will come and get you."

"Very well," she said reluctantly. "I suppose I will need it, for I intend to sit up with him tonight."

"Good," he said and yawned. "I'm off to bed. I'll see you later, daughter." He bent and kissed her cheek and left.

Elijah brought up her chair and she sank gratefully into it. It enveloped her with comfort and a thousand happy memories of her family all together in the parlor.

She missed Leslie. He had returned to Washington in November of last year, shortly after Yancy's last visit. He had written, with vast relief, to tell them that he had joined the 8th Maryland, which was assigned to North Carolina.

It's extremely unlikely I'll ever see Yancy on a battlefield again. Tell him for me, and thank him again. And tell him that I hope we may meet as friends again soon, in a time of blessed peace.

She read the Bible for a while by the single candle in the room, but candlelight was too dim for reading at very long stretches. She settled back in her chair and laid her head back, closing her eyes to rest them. Without really realizing it, she fell into a light sleep.

She didn't exactly dream, but she did have a vague feeling of deep comfort and knew she was in her favorite chair. Airy images floated through her subconscious — her mother, smiling; a warm fire in the parlor; Yancy sleeping.

This faraway picture roused her a little. She stirred and slowly opened her eyes.

Yancy's eyes were open. The swelling in

his right eye had gone down considerably with Lorena's faithful applications of the ice packs. In his half-sitting position he leaned back against the mound of pillows propping him up. He looked relaxed and comfortable, but his eyes were bright and sharp. His expression was not apprehensive and certainly not fearful, but as her father had predicted, he appeared to be slightly confused. "Hello," he said.

"He–hello," Lorena stuttered. She was startled, and the faraway feeling of her dreamy slumber had not yet faded.

He continued to look at her with his fathomless dark eyes.

She sat up straight, smoothed her hair back, and looked at the pendant watch pinned to her shoulder. It was 3:30 in the afternoon, and mindful of what her father had told her about Yancy's probable lack of time perception, sharply she made herself recall that it was Saturday, June 28, 1862.

Calm now, she looked back at him and asked, "Do you know your name?"

He frowned. "Yes, of course. I'm Yancy Tremayne."

"Can you see me clearly?"

"Yes, my vision is clear, but my right eye. . . ." He moved his right arm, but it was immobile in the sling. He looked down at it with some surprise. "What happened to me?" he asked.

"You were hurt. Injured. Do you remember anything at all?"

Long seconds elapsed as he stared into space blankly. "I . . . I remember a big black horse, riding a big black horse. . . ." His vision focused sharply on her face. "I'm a soldier. In Stonewall Jackson's outfit. My horse's name is Midnight, and I'm — I'm a courier for Major Jackson."

"General Jackson," Lorena corrected him gently.

He looked bemused. "That's all I can remember. Riding Midnight. Carrying dispatches for Maj — General Jackson."

"It's all right," she said soothingly. "You've had a head injury, and that's why your right eye is swollen, and that's why you're a little confused right now. It's very common with this type of injury, but it will pass."

He nodded, seemingly satisfied at the moment. His gaze wandered around the room. "What time is it?"

"It's 3:30 in the afternoon. Today is Saturday. It's June — June 28."

"Oh," he said blankly. Then he looked down and touched his bound right arm with his left. "What happened to me?" he asked again.

Lorena hesitated. She was uncertain whether she should give him the bald, frightening facts that he had been shot in battle. But he seemed steady enough and she knew that Yancy was a strong man. She replied, "You're right, Yancy, you are a soldier. You fought in a battle. A bullet grazed your head, and you have a slight fracture, and the wound required stitches. You were also shot in the arm, but the bullet was removed without any problems. The only reason that your right arm is immobilized is because the bullet lodged against your humerus — that's the big bone in your upper arm — and chipped it just a bit. Your arm isn't broken, but it'll be best to keep it still for a few days."

He listened carefully, and still he was expressionless. Lorena really couldn't tell how much he comprehended, but he was not at all distressed. His respiration, she noted, was full and steady, and his eyes stayed clear and focused. "Ma'am, could I please have a drink of water?" he asked at last.

"Of course," she said. She rose and went to the washstand, a solid chest with a marble top and a cabinet and drawers underneath. There was a large bowl and pitcher for wash water, and now Lorena had kept a pitcher of water on ice. She poured him a glass and noted with satisfaction that it was cool but not too cold, as her father had instructed. She brought it to him and hesitated, not really knowing if he was so weak that she needed to hold it for him.

But with no apparent problem he reached up with his left hand and took the glass and drank thirstily.

"More?" she asked as he emptied the glass.

"Please, ma'am."

Lorena was a little troubled by his formality, but she dismissed it as Yancy's natural courtesy. She filled the glass again.

He drank about half of it and then set it on the bedside table. She was glad to see that he apparently moved with relative ease, for the table was on the right side of the bed, by her chair, and he had made the awkward crossover of his body to set the glass down securely. He settled back into the pillows, but they had come disarrayed.

She bent over and pulled up on one slightly. "Can you lean forward a bit, Yancy? If you are able to, I think I can arrange your pillows a little better." It was a test, to see if he could sit up straighter without her help. He did. *He's very strong,* she reflected with a sort of furtive feminine admiration. *He should heal quickly.*

She finished and Yancy settled back. "Thank you, ma'am," he said.

"You're welcome." She studied him for a few moments and he met her gaze with no apparent discomfort. Lorena took a deep breath and her eyes dropped to her hands, folded in her lap. She had become nervous, twisting the fabric of her skirt into little knots. With a conscious effort she stilled her hands then looked up. "Yancy," she said, and her voice had deepened with tension, "do you know me?"

His gaze didn't waver. "I know that you're a beautiful lady and very kind. Like this room, you seem familiar, but it's a very faraway feeling, like you're not really connected to me. It's like — it's sort of like I've seen pictures of you, and this room, a long time ago, in some book."

Numbly she nodded and ducked her head again to hide her distress. It shocked her to realize just how desolate his matter-of-fact answer made her feel.

"Do I — have I offended you, ma'am?" he asked with the first sign of anxiety. "Am I supposed to — are you — have I —"

Quickly she arranged her features to hide the turmoil of emotion she felt and looked back up. "No, Yancy, of course you haven't offended me in any way. As I said, you may have some trouble with your memory for a day or two; you were injured only yesterday, you know. You are in Richmond, in the Hayden home. My father, Jesse Hayden, is your physician, but not only that, you are a close friend of our family's."

He relaxed. "That's good then," he said vaguely. He reached up with his left hand and barely touched the bandage on his head, wincing slightly.

"Are you in pain?" Lorena asked quickly.

"Well, yes, I'm getting the beginnings of a headache. And my arm is starting to hurt some."

Lorena took a brown bottle from the bedside table and carefully measured the light brown liquid into a spoon. "Here. This will ease your pain and help you to sleep."

Obediently he opened his mouth and took the dose. He made a face and Lorena handed him the glass of water. He washed down the bitter medicine with a long drink.

"Do you think you could drink some broth, Yancy?" Lorena asked him.

"I don't really want anything else right now, ma'am," he answered. His eyes were already dulling somewhat, his eyelids dropping. Laudanum was a mixture of the tincture of opium and brandy. Dr. Hayden added sugar to his prescriptive, but it did little to mask the unpleasant taste. Yancy was already feeling the effects of the powerful drug. He blinked slowly, twice.

"When you wake up again perhaps you'll feel more like eating a small meal," Lorena managed to say lightly. "For now, just go back to sleep."

He closed his eyes and breathed deeply.

Lorena now let the anguish show on her face; she pressed shaky fingers to her forehead. Feeling helpless tears rising, she got up and tiptoed to the door. She certainly wasn't going to sit by Yancy's bed and sob like a hurt child.

She had only gone a few steps, when behind her Yancy murmured, "Ma'am? What is your name, please?"

"Lorena," she said, her voice raw. She couldn't help it. "Lorena Hayden."

He blinked, then his eyes closed again.

Lorena fled, running into her bedroom across the hall. It was long minutes before she could stop crying.

" '. . . and so after seven bloody days of battle, once again our heroic Army of Northern Virginia has triumphed over the Yankee invader. The cowardly McClellan with his rabble cowers on the far bank of the James River, his plan to overtake Richmond thwarted by our brave commander, General Robert E. Lee. With a force of barely eighty-eight thousand, General Lee and his fighting commanders General James Longstreet and General Stonewall Jackson pushed the one hundred thousand Federals a full twenty miles from our beloved capital. Even though our army was so vastly outnumbered, they were so overpowering in battle that the well-bloodied Yanks could not run fast enough. In tremendous triumph, General Lee and the Army of Northern Virginia have taken close to ten thousand prisoners and have inflicted nearly sixteen thousand casualties (killed, wounded, and missing) on the enemy. In addition, General Lee has seized fifty cannons and ten thousand muskets for the blessed Confederacy.

President Davis has declared a day of thanksgiving, and rightly so. United, we loyal and grateful citizens of the Confederate States of America thank Almighty God for protecting and defending us and our courageous army, and we acknowledge that the praise for not only this, these Battles of Seven Days, but all victories in this life come only from His sovereign hand. Amen.' "

Lorena finished reading the article from the July 6 edition of the *Richmond Report* and looked up at Yancy.

He seemed troubled.

"What's the matter, Yancy?" Lorena asked.

He shrugged a little, with his uninjured left shoulder only, the way that he would probably have to make the gesture for the remainder of his life. "I dunno, exactly. I'm sure no military genius, like General Lee and General Longstreet and Stonewall. But . . ."

"Yes?" Lorena prodded him curiously. In spite of his words, Lorena had found that he had an insight into the strategic implications of the battles that was very unusual for a mere sergeant who was only one small stitch in the vast complex tapestry of war.

"It's just that I think General Lee would have planned to destroy McClellan's army, and I think he could have, in spite of being outnumbered. We're always outnumbered," he said with an endearing earnestness. "Somehow I just think that this campaign wasn't as successful as the papers make it out to be. We inflicted heavy casualties on the Army of the Potomac, yes, but it didn't say anything about our casualties."

Lorena sighed deeply. "No, the *Richmond Report* is always limited to our triumphs, it seems. But the *Dispatch* reports the casualty numbers daily. They're not good, Yancy."

"Tell me," he insisted.

She picked up the *Richmond Dispatch* and turned to the "Battle Reports" page. "So far, 3,286 killed, 946 missing, and about 15,000 wounded."

"What? Oh no." Yancy groaned and lay back heavily on the pillows. "Fifteen thousand . . . Richmond must be overrun. No wonder I never see Dr. Hayden. He's not working too hard, is he?"

"Yes, and no one on this earth can stop him," Lorena said with exasperation. "Day and night he's at Chimborazo. Sometimes he comes home to sleep for a few hours, but more often he's been staying at the hospital, sleeping in a building they've set up especially for the doctors and assistants. They have matrons attending twenty-four hours, providing meals and laundering the cot linens and cleaning the quarters. Still, he can't possibly be resting for any great amount of time. It's driving us all crazy, even Elijah and Missy."

A small half smile played on Yancy's face. "Sounds like you," he said lightly. "You've been nursing me around the clock for a week now. Not much you can say to your father, Rena."

A surge of joy ran through Lorena as, for the first time, Yancy said her nickname. Only Leslie and Yancy had ever called her Rena.

In the last week, Yancy's confusion and disorientation had cleared up amazingly. He still couldn't recall being shot, and there were still holes in his memory, of times and places. As Dr. Hayden had predicted, he had difficulty sensing the passage of time. Every time he woke up he asked what time it was and if it was day or night. And he had a nagging memory of a short, grizzled man in a red flannel shirt, sitting on a runty chestnut horse, but no matter how he tried, Yancy couldn't put the man into a setting, and he couldn't fathom why he seemed so important. The Haydens couldn't know that he was seeing General A. P. Hill at the Battle of Gaines' Mill when he was shot.

Thankfully, two days ago, Yancy had finally remembered the Haydens, including Leslie, which was a big breakthrough since they hadn't mentioned Leslie to him. Yancy remembered that he was a Union soldier and how Yancy had saved his life.

However, to Lorena's bitter disappointment, Yancy seemed to have no recollection of his declaration of love to her eight months ago. It was obvious that he liked her and enjoyed her company. His manner toward her was warm, but there was no sign of the passionate romantic man that Lorena had known last October.

Until Yancy was wounded, Lorena had held her emotions strictly at bay, in effect forcing them into a far dark corner of her heart, seldom visited. The night that Elijah had brought Yancy home, bloodied and battered, Lorena had suffered anguish she hadn't known since Leslie had been injured. She felt as if someone had taken a dagger to her heart and laid bare the love she had for Yancy with brutal strokes.

It had only grown worse in the last two days, since Yancy had finally remembered her and he had so naturally and carelessly placed her in the platonic position of a sister. She had been overcome with a scalding regret that she had so stubbornly fought her love for Yancy. Indeed, she had triumphed for a time. But now she was afraid that this so-called triumph was, in truth, a grievous defeat inflicted on her only by herself. *What if he never remembers he loves me? What if the memory of that love has been completely erased? What if that part of his heart that belongd to me is gone forever?*

Breaking in on her agonized thoughts, Yancy said, "You're making faces. Leslie said that one day you'll get stuck that way, and then you can be a sideshow at the circus. 'The Angry Woman — Look upon Her Dreadful Countenance if You Dare!' "

"I'm not angry," she said indignantly, instantly forgetting her dreadful worries at the sight of Yancy's inviting grin. He did have such lovely straight, very white teeth. "I'm just — thoughtful."

"Yeah? Then do you suppose you could think up some food for me? I'm kinda hungry."

"Always and forever," Lorena grumbled, rising.

"How 'bout some real grub this time, instead of watery soup?" Yancy wheedled.

"It's not watery soup; it's broth. And your physician has ordered that you stay on a light diet," Lorena said, hands on hips. "In spite of the fact that he knows very well that Missy and Elijah have been sneaking you eggs and bacon and grits and kidney pie."

"Busted again," Yancy said cheerfully. "So how's about you sneak me some of that roast beef? I can smell it, you know. I have a very keen sense of smell, and it's starving me right to death."

Lorena turned and went to the door, her

spine set in a stubborn ruler-straight line.

Yancy called after her, "Rena?"

In spite of herself, a swift secret smile played on her lips and she turned. "Yes?"

"Thanks. For everything. I'm pretty sure that you're my best friend," he said innocently.

Now she smiled happily at him. "I'm pretty sure, too, Yancy. And I'm very glad. One day, perhaps, you may know just how glad I am to be your friend."

CHAPTER TWENTY-ONE

"Yancy, there's a telegram for you," Lorena said, holding it out to him. He read it quickly then looked up with a glad smile. "My dad and Becky are coming. They left Lexington early this morning, so they'll probably be here tomorrow — if the trains are running as scheduled."

"I'm so glad," Lorena said. "When we wrote to invite them to come stay with us, I honestly didn't think they'd come. I mean, travel these days, especially into Richmond, is so complicated, with all the soldiers and supplies traveling everywhere. I had the idea that the Amish are so unworldly that they wouldn't get in the middle of it."

"You're right about that," Yancy said, pulling himself up straighter in bed. "I can't see anyone in the community attempting it right now, except for my father. He's different from the Amish that have always lived in that world."

Automatically Lorena bent over and fixed Yancy's pillows as he talked. They had done this so many times that Yancy had learned just how to lean forward so she could easily rearrange the three fat pillows behind his back, and Lorena knew exactly how to fix them the way Yancy liked them.

It was July 9, 1862. Lorena had been taking care of Yancy for two weeks now, and they had slowly evolved into a familiar routine where Lorena anticipated Yancy's needs, and he was sensitive to when she was tired, when she wanted to talk, when she wanted to be quiet, and when she wanted to read to him or write letters for him. They fit together very well.

Becky and Daniel did arrive early the next morning. The hospital was not quite so urgent now, so Dr. Hayden had stayed home to meet them. He and Lily waited in the parlor. As always, for every minute she was awake, Lorena was with Yancy.

The knocker sounded, and shooing away Missy, Lily and Dr. Hayden rushed to open the door. They eagerly greeted Daniel and Becky as if they were old friends and brought them into the parlor. "We're so happy that you're here. The trains must be running fairly well," Lily said. "Richmond is like a beehive filled with angry bees these

462

days, with lots of buzzing around and in and out."

Daniel replied, "It sure is. But the trains were running, all right, transporting soldiers and lots of foodstuffs and material from the valley. So the trains, it seemed to me, were traveling as fast as they could steam."

"Seemed like about two hundred miles an hour to me," Becky said drily. "It's the first time I've been on a train, and after I get back home I hope it's my last. They're like great black, growling, smoky dragons. I may have nightmares."

Daniel said affectionately, "My wife exaggerates. She's got more backbone than I do."

Becky looked up at him. "Thank you, husband . . . I think."

She certainly didn't look as rugged as Daniel Tremayne, but then, no woman would. The Haydens saw in him a man that had experienced a hard life, and it had toughened him considerably. His reddish blond hair was bleached almost white by the sun. He was handsome in a leathery, rough way, with a chiseled jaw, straight nose, and sharp blue eyes. The scars by his mouth and on his jawbone were pronounced and added to the aura of sinewy strength.

Yancy looked nothing like him, except that he was built like his father. Over six feet, with long, muscular legs, wide shoulders, thick chest, brawny biceps — in this frame they were almost identical. Even their hands looked alike.

Rebecca Tremayne was no fainting flower certainly. Tall and slim, Becky always stood and sat very erect, with a severe grace. With her thick jet black hair, penetrating dark blue eyes and wide, firm mouth, she was the picture of a woman of vitality and fortitude. She was not beautiful, but she was attractive in a magnetic way, even dressed in the sober Amish garments and her modest prayer cap.

Now Dr. Hayden asked, "Would you like some refreshment?"

Daniel answered, "Thank you, but we are very anxious to see Yancy, you know."

Dr. Hayden nodded and rose, motioning them to follow him up the stairs. "Certainly. I'll take you to his room, but it's time for his morning coffee anyway, so I'll have Missy bring up a pot. Would that suit you, or would you care for something else? Tea, or fresh juice?"

"We would dearly love coffee," Becky said gratefully. "Daniel and I are so glad that the Amish don't regard the love of coffee as a sin. I'm afraid we would be tempted to break that commandment if they did."

464

Dr. Hayden brought them to Yancy's room. He could sit up now, for Elijah had brought the wing chair that matched Lorena's up to his room, and he was comfortable in it for long periods of time.

Now he tried to stand up, but Becky rushed to him and threw her arms around him before he could rise. "Oh, Yancy, Yancy, how we've missed you! How frightened we were when we heard you'd been injured!" She released him and stepped back.

Daniel came and gave him a hug. "I'm so glad you're all right, son," he said huskily. "Hearing about you and not being there was the hardest time I've ever had."

"I'm really all right, you know. Good nursing." He winked at Lorena then said, "Becky, Father, this is Lorena. Lorena, meet my father and second mother."

Lorena held out her hand to Daniel, who took it and held it warmly for a minute, and she and Becky nodded politely, as gentlewomen did upon introductions. Lorena said, "Please, won't you make yourselves comfortable sitting on the bed? Yancy just got up a few minutes ago, and I have no intention of letting him laze around back in bed yet."

Daniel and Becky laughed as they seated themselves on the bed. Becky said, "I see you must be a good nurse for Yancy. Don't take any of his nonsense."

"She doesn't," Yancy sighed. "Reminds me a lot of you, Becky."

"I regard that as a compliment," Lorena said primly.

"It is," Yancy agreed.

Becky and Daniel looked Yancy up and down, Becky with narrowed critical eyes. "You look terrible," she said severely.

Yancy rolled his eyes. "Don't waste words or flatter me, Becky. Just go ahead and say what you mean."

"I like a lady that speaks her mind plainly, Mrs. Tremayne. I think that is a sign of honesty and therefore is a virtue," Lorena said.

"Then you and Becky are the most virtuous women I've ever met," Yancy said with exasperation.

"Thank you," Becky and Lorena said in unison, in the same sarcastic tone. They stared at each other in surprise, then both of them giggled like young girls.

"They are a lot alike, aren't they?" Daniel observed, bemused.

Missy brought coffee and served everyone. Becky eyed Yancy again with doubt. "Yancy, I really am concerned about you. Please, how do you feel? How are you progressing?"

Lorena had written to them, explaining his injuries in detail.

"I'm doing well, considering," he answered thoughtfully. He still had not regained his robust color, and naturally he had lost weight. He hadn't required a bandage around his head for a few days now, as the incision was healing nicely. But it was still an angry red streak across his right temple, and the stitches weren't out yet, so the site was thick and still swollen, with the tie ends of the lurid black catgut sticking out.

He continued, "I'm having some headaches, but not so often and the pain gets less every day. And my arm is good. I've been using it a little, but Dr. Hayden says that I need to keep it pretty still for another few days. I just started getting up two days ago." He grinned. "That first time was a real corker. I thought, sure, I can just pop up out of this bed and walk around the room a few times. I stood up and then sat right back down, thank you very much, with the room spinning around me like a top and my eyes crossing with dizziness."

Lorena added, "You can joke, Yancy, but that scared me to death. If Elijah hadn't been here you would've crumpled right down to that floor."

"Maybe," he said carelessly. "Anyway, I took it real slow the next time, and got up a few times, just for a few minutes, day before yesterday. Yesterday I got up and even went downstairs," he said proudly.

"Really? Kinda soon, isn't it? Don't rush it, son," Daniel cautioned him.

Lorena sniffed. "Believe me, he won't do that again for a while. It took him about half an hour to get down the stairs, and then, of course, he was too weak to climb back up. Elijah had to carry him like a big baby."

"He did, too," Yancy agreed good-naturedly. "Embarrassing, that was. But I was so sure I could do it."

"Oh yes, you were so sure, Mr. Smarty-britches, and could anyone talk you out of it? No, sir, not Sergeant Yancy Tremayne, one of Stonewall's Boys," Lorena said disdainfully.

"Yeah, she's a whole lot like you, Beck. Good thing, too," Daniel observed cryptically.

"It is," Yancy agreed, grinning. "I'm really glad."

They talked for a while but it was true that Yancy did still tire easily. Becky and Daniel left him alone, meeting Elijah on the way out, as he was coming to help Yancy

468

back to bed. They thanked him profusely for taking such good care of their son.

They settled in the guest bedroom and then had a very good lunch with Lily and Dr. Hayden. He explained Yancy's mental state more clearly to them. "I'm sure Lorena wrote you that memory loss is a very common result of a skull fracture. Yancy's appears to be fairly slight, but I've found that he has a natural reticence and won't talk much about his feelings, what he's worried about, if he's anxious. It's hard to tell the extent of his amnesia, but he does seem to recall all the most important people in his life — you, his family; us, his close friends; General Jackson; his friends in the Stonewall Brigade. He's very lucid and insightful about the events in the war, so he seems to have retained all of his knowledge of being a soldier and of tactical and even strategic wartime moves."

Becky asked rather anxiously, "So it's clear what he remembers. But what about what he's lost? What memories?"

Dr. Hayden shook his head. "As I said, he's a reserved young man. He doesn't like to confide in me. He and Lorena have grown close, naturally, but she says he won't tell her anything about how his memory has been affected. I was hoping, Mr. Tremayne, that he might confide in you. It's obvious that he respects you, looks up to you, trusts you, and loves you deeply. I believe there's a better chance of his talking to you than to anyone."

Daniel nodded. "I'll talk to him alone this afternoon. And I hope you're right, Dr. Hayden. No one needs to go through something like this alone."

Later that afternoon — after he and Becky rested for a time in their room — Daniel went to Yancy's bedroom and saw that he was awake, sitting up in bed, talking to Lorena.

Lorena shrewdly said, "Mr. Tremayne, if you're going to visit with Yancy awhile, I think I'll go take a nap. Certainly, though, come get me or my father if you should need us."

Daniel sat down by Yancy's bedside and they talked, mostly about home and Callie Jo, who was four years old now, and David, who was a precocious two-year-old. Yancy wanted to know all the news about everyone in the community, and so Daniel told him all the gossip he could possibly think of.

"Hannah Lapp is getting married in November," Daniel told him, watching him shrewdly. Yancy had been very enamored of

Hannah when he was fifteen.

"Is she? Who's she marrying?" he asked with no sign of regret, only curiosity.

With relief Daniel replied, "Nate Raber. You remember him, Sol's middle son. Big beefy boy like Sol, but seems like a gentle and kind man."

"I do remember him, and he was a nice fellow," Yancy agreed. "He'll suit Hannah well. I'm glad for them."

Daniel studied him for a few moments then said quietly, "It's good that you remember people like Nate, that you barely knew. Dr. Hayden's told us that memory loss just goes along with your head injury. So how are you doing with that, son?"

Yancy frowned and stared into space. He was silent for long moments.

Daniel waited patiently and quietly.

Finally Yancy said in a voice that was somehow faraway, "For one thing, I have holes in my memory. They're usually connected to something I do remember. Like Leslie. I remember him, I remember what he looks like, I remember when I brought him here, home, from Manassas, but I can't remember *him,* exactly. I can't remember what he's like, his personality, his expressions. He's not really real to me. I remember him, but not all of him." He looked at Daniel anxiously. "Does that make sense?"

"Perfect sense," Daniel encouraged him. "Go on."

"And then sometimes I have mixed-up memories. I think I remember something, but somehow I don't feel like I'm recalling it right. It's fuzzy or something."

"So, what kind of things do you think have gotten mixed up in your memories like that?" Daniel asked.

For the first time Yancy dropped his gaze and fidgeted with the sheet. "Oh, just little things," he said vaguely. "Just — some things about some people."

Daniel believed one of those "people" was Lorena, but he didn't push him; he knew it wouldn't do any good.

Finally Yancy went on, "And then there's pictures that pop into my head that I know I should remember, but I can't get a grasp on them. One of these pictures I keep seeing is this man, with red hair and a mustache and a beard and a bright red flannel shirt, sitting on a kinda runty swaybacked mare. He's so familiar. But for the life of me I can't place the man."

Thoughtfully Daniel said, "Well, one thing I do know is that your mind is working right; your thought processes are obviously working well. You know, Yancy, Dr. Hayden

472

is fairly sure that you're going to regain most, if not all, of your memories at some point. If you could tell him what you just told me, it would help him to understand where you are in terms of recovery, and then he'd be better able to help you. Do you think you could talk to him like you've just talked to me?"

"Guess so. I just don't like — complaining and fretting to people. You're different. You have to put up with me," he said with a mischievous grin, but then he sobered. "I see what you're saying, though, Father. I will talk to Dr. Hayden. I'll talk to him today."

Two days later, Becky and Lorena were sitting in the parlor with the Haydens' usual afternoon tea. Daniel and Dr. Hayden were with Yancy, and Lily had gone to the market with Elijah and Missy.

Becky and Lorena had hit it off instantly. They had already felt a kinship, because Yancy had told his family much about the Haydens, and likewise the Haydens felt they knew Yancy's family through him. Also, in the last two weeks since Yancy had been hurt, they had exchanged letters. It could be said that though they had actually been together for only two days, Becky and Lorena were already fast friends.

Lorena said, "Becky, I've decided that I'd like to give you a gift. Will you come up to my room with me?"

"Of course," she answered.

They went upstairs to Lorena's room, a cozy space with a white embroidered coverlet on the bed, a fine Persian rug, and paintings of lovely Victorian ladies on the walls. A small secretary was placed in front of the window, with a desk chair and two side chairs on either side.

Lorena sat down at the small desk and motioned for Becky to take a chair next to it. Lorena opened the middle drawer and pulled out a top-bound sketchpad. She skimmed lightly through the pages, stopped at one, and opened the sketchpad to that page. Handing it to Becky, she said, "I thought you might like to have this."

Becky took it and stared down at the drawing with amazement.

The likeness of Yancy was astounding. Lorena had drawn him sitting up in bed, smiling. The scar on his forehead was clear, and she had faithfully represented that his face was somewhat drawn, his cheeks more hollow than usual. But still, she had captured that elusive boyishness Yancy had when he grinned, the sparkle in his eyes, the way they slightly wrinkled at the corners, the way his mouth stretched wide to reveal fine white teeth. She had gotten his proportions exactly correct, his shoulders still broad, and she had even captured his hands, the capable and masculine set of them. Until now Becky hadn't realized that Yancy had Daniel's hands. She loved Daniel's hands.

She looked up. "Lorena, this is simply wonderful. You've captured him, his spirit, his playfulness, even his masculinity. It's sheer genius."

"You know, I never seriously drew anything until the last two weeks," she mused. "I used to doodle, make very quick throwaway sketches of flowers or some child I had seen or a beautiful tree outlined in the evening sun, things like that.

"But when Yancy came and he was so terribly injured, he had to be monitored around the clock for two days. In those first days he was so sensitive to light that he couldn't bear anything but a single candle. I sat with him day and night, and it was too dark to sew, at all, or to read for very long. So in those long hours when Yancy was sleeping so deeply, I started just making line sketches. As the days went by and he could tolerate more light, I started doing these. And I found I was good at it," she finished simply.

"Yes, my dear, you are," Becky agreed. Curiously she looked down at the sketchbook. It was about half full. Lorena had turned several pages back to open to this sketch.

Now she watched Becky and finally said, "You're welcome to look at the others if you like. It's just that some of them are — difficult to see."

"Thank you," Becky said. She turned to the beginning and looked at the first sketch. It was, indeed, brutal. It had been done the first night he had been brought to the Haydens'. The shadows of his sunken cheeks were stark; his cheekbones looked so sharp they were skeletal. His right eye was an enormous dark swelling, and there was a bloodstain on the bandage around his forehead. His other eye was closed. His mouth was tight and twisted slightly, as if he were in pain. "Ohh," Becky said, a half moan, half sigh.

Lorena said nothing.

Becky held the sketchbook up closer, letting the strong afternoon sunlight fall on it. She could see small round spots where the paper was slightly rippled. Teardrops.

Becky turned to the next one. A few days later, it seemed, for Yancy looked better, his eyes open, looking strangely vulnerable. Then there were several drawings of him sleeping, and his face was peaceful, each showing his injuries improving slightly. Then there were several studies of him sitting up, alert. In one of them he had an intent look on his face, obviously listening to something. Becky looked up. "Were you reading to him?"

"Yes."

With satisfaction Becky said, "I could tell. He always looked like that when I read aloud to the family at night. You've captured it perfectly. And I know very well that Yancy didn't sit for these. You did them from memory, didn't you?"

"Except for the ones when he slept," Lorena answered softly.

"Amazing," Becky murmured. She turned to the next one, the last one. It was a full page. Yancy was sitting in the big wing chair next to his bed. His body was completely relaxed. Gentle morning light shone through the window behind and to the side, lighting his face. His head had fallen slightly to the side, as he was sleeping. The lock of hair fell over his forehead. Though he still had the scar, his face in repose was, in fact, beautiful.

Abruptly Becky looked up at Lorena, her

eyes wide. "You're in love with him," she blurted out.

Lorena pressed her eyes closed and whispered, "Yes. Terribly."

"You — you hide it so well. I didn't know until now, seeing these, your drawings of him. I never would have known, except for this."

"No one knows," Lorena said in a choked voice. "I've been very careful to hide it."

"Even from Yancy?" Becky demanded.

"Especially from Yancy. You see, Becky, last October Yancy was here for a whole day and night, which for him is a long visit. That night he told me that he was falling in love with me. He was so certain and sure of his feelings. I — I wasn't. I wasn't cold to him, but I held myself back from him. Purposefully. Because of some things in my past, I just didn't want to feel anything for another man, and I thought I could keep myself from falling in love.

"But the very night he came here, so terribly hurt, and I was so frightened, and he seemed so faraway, it stripped me of all that stupid pride and stubbornness. I realized how very, very much I love him."

"But then why don't you tell him? I can understand that you wouldn't want to complicate things at first, when he was so ill, but now — ?"

Lorena shook her head. "I can't. Because he's forgotten me."

Instantly Becky understood. "Oh no. He doesn't remember."

"No. I think that now he feels for me much like he does his sister, Callie Jo." A crooked smile came across her full lips. "Once he even told me that he was pretty sure I was his best friend. And I am. But that's not all it is . . . was. It was so much more. Yancy is not the only one that has lost something here. I lost the best and perhaps the only chance for happiness I'll ever have." Suddenly tears rolled down her cheeks. She bent her head and sobbed, a heart-wrenching sound.

Quickly Becky came to her, bent down, and wrapped her arms around Lorena's trembling shoulders. "Don't, don't, darling, don't. Your hope is not in Yancy. You must have hope in the Lord. The Proverbs promise, 'The hope of the righteous shall be gladness.' So be glad, dear Lorena. Yancy's heart will bring back the remembrance of love."

July simmered on. In the aftermath of the Battle of Seven Days, Lee and the Army of Northern Virginia remained camped close to Richmond. Eagerly Yancy read every single newspaper he could get his hands on, starving for information about the army and particularly about the Army of the Shenandoah Valley. As always, Jackson managed to keep his movements secret. Journalists could only speculate, and generally their speculations were wrong.

President Lincoln and Secretary of War Steward, frustrated with General McClellan's stubborn reluctance to make any offensive moves with the Army of the Potomac without shrill and unreasonable demands for anywhere from 50,000 to 100,000 reinforcements, finally decided to meet him halfway. They formed the new "Army of Virginia" and put General John Pope in charge of it. All of the Richmond newspapers reported Pope's pompous and blustery speech to his men upon accession to command.

Yancy read as much as he could, but he was subject to violent headaches, so Lorena still often read to him. One hot stuffy afternoon Yancy had given up sitting in his chair, his headache was so severe. He lay in bed in his darkened room with a cool cloth on his forehead, his eyes closed.

Lorena skimmed the newspapers and picked out light, amusing things to read to him. "Listen to this," she said. "The *Richmond Report* reads, 'General Pope bombastically told his men: "My headquarters are in the saddle." When our valiant General Stonewall Jackson heard this, he shouted, "I can whip any man who doesn't know his headquarters from his hindquarters." ' Isn't that hilarious?"

Yancy scoffed, "General Jackson never said that. He wouldn't say anything like that." His voice was weak, with that slight petulant note that came to people in severe pain. His eyes were closed and restlessly he fidgeted with the cold compress.

Lorena rose, took the cloth from his forehead, and dipped it into the icy water in the bowl on the washstand. Folding it securely, she placed it back on Yancy's forehead. "Why do you say that General Jackson wouldn't say that?" she asked curiously. "I had the impression that he's a man with little use for such theatrics."

"He is," Yancy answered shortly. "But that reply is boastful. General Jackson is never boastful. Never."

Wistfully Lorena thought, *He knows and remembers everything about Stonewall Jackson, down to the last detail of his uniform and every facet of his personality. Oh, how I wish he remembered me that well!*

"Yancy, I can see you're in pain," she said quietly. "I know you're trying very hard to get better as fast as you can, but you simply cannot speed up the healing process by sheer force of will. You never ask for laudanum anymore, but today I think you should take just maybe ten drops and see if you can nap a little."

He shifted restlessly. "What time is it?"

"It's only one thirty."

"In — in the afternoon?" he asked.

Lorena was somber when she heard this. Yancy hadn't been confused about the time for a couple of weeks now. This was a definite setback. "Yes, it's early enough in the afternoon that a short nap shouldn't keep you from sleeping tonight."

After a short hesitation he said, "Okay. I do feel kinda tired."

Lorena gave him ten drops of laudanum. "I'll come back and check on you in about an hour," she told him. "But if you need anything, just call. I'll be in my room right across the hall."

He nodded, already drifting off to sleep.

She left and went to her bedroom. Since Yancy had been better, he didn't require constant bedside monitoring, so Lorena left him for naps and at night. But since he seemed somewhat worse today, she pulled up one of her desk chairs right by the door so she could hear him if he called. And then she sketched.

Still, Yancy continued to improve, in spite of occasional setbacks such as the one he'd had that day.

General Pope's Army of Virginia moved northwest of Richmond, arrayed along the foot of the Blue Ridge Mountains. McClellan's Army of the Potomac stayed at Harrison's Landing on the James River, where they had retreated to after the Seven Days battle. It was obvious that the two armies were going to try to overtake Richmond in a pincer movement.

General Lee sent Stonewall Jackson to the north to deal with Pope. This news made Yancy so restless he was miserable, knowing that his Army of the Valley would soon be in battle.

The last week of July he announced that he was going to rejoin the army on August 1.

Dr. Hayden said calmly, "Oh? And what, exactly, are you going to do when you rejoin?"

"I'm on General Jackson's staff. I'm a courier, you know that. They're in the north, and they need me," he answered with a touch of impatience.

"Mmm-hmm. And so, are you planning on riding Midnight to perform these courier duties?"

"Of course. I'm feeling much better and stronger. I'm going to ride for about an hour this afternoon, and then slowly increase the time each day until the end of the month. Then I should be fit to rejoin my unit."

"I advise against it, Yancy," Dr. Hayden warned him. "There is a world of difference between riding a high-spirited horse like Midnight and taking long walks and climbing up and down stairs."

"I've ridden horses since I was five years old, sir. I appreciate your concern, but I'm not at all worried."

But he should have been. He rode Midnight for an hour that afternoon. He returned home with a headache so excruciating that it literally left him bedridden for two days. And his arm, though the hairline crack was fully healed, had not been exercised and was pitifully weak. Trying to control Midnight, which Yancy had taken so much for granted before, made his arm hurt. It throbbed so deeply and incessantly that he finally asked Lorena to bind it up and immobilize it again.

As he lay in bed, fighting the pain but

knowing that he would have to ask for laudanum to be able to rest at all, he came to the bitter realization that he had been insidiously weakened by his wounds. He knew then that it would be some time before he could join General Jackson again.

Dr. Hayden improvised a cautious regimen of exercise, progressing very slowly for Yancy, and he followed it faithfully. But August of 1862 proved to be the most maddening, frustrating month he had ever endured in his life

On August 9, General N. P. Banks, Pope's commander of II Corps, attacked Jackson at Cedar Mountain. A relatively small but bloody battle ensued; in fact, it would have been called a skirmish except for the high number of casualties on both sides. The Army of the Valley sustained about 1,350 casualties — killed, wounded, or missing — while Pope's Army of Virginia lost almost 2,400 men. But General Jackson was once again victorious. Pope's army retreated, and the weary, dispirited troops made the miserable retreat northward to Culpeper.

On August 10, Yancy had another headache, though it was not so painful as those he had endured before. They had been diminishing both in number and severity.

Lorena had noticed that any stress or

worry tended to cause them, as happened when Yancy exercised too vigorously, and mentioned this to him.

He was coming downstairs regularly now, and this morning they sat together in the kitchen while Missy made breakfast. Yancy closely perused each newspaper, frowning. "Where are the casualty lists?" he muttered.

Sitting with him, Lorena said soothingly, "Yancy, you know that it takes a couple of days for those to be published. Be patient."

"It's so hard," he murmured distractedly. "They're my men. They're my friends."

"I know," Lorena said sympathetically. "Every single day of war is hard." She reached over to cover his hand with hers.

He grasped it hard — as if it were a lifeline — for long moments, his shoulders and head bowed. Lorena stayed very still. Then with a sigh he released her and sat up. "It is. I don't for the life of me understand why I miss it. Something must be wrong with me."

"You don't miss war, Yancy," Lorena said gently. "You miss your friends, and you feel a responsibility toward them and to General Jackson. That is an honorable and just motive to wish to return to the war. And I believe you will . . . soon."

For Yancy it would not be soon enough.

On August 17, the Richmond papers were afire with the news that General McClellan and his Army of the Potomac had embarked for northeastern Virginia, to join forces with General Pope's Army of Virginia. It was clear that they now planned to drive toward Richmond from the north.

In the next few days, Lee made his plans and began the brilliant countermoves of the two Federal armies. These maneuvers culminated in not only a victory over them but, in the end, with both Pope and McClellan suffering devastating defeats. These last terrible days of August were referred to as the Manassas Campaign. Once again the humble crossroads was to become the center of a raging war.

To Yancy's vast relief, the newspaper coverage was good, though it dealt with the campaign in generalities. General Lee's movements could not be hidden or kept secret, and so word of the events in the campaign were generally only delayed by one day.

General Lee sent Jackson to sweep around Pope's right and flank him. This movement of the Army of the Shenandoah Valley was kept a tight secret, and ultimately it trapped Pope into thinking that Jackson was retreating from northern Virginia. Jackson's first triumph was the capture of the Federal stores at Manassas Junction, a truly welcome gift for his always hungry and ragged troops.

On August 29, Pope attacked Jackson in force, thoroughly believing in a quick and easy victory. He was wrong. Jackson's army fought ferociously, and Pope flinched. The next day Longstreet arrived. In the Battle of Second Manassas, the Confederates shattered Pope's army, both physically and mentally. McClellan didn't arrive in time to save him. With this humiliating defeat, both armies fell back in ignominy, harried and driven and tortured by Jackson's pursuit, until they finally managed to flee in disarray back over the Potomac River.

On the last day of August, Yancy read of the Confederate's triumph and that they were camped at Chantilly, in northeastern Virginia. It was only twenty-five miles from Washington DC. When he read this, Yancy got chills. He had no way of knowing, but somehow he thought that this might be the critical time for General Lee to invade. Yancy knew that General Jackson, since the days of his Valley Campaign, had continuously called for an offensive action into the North. Now, after the glorious victory at Second Manassas, Yancy just had an instinct that maybe this time General Lee and President Davis might listen to him.

He went to Dr. Hayden, who was sitting in the garden, also reading the newspapers. As Yancy approached, Dr. Hayden looked up, and for an instant a shadow crossed his kind face. He knew.

"Sir, I believe that I have recovered enough to rejoin General Jackson," Yancy said bluntly, coming to stand before him, his arms crossed stubbornly. "I may not be exactly as well as I was before I was hurt, but I feel good and strong."

Dr. Hayden nodded. "You have improved almost miraculously this last month, Yancy. I'm proud of you, for you have shown courage and true determination in your recovery. I am very sorry to see you go, but I have to agree with you. I believe it is time."

Yancy was so eager that he left the very next day. He felt a deep urgency, for he sensed that General Lee would move very soon. At dawn the family was up to see him off, assembled in the foyer. He kissed Missy and Lily and Lorena and shook hands with Elijah and Dr. Hayden.

"I can never thank you enough," he said in a deep voice. "I am so blessed by the Lord to have a second family such as you. Pray for me, and I'll pray for you all to have peace, undisturbed. I — I love you all." A little embarrassed, he hurried outside.

Lorena followed him. Great luminous tears shimmered in her dark eyes, and impulsively she threw herself into his arms, whispering, "Oh, I will miss you so terribly, Yancy."

Surprised, he drew her close to him. For a short moment some shadow, perhaps of recognition, perhaps of remembrance, passed through his mind. But it was like a vapor, a mist that disappears once the light touches it.

Again he kissed her lightly on the cheek. "Don't cry, Rena. I'd rather remember you saying good-bye with a smile."

She drew back from him, scrubbed her eyes with her apron, and then determinedly gave him a smile. "Ride fast, fight hard, and hurry back. I'll wait for you."

Again Yancy had that odd flash of almost-recognition. But this was a hard day, and he had a hard ride ahead of him to enter back into a grim and harsh war. Returning her smile, he gave her a mock bow, turned, and hurried down the walk.

Lorena watched until he mounted Midnight, spurred him, and galloped up the quiet street.

In his heart, he knew she was crying and

told himself it was just because she was worried about his returning to the war, but something he couldn't quite latch on to whispered that it was much more.

CHAPTER TWENTY-TWO

Yancy left Richmond at dawn on September 2. On September 3, just before dawn, he stood at the entrance to General Stonewall Jackson's headquarters tent. He had ridden about one hundred ten miles in twenty-four hours.

The tent flap was open, and Yancy could see the general inside, sitting at his camp desk, reading the Bible by the light of a single guttering candle. He looked exactly as Yancy had pictured him so often in the past two months — dusty, wrinkled, shabby, but still with that indefinable aura of strength and authority that Jackson emanated without effort.

"Sir?" Yancy called softly. "Permission to enter?"

Jackson looked up, squinting slightly, then rose and came forward without hesitation. Yancy stood at strict attention, but Jackson held out his hand and Yancy gladly shook it.

"So, Sergeant Tremayne, I see you're still alive. Glad to see it."

"Thank you, sir. I am, too."

Jackson turned and motioned for Yancy to follow him and sit on the camp stool opposite his desk. "I'll have to write Anna; she's been after me for news of you. I did hear at Chimborazo that Dr. Hayden took you home to care for you. Sounded like good news to me, though I never had the pleasure of meeting Dr. Hayden. Friends of yours, the Haydens?"

"Yes, sir. Very good friends."

"Good, good. Looks like they took fine care of you."

"They did, sir. I'm ready to rejoin. I'm sorry I was away for so long. I wanted to come back as soon as I could."

Jackson's startling blue eyes twinkled slightly. "Missed us, did you?"

"I did, sir. It's hard to explain. I just know I belong here."

"That's explanation enough for me, Sergeant. We're glad you're back, and I'm especially glad Midnight is back. He runs circles around even General Lee's couriers," Jackson said with evident relish. "I would have conscripted him while you were out, but it wouldn't have done any good since he won't let anyone but you ride him."

"Sir?" Yancy said, puzzled.

"You didn't know?" Jackson asked in surprise. "Contrary horse threw half of my aides before we figured out that he wasn't having any rider fumbling around on his back except for you. Even Sergeant Stevens couldn't ride him."

Yancy's eyes grew wide. "Midnight threw Peyton?" he blurted out; then, recovering himself somewhat, he added, "Sir?"

"Sure did. Tossed him onto a caisson and bruised his collarbone. Stevens came back to headquarters riding his own horse with Midnight tethered behind him. Said it made him nervous, that stubborn horse behind him. Felt like Midnight was planning to attack him again, from the rear, at any time. So we went ahead and sent him on to you."

Yancy was amazed at this speech coming from the terse Stonewall Jackson. He didn't think he'd ever heard the general say so many sentences in a row. And then he astonished Yancy again, for he threw his head back and laughed aloud in a creaky, rusty manner. Yancy couldn't help but grin.

Stonewall seemed to have amused himself mightily, for he laughed on and on, and finally Yancy started laughing, since it was contagious. Yancy thought, *This is crazy, me and the great Stonewall Jackson sitting here laughing like the village idiot. Maybe I really did lose my mind when I got shot in the head.*

Finally, though, the madness came to an end, and with a final chuckle, Stonewall rose. Yancy snapped to attention as Jackson said, "You look tired, Sergeant. I happen to know that Stevens's tent is the second one down the lane there, on the right, though I don't know how anyone could mistake it. It's bigger than mine and usually sounds like there's a rowdy party going on there. Go get some rest."

"Yes, sir!" Yancy saluted then turned to leave.

But behind him he heard General Jackson say softly, "Sergeant Tremayne?"

Yancy turned back. "Yes, sir?"

"You are feeling well, are you not?"

"Yes, sir. Very well, sir. I'm ready."

"Good, good," he murmured his familiar refrain. He resumed his seat and put on his spectacles. "You're going to need to be. We're all going to need to be. Dismissed."

Yancy gave Midnight to one of the "cubs," very young soldiers of thirteen and fourteen that General Jackson had adamantly refused to put in the line of battle. He always had three or four of them ostensibly on his staff as "assistants." Mostly they helped Jim with fetching and carrying and took care of the staff's horses.

One of Yancy's favorites, Willy Harper, was feeding apple quarters to Midnight, caressing his nose and murmuring nonsense to him. Willy reminded Yancy of Seth Glick, the young boy who had tailed after Yancy so much when he had first arrived in the community. Like Seth, Willy had red hair and freckles and a friendly grin. He was short and had a small frame. He looked even younger than his thirteen years.

As Yancy approached, Willy came to attention and saluted, and he looked like a little boy playing dress-up in a soldier's costume. Yancy had to stifle a grin, because in Willy's saluting hand was the last quarter of the apple. "At ease there, Private Harper."

"Thank you, sir. I'm glad you're back, Sergeant Tremayne. Did you get hurt bad?"

"Naw, just addled my brains a little bit," Yancy answered, brushing one finger against the scar on his forehead. "I think they're all back in order now. You going to take care of Midnight for me? We've had a long, hard ride. He needs to be brushed good, and then I'd appreciate it if you'd wash him down, Willy. We both got pretty muddy on the road." Yancy looked down at his new thigh-high cavalry boots regretfully. They were splattered with gloppy red mud up to the knees.

"I'll take really good care of Midnight," Willy promised. "And — and then, if you want me to, I'll report to your tent and clean your boots, sir."

Yancy started to say a stern no — after all, Willy wasn't his body servant — but then he realized, perhaps with a wisdom beyond his years, that the boy sort of hero-worshipped him, and probably Peyton Stevens, too, and this was Willy's way of being included with them. So Yancy answered, "That's nice of you, Private. I am tired and I would appreciate it if you'd take care of that chore for me. And bring me an apple, too, if you've got an extra one."

"Yes, sir!" Willy said, saluting.

"Carry on," Yancy ordered.

Like the young boy that he was, Willy led Midnight off, talking a mile a minute to the horse and grinning his goofy smile.

Yancy hurried to Peyton's tent, which indeed was unmistakable. The tent flap was open. Inside Chuckins was stirring a big pot on the camp stove; a delicious scent of stewed beef floated out of the tent. Peyton lazed on his padded cot, reading a novel with a lurid cover. Sandy Owens dozed on another cot.

"Smells good, Chuckins," Yancy said, strolling into the tent. "Daddy come through again, Peyton?"

They all hurried to him and clapped him on the back so many times that Yancy thought he'd be sore tomorrow. After their greetings they settled down to catch up on the last two months.

"First we heard that you got shot in the head," Chuckins said soberly. "We were sure you were dead. But then General Jackson got word about one of the doctors at Chimborazo taking you to his house to take care of you and that you'd been shot twice but not mortally."

Yancy nodded. "True. Bullet grazed my head" — he lifted up the heavy locks of his hair to show them the scar — "and fractured my skull. Another bullet got me in the arm, but it wasn't too bad. I'm friends with the Hayden family, and Dr. Hayden was one of the doctors working at the hospital after the battle. He decided to take me home. I must've been real lucky. I heard there were about fifteen thousand wounded after the Seven Days battle."

This launched a highly detailed, technical description of the battles Yancy had missed. After several minutes of Peyton and Sandy trying to describe the fields and order of battle, the four of them sat down on the floor of the tent and began to draw in the dirt. Chuckins produced some dried beans, and they were arranged to show the different units and their placement in the battles. They started talking about the top-secret march of the Army of the Valley to flank Pope as the Army of Northern Virginia began to march north to meet him.

Peyton told Yancy, "You missed the fireworks then, boyo. Stonewall kept the march so secret he wouldn't even tell the division chiefs where we were going. I was given one fat envelope in my courier's bag and told to go three miles north to the first crossroads I came to and wait there. Didn't know how long, didn't know what for. I found out later that Stonewall told the commanders, 'March up this road. You'll come to a crossroads and there'll be a courier there with orders telling you which way to go. At the next crossroads, the same.' "

Peyton grinned mischievously. "So there I sat, me and Senator, in the middle of nowhere at these unnamed crossroads. Finally, after about six hours, I heard marching and saw a cloud of red dust, and out of it came Colonel B. W. Ripley of the 35th South Carolina, riding like thunder and fury. I mounted up in a hurry to meet him in the dead center of the crossroads. He came up, horse snorting and stamping, and him glaring at me with an evil eye. I handed him the dispatch. He tore it open, looked up at me, and commenced to cussing fit to turn the air blue. His command finally drew up, and he turned in the saddle and yelled, 'That way!' and pointed to the left-hand road. They started marching that way. The whole time they passed by he sat there and cussed me up, down, sideways, and back again."

Through his laughter Yancy asked, "What did you do? Weren't you mad?"

"Not really," Peyton carelessly replied. "It was, you know, impersonal. Like watching a force of nature. I was kinda fascinated, to tell the truth. He ended it when the last troops turned up the road. It was like capping a boiling pot. *Thump.* Silence. He rode off. Kinda hated to see him go."

Another one of the couriers, Smithson "Smitty" Gaines, suddenly stuck his head in the tent. "Oh, hi, Yancy. Glad you're back. Y'all won't ever guess."

Yancy sighed. "We're marching."

Smitty nodded. "Yep. Cook up three days' rations, strike the tents, and pack up tonight. We're leaving at dawn tomorrow." He popped out of view as abruptly as he had appeared.

"I knew it," Yancy muttered.

"You always do, but I didn't think even you could read Stonewall's mind from Richmond," Peyton said with no inkling of how close to the truth his words seemed to Yancy. "You know what, Yance? You're looking pretty rough. Why don't you eat some of that stew and take a rest."

"Sounds good," Yancy admitted. He stood up, took off his boots, and plopped down on his cot. "Except I think I'll eat when I wake up. I'm pretty tired."

The other three tiptoed out and pulled the tent flap shut, but Yancy could still hear his friends talking.

"I'm glad he's back," Sandy Owens said quietly, and Peyton agreed.

Chuckins said happily, "Me, too. I think it's a good sign. Stonewall's Boys are back again."

Yancy grinned as he closed his eyes, and in just a few moments he was asleep.

If he could have, General Thomas "Stonewall" Jackson would have kept their destination secret from everyone in the Army of Northern Virginia except for himself and General Lee and General Longstreet, and he had his doubts about Longstreet. But of course this was not possible. It was known to everyone in the South that on September 4, 1862, General Lee led his 40,000 battle-hardened men toward Maryland.

The first leg of the march was from the army's headquarters in Chantilly to a small Virginia town on the Potomac, Leesburg. Yancy and Peyton were, as usual, riding with the other couriers just behind Jackson's staff, who followed him. The staff officers kept a very loose formation behind the general. Yancy and Peyton had become favorites of the staff, as they were also obviously favorites of their general, so they often let them slowly ride up until they, too, were just behind Jackson.

As they passed through the small village, a woman standing in a doorway suddenly stiffened with recognition when she saw Jackson, her eyes wide. She ran fast, dashed into the road, and threw her scarf down in front of Jackson's horse.

General Jackson halted and stared at the woman on the sidewalk, obviously mystified.

One of the staff officers rode up close to him and murmured, "She means you to ride over it, General."

Now he smiled at the lady, who smiled back as if her face were suddenly lit by heavenly beams. Jackson doffed his cap and slowly rode over the scarf.

Behind him, the staff and aides exchanged delighted grins. Jackson was famous now, perhaps second only to Robert E. Lee. His face was well known from portraits in the newspapers. Ever since his triumphs at Cedar Mountain and Second Manassas, the people along the marches had recognized him. They often crowded Little Sorrel, hugging her; others touching the general's boots; mothers holding up babies for him to lay his hand on their heads; ladies thrusting handkerchiefs up to him to touch; still others handing him flowers and small flags and often, since his oddities had become known, lemons. No matter how often it happened, no matter if it was one lady or a crowd, General Jackson was obviously baffled by the attention, and it made him embarrassed and awkward. His staff loved it.

They marched and marched. On the ninth, General Lee ordered Jackson to his old command and the scene of such drama, Harpers Ferry. The strategic village was once again in the hands of the Federals, and it was vital for Lee to take it to protect the rear of the army, who were to march to Hagerstown, Maryland, and then farther north to engage the enemy.

After arranging his artillery in a careful sweep surrounding the town, Stonewall stood with his staff on a crag of Bolivar's Heights, looking down at the Federals ensconced in Harpers Ferry. The town was surrounded by hills, which made it easy to attack and impossible to defend.

One of Jackson's officers said, "It sure is down in a bowl, isn't it?"

Jackson said succinctly, "I'd rather take the place forty times than undertake to defend it once."

And so, almost before the first rolling artillery volley was finished, the Federals sent up the white flag, and 12,000 men surrendered. Jackson again had captured a rich unspoiled treasure — 13,000 small arms, seventy-three cannons, and countless foodstuffs, supplies, and other stores.

It was September 15, 8:00 a.m. Even before he went down into the town, Jackson called Yancy to him. "Dispatch to General Lee. Double-quick, Sergeant Tremayne."

"Yes, sir." Yancy saluted and Midnight took off in a flurry of dust and smoke that lingered on the air. It was sixteen hard miles, on the old Shepherdstown Road and crossing the Potomac at Boteler's Ford, to Lee's headquarters just west of Sharpsburg,

Maryland.

At three o'clock, Yancy returned. He was covered in dust, his boots wet to the knee. Midnight was lathering, his legs covered with mud up to his hocks. Still he pranced and stamped.

Yancy jumped off and hurried to Jackson, who was still in the village making arrangements to parole the prisoners. "Sir," he said breathlessly, "I have a return from General Lee."

Eyeing him shrewdly, Jackson took the note. He looked up at Yancy and asked, "Did you see the ground?"

"Yes, sir."

"And?"

"General Lee is hard-pressed, sir. Vast numbers of the enemy have massed east of Sharpsburg."

Jackson nodded. Lee's dispatch had said that if Jackson had not overcome Harpers Ferry that day, Lee was contemplating a retreat. He urged Jackson to come to Sharpsburg with all speed.

They marched all night, quite a feat after the last two weeks of marching and maneuvering and skirmishing. But they were Jackson's foot cavalry, and they were relentless. They reached Sharpsburg early on the morning of September 16. Two armies faced each other, intent on destruction, across a winding, cheerful little creek called Antietam.

It was September 17, 1862. Johnny Rebs called it the Battle of Sharpsburg; Yankees called it the Battle of Antietam. Each of the places on that horrendous battlefield carried its own too-clear imprint.

Dunker Church, where the bloodletting began at six o'clock that morning. And where Stonewall Jackson, calm and imperturbable in the midst of screaming bullets and murderous artillery, directed his men in his final counterattack, saving the Confederate left from complete destruction.

The North Woods, where General Joe Hooker's Union troops harassed the Confederate left all the day, visions of blue coats weaving in and out of the soft-wooded shadows, and sometimes storming out in waves, men in gray falling before them.

The East and West Woods, where both blue and gray fought and died, the sweet glades scarred by rifle fire and artillery explosions and men lying on the ground, coloring it scarlet.

The Cornfield, twenty acres of what had been well-ordered rows of sweet corn, with men of both the North and the South lying as they fell, just as the cornstalks lay from the onslaught. On that day the lines surged back and forth over the Cornfield no less than eight times. In the end neither army possessed it, only the dead.

The Sunken Road, which came to be known as Bloody Lane, because it was filled in some places six deep with Confederate dead.

Burnside's Bridge, surrounded in some places six deep with Federal dead.

General John B. McClellan was timid. He imagined General Robert E. Lee as all-powerful, and in his head he always was certain that the Army of Northern Virginia was half again, or sometimes twice as numerous as it was. "Little Mac," as he was affectionately known in the army, hated to risk his men. He could map out grand strategies, but when it came to completely committing his army to an aggressive offense, as General Lee always did, Little Mac would procrastinate, always asserting that the job could not be done unless he had more reinforcements, more cannons, more rifles, more ammunition, more aides, more couriers, more food, more tents, more blankets, more shoes, and more intelligence. Even his defensive moves were halfhearted and ineffective because of his reluctance to fight.

At Sharpsburg he outnumbered General Lee's army almost two to one, with a force of 75,000 facing Lee's army of 40,000. All that day McClellan attacked and defended in a piecemeal fashion. The Confederates cut up those Yankee pieces even more, and in pieces they retreated.

The Army of Northern Virginia lost over 10,000 men, killed, wounded, and missing. Federal casualties were close to 12,500. When the final awful numbers were tabulated, 22,546 men had fallen on that Bloodiest Day.

One thing happened to Yancy that day that should have made him glad. But because it happened at such a grim and critical moment during the Battle of Sharpsburg, he recalled it with wonder, mixed with the pall of dread that overlaid his every image of that battle.

When Jackson had withdrawn from Harpers Ferry, he had left General A. P. Hill's division behind to deal with the parole of their 12,000 prisoners and to inventory and transport the captured guns and material to Sharpsburg. Consequently, he was late arriving on the field; in fact, he arrived just at the moment that the Confederate right was about to crumble, and thus the Federals could easily have flanked them and then utterly destroyed them.

When General Jackson sighted the first of Hill's troops as they appeared on the Shepherdstown Road, Jackson sharply called out for Yancy. He rode up and the general grabbed Midnight's bridle. "General Hill is just arriving on the road, there, to the south. No time to write a dispatch; ride to him as fast as you can and ascertain if he is still at his strength and numbers or if he has lost stragglers along the road. And hurry back to me."

"Yes, sir," Yancy said and hurried off toward the south.

General A. P. Hill was already at the line of battle and was directing the first brigades marching into their positions.

Yancy rode at a blinding gallop to the front, through confusion of soldiers hurrying to get placed along the line. He drew up to the head of the brigade. Then he reined in Midnight so abruptly that he reared and screamed. General Hill turned, and in a single blinding instant, Yancy's mind was filled with images imprinted as surely as if he were seeing them with his eyes instead of his brain:

General A. P. Hill, in his blazing red flannel shirt, shouting orders and cursing at the top of his lungs on the bloody center of the Battle of Gaines' Mill.

Grinning at Yancy. "Orders from Stonewall, huh? What? Attack the North Pole?"

Looking down at his right arm, watching the dark stain spread.

Stunning blow to his head . . . gray . . . then black.

Yancy remembered it all — the noise, the screams, the guns, the smell, the fear, the pain. It filled his mind for a moment, and he had to shake his head to clear it. Then he rode up to General Hill and shouted, "General Hill! Message from General Jackson!"

And so he thought no more about it. He knew he would not have time until much later that night.

As night fell, the few guns firing here and there spluttered out. Lee's officers were expecting an order to retreat. In spite of the fact that the Confederates had undoubtedly driven the Federals from the field in a shamefaced retreat, the Army of Northern Virginia had been mauled badly, and withdrawal would have been understandable and perfectly honorable.

But Robert E. Lee stood his ground.

The Army of Northern Virginia camped

that night. Fatalistically they ate confiscated supplies more plentiful than they had since Second Manassas, anticipating another cruel fight the next day. Faithfully they believed in Robert E. Lee and with certainty believed, in spite of their cruelly reduced numbers, that they would drive the hordes of men in blue from the field once again.

Yancy and Peyton Stevens found a grassy swath under a bullet-scarred oak tree in the West Woods, where General Jackson had set up his overnight headquarters. Both of them were deadly tired, though they only felt a peculiar numbness, and they were ravenously hungry. They built a fire, neither of them speaking, only gathering up wood and hollowing out a shallow hole and going through the business of lighting the wood in a light breeze.

Peyton Stevens was pale and drawn and looked twice his age. Yancy was pasty-faced, the hollows of his jaw deep, his cheekbones sharp, his eyes red. They had fat peaches from one of the orchards they had passed on their march from Harpers Ferry. As always, Peyton had plenty of stores of tinned beef, peas, salmon, and even lobster. Yancy had brought a loaf of fresh bread from the prison bakery at Harpers Ferry that had, miraculously, survived in his haversack, along with some confiscated beef jerky.

As they ate, they slowly began talking, just a little, about the day, telling each other of the dispatches they had taken to which commander, and of the situation at the time. Both of them had been to General Lee's headquarters twice that day, and they compared notes on the beloved "Marse Robert" as his army called him.

"It's too bad that Chuckins can't do courier duty sometimes, as he loves General Lee so much." Yancy stopped, sat up, and looked around blankly. "Where is Chuckins, anyway?"

Peyton answered, "General Jackson called all his clerks together. He's taking them to tour the field hospital to get the information about the dead and wounded."

"Oh," Yancy said unhappily. "I'd rather ride through a hail of bullets than do that."

Peyton didn't answer.

Knowing that General Jackson could call them to duty at any time, after they ate they spread their blankets and went to sleep.

Long after midnight, Yancy was roused from feverish, hateful dreams of blood and gore by a small, pitiful sound. He sat up.

Charles Satterfield sat against the trunk of the oak tree, his knees drawn up, his arms hugging them, and his head resting on them. His shoulders shook. The little noises that Yancy heard was Chuckins sobbing quietly.

Yancy went to him, sat down by him, and put his arms around him. Chuckins buried his face in Yancy's shoulder. Chuckins cried for a long time, but finally the sobs subsided and he drifted off to sleep, leaning against Yancy's side, Yancy's arm still around him. They slept until dawn.

CHAPTER TWENTY-THREE

In October 1862, General Lee reorganized and streamlined his army. Major General James Longstreet was promoted to Lieutenant General and named commander of the newly-created First Corps. Major General Thomas "Stonewall" Jackson was also promoted to Lieutenant General and named commander of Second Corps. The Army of Northern Virginia was now not only in spirit, but also in letter, a cohesive unified whole.

Jackson called Yancy and Peyton into his headquarters tent. "I've just received a promotion, by the grace of God," he said humbly. "And for your outstanding service, your courage, your valor, and your dedication to the army, General Lee and I have agreed to give you field promotions to Second Lieutenant."

He rose, raised his right hand, and, stunned, Yancy and Peyton did the same.

Jackson swore them in with the Confederate Officers Notice of Commission, and then they took the Loyalty Oath. It was some time before Peyton and Yancy could actually believe that they were now lieutenants.

A few days after his own illustrious promotion, Jackson received a letter from Anna suggesting that she take steps to publicize his career. His reply was ever that of the devout Christian that he was:

> Don't trouble yourself about representations that are made of your husband. These things are earthly and transitory. There are real and glorious blessings, I trust, in reserve for us beyond this life. It is best for us to keep our eyes fixed upon the throne of God and the realities of a more glorious existence. . . . It is gratifying to be beloved and to have our conduct approved by our fellow men, but this is not worthy to be compared with the glory that is in reservation for us in the presence of our glorified Redeemer. . . . I appreciate the loving interest that prompted such a desire in my precious darling.

The Battle of Antietam almost claimed another casualty — President Abraham Lincoln. News of the horrendous bloodshed so anguished him that he came very near to physical prostration, and his grief was so great that his advisors, for a day or two, feared that he might suffer a mental breakdown. However, being the keen and stalwart leader that he was, he quickly overcame his desolation and turned again to leading his country in war.

In the aftermath of the shambles at Sharpsburg, Lincoln knew very well that it was the perfect opportunity to destroy the Army of Northern Virginia and shorten the war. He could clearly see that the Army of the Potomac, again fortified to 110,000 men, should pursue Lee's weakened and exhausted army into Virginia and crush them. But Lincoln could also clearly see that General George B. McClellan had no such plans in mind. After Antietam he had trumpeted his great triumph and settled down there to winter, safely and comfortably back across the Potomac and near to the 73,000 troops guarding Washington.

Determined to prod him, Lincoln made a surprise visit to him and the army on October 1. He stayed for three days, much of it spent pressing "Little Mac" to move the army forward. Yet he could sense it was to no avail.

Early one morning the president invited his close friend, Ozias Hatch, to go for a walk. On a hillside, Lincoln gestured with exasperation to the expanse of white tents spread out below. He asked, "Hatch, Hatch, what is all this?"

"Why, Mr. Lincoln," Hatch replied, "this is the Army of the Potomac."

"No, Hatch, no," Lincoln retorted. "This is McClellan's bodyguard."

After this fruitless visit, Lincoln tried peremptorily ordering McClellan to cross the Potomac and engage Lee.

McClellan flatly refused and engaged in a long series of shrill telegraphic demands for more reinforcements and more supplies.

Lincoln reached the end of his considerable patience. On November 5, 1862, he relieved McClellan of duty, directing him to return immediately to his home in Trenton, New Jersey, where he was to await "further orders," which he had no intentions of ever sending.

When he learned of his dismissal, McClellan wrote his wife that night:

They have made a great mistake. Alas for my poor country! I know in my inmost heart she never had a truer servant.

But that November, McClellan saw war for the last time.

For the third time, President Lincoln asked General Ambrose Burnside to take command of the Army of the Potomac. For the third time he refused, again insisting that he was not competent to handle so large a force. But when he learned that if he did not accept, the command would go to an officer that Burnside had long detested — General Joseph Hooker — he reversed his decision.

General Robert E. Lee was uncertain of what this change of command would take. He lamented McClellan's departure. "We always understood each other so well," he remarked to Longstreet with his characteristic modesty. What he really meant was that McClellan was transparent to him. General Lee, from the beginning of his adversary's command, had understood that McClellan dawdled, he was reluctant to seize the offensive, he was an incredibly poor strategist, and that most of his reputation as a military genius was due to adroit political posturing. Lee rarely spoke so harshly aloud of anyone, however, so he merely continued, "I fear they may continue to make these changes till they find someone whom I don't understand."

It was, indeed, a while before General Lee came to understand Ambrose Burnside. It was not because Burnside was clever, however. It was because he was so incredibly incompetent that Lee viewed him with disbelief . . . until he proved it.

However, when Burnside took command, Lee had good reason to be wary, because his army was split in two. This was because at the beginning of November, in the last days of McClellan's command, "Little Mac" had perhaps deep down begun to sense his own downfall. He had begun to slowly deploy the Army of the Potomac into Virginia, creeping down to Warrenton, Virginia, on the east side of the Blue Ridge Mountains. His strategy, as Lincoln had been pressing for months, was to stay astride Lee's lines of supply from the Shenandoah Valley and then to press south toward Richmond, engaging Lee from the north.

The problem, as always, was that McClellan dawdled along so slowly that Lee had been given time to position his army in what would most likely mean another Confederate victory and another Federal rout. Lee sent Jackson and Second Corps to the valley, threatening McClellan's western flank. He sent Longstreet and First Corps to Culpeper, twenty miles to the southwest, directly in McClellan's path.

Still, Lee was no fool, and he understood the peril that his army was in. It was divided in half, which in military terms equaled a weakening of the whole. As always, Lee was terrifically outnumbered — at this time the Army of the Potomac numbered about 116,000 men; the Army of Northern Virginia, 72,000. Again, as always, the Federal army was much better equipped than Lee's men. Lee knew very well that if the Federal army could be led by a daring and courageous commander instead of Little Mac, the odds of a victory for the Confederates would be diminished indeed.

And so, when Lee finally did see the new strategy of Burnside's Army of the Potomac, he was puzzled. On November 19, he learned that Burnside was moving the entire army south, along the east side of the Rappahanock River. Burnside was abandoning a promising opportunity to strike the two separated wings of the Army of Northern Virginia. Also, he was skirting around the Confederates again, a move very reminiscent of McClellan. Lee couldn't understand how Burnside could hope to gain a better position, but that was because Robert E. Lee was a military genius, and it was difficult, if not impossible, for him to comprehend utter military ignorance.

Abraham Lincoln and the War Department did not view General Burnside as ignorant. They had approved his grand new strategy. He proposed to position the army on the east side of the Rappahanock, just across from Fredericksburg, which was a picturesque village that stood squarely midway between Richmond and Washington. Burnside planned to build floating bridges across the Rappahanock River, send across the army quickly and in force, take Fredericksburg before Lee could block him, then move south and seize Richmond.

The plan depended on speed. General Burnside did succeed in marching his forces quickly, a stunning change from the days of "Little Mac." The army began their march on November 15, and by November 19, they were in position, a long, heavy blue line from Falmouth, north of Fredericksburg, some miles south of Fredericksburg at a possible alternate crossing called Skinker's Neck. From Stafford Heights, a series of hills on the west side of the river, Federal cannons brooded menacingly, aimed directly at the eastern shore.

And there and then the Army of the Potomac stopped and stayed, immovable and unmovable. Once again, incomprehensible Union hesitation gave Robert E. Lee ample time to deploy his army and position them on the most favorable ground. Fredericksburg was down in a little valley, with a line of gentle hills just behind it. Longstreet's First Corps was on the right, arrayed along a ridge called Marye's Heights. Jackson's Second Corps was on the left, along a crest of hills that looked down on wide, flat fields that stretched from the river all the way to the steep banks of the hills.

And so the two mighty engines of destruction faced each other across the gentle river and the forlorn little town. And still Burnside waited.

General Thomas "Stonewall" Jackson was not, in war, a man who could tolerate inaction very well. Every day he rode or walked the heights behind Fredericksburg restlessly, eyeing the army across the river with flaming blue eyes, envisioning scene after scene of vicious attacks. He was as cross as a fishwife, so irascible that his staff and aides — though they always accompanied him — stayed at a discreet, safe distance.

But in the last week of November, suddenly General Jackson's temperament sweetened tremendously. He was cheerful, making his clumsy little attempts at wit, smiling more often than anyone had ever witnessed. None of them knew what had caused this sea change in their general, for as always, he was intensely private and secretive.

Jackson had been expecting news from Anna, and finally he received a letter. It read:

My Own Dear Father —
I know that you are rejoiced to hear of my coming, and I hope that God has sent me to radiate your pathway through life. I am a very tiny little thing. I weigh only eight and a half pounds, and Aunt Harriet says I am the express image of my darling papa . . . and this greatly delights my mother. My aunts both say that I am a little beauty. My hair is dark and long, my eyes are blue, my nose straight just like Papa's, and my complexion not at all red like most young ladies of my age, but a beautiful blending of the lily and the rose. . . .
I was born on Sunday, just after the morning services at your church. . . .
                    Your dear little wee daughter

On December 10, Yancy was reading a letter with much pleasure:

. . . and so I hope you like the sketches, and that they may cheer you. I believe that my favorite is the one of Missy in the kitchen, it's such a comforting and homey scene. Remember how many hours we spent in there, reading the newspapers and watching her cook, our mouths watering? Or yours, at least, as always. While you were here I came to believe that Missy is right, your stomach goes all the way down both your long legs to your ankles.

We are going to try to send you some Christmas presents. I find it a miracle that the mail still runs smoothly, by all appearances. I know you'll be glad to know that we get letters regularly from Leslie. He is doing very well and always mentions you and writes of the hope of better days when we may all be together as a family again. (Your second family, of course!)

We pray for you daily, and we miss you very much. I miss you very much. I understand that since you are camped at Fredericksburg along with General Lee, naturally he would send all of the army's messages to Richmond. But we do miss the days when General Jackson's dashing courier would ride in all hours of any day for a visit. Should any opportunity at all present itself for you to come to us, we should be so very glad to see you. Blessed Lord grant that it may be soon!

From your best friend (probably),

Lorena

Yancy perused Lorena's sketches for long minutes, a smile playing on his lips. Mrs. Hayden, smiling down at the artist as she mounted the stairs, candle in hand; Dr. Hayden, putting on his ancient slouch hat and holding his beat-up medical bag, going out the door to Chimborazo; Missy, frowning down at a steaming pot on the stove as she stirred it — these three were all obviously done from memory. But Elijah's picture was blatantly posed. He stood looking straight at the artist, his bulky arms crossed in front of his chest. On his face was a smile so wide it seemed it would split his face. In her letter Lorena had said that he had stood as still as if it were a glass-negative photograph, even when she had told him to relax. He didn't stop posing until she had finished all but the fine shading.

Yancy chuckled to himself. *She's so talented, I had no idea.* He looked over the sketches again and thought, *It'd be great if she'd do some of herself and send them to me. I bet she never draws herself, she's so modest . . . but I'm going to write her and beg her. Bet she'll do it for me. . . .*

He got up and went to the little folding desk in their tent, sitting down with pencil and paper, and began:

Dear Best Friend (I'm pretty sure),

But that was as far as he got. Peyton, who was on courier duty that morning, came into the tent. "Hope you enjoyed your morning off, Yance," he said, going to his storage trunk, taking out a cigar, and lighting it with pleasure. General Jackson disapproved the use of tobacco, so the aides and even the staff officers basically hid and smoked. "We've got an assignment."

Yancy rose, threw on his tunic, and began buckling on his saber. "Are we riding?"

"No. That is, no courier duty. General Lee found out that there are still some holdouts in Fredericksburg, mostly old people and ladies with small children, and it's upset him. He's ordered all of the couriers that aren't riding today and all of the wagons that can be spared to go into town and help them evacuate."

When General Lee had arrived on November 20, he had been greeted with delight and relief from the inhabitants of Fredericksburg, believing that he would save their town from the Federals massing across the river. Regretfully General Lee had explained to the mayor and the city council that it was impossible to defend the little town. Federal artillery was aimed straight down at it from Stafford's Heights, and no number of charges by any thousands of infantry would be able to dislodge such well-placed guns. It was, Lee explained, a basic tenet of warfare that even privates knew. Infantry assailing well-placed defenders on high ground was simple suicide. Sorrowfully the city leaders came to understand this and ordered an evacuation of the town.

Twenty-two couriers and aides went down into town, followed by eight sturdy supply wagons that had been emptied. Peyton and Yancy, perhaps because their horses were the showiest — or maybe because they naturally tended to assume leadership positions — led them in.

Many of the people were already standing outside in heavy traveling clothes, some with trunks, some with their possessions simply knotted up in sheets. On Main Street through the center of town, just down from the Episcopal church, was a boardinghouse — a clean, simple three-story building painted white with neat black shutters.

As they neared it, Yancy could see that there were about a dozen people standing outside, with their trunks and cases on the walk. He reflected that he would start loading these people up first, and he rode to that side of the street.

He guided Midnight up to the hitching post directly in front of the building and scanned the little crowd. Suddenly he drew in a painfully quick sharp breath. His head and hands felt too warm. His vision narrowed until all peripherals disappeared. He stiffened and froze so suddenly that Midnight, sensing the intensity of Yancy's agitation, grew stock-still.

She stood just to the right of the door of the boardinghouse. Her hands were in front of her, holding the handle of a small portmanteau. Her face was upturned as she watched Yancy. It was heart-shaped and she was pale and sad, and her eyes were dark and filled with tears. She was wearing a royal blue mantle, and the cape was drawn up, and soft tendrils of her light brown hair damp in the dismal mist escaped, curling around her face.

Yancy did not see this girl. He saw Lorena. She looked up at him, her soft voice catching in her throat as she told him of her sorrow, the blue mantle framing her perfect face, her eyes shimmering with tears.

I loved her . . . I love her! I—I've loved her for so long! How — how could I have forgotten my darling Lorena? How could I have seen her every day, laughed with her, talked to her, listened to her sweet voice, and not feel this great longing? How, how . . . What have I done? What can I do?

"Yancy," Peyton said softly, touching his arm, "are you all right? You look like you've been struck by lightning."

"What?" Yancy said vaguely. His gaze was still locked on the girl, though in his mind he still saw Lorena.

"Yancy," Peyton said more insistently, "you're almost as pale as a white man. Are you sick?"

With an effort, Yancy tore his gaze away from the girl, took a deep breath, and managed to focus on Peyton's face. In spite of his joking words, Peyton looked concerned. Yancy passed a hand over his brow, realizing that one of his headaches, very rare now, was starting to threaten him with a vague ache behind his eyes. "No. No, I'm not sick. I'm — fine. I just . . ."

He couldn't possibly articulate what had

happened to him. Yancy, private man that he was, had never told his friends about his memory loss after he was wounded. He stole a look back at the girl. Now he could see that she didn't really look like Lorena; this girl was tall and curvy and her features were nothing like Lorena's. There was a very old man standing next to her, holding her arm, and Yancy realized that he must be her grandfather, perhaps, and likely he was the reason she had not attempted to evacuate.

Yancy forced himself to say firmly, "It's okay, Peyton. Don't worry about me. How about we start with these people here? I'll go back and bring up one of the wagons if you'll start organizing them."

He turned and rode back to the line of wagons behind the mounted couriers, taking the few minutes to calm himself and to bring his chaotic thoughts to order. He had a job to do, and it was important. These people needed him to be kind and attentive and reassuring. He would have to put his shocking revelation about Lorena aside for now. Later, perhaps, he would figure out what to do.

The next night, December 11, at 2:00 a.m., Federal engineers started building bridges. The night was smothered in a heavy, wet fog, and it was bitterly cold. Though the sounds were completely recognizable, the clanks of tools and crash of timbers sounded oddly muffled on the thick air. Still, they were enough for the sharpshooters Lee had stationed along the Confederate side of the riverbank.

They fought off the bridge builders all night and all the next day. Supremely frustrated, Burnside fired 5,000 shells into Fredericksburg, reducing it to rubble. Still the sharpshooters picked off the engineers every time they showed their faces.

Burnside ordered the army to cross in pontoon boats, which they did successfully, though with some losses. The Confederate skirmishers fell back slowly, grinding the first line of Yankees down, giving every yard grudgingly. But finally they were threatened to be overwhelmed, and they withdrew to the safety of the heights.

That day, the Union soldiers had literally sacked the entire town, dragging furniture, pianos, paintings, dishes, linens, clothing, books — anything they could get their hands on — out into the streets and destroyed them. They stole every valuable they could find and every scrap of food and drink. Fires raged all over the city from the Federal shelling, and the soldiers often took torches from the houses that burned and set others on fire.

From the grim heights behind the benighted town, Robert E. Lee watched Burnside's army. More and more of them swarmed across the Rappahanock, the pontoon boats crossing again and again, each time full, coming from the east side. Surely, Lee thought, Burnside would not do the unthinkable — attack these unassailable hills. Lee's army was ordered in what was as close to perfect position as could ever be in war. He had the high ground, with almost no cover below in the approaches to the foot of the hills, his artillery arranged so as to inflict sure death over carefully laid zones of fire. No sane opponent would dare attack him.

Yet Burnside did just that. He was not insane, though throughout the Battle of Fredericksburg, Lee and his generals had very good cause to wonder.

On December 13, in the cold gray dawn, Burnside ordered the attack to begin. They attacked Jackson, on the Confederate right, and were beaten back with heavy casualties. They attacked Longstreet, arrayed on the invulnerable reaches of Marye's Heights.

The Federals were routed, with heavy casualties. Again and again, brigade after brigade charged First Corps' guns and massed musketry. The slaughter was horrendous.

Burnside ordered a final assault on the center at dusk. They fell in their hundreds crossing the open ground to those impossible heights. At dark, at last, the guns were silenced.

In one day of massacre, the Union army had sustained 12,653 casualties in killed, wounded, or missing; the Confederate army, 5,309.

On the next day, a truce was declared and the armies recovered their dead and wounded. The truce ended that afternoon, and the Federals resumed their battle formation on the field. Lee, Longstreet, and Jackson readied themselves for another attack. It did not come.

That night a violent rainstorm assaulted the area. The next morning, Lee and his lieutenants looked out over a deserted battlefield.

In the storm, the Federals had crept back across the Rappahanock River. The Battle of Fredericksburg was over.

CHAPTER TWENTY-FOUR

"Yancy, what are you doing?" Peyton asked lazily. He was sprawled on his cot, smoking a cigar, blowing smoke rings into the air.

"I don't know," Yancy answered distractedly. He was pacing, though not in a fast back-and-forth manner. He would sit at the camp desk, stare down at the papers spread out on it, then jump up and stride to the tent opening. He'd open the flap and stand there, staring outside for long moments. Then dropping it, he would go to stand by the camp stove, open it, jab irritably at the coals, slam it shut, and then walk a few paces back and forth. Again he would sit down at the desk and moodily peruse the papers. He had been doing variations of this routine for almost an hour.

"I don't know either," Peyton retorted. "But I do know that you're annoying me to distraction. If you don't stop twitching I'm going to have to kill you."

"At least I'd be out of my misery," Yancy muttered. He put his head in his hands.

Peyton sat up and regarded his friend with concern. "C'mon, Yance. You've been a train wreck ever since Fredericksburg. It was bad, I know, but it sure wasn't as bad for us as Sharpsburg, and you came through that like a trooper. Is it — is it just getting to you? All of it?"

"No, no, it's not the war," Yancy answered bleakly. "It's — it's — I can't explain it."

"Look, you're my friend," Peyton said evenly. "I know you're not much for talking about yourself and your troubles. But just tell me this much — is there anything at all I can do to help?"

"No . . . no."

"Is there anyone that can help you?"

"Not really, no."

Peyton gave up. He lay back down and blew another perfect smoke ring. "Okay, then," he said resignedly. "But don't forget. If you don't calm down, I *am* going to kill you."

Yancy's trouble was Lorena, of course.

After Fredericksburg, the army had camped about twelve miles south of the town, in a serene wooded area alongside the Rappahannock. Jackson's headquarters were at Moss Neck Manor, a gracious

535

plantation mansion with long columned porches. As always, Jackson had refused to stay in the house; he firmly held that soldiers, even if they were lieutenant generals, should quarter in tents. About a week later, however, he developed an earache, a condition that had been cropping up throughout the fall and winter. He bowed to his physician and then consented to use a three-room outbuilding that served as an office, a study, and a library for the master of the plantation, as his office.

The staff had camped nearby on the manor grounds. Peyton, Yancy, and Chuckins were again living comfortably in Peyton's tent. It was January 1, the first day of the year 1863, and they had been at leisure ever since December 18, when the last Union halfhearted rearguard action had finally allowed the last of the demoralized Federal army to cross the Rappahannock.

And Yancy had been in turmoil since December 18, when his entire being was no longer taken up with battle. On that day, as they had retrieved their belongings from the wagon train and had set up their tent, Yancy had found the letter he had started before the war's events had provided a so-welcome distraction.

"Dear Best Friend (I'm pretty sure)," it read.

Yancy had stared at the innocuous words for a long time. Finally, numbly, he had written a peculiar, disjointed letter, clumsily telling her that he missed her and her family, and he hoped to see them soon. He loved the sketches. Then he begged her to do some drawings of herself and send them to him. In this request he tried to mimic the notes he had hit when he had wheedled her for something — a second portion of roast beef, for her to read to him, for her to fix him bacon and eggs late at night. But the tone was false. It read like begging, and he thought that glimpses of his desperation showed through. He tried and tried to figure out how to rephrase it, but Yancy was not a very subtle man, and he finally gave up, signed the letter, "Your friend, Yancy," sealed it up, and sent it to the mail tent by Willy before he could change his mind.

And then the mental torture began. Every day, all day. *She is my best friend, I'm sure. But is that all she feels? It must be. All that time, she was warm and friendly and kind and even loving — but like a sister. Was she relieved that I forgot October? That night, she was so unsure; she wasn't distant but she was so very cautious. Maybe she finally came to realize that she doesn't love me, can't love me. . . .*

But what if . . . what if . . . she does have feelings for me? I was so oblivious, so ready to just be friends, she couldn't possibly have forced herself on me, blind fool that I am. Maybe she thinks that I'm gone forever, that I lost my love for her completely.

The problem was that Yancy had no idea which scenario was the truth. Was he her best friend, or was he her lost love? He didn't know, and it gnawed at him constantly. And he simply could not figure out how to find out the truth. He thought it would be foolish to write her and blurt out that, yes, he'd forgotten he loved her but now he remembered. And by the way, had she fallen in love with him yet?

For the same reason, he didn't ask for leave to go see her. What would he say? What *could* he say? Like running in an eternal, endless, maddening circle, Yancy went over and over these thoughts.

On this day, Yancy had received his Christmas gifts from the Haydens. Dr. Hayden had commissioned Leslie's tailor to make Yancy two brand-new uniforms for his promotion. As an officer he wore a mid-thigh frock coat, double-breasted, with heavy embroidered gold braid on the cuffs and polished brass buttons. On the trousers, a gold stripe gleamed down the breeches.

They also had four fine lawn dress shirts made for him. They had sent him a brand-new pair of leather boots, thigh-high, in the cavalry style. They had even sent him a new kepi cap, with a gold braid.

But the best gift was from Lorena. Yancy had received three letters from her since he had written her that awkward letter from her "friend," but she had never sent any self-portrait, nor had she mentioned it. Yancy was not really surprised. She was modest, and he thought that her beauty sometimes made her feel uncomfortable. It would be hard for her, he knew, to honestly present herself as the very lovely woman that he knew she was.

But for Christmas, for him, she had done it. She had done two drawings of herself. One was full-length. She was standing in front of a window. Yancy knew it well. It was the window in the guest bedroom, where he had spent two months recovering from his wounds. In the picture she held the drapes slightly open, and golden sunlight fell on her face as she looked down at the quiet street. Yancy had seen her like this a hundred times.

The other picture was three-quarter face. She was looking off to her right, smiling a little. It was an uncanny likeness that captured the warmth in her eyes, the long dark lashes, the mysterious half smile on her full lips when Yancy knew she was secretly amused.

When he first saw them, his heart leaped; surely these pictures of her were so personal, even intimate — a gift from a woman that could be made only for her love.

Then his heart sank. Perhaps, in his consuming love for her, he was transferring his feelings to the pictures, giving them a meaning that Lorena had never intended.

And so Yancy had again spun off into his maddening universe whose center was the riddle that was Lorena, staring again and again at the pictures on the camp desk, prowling around the tent like some caged animal, until Peyton had brought him back to a semblance of his senses.

Now, as he watched Peyton peacefully blowing smoke rings, he realized that it was true — not only was he driving himself crazy, he was driving his friends crazy. He determined that he would find the strength to control himself and his riotous emotions. And he would find a way, somehow, to find out about Lorena and her feelings for him. He had no choice. He had to, or he thought that he would, quite possibly, truly go mad.

Chuckins came in, stamping the snow

from his boots, shrugging off his overcoat, humming happily. "Hullo," he greeted them. "Stonewall gave me the afternoon off." He warmed his hands at the stove for a few moments. Then, looking at Yancy's strained face curiously, he walked over and innocently looked at the pictures of Lorena on the desk. He whistled with appreciation. "What a pretty lady. Is she your girl?"

Yancy looked down at the sketches for the hundredth time. "I don't know," he said blankly.

Peyton said with exasperation, "Chuckins, don't ask anybody any questions. Yancy doesn't know anything. I don't know anything. And neither do you. If we don't leave it at that, I'm going to have to kill Yancy. And we don't want that, now, do we?"

"No, Peyton," Chuckins obediently agreed.

"No, we don't. So, Chuckins, whatcha gonna cook us for supper?"

Never was there such a splendor of Confederate generals and colonels as at the dinner that Lieutenant General Thomas "Stonewall" Jackson gave for his favorite tormentor, Major General Jeb Stuart, and his commanding officer, General Robert E. Lee. The dining room at Moss Neck was luxurious. The costly china, crystal, and silverware glowed; and the long, gleaming table was the height of elegance.

But neither the magnificence of the dining room nor the dashing uniforms of the officers — even Jeb Stuart's flamboyant swashbuckling garments — outshone General Jackson. Stuart had sent him a dazzling officer's frock coat, with the traditonal grouping of four sets of three gleaming buttons arrayed down the double-breasted tunic, which was trimmed with gold lace. Even the gilded buttons were ornate, stamped with "C.S.A." The three stars embroidered on the collar and the complex embroidery on the sleeves were of the finest close-woven work. Admirers had given him a gold sash, a new saber and scabbard, and even gleaming knee-high boots.

Of course Jeb Stuart couldn't resist taunting him. Raising his glass, he said, "General Jackson, I must compliment you on your finery. I see that I am outshone, and I resent it extremely. Tomorrow I will endeavor to renew my entire wardrobe."

As always when Stuart teased him, Jackson blushed like a girl. "Couldn't outshine you, General Stuart. You are the biggest and finest peacock of us all."

In the ease of the moment, one of Jackson's colonels added, "At Fredericksburg, when our general first rode through the troops in his new fancy dress, one of the men had said, aghast, 'Old Jack's drawed his bounty money and bought new clothes!' Another grumbled something like, 'He don't look right, like some struttin' lieutenant. I'm afraid he'll not get down to work.' "

Jackson's servant Jim was a wonderful cook, but for this special occasion he had outdone himself. Some of the lesser officers had not seen such bounty since the war began. They feasted on turkeys, hams, a bucket of Rappahannock oysters, fresh-baked white bread and biscuits, pickles, and other sumptuous delicacies. Most of the food was gifts to Jackson from admirers. Ladies from Staunton had even sent him a bottle of wine, which Jackson readily served and which Jeb Stuart badgered him about.

Even General Lee joined in with gentle teasing of his own, smiling at Jackson. "You people are only playing soldier," he said. "You must come to my quarters and see how soldiers ought to live." General Lee's headquarters were, as always, a plain tent near Hamilton's Crossing on the Rappahannock.

There were other — perhaps more modest — dinners that General Jackson gave.

Undoubtedly he enjoyed wintering at Moss Neck. Though it was not a time of battles, neither was it strictly a time of leisure for Jackson. One of his main priorities had always been drill. He drilled his men constantly, and often he directed the drills himself, always demanding and exacting and seeking to better the men.

Another onerous task that he was obligated to do during this relative cessation of hostilities was reports. His last report had been of Kernstown, one of the parts of the Seven Days Campaign back in July of 1862. Since then he had been engaged in fourteen battles in eight months, and as the commander of first the Army of the Shenandoah Valley and then Commander of Second Corps, he always had much administrative work.

During this tedious time, he had found Sergeant Charles Satterfield's help invaluable. Not only was Chuckins a fine clerk, but he also was able to phrase Jackson's reports professionally, succinctly, and with perfect clarity.

One definite pleasure that Jackson had during the long winter months was the friendship of Janie Corbin. She was the five-year-old daughter of his hostess at Moss Neck. She was welcome at his office at any time, and she played for hours on the hearth while Jackson droned his dictation on and on to Chuckins and his other clerks. More than once he paused in his work to watch her, his grim warrior's expression softened to gentleness. Sometimes he would take her on his knee, and then they would do Janie's favorite pastime — he would cut out paper dolls for her, folding paper to fashion figures holding hands.

Every time, she would pull the long line of figures apart and ask, "And who are these, Gen'ral Jackson?"

"Those, ma'am, are the men of the Stonewall Brigade," was always Jackson's solemn reply.

As the winter drew on, Yancy could sense that Jackson grew more and more homesick. Often after work he would take a ride on his favorite mount, Little Sorrel, and wander along the riverbank.

Once he met Yancy, who, needing the fresh biting air of February to clear his mind, was by the banks of the quiet river. He was walking along, leading Midnight, when Jackson came up on him. Yancy came to attention and saluted, but Jackson made a careless gesture and said, "At ease, at ease, Lieutenant. May I join you?"

"Of course, sir, it would be my pleasure."

They walked along in silence for a while. Jackson stopped and stared across the river. "They're still over there," he said grimly. "They've got a new commanding officer, did you know?"

"Yes, sir," Yancy answered. "My friends in Richmond send me the papers when there is important news in them. General Hooker was appointed just a few weeks ago, was he not?"

"Mmm," Jackson assented. "Our intelligence has a lot on him. Acquitted himself admirably during the Seven Days and Second Manassas. Reported to be courageous and a military professional. He floundered at Fredericksburg, as they all did. It's said, and I believe, that it was probably due to deficiencies in his commanding officer, General Burnside. Hooker replaced him."

" 'Fighting Joe Hooker' he's called," Yancy said.

"Yes, and that's why I think that soon there is going to be a fight," Jackson said, narrowing his eyes as if he could see Hooker's thousands arrayed across the river.

Both of them searched that forbidding west bank for long moments, then by mutual assent they turned and started walking again.

At length Jackson said, "Did you know, Yancy, that I haven't seen my home in Lexington for almost two years? And it's been nearly a year since I've seen Anna . . . and I have yet to see my baby daughter."

Yancy was astonished, both that Jackson was confiding in him in this manner and that he had used his given name. It was the first time, he realized, that the formal and reticent man had ever called him 'Yancy.' *He must be horribly homesick,* Yancy thought with great sympathy.

As he reflected on General Jackson's plight, he realized that his own troubles were small compared to his commanding officer's. During the last two years, he had seen his family several times, and he had seen the Haydens and Lorena fairly often. General Jackson's daughter was almost three months old now, and he had never set eyes on her. Yancy imagined that the longing he felt for Lorena was not to be compared with Jackson's yearning for his daughter, especially after he had lost two babies, one with his first wife, Elinor; and then he and Anna had lost their daughter in 1858.

Quietly Yancy said, "Sir, I pray for you all the time, but now I will pray fervently that you may see Mrs. Jackson and your daughter very soon."

"Thank you, Lieutenant Tremayne," he said, returning to his usual cool reserve. They walked on and then he added, "Her name is Julia. Julia Laura. And yes, may the merciful and bountiful Lord grant that I see her soon."

As the winter melted into Virginia's warm and welcoming spring, General Jackson grew restless. At his headquarters at Moss Neck he had too many visitors, both soldiers and civilian admirers. He was entirely too accessible there. Perhaps, too, echoes of General Lee's gentle teasing at Jackson's dinner still faintly hung on in his mind; Jackson knew very well that General Lee always headquartered in a plain soldier's tent, with only his camping equipment, a camp stove, a military desk, and a cot. His only accessory was a hen that stayed under his cot and laid an egg for him every morning.

The fact that Jackson's health had deteriorated during the winter — and his physician's strict orders that he must not camp outdoors — faded from his disciplined mind. He determined to move to a tent headquarters at Hamilton's Crossing, very near to General Lee, and he set the move for March 15. General Jackson demanded promptness at all times and in all endeavors, and so by the evening of the fifteenth he was well established, his headquarters already organized, and his staff fully bivouacked, too. They began their routine again, that of drill and Jackson's endless reports and the mountain of administrative tasks of running an army corps.

On the eighteenth, the weather was particularly inviting. A balmy breeze stirred the air that was filled with spring butterflies and dandelion fluffs. The sun was kind, a pleasant warmth on the shoulders, and a benevolent lemon yellow glow.

Jackson, in an unusually good mood, dismissed his clerks and determined to go outside and sit in the sun for a while and read the Bible. Jim spread a blanket for him under a little dogwood tree just by his tent. It was in full flower, the simple white blossoms dazzling.

Around Jackson, soldiers worked gathering firewood, helping Jim arrange the general's stores, policing the area just around the general's headquarters. His staff and aides were also outside enjoying the day, some quietly reading; some gathered in groups talking about battles, horses, sabers, rifles, ammunition — all the things that all soldiers were interested in.

■ ■ ■ ■

For once Sandy Owens had been able to join Yancy, Peyton, and Chuckins. Peyton had managed to bribe the supply wagon team that was setting up their tents, and they had put up Peyton's tent in a favored spot, just behind and to the right of General Jackson's tent. Today they had set up a friendly horseshoe competition. Naturally, with his artilleryman's eye, Sandy Owens was beating the tar out of the other three.

They saw Dr. Hunter McGuire, chief medical officer of the First Corps, and also General Jackson's personal physician, by his request. McGuire was young, with handsome, sensitive features. When the staff and soldiers saw the stricken look on the doctor's face, they stopped what they were doing and watched him as he slowly walked, shoulders bowed, to Jackson.

Jackson looked up, and seeing McGuire's face, scrambled to his feet.

McGuire came close to him and murmured something to him that no one could hear.

Jackson reacted with shock, his eyes widening and his jaw convulsively clenching. Then, to everyone's astonishment and dismay, he walked — almost stumbled — to a tall stump of a sweetgum tree that had been cut to accommodate the campsite. Jackson sank down on it, bowed his head, and began to sob. This, from the man that had stared dry-eyed at thousands of his beloved men lying on the bloody field at Sharpsburg, was the most heart-wrenching sight that Yancy had ever seen.

Even before they knew what had happened, tears began to roll down Chuckins's face.

The news spread fast among the still, silent men. Little Janie Corbin had died of scarlet fever.

Jackson mourned for her. His men mourned for their beloved general.

Soon, however, General Jackson and his men had cause for rejoicing.

On a dreary Monday, April 20, at noon, Jackson and his escort rode to Guiney Railroad Station. Before the train had come to a complete stop, he jumped up and pushed his way into the coach. There he saw his daughter for the first time.

She was fat, pink, and sleepy. Anna recalled that he would not take her in his arms because of his dripping coat, but he stared at her and made funny little baby coos to her. Jackson had arranged for them to stay at the Yerby home, which was near his headquarters. Once they arrived and were in the privacy of their room, Anna wrote:

He caressed her with the tenderest affection and held her long and lovingly. During the whole of this short visit, when he was with us, he rarely had her out of his arms, walking her, and amusing her in every way he could think of — sometimes holding her up before a mirror and saying, admiringly, "Now, Miss Jackson, look at yourself!"

Then he would turn to an old lady of the [Yerby] family and say: "Isn't she a little gem?" He was frequently told that she resembled him, but he would say: "No, she is too pretty to look like me!"

On April 23, when Julia was five months old, Anna and General Jackson decided to have her baptized at the Yerby home. The ceremony was to be done by Reverend B. Tucker Lacy, a minister who had long been with the valley troops and who Jackson had named the unofficial chaplain general for the Second Corps.

When the staff and aides heard of the baptism, Yancy went to Reverend Lacy's tent. "Sir, many of the aides would like to attend the baptism. May we have permission?"

The chaplain refused, though not in an unkindly manner: "I'm sorry, Lieutenant Tremayne, but it is to be a private service."

"Yes, sir," Yancy said, crestfallen. But then, gathering his courage, he went to General Jackson's tent.

Even with Anna and Laura there, Jackson still attended to all of his military duties. Jackson sat at his desk and called Yancy in at his request.

"General Jackson, sir. I've just been to see Reverend Lacy to ask permission to attend Miss Julia Jackson's baptism. But he refused, saying that it was to be a private service. Several of us aides hoped to attend, so may we at least assemble outside and perhaps see Miss Julia and you and Mrs. Jackson after the ceremony?"

Expansively happily, Jackson waved his hand. "Mrs. Jackson and I would be glad for you and the other aides to attend. I request that you give Mrs. Yerby a list, so that she might know how many people we have to accommodate. But you and the rest of my staff are welcome."

Yancy dashed off to tell the others.

The Yerby parlor, though it was a generous room of large proportions, was crowded that spring afternoon. Yancy and many of the other young men had never witnessed the Presbyterian baptismal rite. He was awed at the solemnity of the occasion and the resounding, profound, eternal words of the ceremony from the *Book of Common Prayer.* Yancy noticed the beatific look on Stonewall Jackson's war-hardened features and thought he had never seen such pure happiness on a man's face.

The Yerbys' hospitality was such that they had prepared light refreshments on the lawn for the soldiers that attended. Two long tables, set with creamy white tablecloths, held a big bowl of fruit punch, gallons of iced tea with fresh mint, fresh-squeezed lemonade, and pitchers of thick, cool buttermilk. On the other table were oatmeal cookies, slices of still-warm nut bread, a tall frothy sponge cake, peach slices, apple slices, fat cherries, nectarines, and, in an amusing bow to General Jackson, a bowl of cheery yellow lemons.

After a pleasant half hour, Anna and the baby came out to sit on the veranda. General Jackson sat by them, motioning the nearest soldier to come up, by which they understood that they might come see the baby. Jackson beamed, his eyes glowing with inner warmth, his glances at Anna and Julia so tender that most of his soldiers could hardly believe he was the same grim warrior they saw on the battlefield. Discreetly, they filed by one by one, no one lingering except to bow to Mrs. Jackson and thank her.

When Yancy came up to them, Anna smiled up at him and said quietly, "Yancy, my dear, how you have grown! I would wish to see you, so that we may catch up on our news, and so that you can tell me everything that the general has done that I must scold him for."

Even at this gibe, Jackson smiled at her then told Yancy, "Unless something untoward happens, I believe you may take an hour or two tomorrow to visit my wife. But that is only if you stay discreet and give her no cause to scold."

"No, sir, I wouldn't ever do that," Yancy said hastily. Bowing, he said, "Then I shall be happy to call upon you tomorrow, Mrs. Jackson. Thank you kindly for the invitation."

"I look forward to your call," she responded graciously.

At two o'clock the next afternoon, Yancy sat at that same table on the Yerbys' veranda with Anna Jackson. Next to her was her maid, Hetty, holding Julia. The plump, good-natured baby looked around her with interest, and at Hetty's low nonsense talk, would sometimes smile.

"She is much like him," Yancy observed. "It's not so much that she looks like him, but she has so many of his features. It's so distinctive, to see black hair and blue eyes. It's quite striking in men or women. And she has his straight nose and the same lips."

Anna said, "Many people have told him that she resembles him, but he always says that she is much too pretty to look like him."

"Well," Yancy said, "maybe it could be said that she looks like the general, only prettified."

Anna giggled, a pleasantly youthful sound coming from a mature woman. "Oh! So true. I must tell Thomas that."

"Don't tell him I said it," Yancy said hastily. "He's not gentle with anyone but you, ma'am."

"I know," she said softly. "No one would ever believe what a loving and tender husband he is. And how jolly and happy he is at home."

"I would never have believed it if I hadn't seen a little of it when I was working for you," Yancy agreed. "And I've never tried to tell anyone about him at home. They'd laugh me to scorn and call me a liar."

Julia started fussing a little and Anna said, "I believe she is ready for her nap, Hetty. You may take her on up and put her to bed."

"Yes, Miss Anna," she said and went inside with the baby.

Yancy said, "It was so kind of you and General Jackson to share Julia's baptism with us. I had never seen a service like that. It was wonderful. I could feel the presence of the Lord the whole time, and it made me remember again how wonderful it is to be saved."

"It is, of all things, most to be cherished," Anna agreed. "And I'm so very glad, Yancy, to see how you've grown, not only to manhood, but to a fine Christian man. I know how hard it was for you to find your own way to Christ, but I rejoice that you did."

Yancy smiled a curious half smile. "For one of the worst days of my life, it was the best day of my life. But you know, yesterday also brought it home to me like never before that I've never been baptized. And it makes me kinda sad, because of course I want my family to be with me when I am. But no Amish bishop would ever baptize me; in fact, I guess I'm still being shunned," he finished sadly.

Anna reached over and patted his hand,

her tiny white hand in stark contrast to Yancy's muscular dark bronze hand. "The next time you come home, I will introduce you to our minister, Reverend White. I'm confident that even if you don't choose to join the Episcopalian church, he would be glad to baptize you. After all, no matter which church we attend, we are all God's beloved children, and sisters and brothers in Christ Jesus. And I know that Reverend White will be glad to arrange a baptism in any way that will be acceptable to your family."

"Thank you so much, Mrs. Jackson. Already I feel much better," Yancy said.

Anna nodded, then a mischievous look came into her dark eyes. "You were always a good-looking boy, Yancy, but now you are a very handsome man. Tell me, surely there is a lady somewhere? Or maybe even two, or three?"

Yancy would never dream of answering Anna Jackson with anything less than the truth. "There is one lady," he answered somewhat shyly. "But we — I'm not sure exactly how we stand. It's so hard, being apart. You and General Jackson know that better than anyone."

Anna studied his face thoughtfully. Yancy knew she could tell that there was much he wasn't telling her. "It is so trying for families and people who love each other to be torn apart by this awful war. But as always, the best and most hopeful comfort we have is in the Lord. I will pray for you and your lady, Yancy. I will pray that you will find each other in these days of turmoil, and that you will learn of each other, and if it is God's will, you may find happiness together."

"Thank you, Mrs. Jackson," Yancy said in a somewhat choked voice. "That is my prayer, too."

"And now," she said briskly, "what is all this that you say you will not tell me of the general. Because you see, Yancy, that I must depend on my friends, like you, to keep me aware of his misdeeds and misbehavior."

Yancy laughed, his discomfort eased. "Mrs. Jackson, you are the only person on this earth that would dare use those two words in connection with General Stonewall Jackson. I can assure you that he has no familiarity with misdeeds and misbehavior. And even if he did," he added slyly, "though I'm glad you call me your friend, I would be scared out of my wits to report anything to you that might cause you to scold him. No, no. I'm afraid, Mrs. Jackson, you're going to have to find another informant. One more courageous than me."

General Jackson spent every single minute that he could spare from his duties with Anna and Julia, mostly in the privacy of their room at the Yerby mansion, where they could concentrate solely on each other and the baby. Jackson could not watch Julia enough; he often knelt by her cradle for as long as an hour, simply watching her sleep. Together he and Anna prayed, and Anna told him she had never known such deep spiritual meaning as Thomas's prayers for her and Julia.

General Lee did call, and Anna obviously was a little nervous to meet this exalted, walking legend. But his courtly, fatherly manners soon put her at ease, and she came to admire him as most people did upon meeting him.

On Sunday she and Jackson attended Sunday service with Reverend Lacy presiding. Jackson was pleased as General Lee greeted Anna with his customary courtly charm; the old bachelor General Early paid endearing homage to her; and many of the other officers were introduced to her and paid her the highest compliments.

For his part, this may have been the best Sunday service that Jackson had ever attended. All that long winter he had seen the other generals' wives with their husbands at Sabbath services, and it had made him long all the more for Anna. Now, with her at his side, he thought his happiness on this earth could not be more complete.

The days passed all too swiftly. It was dawn on April 29. Jackson and Anna slept deeply. The baby had not stirred. Abruptly the coarse noise of boots sounded on the stairs, and then a peremptory knock came at the door.

"General Early's adjutant wishes to speak to General Jackson," an urgent young voice called.

Jackson got out of bed and immediately began to dress. "That looks as if Hooker were crossing the river," he said. He hurried downstairs to hear what the courier had to say then came running back up to their room. "I was right," he told Anna grimly. "Federals are crossing the river as we speak. There is going to be a battle, and you and Julia must hurry south. I'll arrange a transport and send it to you." He went to stare at the still-sleeping Julia for long moments then gave Anna a hasty kiss and left.

Jackson hurried to the front and saw that generals Early and Rodes were already making proper plans to receive the enemy. Jackson quickly went to his headquarters, where intelligence reports were already starting to come in. It appeared that the movement at his front was a feint and that the main force of the Federal army was crossing the Rappahannock in force to the north of him.

In the next two days, Lee and Jackson were to decide where he must concentrate his forces. He must lead them to a hostile track of impenetrable underbrush and stinking marshy ground known as the Spotsylvania Wilderness, for the Federals were mired in it. Two miles from the eastern edge was a rise and a crossroads with an old public house called Wilderness Tavern. Nearby was a farm owned by a family named Chancellor. This lonely crossroads had come to be called by the exalted name of Chancellorsville.

CHAPTER TWENTY-FIVE

In January 1863, Lee had dispatched General Longstreet to southeast Virginia, in the area of Suffolk, where the Federals were investing a nominal force. But it could have turned into a major movement that threatened Richmond, so Lee had sent all but three brigades of First Corps. On April 29, Jackson and Lee had to face the fact that the Federal incursion over the Rappahannock was in force, and they were facing about 130,000 Union soldiers with a force of about 60,000 effectives. The remainder of the Army of Northern Virginia was over 150 miles away, and Hooker was moving fast. He was landing forces both to Lee's north, at Kelly's Ford, and to the south, in Lee's rear, at Fredericksburg.

General Jackson spent all day and most of the night of the twenty-ninth reconnoitering the Federal dispositions, observing the developments of the rapidly changing situation. Reporting back to General Lee, they came to the conclusion that the movement to the south was a feint and the much larger body of the Union army that was crossing at Kelly's Ford was the main attack. On this day they had started slowly making their way through the Spotsylvania Wilderness.

Since both Lee and Jackson were valiant and daring men and leaders of men, they decided to attack. Lee gave the responsibility for planning and executing the attack to his trusted lieutenant, General Jackson. Immediately he sent out engineers, mapmakers, and scouts to reconnoiter the area and give him an accurate, detailed picture of the ground and the Union army's position.

By the thirtieth, Hooker's III, XI, and XII Corps were concentrated at Chancellorsville, in number almost 75,000 men in the little oasis in the middle of the miserable wilderness. He readied them, set them in battle order, and on May 1, he advanced eastward, deploying his three corps into strong positions on high ground along the Plank Road and the River Road.

Jackson moved in, attacking on both the Federal flanks. Stonewall rode back and forth among his troops, always ordering, "Press them, men. Press them." Jackson's hardened veterans did just that. The firefights that erupted on both flanks were fast and vicious.

Then, suddenly, the Federals began to retreat. Hooker had ordered the Federal advance halted, to abandon the ridges, and fall back to the positions they had held around Chancellorsville. Hooker seemed to lose his nerve in this, his first encounter with Robert E. Lee. And so this mighty Union army that outnumbered Jackson's men by more than two to one, fell back to a defensive positon.

That night, Lee and Jackson again met to review the events of the day and discuss their plans. Lee could not help but believe that Hooker wanted him to attack him where he was, and Lee was determined to do so. After more reconnoitering, Jackson found a way to march across the Federal front unseen and circle around to Hooker's right flank. Jeb Stuart had reported that it was "up in the air," which meant it was completely exposed, with no reserves.

Together Lee and Jackson sat on cracker boxes before a small campfire. The conversation that followed was typical of two men who understood each other perfectly.

"General Jackson, what do you propose to do?" Lee inquired.

"Go around here," Jackson answered,

indicating his route on a map.

"What do you propose to make this movement with?" Lee asked.

"With my whole corps," Jackson answered without hesitation.

"And what will you leave me?" Lee asked evenly.

"The divisions of Anderson and McLaws."

"Well, go on."

This short laconic exchange had enormous portent. Jackson was proposing one of the most daring moves ever done in war, against all military tenets and wisdom. He would split their already outnumbered forces, leaving Lee with only 14,000 men as he faced Hooker's 75,000. Jackson would take 26,000 men through the woods to Hooker's right flank, believing that he could roll back that flank, attack their rear, and force the entire enormous army to retreat.

Lee began to write out orders. Jackson left to prepare for the road.

On May 2, just after 8:00 a.m., the head of the column began their march. At a crossroads Lee waited, watching. Jackson, on his faithful Little Sorrel, rode to him. They exchanged a few words no one could hear. Then Jackson gave a familiar gesture. He pointed down the road and glanced at Lee from beneath his cap. Then he rode down that road. Lee watched until he disappeared from sight. He found himself wondering if he would ever see Stonewall Jackson again.

Yancy, as he always did, rode as near behind General Jackson as he could possibly get. Jackson rode in the vanguard, an old oilskin raincoat wrapped about him, hiding his splendid uniform. As always, even with his new cap, he wore it with the brim right down on his nose. But even these eccentricities did not mask the power and the warrior's burning will in the man. Though staff officers sometimes shuffled him aside, Yancy felt the overwhelming magnetism that they all felt toward Jackson when he led them into battle. Stubbornly he stayed close.

It took all day for Jackson's corps to flank the six-mile front of the Union army. Yancy received reports that in spite of the fact that Jackson moved his ten-mile-long train on a track unknown to either side until the previous night, Stonewall was still spotted at least three times, and his moves were reported to Hooker.

Hooker had received the reports, including an assault General Sickles had made on the Confederate rear. From the number of ambulances and wagons in the train, Hooker jumped to the conclusion that the entire Confederate Army was retreating. His staff officers believed it, too, and they relaxed at their headquarters at Wilderness Tavern, sitting on the porch drinking toddies, ignoring all further reports of Jackson's movement.

Jackson got his troops into position on Hooker's unguarded right in the late afternoon. The Federals who were in plain sight of Jackson's column were cooking supper. Jackson looked at his watch, and automatically Yancy checked his. It was 5:15 p.m. Major Eugene Blackford rode up, coming from the front.

"The lines are ready, sir," he reported.

Jackson turned to General Rodes, whom he had selected to lead the attack. "Are you ready, General Rodes?"

"Yes, sir."

Jackson's voice was low and slow. "You can go forward then."

Bugles sounded, men started running, regimental flags flew, and the savage Rebel yell on the air was like a series of explosions.

The enemy, obviously terrified by the sudden onslaught, turned and ran. Hooker's right flank rolled like a tidal wave before them. Jackson's troops had smashed the first line and held the high ground. The army was as panicked as they were at First Manassas. Like wild animals they fled. Plunging, panting, pushing, trampling, they ran into the deep thickets of the wilderness.

The victorious Confederates ruthlessly pursued them. But darkness came, and in the vast entangled forest, Jackson's attack lost its momentum. Battle lines came apart, officers were lost, men got scattered, communications broke down. The Confederates had no choice but to stop and regroup.

Jackson was impatient. As always he wanted to press forward, to pursue his prey and destroy them. He halted on the Plank Road, where he had observed the main body of the enemy retreating. "Lieutenant Tremayne," he called in a low voice.

Yancy hurried to him.

"Go to General Hill; I don't have time to write out orders. You tell him to move forward, relieve General Rodes's men, and prepare for a night attack. Bring me back his answer with all speed."

"Yes, sir." Yancy turned and galloped back toward the edge of the wilderness to General Hill's command.

He found him, having anticipated Jackson's orders, already forming his men up to march. He was wearing his red flannel battle shirt, which always brought strong memories of Gaines' Mill, when he was wounded, to Yancy's mind. He related Jackson's orders, and Hill answered, "Ride back to General Jackson and relieve his mind. My men are already on the move, and I expect them to reach General Rodes within the hour. I'm going to ride forward shortly to join General Jackson in scouting the enemy lines."

Yancy hurried back to the Plank Road.

General Jackson had gone slowly ahead along the unfamiliar ground in the strong moonlight. With them rode Lieutenant Joe Morrison — Anna's brother — Lieutenant Wynn of Jackson's staff, and his signal officer, Captain Wilbourn. Softly they moved, quieting their mounts, whispering, for they didn't know how close they were to enemy lines. Silently, cautiously, they crept forward. It was about nine o'clock, and the full moon rode high. Then, in the near distance, they heard axes ringing and trees being felled. The enemy was strengthening his breastworks.

They were crossing right in front of the Eighteenth North Carolina, who were lined parallel to the road. Earlier that evening they had heard rumors that a Union cavalry attack was forming along their front. As they stared through the thick brush, they saw men — officers, mounted officers in fine uniforms. A quiet order was given, "Fire, and repeat fire."

Musket fire barked along the quiet road.

Little Sorrel reared and twisted right, then carried Stonewall Jackson into the depths of the wilderness.

"Cease firing, men!" General A. P. Hill, who had just that instant caught up with Jackson and Yancy and the others, thundered out through the woods.

Joe Morrison shouted, "Cease firing, cease firing! You're firing at your own men!"

"That's a lie! Pour it on 'em, boys!" It was never recorded who the officer that gave the firing orders was.

Another volley rang out. Jackson reeled in pain and lost Little Sorrel's reins. She plunged into the brush, and Jackson was hit soundly on the forehead by a low-hanging branch. His right hand had been shot. With his left he picked up Little Sorrel's reins and guided her back to the Plank Road, where his frantic escort still was. When he reached them he was slumped over the saddle, bent almost double.

Yancy and Lieutenant Wynn hurried to him and pulled him down, gently setting him on his feet. Then, slowly, supporting him, they took him to a small tree by the road and made him lie down beneath it for safety's sake.

Captain Wilbourn hurried, unafraid, toward the Confederate line of muskets that had shot at them, seeking their commanding officer. Lieutenant Wynn went to try to find an ambulance.

Yancy took off his frock coat and was rolling it up to make a pillow for the general's head, when General A. P. Hill rode up and threw himself off his horse. He hurried to Jackson and said painfully, "Oh, I tried to stop their firing. General, are you in much pain?"

"It's very painful," Jackson answered. "I think my arm is broken. I think all my wounds came from my own men." In the wash of sterile moonlight, Jackson's long face was deadly pale, the gash on the broad forehead colored a gory black.

Major General A. P. Hill threw himself down by Jackson and drew his head onto his lap.

Yancy reflected that it might be said that General Hill was Jackson's bitterest enemy in the army. Through the last two years, they had argued rancorously. Jackson had put Hill under arrest. Hill had made a list of charges against Jackson and submitted them to General Lee. Jackson had accused Hill no less than three times of neglect of duty. Even a few days before they had enjoined this battle with Hooker, Jackson and Hill were still squabbling.

Yancy, of course, knew all this. All of Second Corps did. Now he watched in wonder as the hotheaded and acrimonious Hill ever so gently drew off Jackson's gauntlets, the right one filled with blood, and then removed his sword and belt.

Captain Wilbourn returned, evidently unable to find any officer, and the enlisted men refused to leave the battle line to carry a litter for, as Captain Wilbourn had discreetly said, "a friend of mine that is wounded." Above all they didn't want the men to know that it was Stonewall Jackson, or morale would likely hit solid rock bottom.

Lieutenant Wynn returned and reported that though he couldn't find an ambulance nearby, he had gotten word to the nearest brigade, which was General Pender's, to send their surgeon. "I was afraid to go all the way back to Chancellorsville to get Dr. McGuire," he said anxiously. "I knew Dr. Barr could make it here much faster."

Jackson murmured, "Very good." Then, looking up at Hill, who still cradled his head, he whispered, "Is he a skillful surgeon, Hill?"

"He stands high in his brigade," Hill assured him. "We will have him see to you until Dr. McGuire can come."

Jackson seemed satisfied. Vaguely he looked up at the glowing night sky and murmured, "My own men."

Dr. Barr arrived and examined Jackson. He had been wounded three times — one bullet in the left shoulder, another in the left forearm, and one in the right palm. Captain Wilbourn had tied a handkerchief above the wound in his forearm as a tourniquet and had torn up a shirt to fashion a sling. He had also put strips of cloth around Jackson's right hand. "The wounds are already beginning to clot," Dr. Barr said, "so I don't believe any additional bandaging is needed right now. But he must be taken to a field hospital as quickly as possible."

Hill, who as a major general was the senior officer, ordered Barr back to his brigade. Sounds of firing and shouts of, "Halt, surrender!" sounded in the woods. The booming of artillery sounded closer, and the shells began to light up the woods very near to them. Hill tenderly slipped Jackson's head aside then stood. Now that General

Jackson was wounded, he was next in command. General Hill was the only other major general in the field that night. "I'm going to go form the troops and meet the attack, General Jackson. And I will do my utmost to keep the men from knowing that you are wounded."

"Thank you," Jackson said faintly.

Hill left one of his staff officers, Captain Benjamin Leigh, to help, and another officer, Lieutenant James Smith, had joined them. It took six to carry a litter, so Lieutenant Morrison finally collared two soldiers and made them help. They had four rearing, stamping, spooked horses, so it was decided that Captain Wilbourn and Yancy must lead them, for no one could control Midnight but Yancy.

Once one of the litter bearers dropped his side because he had been shot through both arms. Joe Morrison managed to keep the litter from dropping. Then shells started sailing over their heads, screaming their death song, and by the roadside broken branches and young saplings were crashing to the ground. The other soldier simply lay his side of the litter down and fled. As gently as they could, Morrison, Wynn, Leigh, and Smith laid the litter down as the tornado of fire — canister, grape, and minié balls —

continued.

Leigh ventured into the fiery woods and asked every man that he encountered for help, but they either ignored him and kept firing toward the enemy lines or they would melt back into the shadows. Finally, frustrated, Leigh went to a firing line and yelled, "General Jackson is wounded! We must have help getting him to safety!" Instantly he was surrounded by men, already fighting for the honor. Leigh chose the two stoutest, and they returned to the litter. Under heavy fire but without flinching, they and Yancy and Wilbourn went through the wilderness.

Finally they found an ambulance to transport the general to Reverend Melzi Chancellor's house, where Dr. McGuire waited. He joined Jackson in the ambulance and knelt by the litter. "I hope you are not badly hurt, General," he said in his customary kindly tone.

Jackson answered clearly, with no sign of fear, "I am badly injured, doctor. I fear I'm dying. I'm glad you've come. I think the place in my shoulder is still bleeding."

McGuire attended him as best he could in the jolting ambulance. It was close to eleven o'clock before they reached the Second Corps field hospital. Dr. Harvey Black, the chief surgeon, had heard the grievous news of Jackson's injury, and he had arranged for a special tent to be set up for him and had it warmed. They carried Jackson in and settled him on a comfortable cot, covered with warm blankets. Slowly he regained some color, and his short, painful breaths eased. Two other doctors were in attendance.

Dr. McGuire told him, "We must examine you, General."

Jackson nodded stiffly. It was obvious that he was controlling the pain with his iron will, though Dr. McGuire had given him whiskey and morphia.

McGuire continued, "We will give you chloroform so that you will have no pain. These gentlemen will help me. We might find bones badly broken, General, so that the only course might be amputation." McGuire paused then asked quietly, "If that is our conclusion, do you want us to go on with the operation?"

Jackson's voice was weak, but the answer was firm. "Certainly, McGuire. Do for me whatever you think best."

One of the doctors spread a soothing salve over Jackson's face to protect his skin from the acrid chemical. Then he folded a cloth into a cone over his face and dropped chloroform onto it, the heavy, bitter odor permeating the room. The general breathed deeply several times and murmured, "What an infinite blessing. Blessing. Blessing . . . Bless . . ."

The minié ball was just under the skin of his right hand, and McGuire removed it. He rolled it in his palm and sighed. "A smooth-bore Springfield. Our troops."

It was indeed necessary to amputate Jackson's left arm. The skilled surgeons, each of whom had performed this operation hundreds of times in the past two years of war, accomplished it in record time.

The general woke up a couple of times but slept the rest of the night peacefully.

The next day was Sunday, May 3. It was a pleasant, sweetly clear day. All of the fruit trees were blooming — apple, pear, cherry, and peach. Their delicate scents floated on the still air.

General Jackson's faithful chaplain, Reverend B. T. Lacy, led a small funeral procession of a few of Jackson's aides and staff officers to his family estate nearby, Ellwood. Yancy trailed behind, exhausted because he had not been able to sleep for worry about the general.

The solemn procession went to the Lacy family burial plot, where a very small grave had been dug. Reverend Lacy and the men said the Lord's Prayer. And then they reverently interred Stonewall Jackson's crushed arm.

The Sabbath was always a good day for the general. He awoke and ate a light breakfast and was cheerful. He sent Yancy with a dispatch for General Lee, just a few lines about his wound and the victorious attack the previous night. He visited with Reverend Lacy and told him that he had thought he was on the point of death when he had fallen on the litter, had prayed, and had immediately felt the peace of the Lord enter him, and he still knew that peace. Lieutenant Smith, another of Jackson's young aides, came in with some reports of the ongoing battle, and Jackson received them intelligently.

Yancy rode as if he were being chased to General Lee's headquarters. He didn't want to be away from General Jackson for even a minute. General Lee read Jackson's few scrawled lines, his handsome face grave. Then he quickly wrote a note and gave it to Yancy to take back to the general. Again Yancy pushed Midnight to his fastest gallop, a ride so smooth it was almost dreamy when he stretched out so elegantly.

Yancy brushed by the aides and officers

gathered outside the tent and went in to Jackson. After all, he was the general's courier, and he had the right to deliver his dispatches to him. "General Lee sent this, sir," he said.

Jackson said, "Please read it to me, Lieutenant Tremayne."

Yancy read:

General,
   I have just received your note telling me that you were wounded. I cannot express my regret at this occurrence. Could I have directed events, I should have chosen for the good of the country to be disabled in your stead. I congratulate you on your victory, which is due to your skill and energy.
   Very respectfully, your obedient servant,
                              R. E. Lee, General

Jackson looked embarrassed. Turning slightly away, he said in a choked voice, "General Lee is very kind. But he should give the praise to God."

That night Jackson slept peacefully without waking up and awoke Monday morning feeling well, and he ate well.

Early on, Dr. McGuire had a note from General Lee advising him to move the general to the rear. The Federals were threatening to cross the Rappahannock at a ford nearby, and they might drive in the direction of the field hospital.

Jackson blithely said, "If the enemy does come, I will not fear them. I have always been kind to their wounded, and I'm sure they would be kind to me."

The doctors were still discussing whether it would do more harm than good to move Jackson, when they received another note from General Lee that evening. It was peremptory in tone, which was unusual for the courteous general. He *ordered* them to move Jackson.

The next day they put General Jackson in an ambulance, and Yancy packed up his bedroll in preparation for leaving. Captain Wilbourn was returning to the front, and he came to speak to Yancy as he was saddling Midnight. Yancy came to attention and saluted.

"I know that you and Mrs. Jackson are friends, and General Jackson does seem to have a closer relationship to you than to the other aides," Captain Wilbourn said. "But, Lieutenant Tremayne, do you not feel that you should return to duty?"

"Sir, I am on duty," Yancy answered, staring straight ahead. "I am General Stonewall Jackson's courier."

Captain Wilbourn stared at him for a moment, and then his stern face softened. "I see. Carry on, Lieutenant."

"Yes, sir."

Engineers went ahead of the general's train, grubbing up roots, removing logs and branches, digging up jutting rocks, and filling in sinkholes and ruts to make the ride in the spartan ambulance as smooth as possible. Reverend Lacy, Dr. McGuire, and Lieutenant Smith rode with him. Yancy rode behind, with Jim driving a cart that had General Jackson's belongings in it.

The rule of the road was that the heavier vehicles had the right of way. When the ambulance driver tried to make teamsters pull aside, all he got for his trouble were harsh refusals. But when they were told that it was Stonewall Jackson being transported, they ran their wagons into the ditch, hopped out, and stood bareheaded, some of them in tears as the ambulance passed. From them the word passed quickly up the road that "Old Jack" was coming.

They also passed many men, veterans of Second Corps who were very lightly wounded and were walking to the field hospital. They shouted friendly messages to him, and many of them cried out that they wished they had been wounded instead of the general.

All along the road now hundreds of people gathered. Yancy searched their faces and saw in them the same reverence and sorrow that those who knew him well felt. Men stood with hats in hand; women bowed their heads and wept. Many people now came with gifts, whatever delicacies their meager farms could offer. Yancy and Jim collected pails of milk, cakes, pies, honey, dried fruits, bags of fried chicken, and fresh biscuits until the wagon was filled to overflowing. Jackson was endearingly surprised and grateful at the attention.

He was cheerful and bright most of the day, but in the afternoon he grew weak and nauseated. They stopped for a time and opened the ambulance doors for the general to get fresh air. And Dr. McGuire good-naturedly honored Jackson's old favorite remedy for nausea — cold towels on the stomach. People stood by watching them but remained at a respectful distance. All Dr. McGuire had to do was to ask the nearest man, "Is there a well near here with cold water?"

Half a dozen men and women took off running. The first man that made it back, panting, his face red, had a bucket of icy cold water. When the others came back, they were so crestfallen that Yancy and Jim told them that they were a godsend, too, because all of the attendants were very thirsty and so were the horses. This seemed to cheer them up; it made them feel as if they, too, were helping their revered general.

It was twenty-seven miles to the Chandler farm, a family that Jackson knew slightly. They arrived at about eight o'clock that evening. The Chandlers had taken in many other wounded soldiers, including two that had the highly contagious disease erysipelas, so the Chandlers offered General Jackson their study. It was an outbuilding much like Jackson's headquarters at Moss Neck Manor. It was a small plain building, cool and shady, nestled beneath three huge oak trees.

After they settled in, Jackson said he was very comfortable. He had tea and bread for supper. A spring thunderstorm broke, with the drowsy rhythm of rain on the roof, and Jackson slept.

Wednesday morning dawned a cool and freshly-washed morning. To Yancy's surprise, Peyton rode up and greeted Yancy before he went in to deliver his dispatches. After their hellos, he asked, "How is he?"

Yancy answered, "Pretty good, I think. He seems to be in good spirits. And Jim told me that he's talking about staying here just a few days, then moving to Ashland and resting there for a couple of days, and then home to Lexington to recover. Jim told him, 'And then you can come back and beat them Yankees better with one arm than they can do with two!' "

Peyton grinned, relaxing somewhat. "As he himself says, 'Good, good.' So listen, Yance, these dispatches I've got from General Stuart. He told me that I ought to give them to Dr. McGuire and that it would be best if the general didn't hear. Do you want to go inside and fetch him?"

"Sure. In fact I know General Jackson is sleeping right now. Jim can stay with him while I get the doctor." He went inside and came out with Dr. McGuire.

Reverend Lacy and Lieutenant Smith were seated outside the general's bedroom when Yancy told the doctor that there were confidential dispatches for him, and Dr. McGuire had motioned them to come. Peyton handed him the envelope, and Dr. McGuire read it quickly then looked up. He didn't dismiss Yancy and Peyton; he was not so strict as the officers, and he understood their particular friendship with Jackson.

"General Stuart says that he has received some reports that raiding Union cavalry may be in this district," Dr. McGuire told them gravely. "He advises us that he can't send a guard this far from the front."

"I'll ride around and do some reconnaisance," Yancy instantly volunteered. "I'll watch this afternoon and tonight."

"If there's a Yank around, Yancy will sniff him out," Peyton said. "Indian, you know."

Dr. McGuire grew thoughtful. "If by chance General Jackson is taken prisoner, I am determined to stay with him, to take care of him."

Reverend Lacy said, "I, too, will stay."

"And I," Lieutenant Smith said.

Yancy said, "I go where Stonewall goes. I'm his courier, and it's my duty to stay by his side."

Peyton sighed. "How I wish I could stay with him, too. But without him, the commanders are sending dispatches all over this mess of a battlefield every five minutes it seems. I have to get back. Dr. McGuire, the men are starving for news of General Jackson. Yancy says he seems to be doing well. May I give them a report?"

"Certainly. General Jackson is recovering —"

Peyton interrupted, "Sir, excuse me, but this is so important to the men that I would prefer to write it down just as you say it."

From the courier's bag he took out pencil and paper.

Dr. McGuire continued, pausing to let Peyton write. "General Jackson's recovery is very satisfactory. His wounds are healing cleanly. His spirits are good. He is eating very well considering the trauma of his injuries and the surgery. He sleeps peacefully. He is keenly interested in the progress of the battle and is always glad for news of his men. We expect Mrs. Jackson and baby Julia to join us, perhaps tomorrow."

"Thank you, sir," Peyton said gracefully. "I'll return as fast as I can with this good news." He mounted Senator, gave them a jaunty salute, and dashed off.

General Jackson seemed to be doing so well that Dr. McGuire decided to let Jim watch him while he got a much-needed night of sleep.

Yancy scouted all over the district that day and night and saw no sign of Union soldiers, cavalry or otherwise. He returned at about midnight and was about to bed down when a shadowy figure slipped outside. Jim came to Yancy's campfire. "I'm watching the gen'ral tonight. I was thinkin' mebbe you might like to help me." Yancy was one of Jim's favorites, mainly because he was one of Jackson's favorites.

Yancy jumped up eagerly, and they tiptoed back into the house. Without speaking they took chairs by the general's bed. On the far side of the room, Dr. McGuire slept on a sofa, his face tranquil, his breaths deep and restful.

And so the two kept watch, Jim with uncomplicated affection, Yancy with somewhat more complex emotions. He esteemed Jackson personally, but he also had the sense of separation from him, the chasm between a mere soldier and the great man that is his leader in the bloody business of war.

Neither Jim nor Yancy slept, though both of them got up to stretch and move around a bit, careful to be quiet so as not to wake either the doctor or the general.

Jackson seemed to be sleeping quietly, but around two thirty he started getting restless. Then at about three he came awake all at once, his mouth drawn into a tight line, his face grimacing with pain. His eyes quickly roved around the room, and he whispered, "H–hello, Jim. Hello, Yancy. I don't feel well at all, Jim. Would you get me some cold wet towels for my abdomen?"

"Sure, sir," he said, and left to fetch icy water.

Yancy said hesitantly, "Sir, are you in pain?"

"I am," he admitted with difficulty. "My right side . . ."

"Sir, shouldn't I wake Dr. McGuire to check on you?"

"No," Jackson said harshly. "The man hasn't slept in three nights. Leave him be. The cold towels will do the trick."

But they didn't. Jackson steadily worsened, the vague pain in his side gradually turning into paroxysms of agony with every breath that he took. Still he refused to allow Jim or Yancy to awaken the doctor. He managed to hold out until the first chilly gray light of dawn, and finally he asked Yancy to get Dr. McGuire.

The doctor sprang awake and hurried to Jackson. After listening to his heart and his chest, Dr. McGuire knew what was wrong. Jackson had developed pneumonia in his right lung. Immediately he gave Jackson morphia for the paralyzing pain he was experiencing.

It eased his breathing and obviously lessened his pain. But in his weakened state, the powerful drug affected his mind, and all day he wandered in and out of consciousness, sometimes talking to himself, sometimes talking to people who weren't there.

■ ■ ■ ■

Anna arrived that afternoon with Julia and Hetty. One of the doctor's staff attendants had been dispatched to meet the train. As soon as Anna got into the buggy, she sensed that things had gone wrong. Immediately she asked the young attendant how her husband was.

"The general is doing pretty well," he answered with some hesitation.

Anna asked no more. She had to wait on the porch until the doctors finished dressing Jackson's wounds. Finally Dr. McGuire came to fetch her. As soon as she saw her husband, she knew that he would never return to Lexington. He was well on the way to his final home.

She knew of his wounds and the surgery, of course, but there was no way to prepare herself for the sight of his missing arm, the stump thickly bandaged, and his swollen, misshapen right hand. His face looked sunken and skeletal. He slept, but there seemed no repose in it, for his breaths were short and ragged.

Gently Dr. McGuire awakened him.

He looked up, and the old familiar light came into his dull eyes when he saw Anna.

"My esposa, my love, how glad I am you have come," he said. When he saw Anna's distress he said, "I know you would give your life for me. But I'm perfectly resigned. Don't be sad. I hope I am going to recover. Pray for me, but always remember in your prayers the old petition, 'Thy will be done.' "

Then he sank into a stupor, mumbling incoherently. After a time he barely opened his eyes and murmured, "My darling, you must cheer up and not wear such a long face in the sickroom."

She asked him several times that afternoon when he roused if he wanted to see the baby.

He always replied, "Not yet. Wait until I feel better."

Anna sat all that long afternoon and evening with him. Dr. McGuire only interrupted when Jackson began to show pain, to give him more morphine.

Occasionally Jackson would rouse and speak endearments to Anna. Once he said, "My darling, you are very much loved." Another time he whispered, "You're the most precious little wife in the world."

On Friday, he seemed to rally a bit, though he admitted he was exhausted, and throughout the day he grew noticeably weaker. Again he wandered in and out of consciousness.

On Saturday, he wanted to see Julia, and Anna brought her to him. Jackson beamed at her, obviously completely lucid. His splinted right hand was huge and clumsy, but Julia seemed to have no fear of it as he caressed her. She smiled at him and he murmured, "Little comforter . . . little comforter."

That afternoon Jackson wanted to send Yancy to get Reverend Lacy.

McGuire frowned. Upon his examination he had found that both of Jackson's lungs were filled with fluid. His respiration was shallow and fast, like a hoarse panting. "I beg you, General, I don't think it would do you good to converse with the reverend just now," Dr. McGuire said.

But Jackson insisted, and Yancy fetched Reverend Lacy. Jackson's first concern was to learn if Reverend Lacy was continuing to work on an armywide observance of the Sabbath. Lacy assured him that he was. Then Jackson spoke for a while of his favorite topic in this world — spiritual matters. In spite of his determination to see the chaplain, Jackson was utterly exhausted when he left.

His condition steadily worsened. That night, as Anna sat with him, she asked gently, "Thomas, might I read some Psalms of consolation to you?"

Vaguely he shook his head and mumbled, "Too much pain . . . to be able to listen." But in a few minutes he roused somewhat and said apologetically, "But yes, Anna, please do. We must never refuse that."

She read in her soft voice.

After a bit Jackson said, "Sing to me."

Anna, who had managed to remain calm and steady as she read, knew that she couldn't sing Thomas's favorite hymns without crying. She went and got her brother, Lieutenant Joe Morrison, who after he had helped Jackson that awful night had stayed on to attend to him. Together brother and sister sang.

As the night wore on, Jackson's breathing became short, wheezing gasps. But after they had sung several hymns, Anna said, "The singing had a quieting effect, and he seemed to rest in perfect peace."

In the morning, Dr. McGuire had a somber meeting with Anna and gave her his tragic prognosis. "I believe he will die today, Mrs. Jackson. I do not think he will see another night."

Calmly Anna nodded and went back to her husband's bedside. Long before, Jackson had told her that he had no fear of dying, but he hoped that when that time came he would "have a few hours' preparation before entering into the presence of my Maker and Redeemer."

She steeled herself for this last and most difficult service for her husband. She roused him from his stupor and said quietly, "Do you know the doctors say that you must very soon be in heaven?"

His eyes were open, and he looked at her but said nothing.

Anna repeated it and added, "Do you not feel willing to acquiesce in God's allotment, if He wills you to go today?"

He stirred a little but apparently didn't comprehend what she was saying, and so she repeated it, softly and clearly. This time he focused on her face and said, "I prefer it." His words came out slurred, just a little, so he repeated, more firmly, "I prefer it."

They talked a little while longer, and then the surgeons came in to examine him, though they did not redress his wounds. They disturbed him as little as possible. He sank into a stupor when they left.

Later he roused again to see Anna kneeling by his bed. Again she told him that before the sun went down he would be in heaven.

He thought for a moment then asked,

"Will you call Dr. McGuire?"

Instantly his faithful physician was at his bedside.

"Doctor," Jackson said, clearly and alertly, "Anna informs me that you have told her that I am to die today. Is it so?"

Always gentle, always warm, Dr. McGuire replied, "General, the medicine has done its utmost."

Jackson pondered this for a bit, staring up at the ceiling. Now, instead of his habitual "Good, good," he already seemed to be seeing a higher plane, and he said, "Very good, very good. It is all right." And then he comforted Anna, who at last was weeping.

She stayed, and they talked from time to time. Jackson seemed to have recovered his full senses. Later he said, "It is the Lord's Day . . . my wish is fulfilled. I have always desired to die on Sunday."

In the warm, bright afternoon, he again wandered. He gave orders, spoke to his favorites on his staff. He mentioned Yancy once, murmuring that he should ride hard and return quickly. He fought battles, was at home in Lexington with Anna and Julia, was praying. He fell silent.

Only Anna was at his bedside, holding his bandaged hand, crying silently.

The clock struck three sonorous notes.

His breathing grew shallower; his chest barely rose.

At 3:15, his eyes closed. Clearly and gladly he said, "Let us cross over the river and rest under the shade of the trees."

And so he did.

CHAPTER TWENTY-SIX

The once-splendid uniform that Jeb Stuart had given Stonewall Jackson was blood-stained and slashed to shreds. Jim had found a suit of civilian clothes to fit, but then he was so distraught that for the first time he could not attend his general.

Yancy, Lieutenant Smith, Dr. McGuire, and Reverend Lacy dressed General Jackson in the clothes then wrapped him in a military cloak. They covered the coffin in spring flowers and banked lily of the valley at the head.

Anna stayed with him most of the night. He showed no trace of the suffering he had endured in his last days.

The next day, Monday, May 11, 1863, the funeral party left for Richmond.

Yancy didn't want to leave Midnight behind, so he wrangled an empty cattle car and settled the skittish stallion in it. Midnight didn't do too well on trains, so Yancy planned on staying with him.

To his surprise, riding as if a bandit was on their heels, Peyton, Chuckins, and Sandy came flying up. They spotted Yancy and without prelude started loading their horses into the boxcar with Midnight. Their faces were grim, and Chuckins had traces of tears on his face.

As they settled in the car, Yancy asked, "How did you get leave? General Lee wouldn't let the Stonewall Brigade take leave. He wouldn't even leave the field himself." The Battle of Chancellorsville was still raging.

"Most of the staff and aides got leave," Peyton answered. "Since General Stuart took over command of Second Corps, he's used some of us, but he has his own staff and couriers aplenty, you know."

"But what about you, Sandy?" Yancy asked curiously. Sandy was a pivotal part of General Pendleton's battery. He had consistently gotten praise for his bravery and daring in every battle they fought, and he was the number one gun captain. Many men asked to be on his gun crew.

Sandy shrugged carelessly. "I went to General Pendleton and requested leave. He refused, telling me about General Lee's stand on furloughs right now. So I said that

I was giving him notice that I was deserting, and since the penalty was either getting arrested or getting shot, I told him I'd appreciate it if he'd take the next few days to decide which it would be. I would report back after General Jackson's funeral and he could do whatever he wanted. So he gave me leave."

For most of the trip the four friends stared into space, remembering. Every once in a while one of them would say, "Remember First Manassas? He stood there, the bullets whizzing by him, as calm as a summer's day. . . ." And another memory, and another. "Do you remember . . . remember . . . ?"

When they neared Richmond, they got up and groomed the horses until their coats shone like polished glass in sunlight. Then they worked on their uniforms, polishing buttons, arranging their sashes just so, making certain that their sabers hung just right, the scabbards spotless, polishing and repolishing their boots, flicking every single speck of dust off of their tunics. The four looked splendid together. Peyton's and Yancy's long tunics, with collars and cuffs of infantry blue, had gold lieutenant's flashes on the collar and elaborate gold embroidery on the cuffs. They wore dark red sashes, the regimental color of the Stonewall Brigade.

Chuckins and Sandy were still sergeants, so their sleeves had the distinctive three chevrons. Chuckins's sash was the regimental dark red, but Sandy's insignia and sash were the bright scarlet of the artillery. Motionless and silent they stood for the last few miles, not wanting to sit down again on their blankets and get dusty. They were determined to show nothing but perfection for General Jackson.

Black-draped carriages had been sent for Mrs. Jackson, Hetty and the baby, and two ladies that accompanied her, and for the staff officers escorting the general.

One of them, an older man who had purchased a commission as a captain, was an Episcopalian minister — for Jackson had several ministers on his staff — and was a notorious stickler for rules and protocol. As the officers helped the ladies into their carriage, he muttered to a lieutenant, "What are those impudent boys doing? We had not planned for a mounted escort. Go tell them to fall back and follow at a discreet distance."

Anna followed his critical gaze, and her weary, reddened eyes softened. "No, sir," she said with uncharacteristic curtness. "Leave them alone."

The captain looked vaguely disapproving but said no more.

In truth, Anna felt it was very fitting that they should escort General Jackson. Yancy, Peyton, and Chuckins were the only members of the Stonewall Brigade there, and Sandy was one of the few VMI cadets that had left the institute to follow Jackson into war. For a fleeting moment, the sight of them made Anna forget her overwhelming sorrow. They looked so noble, so dignified, and they were all such handsome young men.

Leading this group were Yancy on Midnight and Peyton on his gorgeous gold palomino, Senator. To each side were the smaller horses, Chuckins's pinto, Brownie, and Sandy's elegant buckskin mare, Jasmine. Even the simple Brownie seemed to sense the solemnity of the day, for she held her head high and tossed her glossy mane and stepped proudly.

Slowly the procession made its way the two miles to the executive mansion. Throngs of people crowded the streets in uncanny silence, merely watching the funeral cart with its flower-draped casket go by. They stood still, their grief-stricken faces imprinted in Yancy's memory. Most of the women, and many of the men, were weeping.

When they reached the mansion, Governor Letcher met Anna, and Mrs. Letcher took her to the governor's private rooms, where mourning clothes and a veil were waiting for her. The staff officers knotted in little groups, planning where they would stay the night.

Yancy told his friends, "I'm going to the Haydens. Right now. I just won't wait any longer. I just can't."

Chuckins and Sandy had no idea why he spoke that way. But Peyton, for all his lackadaisical ways, had come to understand that Yancy was in love with Lorena Hayden — the lovely woman in the drawings — and that there was some problem, insurmountable it would seem, between them. He nodded encouragingly to Yancy. "Go. Chuckins and Sandy are staying with me." Senator Stevens had an enormous mansion on the James River.

Without another word Yancy turned and rode off.

Chuckins turned to Peyton, his honest face puzzled. "What was all that about?"

Peyton answered with his old litany, soberly this time. "Yancy doesn't know anything. I don't know anything. Sandy doesn't know anything. And neither do you."

Recklessly Yancy rode Midnight hard through Richmond's streets. Although the way from the railroad station to the executive mansion had been congested with people, the side streets were all but deserted.

He clattered up to the Hayden home, as he had done so many times before — but this time was different. He jumped off Midnight and started to run to the door but then paused. Again he wiped off his dusty boots, straightened his tunic, swiped the buttons to make them glow, checked his sash and saber, then smoothed back his hair. The errant forelock promptly fell down over his forehead again, but he scarcely noticed. Taking a deep breath, he went to the door and knocked.

Missy answered it. Without a word to him, she took him in her arms and hugged him. "I'm so sorry you lost him, Yancy. It's a sad day for everyone in the South."

"Thank you, Missy," he said. "It is a very sad time."

"They's in the parlor. Go on in," she said, wiping her eyes with her apron. "You're family. Ain't no need for me to announce you."

Yancy went to the parlor and hesitated, standing almost at attention in the doorway. Ever since General Jackson had died, he had not felt at all like himself. His mind, for one thing, seemed to have come to a screeching halt, stopped in that warm room where Stonewall took his last breaths. He felt like one of Stonewall's Boys, bereft and lost, stuck in time as Yancy the soldier, stiff and unyielding.

The only other thing he felt was a tremendous desire to see Lorena. He had no plan of what he would say to her; he couldn't picture it in his half-blank mind. He just knew he had to see her.

At the sound of his footsteps and the slight metallic sound of his scabbard, Dr. and Mrs. Hayden looked up.

Yancy, frozen in the doorway, could only manage to say, "Hello. I — I came with — with — escorting General Jackson."

Lily Hayden hurried to him and hugged him much as Missy did. "Oh, Yancy dear, we are so very glad to see you, but so very sorry it is in these tragic circumstances. Are you all right?"

"Yes, ma'am."

She held him at arm's length, and she and

Dr. Hayden looked him up and down. They both seemed puzzled at Yancy's obvious distance.

He couldn't frame the words to say to reassure them. Finally he blurted out, "Where's Lorena?"

"Why, she's in the garden, dear," Lily answered after a slight hesitation and a glance at her husband. "Why don't you go on out to see her?"

Without another word, Yancy turned and marched out to the garden.

She was there, cutting flowers. Her dress was a cheerful spring muslin, with tiny sprigs of peach-colored roses entwined with little tendrils of ivy. She wore a wide-brimmed hat with a peach ribbon tied under her chin. The setting sun barely touched her face, lighting it with a soft golden glow. Lorena didn't look up, as she was humming to herself and obviously didn't hear his approach.

As Yancy hesitated just outside the kitchen door, watching her, she began to sing. It was a song he had never heard before. Her sweet, clear, high soprano voice, and the hymn itself, rent his heart, a confused torrent of great joy mingled with inconsolable sorrow.

Hark! Hark my soul! angelic songs are
    swelling,
O'er earth's green fields and ocean's
    wave-beat shore:
How sweet the truth those blessed strains
    are telling
Of that new life when sin shall be no
    more.

Angels of Jesus, angels of light,
Singing to welcome the pilgrims of the
    night!

Onward we go, for still we hear them
    singing,
'Come, weary souls, for Jesus bids you
    come';
And through the dark, its echoes sweetly
    ringing,
The music of the Gospel leads us home.

Angels of Jesus, angels of light,
Singing to welcome the pilgrims of the
    night!

Angels, sing on, your faithful watches
    keeping;
Sing us sweet fragments of the songs
    above,
Till morning's joy shall end the night of

weeping,
And life's long shadows break in
cloudless love.

She began to hum the refrain again, but something unseeing touched her, and she looked up, right into Yancy's eyes. Much like him, she froze.

Long moments passed.

Yancy, in a choked voice, said, "Lorena . . . ? Lorena . . ."

She dropped her basket, dropped her shears, dropped the red, red rose she had just clipped. She ran to him so fast that her hat tumbled over her back, held by the ribbons. When she reached him she threw herself into his arms, and even though she was such a tiny woman, she moved so fast and hard that he almost staggered as he embraced her.

"Oh, Yancy, Yancy, you've remembered, haven't you?" she cried against his chest.

"Yes. Finally . . . I've come back to you," he murmured. "Lorena . . ."

"I love you! Desperately!" she said, pulling back and putting her hands on his face. "I've loved you for — forever!" Then she pulled him down to her and kissed him long and passionately.

He lifted his head and stared down at her.

"Are you sure? You love me?"

"Oh, yes, yes."

He sagged a little, his shoulders bowed, and he dropped his head. He still held her in the circle of his arms.

She waited.

In a voice so low she could barely hear him, he said, "That's — that's good, Lorena. Because I not only love you, I — I need you. Much, much more than when I was hurt and sick. I need you now, so much, because — because —"

"You grieve for him," she said softly. "You've lost him. I know, all too well, what it is to lose someone you love."

"I do grieve, and I did love him," Yancy said with difficulty. "And all I've been able to think of to comfort me — is you."

"I will do that," she said. "From now on, forever, I will guard your heart as if it is my own."

He pulled her to him with a low groan. Yancy had not shed a tear in all this horrid war and did not cry when Stonewall Jackson died. And now, as if he were a lost child, he held her close and sobbed.

Yancy and Lorena went to speak to Dr. Hayden and Lily, returning from the garden where they had, both literally and figuratively, found each other. They went into the parlor, hand in hand.

Lorena's parents looked up as they entered. Dr. Hayden looked mystified, but after seeing their glowing faces, Lily smiled.

"We — we have something to tell you, sir, ma'am," Yancy stuttered. He shifted from one foot to the other awkwardly. "We — I mean, Lorena and I —"

"Just say it, Yancy. It's quite all right, you know," Lorena said with her old exasperation.

Yancy blew out a long whistling breath. "Okay. Okay. See, Dr. Hayden and Mrs. Hayden, we — I mean, Lorena has said — I asked her —"

"We're in love," Lorena blurted out. "And we're engaged."

"What?" Dr. Hayden asked, bewildered.

"Finally," Lily muttered. She rose, went to them, and kissed each on the cheek. "Come, come, Yancy, I'll bet you didn't look nearly so terrified when you were riding into one of those famous battles we keep hearing about."

"Yes, ma'am. I mean, no, ma'am." He and Lorena sat in their old chairs, but they reached across to hold hands.

"This is wonderful, perfectly wonderful," Lily said happily, taking her seat by her husband. "Although for a long time now we've looked at you as a son, now you truly will be, Yancy. I couldn't be happier, both for you and for my Lorena."

"Thank you, ma'am," Yancy mumbled. He seemed almost — but not quite — as stunned as Dr. Hayden.

Lily asked eagerly, "Have you made any plans yet? Set a date?"

Now a shadow crossed over Yancy's face, and he focused and became intent. "No, ma'am. I thought, somehow, that Lorena might want to wait until the war is over before we got married —"

"No," Lorena said firmly. "No, I don't want to wait."

"I don't either, once I thought about it," Yancy agreed. "I've thought about a lot of things since General Jackson died. One thing I realized, since I knew him and Mrs. Jackson before, they didn't waste time. They took every possible minute that they had together and treasured it, no matter what the circumstances. I know that if you had told Mrs. Jackson before she married him that he would die so soon, so young, after they'd been married less than six years and when their only daughter was only four months old, she would say that she wouldn't hesitate, she would marry him anyway, as soon as she could. And that's the way we feel," he finished firmly.

"Exactly. I'm just sorry that we can't get married today," Lorena grumbled.

"What?" Dr. Hayden said again.

"General Jackson is going to Lexington, to lie in state one day. And then on Friday he's to be buried. With your permission, sir, ma'am, I'd like for Lorena to come to Lexington, to be with me these next few hard days. It would be such a comfort to me," Yancy said, now confident. "And then I would like for us to visit my family on Saturday. I will bring her back on Sunday. And then I have to return to Chancellorsville."

"Of course," Lily agreed instantly. "That will be perfectly fine. Missy can go as your chaperone, dear. I only wish that Jesse and I were well enough to travel to Lexington for General Jackson's funeral and then to go visit Becky and Daniel. But I think it would be too much of a strain, don't you, dear?"

"Hmm? Oh. Oh yes. A strain," Dr. Hayden repeated.

Lily patted his knee. "Poor dear, he hadn't a clue. Of course, I knew all along."

Lorena put her head to the side, like a small bird. "You did? However did you know, Mother?"

Lily smiled, a sweet expression that was often on her face. "I hope you find out, my darling Lorena, because only then will you understand. Mothers know. Mothers always know."

"I want to know," Lorena said softly, looking at Yancy. "And I dare to hope it may be soon."

On that night they embalmed him.

The famous artist, Frederick Volck, and his assistant, Pietro Zamboggi, made his death mask. Oddly enough, Volck had visted Stonewall Jackson's camp in December of 1862, at Fredericksburg, when Lee, Jackson, and Longstreet were camped on the heights above the town and faced Burnside's doomed troops below. Volck had even done some sketches of Stonewall after his staff persuaded him to pose on a stool. As he was prone to do, Jackson fell asleep, and the staff roared with laughter, which woke him up. He was embarrassed but good-natured about it. The work which the artist did this night was very different from that cheerful scene.

He lay in state the next morning at the executive mansion, in the Reception Room. The public was not allowed in there, but any person who could scrape up any connection to the Confederate government and came to the mansion that night was allowed to view the shadowed features. Many lingered for long moments, and many more tears were shed.

Without being asked, and without consulting anyone, Yancy, Peyton, Chuckins, and Sandy came to the executive mansion at dawn that Tuesday. They were greeted at the door by a disdainful butler. "And you are . . . ?" he asked snootily.

"We are General Jackson's honor guard," Yancy answered firmly.

"I have no knowledge of this," the butler said suspiciously.

Yancy stepped up to stand very close — too close — to the butler. He looked down at him; the man was at least a foot shorter than Yancy. In a soft tone that brooked no nonsense and may even have had a bit of menace in it, he said, "Then you may go wake up Mrs. Jackson and ask her about us. She has given us permission to escort her husband all the way to his resting place." This, of course, was not strictly true. But Yancy knew Anna Jackson, and he knew that she would, and did, wish it.

The butler took a hasty step back, almost stumbling. "No, no, of course I wouldn't dream of disturbing Mrs. Jackson. Please come in and follow me to the Reception Room."

Yancy took his place at the head of the general's coffin with Peyton at the foot. They stood unmoving at strict parade attention, staring straight ahead. After four hours, Chuckins and Sandy relieved them. They took these shifts until the afternoon, when General Jackson's pallbearers and funeral procession arrived, and Jackson was taken to the House of Representatives.

His coffin was placed in the hall and put on a white-draped altar before the speaker's bench, with the Confederate flag draped over it. The assembled crowd to witness the placing of General Jackson in state included President Jefferson Davis and his aides, several generals and other high-ranking officers and their staffs, the governor, the cabinet, Richmond city officials, and a number of Virginia and Richmond politicians. They had a long prayer.

After it was over, Yancy pushed people aside and the four friends marched to the general's casket. The crowd seemed stunned, but before anyone could say anything, Anna went to Yancy and put her hand out. He took it in both of his.

"Thank you, Yancy," she said softly, but it echoed throughout the silent room. "He was very proud of you, all of you. He would be glad that you are here." She turned and swept out, her long black skirts whispering on the polished floor. Immediately the crowd broke up and followed her. Yancy and Peyton took their stations guarding the general.

More than twenty thousand people filed through the hall that day and evening. They piled so many flowers about the bier that some had to be taken away to make room for people to pass by the coffin. As it grew later, officials made several attempts to close the doors, but they were soundly shouted down by the hundreds and hundreds of people who had waited in the line of mourners so long and so patiently. Taking pity on them, Governor Letcher ordered the doors left open until everyone who wanted to see the general had filed by and said their good-byes.

Yancy, Peyton, Chuckins, and Sandy guarded him all day until midnight. They never showed any weariness at all. They never wavered. They stayed at his side until the last mourner left the hall of the House of Representatives.

The next day, Stonewall returned to the institute for the last time. By train he went to Gordonsville and then Lynchburg. At each stop the station was crowded with hundreds of people. They pressed close to Anna's special car, crying out to her. Many times they called out, pleading to see Julia. Anna took pity on them, and Hetty held Julia up to the window dozens of times to be kissed. Julia bore it well, never crying, never fussy, often smiling.

From Lynchburg they took a canal barge to Lexington. The four friends insisted this time on leading the funeral procession to the institute. There VMI cadets took over the escort, marching with their arms reversed. Jackson's big gray horse that had been a gift from an admirer was the riderless horse. He was led by a VMI cadet, empty boots in the stirrups turned backward.

They took Stonewall to his old lecture room, which had not been used since he left. There he lay the entire day, and another long procession of grieving men and women passed by the window. Roses were piled high beneath it. All day the slow, mournful firing of the institute's cannon sounded, mourning the loss of their most revered and valiant soldier.

Daniel, Becky, Lorena, and Missy stood at the front of the crowd that lined the way to

Virginia Military Institute. Yancy, Peyton, Chuckins, and Sandy led the funeral procession with great somber grace. When the cadets met them, the four friends returned the cadets' salutes, turned and rode to the rear of the procession, then turned to the side and dismounted. Yancy hurried to join his family.

After Stonewall Jackson had been placed in state at the institute, they all returned to the farm. Daniel had brought the buggy, so Becky and Missy rode with them, while Yancy rode Midnight.

The Shenandoah Valley was breathtaking in spring. Every scene was richly colored in a hundred shades of green, every field had riotous wildflowers blooming, every house they passed had luxurious gardens surrounding them. Lorena couldn't see well enough out of the buggy's back window, so, being the outspoken lady that she was, she demanded that Daniel let her sit with him on the driver's bench. Of course, Becky was just as demanding, and so she climbed up with them, and the three of them sat crowded together, shoulder-to-shoulder.

Yancy laughed at them. Since he had at last found his comfort in Lorena, his mind and soul and even his body felt lighter, more alive. He could smile and laugh now.

As she had done countless times before, Zemira came out onto the porch to meet them. Behind her scooted Callie Jo, now five years old, and David, who was three. They weren't shy children at all.

Callie Jo ran to Yancy, supremely unmindful of Midnight's prancing hooves, while David waddled to the side of the buggy, held his arms up, and lisped, "Hold 'im."

Yancy jumped down and swooped Callie Jo up high in the air. "Hello, Jo-Jo. Missed me?"

"Yes, Nance," she answered in her little-girl voice. "Now, ride me on Minnight."

"Not now. Later. Right now I want you to meet my friend Miss Lorena. You'll like her."

Zemira came straight up to Lorena when she climbed down from the buggy, threw her arms around her, and hugged her soundly. Then she stood back and looked at her with dancing eyes. "Well, if you aren't just the tiniest little bitty thing I ever saw in my life. And Becky says you can boss Yancy just fine. Big trouble in a little package, I'll bet."

Holding Callie Jo, Yancy came up to them and said, "You know it, Grandmother. But she's pretty nice. Most of the time."

They all went into the house, talking. As usual, Zemira had cooked an enormous meal for them — ham, fried chicken, new potatoes, sauerkraut, green beans, creamed corn, and, of course, Yancy's favorite, Amish Friendship Bread. They found their seats, Callie next to David, in his homemade high chair, and Lorena sitting by Yancy. Without a word, Daniel, Becky, Zemira, and even Callie Jo and David bowed their heads. Lorena glanced at Yancy, and he bowed his, too. Silence ensued. Yancy looked back up as he realized Lorena might be puzzled at their silent praying as he was when he first came here. After a few moments, he pinched her arm, and she looked up to see everyone starting to help themselves to the delicious food.

They kept the conversation light during the meal, mostly talking about the farm, the crops, the doings in the community. No talk of war or death shadowed this family time together.

After they finished and cleared away, Becky and Zemira put the children to bed and they all gathered in the parlor. It was a cool night, and Yancy and Daniel built a small, cozy fire.

Yancy and Lorena sat close together on the settee, and across from them Daniel, Becky, and Zemira sat on the sofa. Yancy reached over and took Lorena's hand. "I have two very important things to tell you," he said. "The first is that I spoke to Reverend White, the pastor of the First Presbyterian Church in Lexington. Mrs. Jackson had been kind enough to write to him and tell him of my situation. You know that I've been a Christian for almost two years now, but I've never been baptized. I want you to be with me when I am, of course. But I know that no bishop in the Amish church will baptize me. Mrs. Jackson explained this to Reverend White, and he's agreed to come out and baptize me here, so that you can all be present."

"Thank the Lord!" Zemira exclaimed, beaming. "That will be a day of rejoicing, for sure and certain, grandson!"

"It will," Daniel agreed. "I had thought about this, you know, Yancy. But I didn't know how to solve it. Many ministers would be wary of baptizing someone that is not in their congregation."

Yancy nodded. "I can understand that. Mrs. Jackson understood immediately. I had the opportunity to be there when she and General Jackson had their baby baptized, and I visited with Mrs. Jackson the next day. She told me of Dr. White, and she must have written to him that very day. Pretty soon I got a kind letter from him, welcoming me into the service of God and assuring me that he would be honored to baptize me at any place I chose."

"I will write to Mrs. Jackson and to Reverend White to thank them," Daniel promised. "It's good to have faithful and caring brothers and sisters in the Lord."

"Even if they're not in the community?" Zemira, the lifelong Amish woman, asked suspiciously.

"Well?" Daniel countered, grinning. "Even if they're not?"

"Hmm. Even if they are those English, I suppose," Zemira agreed. Somewhat.

"Which sorta brings me to the next thing I want to tell you," Yancy said. "I'm sorry to say, Grandmother, that I have asked this English to marry me. And she's been fool enough to say yes."

With glad cries, Zemira and Becky jumped up, pulled Lorena to her feet, and hugged her so many times that she felt bruised. Daniel and Yancy stood and solemnly shook hands as men do.

Finally they all regained their seats, Yancy and Lorena glancing at each other and exchanging beaming smiles. Happily Becky asked, "When? When, Yancy?"

He sobered, though he didn't wear the same desolate face that had so marked him a few days before. "I have to go back, you know. After the funeral. The Yankees at Chancellorsville are still making noise, and General Lee says that we have to stay and be vigilant, for no one knows when the next battle will be."

Zemira sighed. "Very true. All we know is that there will be another, and another, in this wicked old world. But" — she brightened — "you children look so happy. I know that you will have a good life together. And won't you have some pretty babies!" Both Lorena and Yancy blushed, and Zemira laughed at them.

"Anyway," Yancy continued, "just as soon as I can, when we may see a few days of peace ahead, I'm going to ask for a furlough. Then I'll come home and bless Reverend White again. He said he'll marry us anytime, even if it's only with an hour's notice. But you know that I'll try very hard to make it a time when you all and Dr. and Mrs. Hayden can be there. Neither Lorena nor I can imagine getting married without our families."

"Then we'll pray for days of peace ahead," Daniel said. "Many of them."

They talked long into the night before Daniel, Becky, and Zemira finally headed off to bed.

■ ■ ■ ■

Yancy and Lorena sat out on the porch for a few minutes before they retired. They stood close together at the porch steps, looking at the vast tapestry of stars blanketing the blessed valley. "New moon," Yancy murmured. "New love. New life." He turned to her and took her in his arms.

Lorena said, "I knew I had already found true friends in Becky and your father, but now I know that they and your grandmother have already begun including me in the family. I don't think I've ever been happier. I will never forget this day."

"And I will never forget you again, Lorena," he promised. "And I will never leave you again. No matter what happens. No matter where I am. I'll be with you always."

"And I with you," she whispered. "For always . . . beginning now."

EPILOGUE

On the next day — another innocent, pretty Virginia spring day — General Stonewall Jackson took his last journey. Reverend White conducted a short service. Then the procession went to the Lexington Cemetery. In the shadow of the hills he knew so well, in the valley that he loved so much, Stonewall Jackson was finally at rest.

After the earthly good-byes were said, Anna Jackson, crying softly beneath her veil, turned and walked away from her husband's coffin. She didn't look back. The attendees followed her out of the cemetery. . . .

Except for four boys, whom Stonewall Jackson had taught to be men. They came to stand by his coffin, with their beloved flag draped over it. Mounds of flowers surrounded them, the air heavy with their heavenly-sweet scent.

"Atten–tion!" Yancy ordered in a low voice.

Together, very slowly, they raised their hands to give one last salute. They held it for long moments then together snapped back to attention. In silence they stood.

"I will always believe we were closer to him than the others," Peyton said quietly. "Guess no one else would believe it."

"I do," Chuckins said staunchly.

"I do," Sandy agreed.

Yancy said, "It's the truth. We were Stonewall's Boys."

ABOUT THE AUTHOR

Award-winning, bestselling author, **Gilbert Morris** is well known for penning numerous Christian novels for adults and children since 1984 with 6.5 million books in print. He is probably best known for the forty-book House of Winslow series, and his *Edge of Honor* was a 2001 Christy Award winner. He lives with his wife in Gulf Shores, Alabama.